Tangled Thoughts

Book Three of the Sententia

Cara Bertrand

www.carabertrand.com

Paperback ISBN: 978-1-941311-94-3

Cover Design by Brit Godish
Images courtesy Shutterstock.com

LUMINIS BOOKS

Meaningful Books That Entertain

Tangled Thoughts

Book Three of the Sententia

Prologue

Lainey

What would you do, if your choice was between your love or your life?

That's a trick question, because it's not really a choice at all.

You live.

That's what I did.

Or at least I was trying.

Carter

I thought I understood heartbreak after my father died.

I was wrong.

I thought I understood betrayal the day Lainey left.

I was wrong then too.

Chapter One

Lainey

ollege was *different*. Without the rigid schedule of high school, my days felt open and unpredictable. Liberating, too, but…different. Free time was a taunt, always waiting and in abundant amounts, with a city full of amusements and antique shops to spend it in. I was glad Boston was already my home, that I'd spent an entire summer exploring every last hidden place.

I was glad, too, that I'd spent so many hours during my wayfaring life before Northbrook studying on my own. The entire college experience had to be a challenge for the un-self-motivated. Of which there were many, including my roommate, Natalie. There were all kinds of *everyone*.

Maybe the most freeing thing about college was the ability to be yourself.

Or to be whoever you *wanted* to be.

Who was I? I never realized how difficult a question that was to answer. It depended, in part, on who was asking. To some, like the university registrar, I was the basics: I was Elaine Rachel Young, daughter of Allen and Julie, deceased; adopted daughter of Teresa Espinosa, artist and professor; eighteen-year-old freshman.

Some others seemed to see me only for two things, both of which I'd inherited: wealth and beauty. I thought that said more about who they were than who I was.

And then to a select group, I was something more. Among the Sententia—the people, like me, gifted with cognitive abilities that we called Thought, and the rest of the world called something like extrasensory perception—I was special. I was the last Marwood, the last known living Hangman.

I wondered what everyone would think if they knew they were walking around campus with the most dangerous Sententia alive, a girl who could kill anything with just a touch and a Thought. I was afraid of her, and she was me. But the thing was: I didn't have to be that girl.

When I'd made my bargain with Daniel Astor—Sententia leader, Carter Penrose's sort-of uncle, and all around bad guy—agreeing to leave Carter in exchange for a little thing called my life, I'd earned my freedom—from him, but also from *her*. Like I'd dreamed from the first day I'd learned the truth about myself, being Sententia was something I could leave behind.

Safe and anonymous in my first year at the University of Boston, I'd decided to take it all the way: no Sententia involvement *at all*. I wasn't even going to use my abilities. Even though it was in me, it didn't have to define me. *I* could define me.

How powerful was that?

I could be any *me* I wanted to be.

Of course, I quickly realized I was a work in progress. I stumbled into my dorm room in the International House out of breath and very nearly out of time, thankful as ever our building was in almost the exact middle of campus. It helped when you didn't know where you were going.

"Hello?" I called. Silence. *Damn.* No one was home!

The four of us were the only freshmen in the whole house, and only one of us was an actual International Student—Jin Hee, or Ginny as she asked to be called, from Korea. She was in the business school with me and I *thought* she was meeting me so we could go to discussion together.

I did mostly like my roommates, even if I might not have chosen them, but that was the point. It was exactly why despite having purchased an apartment within walking distance of campus, I lived here. We called ourselves the Ex-pats, because it sounded cute.

I kicked open the door to my room and screamed. Sitting in the middle of her bed was Nat, the slacker.

"Jesus," she said. "Scared much?"

"Didn't you hear me come in?!" She shrugged, and I wanted to scream again. I dumped my bag and keys on my bed. Only a dresser separated it from where Natalie lounged on her own bed. Our suite might have been bigger than the typical freshman shoebox, but our bedroom was small and beige. It's kind of strange when your college dorm is a step down from your high school one. Part of the experience, I reminded myself. "Where's Ginny?"

"Shopping? I don't know. Not home." Nat shifted focus back to her phone.

"Oh." *Crap.* I took a deep breath and resisted the urge to snap at Natalie. It wasn't *her* fault. "I guess I'll just see her in discussion then." I was really hoping she knew where it was.

"I think she said something about switching?"

"What? Damn!"

Nat's eyes flicked to me for a second. "You have charcoal on your shirt."

"What?"

"Charcoal. On your shirt." Before she went back to playing her game, she added, "And your face."

Sure enough, in the mirror I saw black smudges all over my t-shirt and more across my cheek and nose. "Shit! What the hell?" Apparently they'd come from my hand, which was smeared black with dust.

"Kendra," she said without looking at me, naming our other roommate, the artist. Nat gestured vaguely in the direction of the door, whose handle was as black as my hand. And shirt. And face.

"Shit!"

WHICH IS HOW I ended up the very last student to arrive at the first discussion section for my most important class—Intro to Business. I swore discussion locations were intentionally assigned as torture for freshmen, to ensure we got lost and give us maximum exposure to the randomest, hardest to find places on campus.

The room turned out to be small, windowless, and in the basement of a building I'd never even heard of before, let alone been to. The other students all watched as I stumbled into the closest open seat at the table, bumping the girl next to me; I actually recognized her from lecture.

"Sorry," I whispered.

"Welcome, latecomer," called the TA, whose back was to the door as he finished scrawling an office location and time below the name *J. Kensington* on the white board.

"Sor—" I started, and then the TA turned around. I half choked and had to start again. "Sorry."

J. Kensington was *hot*.

"Not a problem." He met my eyes and smiled. Blushing like a stupid freshman, I fumbled for my pen. "But try not to make it a habit. The sooner we start, the sooner we get done. Elaine, right? You're the last one on my list."

"Yes," I squeaked and cleared my throat. "But I prefer Lainey. And sorry. Again. I'm not usually late, I swear." I smoothed my hands across my notebook. I was literally the only student in the room without a laptop or something in front of me, as if the pen and paper were a set of my beloved antiques.

"Not a problem," he repeated, handing a piece of paper to the student closest to him. "Pass this to Lainey, if you would. As I was saying, I'm Jack. Please don't call me Mr. Kensington, ever. My info is everywhere—on the board, on that paper, and online. Believe it or not, I want to see you at office hours. Business relationships are developed in person…"

I was trying to listen, I really was, but J. Kensington—Jack—was distractingly attractive. TAs were supposed to look like…I wasn't sure, but not like Jack: maybe six feet tall, medium-length dark hair styled just the right side of messy, brown eyes meant for staring at, and a dimple that came out whenever he lifted one corner of his full mouth.

He'd rolled up the sleeves of his slim button-down and wore a quirky tie that, paired with the dimple, made him basically adorable. I assumed he'd come to discussion straight from a GQ photo-shoot of Future Business Leaders of America. I couldn't quite figure out if the letters running across his tie spelled something—

I dropped my pen when my neighbor touched my elbow at the same time Jack said, "It says, *Do not read this. Violators will be prosecuted.*" Once again, the entire group was looking at me. And laughing. Shit. It was just not my day. The only positive so far was the guy at the head of the table I was making a fool of myself over. At least he was smiling at me.

"So, Lainey, that means you have the privilege of starting our required awkward let's-get-to-know-each-other session. Name, rank, where you came from, all that good stuff. Go."

The rest of the hour went better from there. It was actually fun. The opposite of awkward. And I think that was all because of Jack. When we'd gone all the way around the table, he said, "It's only fair I tell you mine, so, I did high school in San Francisco, college in New York, a year of work, and now I'm adding a stop on my tour of major cities here."

"So what you're saying is, you get around?" the girl next to me said. My mouth dropped open, but most of the class laughed. I'd never have had the nerve to say something like that. I glanced at my neighbor and she grinned at me while at the front of the room Jack smiled like the devil.

"Exactly," he said. "Was it Serena?"

"Yeah."

"Excellent. Everyone, let that be your first lesson: don't be afraid to ask the hard questions."

"So where do you like best?" someone else called out.

"Another excellent question. Believe it or not, I moved here probably the same day you guys did, so I can't tell you how Boston compares—yet—but confidentially I can say you're the best discussion group of my half of the class, and, also confidentially, you're lucky to have landed with *me*."

We all laughed again, and I was sure he said that to each of his groups, but also that the last part was probably true. He even made the rest of the time discussing a few key points from lecture interesting. By the end, I was wishing we had discussion more than once a week. Serena, the girl next to me and also now my partner for the first of our million group projects, agreed.

Before leaving, she half whispered, "I think this just became my favorite class," and I laughed.

"Maybe mine too."

We were almost out the door when Jack called, "Latecomer! Hang on a second. If you don't mind."

No, I didn't mind. I said goodbye to Serena and backtracked into the now-empty classroom where Jack was perched on the edge of the table. "Sorry again about being late, uh, Jack."

He nodded somberly. "That's what I wanted to talk about." I was starting to worry he'd been hiding his inner hard ass when his face broke into a smile. "I'm sorry for giving you a hard time. And for just doing it again. I'm still figuring this whole TA thing out, so I thought I'd better apologize. You're really tall, by the way."

I laughed. With the way he was leaning on the desk, we were on eye-level. "I'm sorry. In addition to being on time, I'll try to slouch from now on."

"Nah, definitely don't. It'll intimidate people. You want to cultivate that."

"Okay." I stood up a little straighter. He was smiling and casual, and I wasn't quite sure what to do, if I was dismissed or what. I wanted to keep talking to him just because. "I will. Any other suggestions?"

He surveyed me from head to toe, as if taking my measure or…but he couldn't be checking me out, right? With a keen nod of his head he said, "Yes. Go to lecture, but you already do that, I can tell." He glanced up at the messy bun on top of my head. "And, also, wear your hair down." After a pause he added, "It will cover the smudge of, is it pencil? Right here."

And so lightly I wasn't sure he'd really done it, he touched a place on my jaw right below my ear.

Chapter Two

Carter

I was a fucking cliché.

I pulled the well-worn piece of paper from my pocket and unfolded it for an innumerable time. The words were fading and creased but it didn't matter; I could still read them.

I will love you always.

I didn't know why I bothered looking at it, since I could see an exact replica any time I wanted. All I had to do was close my eyes. I laid back on my couch and did just that while the note rested on my chest.

Everything was different in Washington. I was different.

I was alone.

It hit me during the four hundred mile drive to DC, after the rapid rearranging of my future Uncle Dan had accomplished in a matter of days. I was on my way to an apartment I'd never seen and couldn't afford but for the generosity of my uncle, in a city I'd never even visited, and I was alone. Uncle Jeff offered to drive with me, but Aunt Mel needed him. This was a big change for all of us. Uncle Dan was in the city, but he was a busy man.

And then, waiting in my office cube like the light at the end of my stupid, sad tunnel, was Alexis Morrow. It was a surprise when I saw her, even though I knew she was interning for my uncle too. I hadn't known she'd be working with *me*.

She took one look at me and said, "Hey. Listen, I didn't really like her, you know that, but I'm sorry. That sucks, and I'm sorry."

Of course she already knew. But something about the way she said it, the look on her face, made it one of the truest moments we'd ever had. It made me smile.

I said, "Well, you warned me."

She smiled back, and that was it. "Yeah," she said, "I did."

I hadn't forgotten how beautiful she was either, but when faced with it directly, her beauty was a physical thing that knocked you over. Also: she looked like Lainey. Now her beauty was a punch to the heart. It crushed me, and I craved it.

It didn't take long. Lunches became nights out with the other interns became nights out together became nights in at my apartment. *I* kissed *her*. Unlike our first kiss, she didn't push me away.

Being with her was a strange mix of comforting and uncomfortable. She was something I knew, something from home, but different here. And different from what I'd grown used to. I shouldn't have been with her or anyone. But something about it being a broken promise made it even better. I could let myself do all sorts of things I wouldn't before.

Lex made life fun and school made life bearable. I wished I'd taken *more* classes, but I didn't want to push it. American had bent over backwards for me as it was.

Well, not entirely for me. For Uncle Dan. I knew he'd made a do-nation to compensate for my last minute switch. He'd made one to Harvard too.

Thinking about Harvard was forbidden, because thinking about Harvard led to thinking about Boston and everything there. Downtime was forbidden too. Work and classes were over for the day, and I'd already run plenty of miles that morning. I could run again, but that felt obsessive. When something felt obsessive to an obsessive you knew you were in trouble. I gave myself three more seconds to look at the note before I put it away and called Alexis.

"Hey, babe. You sound like you need to come over here."

She always knew. "What are you up to?"

"Party. Wanna join me?"

She knew I did. Or really that I didn't, but I needed to. "Where?"

THE YOUNG SOMETHINGS-or-Other for Democracy were partying not far off Georgetown's campus, at the shared house of what had to be ten young politico dudes. Judging by the house, I'd have guessed they had more idealism than money, but once inside I saw the signs. Expensive electronics. Furniture that was decent, even leather. Tennis rackets—a sure giveaway. At least one of them had some bucks, which meant his parents probably did too. Now I understood why Alexis was here.

As I nursed my warming beer and watched guys and girls get drunk and try to hook up with one another, I wondered if I'd have enjoyed this—college, and everything that came with it—more if I'd gone right away. Which was a stupid thing to wonder.

Of course I'd have enjoyed college more back then, when I was seventeen and an idiot. Back when hooking up was still my other hobby. Classes that made me think and, literally, thousands of girls I might find a way to sleep with? College would have been my nirvana.

This party was not helping me feel better. A hand appeared in front of my face, waving, and I blinked.

"What's up, man whore? I know what you're thinking."

God fucking bless Lex. Her brown eyes lit with amusement as she blocked me into the little space I'd carved for myself against a wall. I pulled her right up against me. Her height, the curve of her hip where it touched mine, the length of her deep brown hair that tickled my neck—its familiarity always made me breathe a little deeper, even if it was a sensory memory of someone else. "Oh yeah?"

"Yeah. You're far more transparent than you think, bad boy. So, see anything you like out there?"

"I do now."

She dragged me to a couch and sat on my lap, mercifully saving me from having to mingle on my own. While we lounged, new friends came and went, courting her favor. I couldn't decide if it was a shame or blessing Georgetown didn't have sororities. Alexis Morrow would have ruled them, but it wouldn't have made her better. As it was, the layers of bitchiness high school had polished to a gleam were slowly dulling and wearing away. I liked her better this way.

She swirled a finger around my fully warm drink. "You should actually, you know, *have* a beer."

"No thanks."

"Carter, seriously."

"Have you ever tried to run with a hangover?"

"I've played entire field hockey games while still *drunk*!"

"That doesn't sound fun."

She sighed dramatically, the way she always sighed, and shifted so we could see each other. "It wasn't. But I still scored two goals, and you know what *was* fun? The night before."

"I'm having fun," I lied.

"Liar."

"I'm *trying* to have fun."

She turned all the way around and leaned in, face right up to mine. "Babe, do you know how? To have fun?"

I kissed her. It was its own answer, and also because I didn't know how to answer. But I knew how to kiss.

"See?" I teased, as Lex disentangled her arms from around my neck and herself from around me. I brushed a lock of her hair over her cheek. "Having fun."

Behind us, someone called, "Nice show, Lex," and another girl whistled.

Lex muttered, "Douches," but she was still smiling and I wasn't fooled. Exhibition was arguably her favorite pastime. "So you don't want to leave?" she said to me. "Now that we're 'having fun'?"

I did. I'd a million times rather have hung out at my apartment instead. But the party had barely started and she *didn't* want to leave. She deserved for me to try. "No, I don't want to leave."

"Liar."

"I mean it. I don't. Because you don't."

"You don't have to stay for me, babe."

"I. Want. To."

"Good." She shifted, ready to get back into the fray. "I want you to, too. Now could you maybe *try* to mingle?"

When I heard myself saying the next words, I was ready to punch myself before I was even done. "Is there anyone here my age?"

She slid backwards off my lap, shaking her head. "You mean forty? No. I don't think so." She stood and stretched her arms out, the hem of her sweater giving a sweet peek at the smooth skin underneath. When she saw me watching, she grinned and raised her arms higher. "Pretend you're at the bookstore, okay? Get people drinks or something. Flirt with some girls and talk about sports or whatever the hell with some guys. Just don't get in any trouble."

"Right. No trouble. Get drinks." I saluted her as she turned to disappear into the party.

"Just," she said, "be yourself. But, like, a *relaxed* version of yourself."

That, I thought, was the problem. I couldn't relax. Maybe I really *didn't* know how to have fun, not in a crowd of strangers. I used to think I knew myself well, but I hadn't known there was so much I *didn't* know. I hated feeling so anonymous, like nobody. Standing in the beer-scented kitchen of people I didn't know, pouring myself a drink I didn't really want, felt as far from who I thought I was as I could get.

But sometimes, when people had no idea who you were, they spoke freely.

From behind me, I heard my uncle's name. He wasn't being discreet about it either, this kid, pronouncing *Astor* like it was the punchline to a joke. Everything about him was familiar, though I'd never seen him before. I knew plenty like him from the Academy, with mouths too big and dicks too small, and trust funds large enough to make up for both. Typical Rex Madsens, the kinds of guys Alexis was *supposed* to date.

When he threw Lex's name into his conversation, I started paying attention. He knew her, obviously, and it sounded like he'd just suggested—

"Who the fuck are you, dude?" The kid was looking right at me, giving me a full up and down with more hostility than seemed necessary. He flicked his too-coiffed hair to the side with a quick snap of his head.

"Excuse me for a second," I said to the girl standing behind me at the keg and handed her my untouched beer. She and her friend gave me plenty of space as they leaned their blonde heads together to whisper. Everyone in at least a five person radius was suddenly quiet. I stepped toward the kid. "Were you just talking about Alexis Morrow?"

"What do you care?" He puffed out his sweater vest and I knew exactly where this conversation was headed. I was going to let it, too.

I wanted him to keep talking so I said: "I'm on staff with her."

"Really. You work for that prick too? *That's* interesting." His smug smile told me he thought he was hysterical. I gritted my teeth and shrugged. While giving me another once over, he said, "So, have *you* boned her yet?"

I shrugged again. "Not today."

"Okay, tell us this—think it's worth sharing her mouth with every dick in the District?"

"Is that why you keep staring at mine?"

I wasn't sure who punched who first.

But I knew I hit him harder.

Chapter Three

Lainey

The other thing about college: it went *fast*. Faster even than high school. In the time it took me to blink, we were a few weeks into the semester. So far I'd turned in all my assignments on time, joined a volleyball team, and was actually starting to feel like I had half a clue what I was doing. Except for one little thing: the morning I woke up and my first boy-related thoughts were about Jack, not Carter, I knew I was in trouble.

But maybe it was the good kind of trouble, the kind I needed to get into.

Classes were over for the day, and I was enjoying the crisp air and the miracle that was the street on which I lived. It was a tiny haven, tucked between the main campus buildings and the Charles river, lined on both sides with trees and old brownstones and with an actual castle at one end. A small one, but still. Autumn was officially invading the city and it was invigorating, blowing out the heat of summer and turning everyone's cheeks a fresh pink. I called Amy as I reached the steps of my dorm.

"I think I have a crush on my TA," I blurted as soon as she answered. The truth was I didn't think it, I *knew* I did. The way my heart beat faster and my palms got hot when I saw him at discussion today was a clear giveaway.

"Hot! So *spill*. What's he like?"

"Hot," I admitted, and she giggled.

"Obviously."

I thought for a second. What *was* he like? "Different," I finally said.

After a pause, during which I knew she was thinking about exactly the difference I'd left unspoken, she replied, "Different is good, Lane. Different is good…and so's hot. I mean, I *wish* I had a crushable TA. I'd even settle for a crushable lab partner, but noooo, I've got the vampire girl who never seems to sleep or see the sun. How about some details here? I've got some vicarious crushing to do."

After my rundown and her noises of approval, I added, "Hey, you want to come slum it on my side of the river tonight?"

I heard her close her laptop with a snap, which told me the answer was already yes, like she'd just been waiting for me to ask. "Do I get to meet, Mr. H-O-T, aka Hot Older TA?"

"No," I laughed, "but that band you told me about, with the bass player and no shirt, they've got an eighteen plus show and I've got passes." I pulled the passes out of my pocket and slid them back and forth against each other. A kid doing promotions had handed them to me on the way through campus and I'd taken them automatically. When I'd set them on the table in discussion and read the name, I realized not only had I heard of them, they were supposed to be *good*. Amy had too much free time too, so her new hobby was discovering indie bands.

Her fingers made a metallic tapping on the computer's cover. "Interesting. You know we wouldn't be stuck with only eighteen plus shows if you'd just…"

I interrupted her with a well-practiced sigh. "Ame, I'm not going to do that." I preferred the stress of her trying to convince me to get a fake ID to the stress it would cause me actually trying to use one.

"Lane, seriously, use some of your stacks of cash for fun. You could buy the best fake ever."

"Not only would I not know where to get one, I buy fun things all the time."

She laughed. "Your eighteenth century armoire is not fun."

"Yeah, but new shoes are…" I dangled it there, knowing what would tempt her. It was still plenty early to go shopping before the show.

"Okay." Her voice was serious, but I could tell she was grinning like she'd just won an argument. "Provided you wear new shoes that are *super* sexy *and* I get to crash at your apartment, I'll meet you at Copley in an hour. Bye."

She hung up before I even had time to agree.

MY NEW SHOES were definitely sexy. Except it was October and my toes were freezing, turning bluer and making me less sexy every minute we stood in line.

"Stop fidgeting," Amy scolded.

"Says the girl in new boots. *Warm*, toe covering boots." Not to mention the shot—or was it shots?—she'd done with my roommates before we left.

She stuck her tongue out at me. "We're almost in."

One of the two guys in front of us stage-whispered, "That's what she said," and his friend snickered. They glanced back at us again, and the one who'd been stealing looks at Amy's cleavage since we'd stepped up behind them actually smiled. He wasn't bad looking, except his eyes couldn't find their way north of chin-level.

Amy smiled back and leaned forward enough to distract him again before deliberately buttoning her coat. "Those," she told him, "are reserved."

"Oh yeah?" He thought she was flirting with him, so he stepped away from his friend and closer to us. "How do I get on the list?"

Amy's grin grew wicked. "Be. Someone. Else," she said, enunciating each word before she brushed past him up to the door. His friend had just gone in without him, leaving us next in line.

"Hey!" the kid said, but the two bouncers were already putting us through, slapping a drink bracelet on Amy's wrist and mine too. Obviously the guy had been too busy looking at Amy's boobs to actually look at my license.

"Nice show," my bouncer said to Amy at the same time the other one said, "Enjoy the show."

Amy winked at them and flounced down the entry hall.

Like the tunnel that led to it, the music hall was almost entirely black, except for the two giant pillars that flanked the stage, painted to resemble silver trees. It was a quirky place and I liked it; it felt intimate, as if you were in someone's basement with slightly better than average acoustics. An open floor led straight up to the stage, low enough that the band was right there. There was a mezzanine that ran around the room, with a second bar and a relaxed vibe away from the stage.

The lower level bar across from the stage was busy, but we stepped right up to it in a lucky opening.

"Ladies," the bartender said with a practiced smile. "What can I get you?"

Before I even had the chance to open my mouth, Amy was ordering a beer for both of us.

"Ame…" I started, but the caps were already off and two bottles set on the bar. She paid for both and practically pushed mine into my hand.

"Re. Lax. One drink with me, Lane. That's all. Pretty please." She batted her eyes and I laughed, taking an only partly reluctant sip. Amy's enthusiasm was, as always, infectious. "That's my girl!" She clinked her bottle with mine. "To new crushes and hot TAs."

"Cheers," I said and we turned to survey the room.

Naturally, leaning on the other end of the bar and talking to some friends was Jack Kensington.

Recognition lit up his eyes when he saw us, and he gave me a not entirely subtle glance up and down. "Lainey!" he called and started in our direction.

"No way," I said under my breath. Of course he was here. I tried to hide the drink I hadn't even wanted behind my back, since Jack definitely knew how old I was.

Amy looked at my blushing face and back to Jack. Threading her arm through mine, she said, "Guess I know who that is. Nice, Heartbreaker. Very nice. And you thought I wouldn't get to meet him."

"You do always seem to get what you want."

"Truth." She tilted her head, appraising. "You know, he kind of reminds me of—" but before she finished, Jack had reached us.

"Nice shoes," he said, smiling like Prince Charming.

"They're new," I replied stupidly. I could feel Amy's grin lighting up the space next to me. Before I had the chance to get my brain working well enough to make the introduction, my TA-slash-crush was doing it for me.

"Hi. I'm Jack." He held out his hand.

Amy took it in her free one that was still looped through my arm, pulling us all closer together. "Amy, Lainey's bestfriendinthewholewideworld and, unfortunately,"—she paused here, giving Jack an even less subtle once over than he'd given me—"not single. Unless…?" She raised her eyebrows suggestively and he laughed.

"Not single right now either," he said, then added, "unfortunately." He might have glanced at me when he said that last word and Amy definitely noticed.

"Too bad," she pouted, nudging me another step closer, until Jack's arm was touching mine. "Who's the lucky…guy?" Her eyes scanned the group he'd been standing with. They were all guys, but none looked like a clear contender for a boyfriend. Wishful thinking had completely blocked the possibility that he might have any kind of significant other, girl *or* boy, from my mind. Disappointment was just settling in my stomach when Jack laughed.

"The lucky *girl*," he said and, deliberately, put his arm around my shoulder, "is Lainey…" Amy beamed, and I stood there mute, stunned by his proclamation and his touch. Those disappointed feelings were being swarmed and devoured by an entirely different kind of butter-flies, when he dropped his arm and continued, "…and about two hundred others in her Intro to Business that I TA for. Unfortunately, I'm dating my job right now."

Amy's smile barely faltered. Though he'd taken his arm off my shoulders, it was still touching mine, and I knew she saw that. He could have, actually probably *should* have, moved away but didn't. "Two hundred girlfriends is a big commitment, a lot of papers to grade. Your stamina must be *excellent*," Amy purred and Jack laughed again, finally taking a step away from me.

"I like you, Lainey's bestfriendinthewholewideworld. Do you guys have a spot? Come watch with us upstairs." Amy immediately agreed for both of us and I followed them up to the mezzanine, still in a bit of a daze.

Chapter Four

Carter

Did *winning* a fight qualify as trouble? That's what I was thinking when I—finally—heard Alexis's voice mixed with the rest of the shouting. Most of which was for me to kick his ass. Whoever this kid was, he was a known asshole.

"What the *hell?!* Carter! Shit. MOVE!" I stood, breathing heavily, more from adrenaline than exertion. Lex grabbed my arm. "What's going—" she started to say, before Asshole rocketed off the ground into me, taking Lex down with us.

We landed in a hard tumble as the onlookers stepped cleanly out of the way. Alexis shrieked when we hit, a noise of pain and outrage. I turned to see her cradling her wrist as two girls helped her up. Which is when the kid got in one lucky shot, catching me right in the eye. My head rocked back, stars blooming. I just got my arm up to block his next swing.

Lex was shouting and struggling, the same girls now holding her back.

I shoved the kid over, rolling to the side to get him underneath me. He pushed back, but I was bigger, more sober, and stronger than him. I slammed my fist into his face with a wet thud that echoed in the crowded room.

His head smacked the floor and stayed there, a nasally groan escaping him as blood spurted between his fingers. "I think you broke my fucking nose!"

"I think you're an asshole." I stood and stepped back, trying not to flex my fingers and failing. It hurt punching someone in the face, even if he deserved it.

"What the actual *hell*, Afton?!" Hell hath no fury like Alexis Morrow. "*Carter?!*"

"Is his name seriously Afton?" I asked and at least one person in the crowd laughed. Not that my name wasn't ridiculous, but Afton? Pretty sure it meant Asshole in some Celtic language. "Want to repeat what you were saying, *Afton?*"

Dear old Afton had gotten himself to his knees, trying to stand without taking his hands from his face. No one seemed to want to help him. He inclined his head in Alexis's direction. His voice was muffled by his hands, but more than clear enough for everyone to understand. "That she's supremely accomplished at 'negotiating' from this position? It's no secret, dude. I bet you know better than anyone, except maybe her senator."

A collective gasp escaped the crowd, and Lex snapped straight to her full height. Before I could *really* break something, she leaned down and flicked the spot where his nose was hidden, bringing tears to his eyes. "You're a jealous idiot," she pronounced, eyes flashing.

And then she kicked him in the balls.

"YOU OKAY, BABE?" It was two blocks up to a decent spot to catch a cab, but it would only take a minute the way Lex was striding.

"*You're* the one with a black eye," she said. Her high heels made angry taps on the concrete.

"This?" I pointed to the swollen, darkening skin. It didn't hurt yet, probably wouldn't until tomorrow. "Don't you think it's sexy? I thought you would. I let him hit me on purpose."

"Shut up."

"I'm serious."

"*You're* an idiot, too." Her still stormy eyes flashed umber as her Sententia gift sparked to life, just like at the party.

"I've known *that* for years. You don't have to convince me."

"Sorry. Sometimes it just happens." Like now, when she was at a minimum buzzed, and because she'd been using her Herald's charm all the time in the employ of my uncle. Alexis was preternaturally convincing. If everyone hadn't believed her assessment of Afton before she'd made it, they did now. Fortunately, I was the only witness to her assessment of *me*. She gave me a tiny, sideways glance of apology. "But you *are*."

"I know." I scrubbed my hand over my head. "But what's *his* problem? Did he ask you out or something?" Her beauty queen smile told me my guess was right on.

"Before you. Long before. His family is old money friends with Daddy. I saw him for the first time in years at orientation."

"Obviously you declined." I raised my hand at the first cab we saw but it zoomed past.

"Like I'd go out with a wank like that! God, where are the cabs!" She stamped her feet before leaning on the side of a bus stop. "Plus," she added, "I don't tend to date gay guys either."

"Except for me." I knew you shouldn't poke an angry bear, but it amused me how Lex used to suggest to most of Northbrook that *I* was gay. She punched my arm with her good hand, and then hailed the next taxi herself. Naturally it stopped. I slipped my arm around her shoulder for the ride to my apartment. "So what was old Afton doing asking *you* out then?"

"Afton is hiding so deep in the closet he can't even find the light switch. He might be *slightly* less of an ass if he weren't overcompensating so hard for who he is. He'd kill to work for your uncle and he makes a good show of dating girls, but besides wanting my job, he's really jealous I have *you*, hot stuff. Not the other way around."

"Huh." That made a lot of sense, actually. "Does everyone know that?"

"Everyone but Afton." After some miles of quiet, Alexis said, "So really though, do you feel better now?"

"I'm sorry?" I turned to look at her, her profile disappearing in and out of shadow as we drove.

"Can we admit that wasn't really about me?"

"Who do you think it was about?"

"You."

"*Me?*"

"Yes. You."

I was feeling like I'd been punched again. I took my arm from around her. "Do you really think I'd just stand around while he said those things about you?"

She tapped me on the chest. "*And* your uncle."

"And my uncle," I agreed. Would I have provoked him if he'd only been talking about Lex? She seemed to think not. It wasn't a question I wanted to examine. The cab pulled up outside my building and I hastily paid the fare before continuing our argument on the sidewalk. "I wasn't going to let him talk like that," I reiterated. "About either of you."

Despite that she, obviously, cared, she said, "What do I care what that dipshit thinks?"

"I don't care what he *thinks* either. He was doing more than *thinking*."

"Whatever. What he says still doesn't matter."

"It matters *to me*." And it did. I held open the outer door and followed Alexis into the elevator.

"Well, thank you for defending my honor." She flicked her hair over her shoulder as we rose. "But really, you just wanted to work your aggression out. Afton was a good excuse."

"What aggression?"

"Babe, really?" She glanced back at me. "About *her*. You've wanted to beat the shit out of *someone* since the last time you saw her, but so far the only good candidate has been yourself."

Shit. "That *wasn't* about her."

"Sure it wasn't."

"Fine. I'd rather not talk about her." We were at my door now, and I stepped around Alexis to unlock it. I contemplated leaving her in the hallway.

To my back, she said, "For fuck's sake, Carter, maybe we should. She's always here anyway."

"No." I yanked the door closed again and spun around. Lex let out a little squeal of surprise when I pulled her tight against me and my back banged into the door. "*I'm* here. And *you're* here."

"Oh yeah?" She leaned into me and reached around my waist, slipping her hand into my back pocket, where the note usually lived. It was empty. She tensed and straightened to look me in the eye. Hers were shiny and surprised. "Wow. Okay."

I nodded once and held her gaze. Alexis's eyes were hers alone, deep and brown and wanting to trust me. "That *wasn't* about her."

"Okay," she repeated, relaxing into me. In my ear, she said softly, "*Thanks.*"

"I'm here and you're here. That's it."

This time when her fingers reached around my waist, they found the door handle and opened it, pushing me through. Then they found their way to the top button on my jeans. I closed the door behind us.

"You know what?" She made quick work of the button and was easing down the zipper now.

"What?"

"Afton was right about one thing—I *am* good at this."

When she pushed me down on the couch, I let her.

I hated myself, but I let her.

In the morning, after Lex was gone, I folded and put away the pair of jeans I'd hastily changed out of before the party. I looked at the note briefly before transferring it to my wallet. Later, at the fitness center, I'd find one of the heavy bags and pretend it was me.

Chapter Five

J ack's friends had staked out a decent spot on the side, with a clear view of the stage below. He barely had time to introduce us before the first opening act started up. The band was surprisingly good for an early act. Concentrating so hard on their music was helping me ignore how nervous I felt. I couldn't relax and the beer I was still holding and not drinking wasn't helping.

Next to me, Jack seemed at ease and, well, really attractive in his expensive jeans and button down shirt with the sleeves rolled up. He knew how to wear clothes that fit, I'd give him that.

Yeah, I was completely crushing on this guy.

Those flutters in my stomach, the ones I'd wondered when I'd ever feel again, were not entirely welcome. First of all, they weren't for Carter. Even though we weren't together, would never be again, I couldn't shake the tiny feeling of betrayal creeping around my brain.

Second, Jack may have been hot, and friendly, and had at least decent enough taste in music to be at this show, but he was still my TA. I didn't think hanging out with him was even appropriate, let alone the *other* things I was thinking.

Jack lightly touched my arm and I nearly jumped over the railing. The band was playing an acoustic number, quieter, maybe their last song. "I'm glad you're here, by the way," he said in low tones.

"Really?" is what came out of my mouth, probably too loud and definitely embarrassing. I wondered if he'd caught me checking him out.

"Sure, why wouldn't I be?"

"Um…" I didn't know how to say it without sounding like a nervous freshman, or terribly uptight, both of which Amy would probably have told him I was. She'd already peeked over her shoulder at me with a look that said as much.

But Jack smiled like he could read my thoughts. "Is it weird to hang out with your TA?"

I held up two fingers an inch or so apart. "Little bit," I admitted and felt better immediately.

He nodded. "How about we consider each other off-duty? I promise I'm not grading you right now, but knowing you have good taste in music *might* positively affect your grade going forward." He touched his hand to his heart like an oath and I couldn't help but laugh.

"Then I'm glad you're here too. I could use all the help I can get!"

"Nah," he said. "You actually go to lecture. You're already ahead of sixty percent of the class. But no more talking about class. Off-duty, remember?" I smiled and, without thinking, started to take a sip of my drink. When I realized Jack was watching me, I dropped it back down to my side. I wished I'd just left the damned thing on the bar.

"I don't like warm beer either. Why don't you let me get you another one?"

"Um," I repeated, blushing. Again. And, once again, Jack saved me from my own awkwardness.

"Lainey, listen. I meant it when I said I'm glad you're here. Probably I shouldn't have offered to get you a drink. Actually, it could probably get me fired, but I don't really care if you're drinking. You've got a bracelet. And, listen. I'm new to the city, you seem cool, and we're here, right? If you want a beer, I'd like to get you one." I hesitated, and he said, "Or I'll just leave you alone, if you want. Sorry." He cleared his throat. "So, could I get you a drink?" He finished with a duck of the eyes and the most self-effacing smile, the combination of which seemed to erase all my reservations.

I'd been planning to tell him I'd just have a water, but what I said was, "Sure. I mean, please." I was a little surprised when I said it, but I actually *did* want a drink, so why not? Let myself have some fun, as Amy would say. I suddenly felt bold and uninhibited.

Jack came back from the bar with a round for all of us just as the second act was starting up. On the talent spectrum, they were on the low end, which they made up for with volume.

Amy made a horrified face while covering one ear with her free hand. "I'm going to need at least one more of these," she shouted, taking a sip of her beer, "to make it through *this*. When does my shirtless bass player get here?"

Jack leaned down and shouted back, "You guys want to sit this one out?"

Did I ever. My new shoes *were* sexy, but still new. Near the back of the room and half hidden behind the bar was an unoccupied couch. We moved aside some coats that had been tossed there.

"God, this girl is an insult to music!" Amy flopped down dramatically, forcing me to scoot closer to Jack. The band rampaged in the background, the lead singer wailing into the mic. It was mercifully quieter in the corner where we sat, but also brighter. The music hall was definitely a place best enjoyed when the lights were down. Amy gulped her beer and said, "You were serious about slumming it. Are all the places around here this dingy?"

"You know full well there are plenty of dingy places on your side too." When Jack gave us a curious look, I explained, "Amy goes to MIT and thinks the clean water flows on the Cambridge side of the Charles."

Jack laughed and Amy pulled a face. "It does," she pronounced primly, taking another drink from her bottle. "Though I don't suppose either of *you* would understand."

"You grew up in Chestnut Hill," I reminded her and she huffed at me.

"How long have you two known each other?" Jack asked.

"Two years and forever," Amy answered. "Right, Lane?"

"At least."

Amy leaned over me to look at Jack, shoving me a little closer still. "You didn't go to Harvard or something, right? Because you kind of have that look and maybe I'd like you even more then."

Carter was supposed to go to Harvard, I didn't say, and Jack said, "No," with an easy smile. "But I *do* want you to like me."

"So where *are* you from?"

"Here, for now, by way of Albany, California, and…a few other places."

Amy squeezed my arm and said, "Lainey's a little bit of everywhere too."

Jack regarded me. "Makes you feel at home nowhere and everywhere, right?"

I nodded, wondering how he'd managed to put into words exactly what I'd always felt.

"Army brat?" Amy pressed.

"Good grief, Ame, with the inquisition?" My neck was flushed and I resisted the urge to lift my hair and run my cold beer across it. Amy probably would have told me to do it.

"*What?* I'm interested!"

"It's fine," Jack said. He bumped my shoulder with his. "I don't actually mind. Not Army, no. More of a family brat, I guess you could say."

"Uh oh. Don't tell me you're the black sheep?" He seemed so...perfect, I couldn't believe that.

Next to me Amy giggled and went *baaa, baaa* as she took the last swallow of her beer.

Jack laughed, shaking his head. "That's my father, actually."

"Really?!" I wasn't sure if I said it, or Amy did, or both of us.

"How so?" For sure I said that.

"My father," Jack said, "married for love, much to my Grandparents' chagrin." His voice was steady, even, like he'd told this story a hundred times and now they were just words he repeated.

I gasped. "What's so wrong with marrying for love?"

"Nothing, unless it's the 'wrong' person." Jack stood. "Another?" He gestured to Amy's drink and she nodded.

"Well," Amy pronounced, watching Jack walk up to the bar. "He's *interesting.*" I glanced sideways at her. "By which I mean *hot. And* interesting."

I sighed. "I know."

"You should seem more excited about that, Lainey baby." She laid her head on my shoulder as Jack turned around with a fistful of drinks. "Don't think I haven't seen him eye-fu—"

"Amy! Please."

"I'm just saying. Clearly, he digs you."

He returned with drinks for all of us, even though I didn't really want another one. "Handsome *and* thoughtful. I like you, black sheep." Jack bobbed his head chivalrously to hide a grin. Amy plucked two beers out of his hand and stuffed one into mine.

It was in between sets by then, the wailing over but still ringing in my ears. In the few moments of quiet, I said to Jack, "Don't you want to hang out with your friends?" Amy nudged me with her elbow but I ignored her.

"Bored of me? Or were you trying to meet someone here? Sorry, I didn't even think—"

Amy laughed, saying, "We were trying to meet *yo*—" and I elbowed her harder.

"*No*," I said. "No no. It's not that. Either of those things. I just thought…" I didn't know what I thought. Or I *did* and I shouldn't say it.

Jack grinned and relaxed on the couch, throwing his arms across the back so one was sort of behind my shoulders. "Is this another awkward TA moment?"

"No." *Sort of.* I was having inappropriate thoughts about a TA, so did that qualify?

He nodded thoughtfully. "Then usually I'd say you were expecting me to say something like '*of course not, you're way more interesting than they are*'—you know, flattery—but I don't get that vibe from you." I must have looked mortified because he laughed. "But seriously, you *are* more interesting than those guys. We play basketball together; I barely know them."

"Oh."

"Lane, remember how we've talked about *relaxing* before?" Amy deposited her already empty bottle on the floor and took the other one out of my hand. "Let's try that." The main act played its first notes before I could glare at her. She squealed and grabbed my hand, tugging me to my reluctant feet. "C'mon! We'll work on relaxing on the dance floor!" Over her shoulder she called, "Black sheep, meet us there with another drink!"

We waved to Jack's friends on our way down to the packed floor. I could see why Amy liked this band. They were good, and true to her word, the bass player was shirtless by the end of their second song. Being in a band was apparently a decent work out.

When fingers touched the inside of my elbow, I whirled around. It was an unexpected feeling, an intimate kind of gesture. But it was just Jack, with new drinks and a smile. He handed off a beer to a delighted Amy and made a decent effort at bopping along to the music.

I leaned closer so he could hear me better. "You're a good sport, you know?"

Jack nodded. "Anything for the cause."

I laughed. "What's your cause?"

He lightly bumped me with his shoulder while he swayed. "Isn't the cause always to spend time with beautiful girls?"

"I'm not sure you should be saying that to me." Despite that I was smiling like an idiot.

Amy, giggling, said, "Ignore her, Black Sheep. *I'll* be your cause to-night." She danced toward Jack, sliding down the length of him, and shoving him closer to me as her breasts brushed his side. I wasn't en-tirely sure the second part was intentional. I started to count in my head the number of beers she'd had.

I got to four before Jack said, "Maybe I should have said *team*. We're a team, right? Not that you're not beautiful, bestfriend-inthewholewideworld," and I lost count. The one in her hand was empty, when it seemed like it had been recently full.

Amy shimmied next to him again. "No one's more beautiful than Elainey, right? Ha! E-Lainey! Lane, that would be your Disney Chan-nel show."

That's when I started to get worried.

"Ame, maybe we should go soon…" I called over to her, loud enough to sound like the total buzz kill I, well, was. A couple people around us booed me.

Amy laughed and kept wiggling. I was starting to think the dancing was a byproduct of the drinks. "Consensus says no, Lame-y. C'mon be on the *team*. What's our mascot, Black Sheep?"

"Wolverines," Jack provided promptly.

"Rawr!" Amy spun around. The band was getting louder and faster, and the crowd, except for me, more into it.

Wolverines? I thought. "Where did you say you went to high school again?" I asked Jack.

"California," he said over the noise. But did he look away when he said it? I was having trouble concentrating between the band, the alarm bell ringing in my head, and Amy's wild swaying.

But I knew that mascot. I could have sworn—"Didn't you say you were from San Francisco before? What was the name of your school?"

Finally, Jack looked at me, really *looked* at me, and said, "I went to Webber, Lainey."

I went rigid. *This could not be happening.*

"Hey! Isn't that—?" The West Coast Sententia school? Yes. But Amy didn't get the chance to say it aloud. She was half turned back to us when she started to fall. "Whee!" she laughed—*laughed!*—as she headed toward the ground. Jack and I managed to catch her before she landed, his hand touching mine as we hauled her up, and I yanked it away as soon as she was standing.

"We're leaving," I told her. "Now."

"Lainey—" Jack said.

"I think that's a good idea," Amy slurred as she started to tilt toward the ground again.

Jack caught her and propped her up with an arm around her waist. "Lainey, listen—"

But I was *not* going to listen. "No! We're leaving! Amy, c'mon." I took her arm and started to lead her toward the door, but she stumbled.

"When did I get so dizzy?" she asked of no one in particular but Jack was there, holding her again. "Black Sheep! I'm so dizzy. Carry me home?" In the periphery, I could see a few people looking concerned, and a bouncer starting to watch us.

"*Shit!*" was all I could say. I repeated it a few times.

"At least let me help you get her outside," Jack pleaded.

And though I couldn't look at him, I nodded.

IF I WAS into understatement, I'd say the taxi ride to my apartment was tense.

Really, it was two miles of nightmare.

Amy was propped up in the middle. I busied myself by petting her hair and praying to every god I could remember that she wouldn't be sick in the car. The driver had already threatened us with the fifty dollar cleaning fee.

And I—I was trying not to throw up myself.

I wanted to. So badly. Jack knew about me, obviously. Somehow. He had to. He was one of us and he *knew*.

When Amy started singing a song about *feeling sentimental*, I basically wanted to kill her. But not as much as I wanted to get us out of the taxi, so I gritted my teeth and counted seconds in my head. We hit every stop light on the way.

At a particularly long one, Jack turned to look at me, saying, "Lainey, can I just—"

"*No,*" I gritted out. "So don't try."

"We promised we weren't grading each other tonight."

"I'm not. I'm just not speaking to you."

Amy chimed in with, "Somebody's got a seeeeccrrreet. Oh." The cab went over a bump, which mercifully made her quiet as she tried not to puke and I did my auntie's yoga breathing for the last thousand feet.

"Lainey, I—"

"No!" With a final jerk, the cab stopped at my apartment, which I'd never been more thankful to own than that moment. Dragging Amy up all the stairs of my dorm would have been an even bigger nightmare than this already was. I threw open the door and jumped out just fast enough for her to lean over and throw up next to a BMW parked at the curb. Before I could pay the cab driver, Jack gave him a bunch of cash and asked him to wait.

"I feel a little better now!" Amy called, seemingly proud of herself.

With difficulty, Jack helped her back out of his door without getting hit by oncoming traffic. Between the two of us, we got her into the building. Jack and Luis, the night doorman, nodded at each other as we went through. The tiny elevator took approximately a year to reach the fourth floor.

Amy broke into giggles as we went down the hallway with her propped between us, singing, "Lions, and tigers, and bears, oh my!" On the other side of her, I could see Jack laughing silently, but I couldn't find a single thing funny about the entire situation. After a few choruses, she swallowed. "Starting not to feel as good, Lane," she warned, but we were—finally!—at my apartment. If unlocking a door had been a rodeo challenge, I did it with winning speed and tugged Amy through behind me.

With little more than a second glance, I said, "Thanks for your help," and let the door slam in Jack's face.

Chapter Six

Carter

My apartment was further outside my budget than I wanted to admit, but when Uncle Dan made the arrangements, I was in no shape to refuse. He wouldn't have accepted a refusal anyway. I was situated less than a mile from a vast park where I could run, close to a metro stop, and a few blocks from the one place that made me feel closest to home: a bookstore.

I suspected the store's proximity was in large part responsible for my current address. It was the first place Uncle Dan took me after I arrived, and they greeted him by name. Of course he was known there—he was a senator as well as a scholar with three books to his name—and he made sure they knew me too.

Inside was a coffee shop and I treated myself to coffee every day and books more often than necessary. It wasn't like Penrose Books at all, except for the scent. The particular smell of a bookstore in the morning was the thing I missed almost as much as…my hand strayed toward my back pocket, but I caught myself. I shoved open the store's door with more force than necessary.

The coffee shop interior was warm and mellow. A glance told me the big chalk board menus were slightly different from the day before. If I thought about it for a few seconds, I could figure out exactly what was different, but I didn't need to. I always ordered the same thing. It was just one more image for the mundane collection stuffed into my brain's infinitely crowded filing cabinet. I wondered if one day my head would explode from it all and a million useless memories of menus and Lainey's goddamned note would flood the ground.

"Senator's Son!" The barista greeted me as she did every day.

"Nephew," I corrected, like always. I tried not to touch my eye when I could tell she was looking at it. I tried to pretend it didn't hurt, too. Training, politeness, or possibly the fact that she'd seen everything kept her from mentioning it.

She was already pouring me a cup when she asked, "One or two?"

"Two," I answered and she poured a second, setting it on the counter with a mountain of pink packets stacked on top.

As she made my change, she said casually, "Hey, saw the senator here on a date a few days ago."

"I'm sorry?" I realized I was still holding out my hand with the dollar and few coins sitting in it, so I dropped them in the tip jar. To my knowledge, Uncle Dan wasn't dating anyone. He hadn't been with anyone seriously for years. And now, it was kind of difficult when you were running for president.

Her smile slipped a little. "Senator Astor. He met a woman here the other day. She was pretty. I've never seen him with anyone who wasn't obviously an aide or you. Who was she?"

"I don't know," I admitted. "Probably a reporter." A line was forming behind me.

Her eyebrows went up in a way that said it hadn't looked like business. "They seemed awfully friendly. Must have been a good interview."

"I'm sure," I said, which sounded stupid even to me. "See you tomorrow."

At my building, I met Lex in the elevator. She was clearly on her way back from the fitness center, wiping absently at her neck with one of their towels while scrolling her phone. She didn't even look up when I stepped in the car.

I leaned on the wall next to her, close, and I could see her readying her best *back off* when I said, "You could just run with me, you know."

She squeaked, and her phone slipped from her fingers, but she caught it before it could hit the floor.

"Jesus. I thought you were some dickhead creeper."

"Just the one who brought your coffee."

"You're lucky I didn't knee you in the balls."

"You're right. Then I would have dropped the coffee." She took it and kissed my cheek in thanks. "You *could* run with me though," I added. I tapped the cup in her hand. "It would be warmer that way."

"I hate running."

I swallowed my coffee hard. "You were *conference* in field hockey."

"I know."

Back in my apartment, I sat at the dining table and continued to sip my coffee.

"What's the matter?" Lex dropped into the chair across from me.

"What?"

"You just ran a zillion miles, it's nice out, you've got coffee and smelled books. Why are you so quiet?"

I picked up my cup and found it light, almost empty. I'd been sitting there for longer than I realized. "Do you know why my uncle is going to Arizona next weekend?"

"No? Politics? Because the best spas are there?" I told her about my conversation with the barista and her eyebrows shot toward the ceiling. "Well, *that* would be juicy news. Maybe he's taking *girlfriend* to L'Auberge. Scottsdale's pretty nice, too."

"Don't you think he'd have told me if he was dating someone?"

"My dad doesn't tell me every time *he's* dating someone."

"Lex, Jesus." I'd been spinning my cup in circles and it clattered to a stop on its side. "That's not true."

"Of *course* it is. Dad has more girlfriends than I do. Mom gets new jewelry every time he gets a new secretary."

"Fuck." Out of habit, I wiped a hand down my face and winced as I passed over my swollen eye.

"Don't pretend you didn't know."

"I *didn't.*"

Alexis shook her head. "That's because you think everyone is sweet and good."

"*I'm* not even sweet and good."

"Yes you are. In here." She leaned forward and tapped my chest. It felt warm under her fingers.

"I haven't always been."

"Carter, seriously." She stood and came to my side of the table, pushing it back with a scrape until she could settle herself comfortably on my lap. "I know I joke about it, but really, you're a good, good boy. I bet even all your love-'em-and-leave-'em townie girls still pine for you."

"I'd take that bet." I knew they didn't. I hadn't stayed with any of them for very long. I hadn't loved any of them either. They *all* knew that. Some of them had wanted me to. "And don't be crass."

"See?"

"What?"

"'Don't be crass'—who says that except *good* boys? Listen, I know you're good because *I'm* not. *You* are just like your aunt."

"*You* are not bad either."

"Ha!"

I pulled her snug against me. "You're not. I wouldn't be here otherwise."

"I think," she said, "you bring it out in me. The good." There was a softness in her voice, the sometimes sharp edge of it dulled by sincerity. I skimmed my fingers across her cheek and tucked a strand of hair behind her ear. She smiled, a small curving of her lips that was the shyest thing she ever did.

"Maybe," I said, and kissed that smile. "But see? It's already *in* you. You don't need me."

With one hand on my chest, she leaned close and whispered, "Don't bet on it."

She kissed me back, a good one, her tongue searching for mine, and for a while I forgot all about the conversation in the coffee shop. My hands fixed on her waist to keep her balanced, but the longer we kissed, the more they wanted to stray. Alexis arched her back, pushing the table even further away with a screech, and wrapped her legs around my waist.

She pressed against me once and that was it. My brain switched off in favor of other things. I stood, bringing her with me, cinched tight. Without a second to consider it, I Thought the table back toward us and set her right there. Alexis's eyes popped open as it made the same awful screech as before.

"Oh!" She jerked her chin in surprise and caught me right in the swollen eye.

Hissing, I fell back into my chair.

Lex sat up on the table, rubbing her chin. "Shit."

"Yeah," I said, shaking my head to clear the stars.

"Sorry. That was weird. Like the table moved itself."

I froze, one hand over the throbbing half of my face, and cursed myself for being such a fool. Only five people in the world knew the secret of my Thought Moving ability and Alexis wasn't one of them. *Fool*, I thought again, gritting my teeth. "I—moved it with my foot," I lied.

"Oh. Duh. Sorry," she repeated, gentler this time. She kissed my cheek, then the hand still covering my eye before tugging it away. I squinted at her and she laughed. "I wonder what your uncle's going to say when he sees you?"

"WHAT'S HAPPENED TO your face, son?!" Uncle Dan and a guest had just stepped into my cube. There was a moment where my uncle opened his mouth, ostensibly to introduce his companion, before he actually looked at me. It was almost funny.

Self-consciously, I touched it. It was better, but the skin around my eye was still blue and yellow. I could have lied, said anything. But I hated lying when I didn't have to, so instead I smiled. "Let's just say there's nothing I won't do to support you, sir."

Uncle Dan laughed, though I could see he was still curious. "I've certainly never doubted your dedication. I hope you were equally convincing?"

"More thoroughly, actually."

His companion laughed then too, and I wondered who he was. His suit wasn't nice enough to make him a likely donor, and something about him reminded me of Uncle Jeff. They looked nothing alike, as this guy was a good half a foot shorter than Jeff and some part Pacific Islander. Or did they? It was how he stood, a readiness, and his eyes. They missed nothing. *Military*, I thought.

Uncle Dan, still chuckling, clapped me on the shoulder as I came around my desk. "Carter, this is Manuel," he said as we shook hands. "Manny, my nephew Carter."

"Nice to meet you," I said, though I still didn't really know who he was.

"Likewise," Manny replied.

"Join us for a minute, would you?" my uncle asked and I followed them around the corner to his office.

Once inside, Manny closed the door and stayed by it as if that was his station. Uncle Dan nodded toward his seating area, and I took one of the wingback chairs. "Manny," he said to me, "if you haven't guessed it yet, is an agent with the Secret Service."

That certainly made sense. I glanced at him again, then back at my uncle. "Is he *your* agent?"

"He is. There'll be a few others on rotation, but Manny is my detail leader. There may occasionally be private security as well."

"But…why?" It wasn't common for senators to have assigned security, and it was still early for presidential candidates.

Uncle Dan rubbed his eyes and I realized he looked tired. I always thought of my uncle as indefatigable. "There have been some…threats," he said. He met my eyes and I sat up straighter.

"What kind of threats?"

"The not very nice kind." He chuckled again, but it lacked the humor from before. "It seems," he continued, "some people take umbrage with, well, many things about me. My 'unconventional' family, for one." He meant Jill, I realized, his daughter-out-of-wedlock. And possibly the fact that he wasn't, had never been, married. "My wealth. My voting record. Also, we believe, my father."

I sucked in a breath. Other Sententia wouldn't *threaten* him, would they? "Are they—?" I cut another glance at Manny, who wasn't obviously listening but surely heard every word.

"You may speak freely," Uncle Dan said, nodding in Manny's direction. "Manuel is discreet in all manner of my activities. In fact, I think you have much in common."

Manny grinned at me, a flash of white teeth. "Never forget a face," he said, tapping his temple.

A *Lumen* then, and a handy skill for a security agent. I should have suspected he was one of us. "I never forget anything," I told him and he chuckled.

"I won't forget *that*," he said. We all laughed, and I liked Manny already. If Uncle needed protection, I was glad it was someone like him. Like us.

Uncle Dan cleared his throat. "To answer your question, it's unlikely fellow Sententia. But—" He shrugged. "It's not impossible. You don't carry my last name or responsibilities without picking up a few enemies along the way."

"Sir, I—" I didn't know what to say. I hadn't realized I should be worried about my uncle. "I had no idea."

"Nor should you have." Uncle crossed his legs, the way only a man steeped in old money could. "We've kept it quiet—and intend to. For now. Publicity will only fan the flames. But," he said, sitting straight and leaning forward, "I want you to know this—we believe the danger is only to me. If there was even a *hint* you or any of the family were a target, I'd have the entire Service on your detail. Please believe me."

"Of course," I said automatically. "Of course I do. I'm not worried about myself." I squeezed my hands against my thighs to keep from rubbing my hair, a habit I was desperately trying to quit. "Can I do anything?"

Uncle Dan stood, which meant I stood too. He touched my shoulder again. "Just your being here helps," he said and I looked at my feet. I hated him to see how much comments liked that pleased me. "It's time for me to go. Sorry to leave you with such…uncomfortable news, but really, you shouldn't worry. Especially now with Manuel here."

I glanced over at Manny again, and he inclined his chin minutely in acknowledgment. "I'll...try not to," I promised. "Have a safe trip." I said it so frequently, the same way Aunt Mel always told me to *drive safely* whenever I picked up my car keys, I knew he hardly heard the words anymore.

Uncle Dan nodded like always and I knew I was dismissed. I'd completely forgotten to ask why he was going to Arizona. Just before I was out his door, he called, "Cartwright?"

I turned. "Yes, sir?"

"Thank you." So maybe he did hear.

"And Cartwright? I love you, son. I know I don't tell you that very often, but never doubt it."

"I won't, sir," I said softly. I never had.

Chapter Seven

Lainey

Amy rolled out of the guest room the next day looking not like something the cat dragged in, but something the cat had dragged behind a car and then run over for good measure. I, on the other hand, looked like someone who'd been up all night worrying her not-so-best friend would make it to and from the bathroom without puking on the carpet or dying because:

"I'm thinking about killing you," I told her. "Also, good morning."

She fell into a chair at the table, peering at me through eyes red as fire and still smudged with last night's makeup. Her skin was approximately the color of the Wicked Witch of the West. "I'm not sure you'll have to," she rasped. "I'm dying. And have I mentioned before that this kitchen is far too *bright*." She propped her elbow on the table and dropped her face into it, covering her eyes. "Seriously, let's get you some lower wattage light bulbs or something."

Only Amy would still say words like *wattage* when epically hungover. I tapped my fingers on the table because I knew it would annoy her. "The wattage of my light bulbs is not going to matter once I've killed you. Or let the alcohol do it for me."

She sighed. "I'm sorry."

"I'm sure you are." I tapped my fingers some more. She peeked at me but said nothing. After a few moments, I got up to pop a frozen waffle in the toaster and retrieve a cup of coffee and some aspirin for her. Despite the green tint to her complexion, I didn't think she'd throw up again. She'd already done so much of it, what could possibly be left?

She thanked me and downed some of both, rolling her head back and forth before taking another sip. When the waffle popped up, I brought it to her dry. "Thank you," she repeated. "Think you can make me forget last night?" She held out her wrist, which looked clammy and limp.

"Even if I could, it wouldn't cure the hangover."

"Shit."

"Pretty much."

"What good are mental superpowers if they can't even make us forget our mistakes?" She took a bite and chewed slowly.

I went back to tapping my fingers on the table, louder, until she narrowed her eyes at me. "If I *could* erase what you did last night, you'd just do it again."

Muffled by waffle, Amy grumbled, "So you're saying this is all to teach me a lesson, right? Thanks, Mom. I won't do it again." She held up one of her fingers, and I laughed.

"Were you trying to tell me 'Scout's Honor'? The Boy Scout Salute involves a few more fingers."

She waved her finger at me. "No, I think I got this one right."

"All I'm saying is now it will be awhile before you do it again—because you know you will—and by then I'll be feeling charitable again."

She sighed and I made myself another cup of coffee. While I was mixing in my sugar, she finally said, "You know it's going to be your turn one of these days. I promise not to gloat. Much."

"I'll hold you to that. Besides, I've had hangovers."

"A little headache after two glasses of wine where you go jogging or some shit to feel better does *not* qualify." She rose from the table as if in slow motion, taking special care not to move her head at all. "Excuse me while I go die on the couch."

"Just be warned, my group partner will be here soon. No more talk of mental superpowers."

Her head snapped in my direction and she groaned, slapping a limp hand to her forehead. I resisted the urge to laugh at her. "Ugh. But, what? You mean someone's coming here? To your apartment?"

I shrugged. "I had no way of knowing when, or if, you'd wake up. So yeah, I invited her here. She's cool." Usually I kept college and my home separate. It was important to me for reasons I had trouble explaining, even to myself, but Amy seemed to understand.

"Okay. I—I'm sorry." She really meant it this time. "And, just real quick, a little more superpower stuff. Have you talked to Jack?"

"No! And *we're* not going to talk about it either." She opened her mouth to say something and I sighed. "So much for hoping you wouldn't remember."

A laugh popped out of her, followed by a groan. "Oh, crap, that was painful. Don't make me laugh, Lane. I may have been drunk, but I wasn't oblivious. Like I'd forget *that*. He's—" The look on my face must have really been something, because she actually quit talking. "Okay. Later," she said and changed her trajectory toward the shower.

Serena arrived while I was still *in* the shower, which is how I found her and Amy sprawled in the living room, becoming fast friends. Amy was stretched out on the couch and I pushed her feet out of the way so I could sit down.

"I like your friend," Amy said without opening her eyes.

Serena propped her feet up on the ottoman. "So, let me get this straight. *You* live here, like you, by yourself. This is *your* place—and you spend all your time in that crappy dorm why?"

"See?" Amy said. She kicked me with her foot. "I like her."

"My dorm is pretty nice," I countered.

Serena nodded. "Yeah, actually, it is. But it's not *here*." She looked around and I wondered what she was thinking. I felt strange, exposing this side of my life to new people.

"I—" I started to explain, but Serena grinned and waved her hand.

"I get it. You got problems but money ain't one. It doesn't bother me."

"Thank you." It was an odd sentiment, but I couldn't stop myself from saying it. I shouldn't feel like I had to apologize for my inheritance. I hadn't stolen it. Serena and Amy shared a look and if I hadn't already been regretting coming here for the day, I immediately regretted introducing them. They were too much alike and together were sure to cause me trouble.

"Maybe thank me *now*," Serena said, pulling a slightly grease-stained brown bag from her satchel and holding it out to me. "Because I brought the goods."

I practically dove across the coffee table to snatch it out of her hands. In the apartment, I kept almost no food, only basic non-perishable or frozen things. In other words, *nothing* like the huge, perfect, bacon-egg-and-cheese sandwich I was now stuffing into my face. It was even still a little warm. Heaven.

"Thank you," I mumbled through my full mouth and Serena laughed. While I chewed, my friends continued to bond against me.

"So you're the genius I always hear about?" Serena asked.

"Every fabulous inch of me."

"So you couldn't, like, calculate the ratio of alcohol to food to body weight or whatever and not get drunk?"

I snorted, and Amy pulled out one of her most dramatic sighs. "I *could* have, I suppose, but I was distracted by shirtless bass players and Lainey flirting with Mr. H.O.T., aka Hot Older TA." Shit. If I'd been close enough, I'd have made Serena forget Amy just said that. Instead, I had to settle for smacking my best friend probably harder than I should have. "Ow."

Serena looked back and forth between the two of us, and before I finished swallowing to say *something*, she said, "A hot TA? *Our* TA? J. Kensington?"

Amy positively glittered. "If the J. Stands for Jack, then yeah. Oh, yeah."

"I *wasn't* flirting," I finally got out.

It was Amy's turn to snort. I glared daggers at her, but when did that ever do anything but encourage her? "You were Lainey-flirting so hard."

"I don't even know what that means!"

"*I* do," Serena said. "I've seen you in class. You're most deadly when you're *not* flirting, doing your whole sweet-and-innocent thing."

"I'm not—it's not a thing!" I interjected, but they were ignoring me now.

Amy did her best—which was really good—impression of my voice. She flipped a piece of hair over her shoulder. "Hi helpless boy, I'm over here blushing and stammering atop my mile-long legs. Which do you want to do first: fall in love with me or buy me a beer?"

"I still haven't decided against killing you. Remember that." I flicked my fingers at her before I got up to throw out my trash. I knew full well they were going to continue talking about this as soon as I stepped away. So I listened from the kitchen, curious yet hating myself for it at the same time.

"Are you busting her balls or is this serious?" Serena asked. She'd lowered her voice, but I could still hear them just fine.

"Both," Amy admitted. I could hear her shifting on the couch, probably rolling over so she could better see Serena's reaction.

"You better tell me *all* of it! I *thought* he always seems a little extra into her in discussion. In a good way."

"Oh, he's into her all right. I'm pretty sure—by which I mean *entirely* sure, because I *am* a genius—if it weren't for the pesky TA thing, he'd have been taking her home by the end of the night. Or sooner."

I suppressed a squeak of outrage. I was *not* that kind of girl. Serena made this kind of hissing sound through her teeth that seemed like approval. "Hell, yes. This is perfect. Why does she seem freaked out about it?"

"Because that's how Lainey *is*. This is *exactly* what she needs, so she'll completely try to avoid it. Plus, she has some…baggage. And an ex—that *she* made an ex—but I think…" Amy had been dropping her voice lower and lower, forcing me to creep closer to the living room door, so I had no trouble hearing when she shouted "…that she's *totally* eavesdropping and might as well just come back and *talk* to us!"

Busted.

"This is *not* what I need," I told them as I returned to the living room. I pushed Amy's feet out of the way again so I could sit. When she tried to plop them back in my lap, I pushed them off then too.

She huffed, but despite her renewed energy around the topic of my not-so-love life, she was still in no condition to fight back. Words always worked fine for her though. "Just by saying that," she said, one arm back covering her eyes, "you've proved it true."

"It's not!"

"Lainey," Serena soothed. "Tell me you haven't thought about it."

I opened my mouth to lie and silence fell out. Amy snickered and I slapped her foot. "You need a bigger couch!" she grumbled. "And to get la—"

"AMY! Jesus. Could you not? That's not happening."

"Would you like it to?" Serena countered. Amy held out her fist and Serena tapped it.

"God. The two of you. This was a mistake."

"On the contrary, Lane, I think this—and one H.O.T.—is just what you needed."

"Shut up."

"I like your friend," Serena said, smiling with all her teeth.

"*I* don't. And," I added, unable to let it go, "just for the record, I would *not* have gone home with him. I'm not that kind of girl."

Serena kind of snort-laughed, while Amy rolled her eyes. "If you say so."

"I do. And I'd like to stop talking about this, please."

Amy sighed. "So this is about to get boring? I'm going to take a nap. I've got to rally." She poured herself over the edge of the couch and trudged toward her room. With a little wave, she called back to Serena, "Nice meeting you."

"You too," Serena replied, before she turned earnest eyes on me. "Lainey, for real though, if he—"

"Please let's drop it."

"Just hear me out—if he's into you, and you're into him, what's the problem? The TA thing will end soon enough. It's not complicated."

Behind me, Amy froze a step before continuing on. I sucked in a breath and let it out, slowly. Amy had once said something so similar to me. About Carter. And I'd believed her at the time.

But it *had* turned out to be complicated—so complicated. And no matter what Serena said, the Jack situation was *already* complicated. It wasn't what I needed; it was everything I was trying to avoid.

Wasn't it?

BY THE TIME Serena and I were wrapping up, Amy was back and looking more human. And I, well, I'd done a good job for a while of ignoring a familiar twist in my stomach.

"I think you'll get an A," Amy said.

"I hope so." I closed my laptop along with my eyes and leaned my head back on the couch. I was exhausted.

"We will," Serena said, not in a way that sounded like convincing yourself, but like she believed it. I envied her confidence. "You know," she added, giving the living room again an appraising eye. "For all you want to do all our projects on antiques, this place doesn't *look* like it's full of old things. Except for that." She pointed at my armoire, which did happen to be the oldest piece in the apartment, though not the oldest I owned. "And that." She indicated the early 1900s copy of *Modern Poetry* on one of the end tables.

"Oh, God," Amy said. She set her mug of tea on the coffee table rather dramatically and covered her ears. "Please don't get her going."

"*You* can go any time, you know." She stuck her tongue out at me and made no moves to leave. "They're not all strictly antiques," I told Serena, "though you're right, that one *is* old. It's French, early 1800s." It was beautiful and gleaming, with a color so deep it was almost black.

"It cost more than a car," Amy interjected and Serena's eyes went a little wide.

"It didn't," I said, but after a look from Amy, I conceded, "it didn't cost more than a new"—Amy narrowed her eyes—"*most* new cars. But anyway, the rest of the living room is mostly fifties. Because antique couches aren't always comfortable or practical."

"Because white is practical?" Serena slid her fingers over the creamy leather.

"It washes we—" I started to say before I recognized she was grinning at me and Amy couldn't stifle a giggle. "Oh, the two of you! Jesus. I should *not* have introduced you. Leave my furniture alone."

"Aw," Serena soothed. "Don't get upset."

"We kid because we care, Lane." Amy yawned and stretched, but still made no moves to get up even while Serena was packing her things.

"It's cute," Serena continued. "I like your…well, it's more than a hobby."

"Yeah," I said. "It is."

"How did you even get into it?"

"Skills of a misspent youth," Amy piped in. "This is what happens when you don't go to school."

"I went to school." I stood, ready to see Serena out, but she was looking slightly confused. "You know about my aunt, and how we traveled a lot. She always liked to go to antique stores, flea markets, things like that, for inspiration. Salvage yards too. I've seen so many rusted out and cool old cars, I should have taken up photography. Anyway, I liked them too, the shops, with all the old pretty things. I had tutors and school work goes a lot faster when you're the *only* student."

"So you spent your free time studying antiques?"

"Some of it, yeah. It's hard to have friends when you're constantly on the move…but everywhere we went, there were new antique stores."

Serena threw her bag over her shoulder, saying, "You know, now that I see this place and everything…I get you more. That's a compliment," she added quickly. "You're interesting. I get why your homework is always done early. I get why"—she cut her eyes to a still-lounging Amy—"what did you call him again?"

"H.O.T.?"

"Yeah," Serena said. "I get why Mr. H.O.T is into you, too."

"He's not—" I started, but Amy made a noise in the back of her throat, and Serena cut me off before I could say anything more.

"He is." I kept my mouth closed, because that twist in my stomach was rolling again, and I was half hoping, half hating that what she said might be true. "I get it," she repeated. "And thanks for letting me come over. I get why you don't invite people here too."

She gave me a quick hug as we said goodbye, and I closed the door behind her feeling like I—finally—had another friend.

My old friend was still waiting for me in the living room. I settled back onto my end of the couch and put my feet up on the coffee table.

"What're you doing tonight?" Amy asked as I sat down.

"I think you're looking at it." I glanced over at her. Maybe this was what she wanted to talk about. "Did you want to just stay here? Get takeout and watch a movie?"

She shook her head. "I mean, I do, but I should go. I have a date later."

"A *what?*"

She grinned. "A *phone* date."

"On Saturday night?"

Amy wrapped one of her curls around her finger. "It's the only time Caleb's roommate isn't around."

"What difference does—" I started to say, but I figured it out by the way Amy's grin had spread. I felt my cheeks light up and I put my hands over them. "Ew. Okay. Well, have fun then."

She opened her mouth to say something, then paused. Instead of whatever she *really* wanted to talk about, she nodded toward the door and said, "She was cool."

"She is," I agreed. "She's...kind of like you; I wondered if you'd get along."

Amy cut me a look. "You doubted me? I get along with *everyone.*"

"Oh yeah?" I laughed. "Since when? You tolerate your roommate, you hate your lab partner, and let's not even *mention* a few names from high school."

Bingo. A look passed over Amy's face, like I'd just opened a door she'd been locked on the other side of. She cleared her throat delicately. "Speaking of high school—"

"No, Ame."

"We can't even talk about it?"

I shook my head. "I shouldn't have mentioned it. I'm not coming." Next weekend was homecoming. I stood up and walked over to my fireplace. On the mantel were two silver candlesticks, one of them dented. I touched that one, letting the familiar hum of its macabre history buzz beneath my fingertips, though I didn't let the vision come.

Amy was standing now too. "Don't you want to see our friends?"

"I do," I said while I bent to turn on the gas burner so I could light the flames, "but I'm not going."

"What about Brooke?" she pressed. "Don't you miss her?" That hurt, and Amy knew it. My lips flattened into a thin line, but I didn't say anything. I did miss Brooke. I felt shitty enough about how I'd left our friendship, and the urge to text her, to apologize was strong. But I just couldn't do it. Brooke was Sententia, and if I stayed in touch with her, I'd still be connected. I'd had to let her go.

"Lane," Amy continued, and the tone in her voice finally made me turn around. She didn't look angry, or irritated, which I'd have preferred. She looked…sad. It hurt to think I was making her sad. "I don't understand." She sank back onto the couch and I moved to sit next to her.

"I know. But I do. You don't have to make excuses for me. Just say hi to…everyone for me."

Her pretty brown eyes, which were tired but clear now and always too smart, didn't waver from mine as she asked, "Is Carter part of 'everyone'?"

I blew out a puff of air. Hearing her say his name hurt too. "I think it's best if you just don't mention me to him at all. If he's even there."

"That's really why, right? You don't want to risk seeing him?"

"It didn't go well last time."

"That was months ago, Lane."

I shrugged. It didn't matter how long ago it was; it hadn't been long *enough*. Visiting him in DC at the end of the summer had been a Mistake with a capital M. I could still picture Alexis Morrow's cold smile through the window in the conference room door, as she leaned over Carter and his unbuckled pants. I could still feel the breathless surprise that he'd followed me into the bathroom. Still feel the way he'd kissed me there, his lips on mine and trailing down…

Amy was looking at me funny, at my neck. I realized I was tracing the path of his kisses with my hand and dropped it into my lap. In a calculated way she said, "You know he's moved on."

"I've moved on too."

She tilted her head and looked again at where my fingers had brushed my neck, at the necklace tucked under my sweater. "See, I don't quite think you have and I don't—"

"Northbrook is his home," I said, cutting her off. "This is mine. I'm not going back."

"Oh-kay," she dragged out. When I looked back at her, she repeated it, softer now and with more understanding. "Okay." I wondered what my face looked like.

"I'm sorry," I said, because that's what I always said when I disappointed someone, including myself.

Amy shook her head. "It's okay. I *don't* understand"—she held up a hand to keep me from interrupting again—"but I don't have to. It's your decision."

"Thank you." Without warning, I hugged her, a load of tension slipping off my shoulders.

Amy hugged me back. "Thank you, too. For taking care of me."

I thought that would be it, she'd said her piece and would be ready to leave, but Amy bit her lip, hesitating again. "What is it? Is there something you're not telling me?"

Her curls bounced when she shook her head. "No! Just…listen, okay?" she started, and I knew exactly what she wanted to talk about.

"Goodbye, Amy," I said, turning back toward the fireplace before she could say anything more.

Behind me, I heard her shuffle. "Okay, I get it, you don't want to talk about him either, but have you considered maybe you were *meant* to meet Jack. He's *like* you. He's someone you could be yourself with, *everything* about you. Isn't that a *good* thing?" She paused, waiting for me to respond or for her words to sink in, I didn't know. When I didn't say anything, she sighed. "Okay. Bye, Lane. Just think about it, okay?"

I didn't move until the door closed behind her and I flopped down on my couch. Everything from last night to Amy's last words raced through my head. I hadn't wanted to think about it, but now I couldn't think about anything else.

All I'd wanted to do was forget, to be *free*, from Sententia and from everything. But how could I be free from who I was? Maybe that was just a foolish dream. I fell asleep there in my living room and dreamed of Jack Kensington instead.

Chapter Eight

Carter

Flying sucked. In the time it took me to pry my fingers off the arm rest, Alexis was already wheeling her—surprisingly—compact bag down the aisle with one hand while dialing a car service with the other. It was obvious to anyone watching she'd been born holding her passport, ready to be stamped. Just another of the considerable differences between us.

"I still can't believe that was your first time," she said, as she zoomed around slower-moving travelers in the concourse. "I mean, you're *twenty* years old."

"I thought you'd be happy to be my first partner for *something*."

"Ha! Who's funny now? Did you get your little set of wings from the Captain? You were a *very* good boy on the flight."

She didn't ask if I'd liked it, the flying. I'm sure the answer was obvious. Being cooped up and powerless were not high on my list of enjoyable activities. I didn't look forward to doing it again in a few days. But for now, I was home, or almost.

An hour into the two hour ride from Boston, Alexis's hand landed on my thigh, stilling its bouncing. As if she knew what I was thinking, Alexis said, "So, are you just going to work all weekend, or will we actually get to have some fun?" She was looking at her phone, not directly at me.

"It's still my business too, babe." When she'd said she wanted to come, I was all for it. But *Homecoming* meant something different to her than it did to me.

"I know." She dropped the pretense of the phone and leaned her face toward mine. "But it's been running just fine without you for months now. This is a *getaway*, not a workaway."

"We'll see."

She groaned. "You're impossible." I had no defense for that. "You're *at least* coming to the bonfire."

"We'll see."

THE NEXT DAY, I ran close to ten miles. My feet didn't want to stop and my lungs urged me to go farther because the *air*. The air tasted clear and smelled *right*. The way air should, like evergreen and freedom. If I ever made it to heaven, the air would be exactly like it was here.

It felt so good to be on my home ground, but also, strange. *Everything* seemed larger or smaller or somehow *different*, but also exactly the same. Was this what everyone felt like when they left home and came back? It was all familiar yet vaguely unfamiliar at the same time. Now I compared home to another place in a way I'd never done before.

Another thing I'd never done before was attend the Northbrook Homecoming bonfire. I always gave the store as an excuse—it was our busiest weekend of the year—but in truth I just hadn't wanted to. Until last year, I *would* have come with Lainey, but we had dinner with Uncle Dan instead. So maybe I was glad it was something I'd never done. I only had memories of *not* being here with Lainey.

From the shadows between two pine trees, I observed the party. The heat of the fire didn't quite reach where I was hiding, but the air was slightly smoky and perfect. Sparks drifted toward the tall forest while voices competed with the crackling of the fire. Juniors, seniors, a few sophomores, and Academy faculty mingled with alumni. I scanned the crowd for the headmaster, but didn't see her blade-like form anywhere. She saw me, though.

"Mr. Penrose." I froze for half a second before I glanced over my shoulder toward the sound of her voice, but I wasn't that surprised. I had just been looking for her.

I nodded. "Headmaster."

She glided to a stop next to me, comfortable on the outskirts like I was. "I'm surprised to see you here."

"Pleasantly?"

Her thin smile made me proud. I could still get under her skin with a single word. "If memory serves," she said, "this is the first bonfire you've attended."

I shrugged. "I wouldn't say I've attended it yet."

"No, I suppose you haven't. You always were content just to loiter in the shadows."

I gritted my teeth and said nothing. Constance Stewart had been a near constant presence in my life, like a wicked aunt I didn't choose and couldn't get rid of. Lainey had liked her, though. She said I misunderstood her, but she was wrong. The headmaster and I understood each other *too* well.

"Are you well?" she asked after she'd given her dig long enough to sink in.

Carefully, I said, "I'm keeping busy," because it was true. It was pointless to lie, even politely, to the Perceptum's best *Vidi Veritas*—lie detector—in a generation.

"I'm glad to hear it," she said and I cut a look at her. It wasn't a pleasantry; Dr. Stewart didn't deal in them either. I felt off balance. I'd been gone too long to know what her game might be. I didn't want to walk into a trap. Before I could decide what was safe to say next, she continued. "How do you find your work for the senator?"

"Challenging. In a good way."

She nodded. "You've always needed more challenges than we could provide here. Even if now I have to look at my clock, rather than out my office window, to know when it's time to begin my day."

Well, well. "I knew you'd miss me," I said, grinning with all my teeth.

With uncharacteristic softness, she said, "I find I miss them all," and I gaped at her. "Well, some more than others," she clarified, straightening her spine.

"The graduates?"

"Last year's, yes. They were my first class, or perhaps you don't recall." Now that she said it, of course I did. She became headmaster the same year Alexis and Amy started here, in the seventh grade. Technically the same year I started the Academy, in ninth. "I'm glad to see so many of them here. Though a few are missing." She looked back toward me, and there it was. The trap was sprung.

I said nothing. I could feel her eyes still watching me, but kept mine on the fire.

"I don't suppose Miss Young will be joining us this year?" she asked, hopeful, and I shook my head.

"I'm not the right person to ask."

"I was…surprised," she said, "to hear about your…parting."

Now I did look at her. She said *surprised* but she also meant *sorry*. Not in a taunting way, but genuinely. "So was I."

"She was…good for you, in a way."

She was good for you, too, I thought, because by God, Constance Stewart was *trying*. She actually felt sorry for me, a Penrose, something that never would have happened before Elaine Young appeared here and cast her magic on all of us. "She was a challenge," is what I said.

The headmaster half smiled. "She was that. But perhaps she needed a different kind of challenge." She sighed. "Still, I'd have liked to ask her some things."

"Those are some answers I wouldn't mind your sharing with me. Now that I know how much you miss me." I turned my toothful smile on her and she actually chuckled.

"Yes, well, perhaps next year we'll get the chance. Now, go Cartwright." She gestured toward the fire. "Attend the bonfire. Think of it as another challenge," she added, and I smiled for real. "And give my regards to the senator."

I nodded and lifted my hand in farewell before wandering forward. I wondered what it meant that the good Dr. Stewart was as doubtful about Lainey's and my breakup as I'd been. It had my head all in the wrong space and I considered finding Alexis to tell her I was going home.

But then I heard her, the throaty, unmistakable sound of her laugh drifting over the crackle of the fire and the annoying noise of my own brain. Amy Moretti. I edged through the crowd until I caught sight of her. She looked great. Older. Some of the roundness was gone from her face, making her less sweet and more beautiful. I'd wondered if— hoped?—she'd be here.

When she turned in my direction, I waved and a huge grin broke across her face. As soon as I was in reaching distance, she threw her arms around me. I held on for a long time.

"I knew I heard your laugh," I told her.

"I knew I saw your ass," she said to my chest, and then pinched said ass. Ah, Amy. I missed her. I'd called her at first, when Lainey wouldn't take my calls, but it didn't help. All our talks amounted to was pity, and I couldn't stand that, so I stopped calling. She reached up to muss my hair. "It's so short. I love it. Gawd, you look good, Penrose. Except for *this*." She touched the shadow still lingering under my eye. "I won't even ask. But seriously, you're more handsome, I think. How's that *possible?*"

I grinned. "You look good too, Moretti. And it's good to see you. What are you doing here?"

"*Me?* Like you thought I'd miss this?! The real question is what are *you* doing here? You never came when you *lived* here!"

I shrugged. "I miss here. More than I thought I would." Which was saying something. I didn't mention that Lex had all but dragged me across the street. "Is Caleb here?" I asked before I realized it was an assumption.

But all she said was, "No," and shook her head. "He wanted to be but, you know. Iowa. And plane tickets."

"So you're still…?"

She laughed. "Yeah, of course." Of course. At what must have been the look on my face, her cheeks reddened and she fumbled, "I mean, you know, last year we worked it out and everything—So. How're classes? College is different, right? It's harder, but classes were hard here too…"

We talked and joked for a while, slipping back into the easy banter that had always made her my friend, even before Lainey. But the absence hovered, the conspicuous hole in the space between us. Finally, I gave in. I told myself I wouldn't ask, but now, after the headmaster had brought her up, I couldn't stop myself. I needed to know.

"Is she coming?" Amy knew who I meant. She opened and closed her mouth before shaking her head. I put my hands in my pockets. "How is she?"

Amy sighed. "Do you think that's a wise question?"

"I know it isn't."

After another sigh, she gave in, as I knew she would. "She's good, hon. She's good."

"I'm glad," I said, and I almost believed myself.

"I think…God, I probably shouldn't even say this, but I think she missed you, even though she, well, you know. But she's good." I didn't miss the past tense in what she shouldn't have said. She shifted on her feet next to me, holding her hands out toward the fire.

"Is she…with anyone?"

She shook her head. "Not yet." Which meant there was someone.

"Would I like him?"

With a sideways glance and a little laugh-cough, she said, "Um. Probably not." Before I could ask something more painful, she added, "Speaking of…Seriously? Alexis?"

"She's not as bad as you think."

"She's the devil in a dress, Carter!"

"Then maybe I'm not as good as you think."

"Carter…" I went to turn away, but she caught my arm and held it. "Hey, c'mon. I'm sorry. She and I…well, you know."

"She helped keep you from being expelled last year."

"I know," Amy said. "And I appreciate that. But she didn't do it for me."

And there she was again, Lainey. Right there in between everything, even Amy and Lex. I blew out a breath. All around us were friends and familiar faces, laughing, joking. Happy. "Speaking of, I should go find her."

"Hey." Amy's voice softened and the corners of her pretty lips turned down. She was still holding my arm and her eyes searched mine. "How are *you*? Are you happy?"

A genuine question deserved a genuine answer. The fact was this: "I don't know."

"Oh, Penrose."

Her eyes got this wet shimmer, like she might cry for me. She hugged me again, and I hugged her back, but this was my time to exit. Once again our conversation had devolved into pity. It was worse than on the phone—I could *see* it. Hell, I bet others could too. Some of the other kids were sure to be watching us. Funny how I'd never been concerned about that before. Everything about me had grown pathetic.

Alexis emerged from the woods then, saving me from searching for her. Her cheeks were pink and eyes glassy. Her arm was slung around her cousin, Mandi, who was probably the only freshman brave enough to come to the alumni bonfire.

"I really do have to go," I said to Amy, who released me and followed my gaze. Her expression turned dour.

"Me too. The other way. I..." We hung in a moment of awkward, something we'd never had before. There was a line; I'd crossed it. Alexis was waiting for me on the other side. Finally, Amy just said, "Bye, Penrose. It was good to see you."

I kissed her head. "Stay out of trouble."

She laughed. "Too late for you, huh? See you." She waved and was gone, melting back into the crowd.

They were giggling when I got to them. "Hi Carter!" Mandi trilled. She clung to Lex, arms around her waist, big smile on her perfect little face. Her eyes were huge and glassy. I nodded at her and kept my distance. Mandi was dangerous, too young and too pretty and too unstable. I hadn't forgotten what she did to Amy and Caleb last year, and I didn't excuse it. "We were in the wooooddsss!" She dissolved into more giggles.

"I can see that."

"Hey, baby." That was Lex, big eyes and big smile a mirror of her little cousin's. She dragged Mandi with her until we were a threesome.

She threw an arm around me, put her face close to mine. "Having fun?"

"Not as much as you." It was colder away from the fire, but I didn't think they felt it.

"You should have come with!" Mandi said. "Lex says you could use it." My eyes snapped hard in her direction, but then she was squealing, "Patch!!" and tearing away from Alexis to take up the same position at the side of a junior douchebag.

"Really?" I said to Alexis.

"What?" She grinned and snuggled closer.

"You took your freshman cousin with impulse control problems 'into the woods.'" *Into the woods* was code for a lot of things at North-brook. There were a lot of things you could do out there, away from supervision.

Lex nuzzled into my neck. "You *should* have come with us, then you wouldn't care."

I pushed my hand through my hair, took a deep breath and let it out, trying not to let her goading work. I thought again how different a year could be. I never thought I'd be here, with Alexis, like this. But I wanted to. It felt both wrong and good, and somehow that combination felt even better. "Did you miss me?" Lex kissed my chin and batted her eyelashes as we inserted ourselves back into the mix around the fire.

"I talked to Amy." She was just at the edge of where we could see her, talking and laughing with people that, a year ago, I'd have been talking and laughing with too.

"How's that skank doing?"

"Don't."

"Sorry. Old habit. I don't even think she's a skank, not really."

"She's not."

"She's more like a bitch."

I sighed. "She thinks the same of you."

Lex smiled. "So how's that bitch doing?"

"Pretty great."

"Yeah?" She blew out a breath. "Then how's the other *skank* doing?"

My arm locked around her. "Lex."

"What? It's obvious you talked about her."

Was it? "She's not—"

"A skank. Sure. Of course she's not. She's a saint."

"What the fuck, Lex? Are you *trying* to pick a fight?" I tugged on my hair again. I was more conscious of doing it, now that it was so short, but I couldn't stop myself either.

She leaned in, mischief in her eyes as she planted a kiss on the edge of my jaw. "Maybe. You're sexy as hell when you're angry, you know. I might just want to take you to the Cove."

I exhaled a long breath. "I'm ready to leave."

"Wait," she said softly, into my collar. "Sorry, babe. Really." She kissed at my chin again. "I'm sorry."

"Okay."

"I just wanted one night where she didn't intrude."

Here? As if that was possible. Besides which: "*You* brought her up."

Her mouth opened like she was ready to snap at me, before realization settled in. She giggled, nuzzling into me and looking up with glassy eyes. "I did, didn't I? My bad." We stood there for a moment, before Lex laughed again. "C'mon, let's mingle! I haven't even said hi to some of these assholes!"

I laughed and instead of what I always said—no—I agreed. "Lead the way, m'lady."

I SLEPT LATE the next morning, from some combination of exhaustion and content. I'd run forever the day before, stayed up late, and didn't *have* to get up. So I didn't. The lure of my own bed, in my own room, in my own house was undeniable. Even after I woke up, I laid there a while, watching the familiar pattern of shadows change with the growing daylight. I watched Alexis for a while too. All the calculation she carried while awake, her style and precision, disappeared while she was asleep. She looked younger, more innocent. I liked it. It reminded me…

I stood up, fast. The bed shook and the floor creaked where my feet slapped it. Next to where I'd just been, Alexis stirred but didn't wake. With more care for quiet, I slipped on a shirt and out into the hall. Aunt Mel was at the kitchen table.

"Hey."

"Did you have fun last night?" she asked, taking a sip of coffee and pretending she hadn't been waiting for me.

"Actually…yeah. I didn't hate it." I poured my own coffee and helped myself to a muffin before I sat across from her. God I had missed these muffins. It was apple cinnamon and still warm. She must have gotten up early to make a fresh batch. I ate it in three bites.

Aunt Mel smiled. "So are you sorry you never went to one before?"

Was I? "No. But I'm not sorry I went to one now." I helped myself to another muffin. "How were sales?"

"Not as good as last year, but strong."

It was strange even asking that question, worrying about the store but not being actively involved day-to-day. I couldn't decide if it made me sad or proud that it was still standing, without my holding it up every day. My whole life had been Penrose Books, even before I was old enough to read. What did it mean when your whole life kept running without you? That you'd helped prepare it well, or that you hadn't been that important to begin with? I didn't want to think about that.

"It's not the same without you, you know." It was like Aunt Mel could read my thoughts.

"How could it be?" I said and grinned before I ate the last half of my muffin. She punched me in the shoulder, but she was smiling too. Dad's smile. I thought I wouldn't think of him as much, now that I didn't spend my days surrounded by things that reminded me of him, like his sister. But I did. Whenever I looked in the mirror.

I'd always known we looked enough alike for it to be obvious, but I never used to see him in my reflection. Not until my heart was broken. Dad had worn heartache like a shroud my whole life. I'd hated it because it was my fault; I took my mother from him just by being born. And now that I understood, I hated it more.

"I mean it though," Aunt Mel continued. For a second, I'd forgotten she was there. "No one will ever find books as fast as you. Or read so many. Did you see the galleys I left in your room?" I nodded. Of course I did. I'd already packed the ones I wanted to take and rearranged the rest in the boxes under my bed. A funny thing about selling books: you drowned in ones you got for free. "Nonfiction is down without you," she added.

"I thought you were trying to cheer me up."

"I thought a trip to Dad's would do that," she countered. It would, but I shook my head. Aunt Mel darted a look over my shoulder, down the hall toward my room, and came around the table to hug my shoulders. "Not ready for that step yet, huh?"

I shook my head again. I couldn't. Not Dad's Diner, not with Lex. Not to the place I'd only ever taken Lainey. "Not yet," I said. Maybe never. Aunt Mel let me go so she could grab the coffee pot to warm my mug and hers. She sat back down with the sugar bowl and stirred.

"Do you think she'll be here at all this weekend?" Obviously she wasn't talking about Lex.

I shook my head. "No."

"Do you want her to be?"

Did I? No. Yes. *No.* I caught myself just before touching the skin below my eye. I let my hand continue up to run through my hair instead, even though I was trying to break up that habit. It felt good.

I didn't want to lie to Aunt Mel, or to myself, so I said, "Maybe?" My voice sounded too hopeful and I hated it. I wanted not to want to see her, but I did. Want to. "I hope—"

My door opened and shut, releasing a bleary-eyed Alexis into the kitchen a few seconds later. I wondered if she'd been listening, for how long and how much she heard. She didn't look like it though. She looked groggy and hung over, if that was the right word for it. I wasn't worried Aunt Mel would disapprove. She wasn't like that. She'd already forgiven Alexis for plenty of her less than stellar behavior in the past. Also, I was pretty sure she'd visited the woods with her friends many times.

"Good morning." Alexis yawned. "What's the matter, babe?" I dropped my hand from my head to around her shoulders and kissed her cheek.

"Nothing. I was waiting for you before I went downstairs."

She nodded absently, and Aunt Mel smiled. "Can I get you something, sweetie? Looks like you had more fun than Carter last night."

"Always." She flashed her perfect, white smile. "Coffee sounds really good, thanks. Ooh, are those muffins?"

I hesitated to leave Lex alone with my aunt, but there was nothing either could say that they didn't already know about me. It felt good to spend the day in the store. I'd meant to stay out of the way and poke around in the background, but by noontime I was immersed in my old routines. Busy at work, for the first time all weekend, I relaxed.

Nothing had changed. Penrose Books was still mine. I still fit here. I still *wanted* to be here. For the first time in months, the dogging worry that I would leave and everything would change, was quiet. I felt good. I felt *home*.

The bell over the door jingled and in spilled Lex with an entourage of girls nearly but not quite as beautiful as her and cups from Anderson's. I smiled. No, things hadn't changed, but then again, they had. When Lex saw me, she scampered over, kissing me roundly and without an ounce of apology. She looked glossy and fresh, all traces of her exploits of the night before gone.

"Hey, babe. It's sooo nice out today, like a real fall weekend, finally. I brought you this, figured you'd need one by now." She stuck a coffee into my hand and kissed me again before flitting away in a whirl of dark hair and confidence. Lex settled in the lounge with Brooke Barros and some of her other friends who hadn't graduated. The next time I passed by, they called to me.

"Hey, Carter!"

"We missed you!"

"Why don't you come stoke my fire?"

I obliged.

I had missed this. Really missed this. Yet, as I settled more wood in the fireplace and bantered with the girls, I felt suddenly shitty, realizing that. I'd missed the store, and my family, and my *life*, but I'd missed, too, the feeling I wouldn't have named before: of being a big fish. This was my pond. I'd jumped into a much bigger one, an ocean, and found I barely knew how to swim.

No one liked drowning. No one liked realizing they craved the attention of a captive audience either. I thought of it for the first time, how I was getting older but the students weren't. Collectively, they'd always be no more than eighteen. I was almost twenty-one. I felt at once too-old and foolishly young. When I left the girls in the lounge, I kept my smile in place, but it lacked the ease it used to have.

And for the first time, I felt ready to leave, to go back to DC.

Chapter Nine

Lainey

The next week, I glided into my seat in discussion next to Serena right on time, not a second early, and spent most of the hour with my eyes trained on my notebook. It was possibly the longest hour of the entire semester. I'd thought about skipping outright, but I couldn't do it forever, and besides, I didn't like skipping. It made me feel guiltier than…whatever I felt about Jack.

When it was finally over and time to pass around our previous assignments, I barely looked at the stack before pulling mine off the top and passing it on. I was ready to dash out of the room until I was distracted by the bright pink sticky note covering the grade on my assignment. For the first time, it read:

Come see me during office hours

Ugh! I tried to look at Jack without looking at him. There was no way my assignment was that bad. *No way*. And he'd *promised* we weren't grading each other at the show. If I wasn't already so pissed at him, I'd have been pissed.

I went to rip the note off and check the damage, except I realized it was two notes. Underneath the ominous one was a second sticky.

Let me explain. Please?

Beneath that was a B+.

I peeked at Jack again to find him watching me, his expression the very definition of chagrin. I sighed. I couldn't avoid this—avoid him— all semester. He was still my TA. In the brief second our eyes met, I nodded. His expression melted into relief, a tiny smile bringing out that damned dimple. God, he was cute, and I was afraid—no, *sure*— my attraction to him was clouding my judgment.

I WAITED UNTIL near the end of Jack's office hours to arrive. Then I waited at least three more minutes in the hall. I stood there doing some covert yoga breathing and *trying* to work out my emotions. I'd been trying to work them out for over a week now. The problem was I couldn't decide if I was being rational or just emotional. Or something. It wasn't Jack's fault he was who, *what*, he was, but I was still scared. If anyone had reason to be, I felt like I did.

"Office hours are usually *in* the office," Jack said from the door and I jumped so high I was surprised I didn't hit my head on the ceiling. "Sorry."

He looked good, leaning there, in his perfectly worn in shoes and Brooks Brothers casual. I wasn't used to guys who were so…put together. It didn't seem like he *tried* to dress like an executive-in-training. More like he was born to it. The look suited him and he owned it.

When I didn't move, he cleared his throat and said, "I'm glad you came. Did you want to come in? Or if not…well, I can apologize out here just as well."

"That's the thing," I said, finally finding my voice. "I'm not sure you actually have anything to apologize for." *Also, I was just blatantly checking you out which I should* not *have been doing.*

"Why don't you come in and we'll figure it out. Fair?"

I nodded and followed him into the office. I wasn't sure what I expected, but it wasn't this. It was small and cramped and windowless, a rather miserable place to have to spend time, especially if any of the other three TAs were around. The scent of someone's cologne still lingered, which made me wonder how powerful it smelled when the wearer was actually *there*.

Jack sat at his assigned desk, furthest in the corner, forcing his visitors to sit awkwardly out past the other two. I called to him, "No offense, but how do you stand it in here?"

He grinned. At least I think he did, in the murky office distance. He rolled his chair forward, past the other desks, until he was positioned across from me on the opposite wall. "What?" he said. "You don't like my cave?" I laughed, breaking a bubble of tension that had lingered between us. "I assure you," he went on, "my cavemates are as charming as our shared space. Maybe you'll even meet them."

"If I'm lucky, right?"

"Right." He leaned back in his chair, more relaxed now. Glancing at his watch, he pushed the door until it was almost closed. "Do you mind?" he asked, looking at me and waiting for permission to close it all the way.

Strange, I thought. In high school, this would never have been allowed, being closed together in such a...*private* space. The hardest thing to get used to in college was *freedom*. Plenty of opportunity to make your own decisions, and your own mistakes. I hoped this wasn't one. I nodded.

"Thanks," Jack said. The door closed with little more than a click. "Hours are almost over anyway. I thought our conversation could benefit from a little...discretion." He looked at me when he said this, and I cleared my throat.

"Yeah. Probably. I kind of got out of the habit of worrying about that."

"It's nice, isn't it?" he agreed. "My grandfather liked to say my most important class every year at Webber was discretion. My father, on the other hand, called it *stress*. You don't realize how stressful it is *actively* keeping a secret every day until you don't have to do it anymore. I assume it's the same at 'Brook."

"'Brook?" I teased. "Is that the slang?"

He grinned. "It is. For us anyway. I guess I don't know if it's derogatory."

"Why even bother? It's not like *Northbrook* is so long. It's the same number of syllables as Webber!"

"But it's a compound word. Much more snooty sounding."

I laughed. We were joking. About secrets and *compound words*. I'd come here a ball of stress and now I was sitting casually with my knees tucked next to me and my bag thrown on the floor. I wasn't even sure how it happened.

"Well, that's certainly better than the expression you left me with the other night. Maybe I haven't completely fucked this up?" Another thing that would never happen in high school. But he was smiling, not tense but more like hopeful. It made me unsettled, though not necessarily in a bad way. Like the dichotomy of power between us wasn't all that uneven.

"About that…" My lips were dry, so I wet them, and I was pretty sure he watched the movement with interest. I didn't know how to put into words what I'd been feeling without examining all the underlying mess more closely than I wanted to, but Jack saved me from it. He held up his hand.

"I think I understand. And I'm sorry."

"I *think*," I said, "I'm sorry too."

"No no." He shook a finger at me and I tried not to giggle. "This is *my* apology. I get what happened now. I'd never seen someone react so negatively before. Usually, I mean, there aren't *really* that many of us, despite how it feels when we're all smashed together at our academies. Other people I've met are always excited. But I understand why it was different for you: because I knew something about you that you didn't know about me."

Yes. That was exactly it. I nodded. "I mean, I guess just because someone went to Webber doesn't guarantee they're Sententia—"

He let his eyes widen. "What? What's that?"

"Oh. Sorry. For guys? It means impotent…"

"*Definitely* not Sententia then."

Laughing, I asked, "So what *are* you?" I knew the impropriety of asking so directly, but we were already being improper.

After a beat he said, "My grandfather says I'm a no-good Herald," and winked. I must have pulled a face because he laughed. "What? Don't like Heralds?"

"No!" I said, then blushed as I realized how that must sound. "Shit. I mean no, it's not that. I don't even know many of you. It's just that one of them…isn't my favorite person." Heralds were what I thought of as just below Thought Movers in the Sententia hierarchy. Their gifts projected onto others. They didn't have impetus—they couldn't force anything—but they had influence. Alexis Morrow was a Herald.

Jack produced a slow, knowing smile, one that was strangely seductive. It made me think he had secrets, ones I'd like to find out. I didn't realize I was distractedly staring at his lips until they moved. "A rival, huh?" he said.

I was pretty sure my blush got deeper. "No." Lie. "Well, sort of. But mostly she was just a bitch."

"I've known a few of those myself," he said, nodding. "Sometimes it comes with the territory. There's plenty of conceit to go around when you're…special, like we all are, but I think Heralds tend to be the most conceited of the bunch. It's easy to get caught up in the effects of your own abilities." I understood that fully, since my abilities inevitably gave me moments of morbidity. "And you?" he prompted. "If you'd care to share."

"What, it's not in my file?"

He gave a little smile and shake of his head. "Unfortunately, they don't note it on your transcript. Though if your grades are any indication, I'd suspect you were a *Lumen*."

On a whim, I told him, "I'm a Thought Mover." It was mostly true.

"Really?" He seemed…surprised, but pleasantly so. He smiled again, appraising me.

"What? Don't like us?" At that he outright chuckled, a deep sound that made my toes tingle. I shifted my legs out from under me. "Or maybe you've never met one before?"

"Never one so pretty," he quipped, and it was the kind of thing he *shouldn't* say, that should have had me bolting from his office out of anger or at least a sense of self-preservation. But whether I should or not, I liked it. Which fact *also* should have sent me running, but instead had me blushing and looking at my knees. "Or so dangerous," he added, and my euphoria disappeared.

I jerked my head up so quickly it almost hurt. "What?"

Jack held up his hands, palms out. "Sorry," he said, and it sounded sincere. He cleared his throat and straightened his funny tie—unnecessarily, since he seemed to prefer it a little askew—smoothing his fingers over the silk. "I was going to say you move my thoughts without trying, which is the truth, but entirely inappropriate. Like several things I've said today. So. Sorry," he repeated.

His chair creaked as he shifted, and I blushed harder. I couldn't understand why I hadn't passed out yet, because all of my blood had to be in my face. "Apology accepted," I said finally.

He wiped a hand over his face. "God, this job is harder than he made it sound!"

"Who?"

"What?"

I giggled. "Harder than who made it sound?"

"Shit," Jack muttered before he stood abruptly and strode to his desk, back turned to me. In the small office, I felt his breeze as he passed. "Professor Gupta, of course." He checked his phone and typed a few letters before shaking his head and returning to the chair across from me. He turned the phone over in his hands as he spoke. "This...wasn't my plan. But the offer came and I couldn't turn it down. I hadn't wanted to, but even if I did, Grandfather would have, uh, convinced me otherwise. And it's turned out to be not what I expected."

"I'm sorry."

"No! God, I'm a complete ass. Complaining while I sit here with you. It's not what I expected in bad and good ways, don't worry. Never worry about me."

"I'll...try not to," I said, because I couldn't promise I wouldn't. I was intrigued by this moment, where Jack's easy charm had slipped to reveal someone who was maybe a little unsure and still trying to figure things out. It made him seem so *real*, so like me, and I wanted to know that Jack as well as the cool, relaxed one. "Your grandfather sounds pretty tough."

He exhaled forcefully through his nose. "That's a nice way to put it. But you didn't come here to talk about my family issues."

"That is *exactly* why I came here," I said and he cracked a smile. "Don't we all have family issues?"

"Do we? What are yours?"

If only. My *real* family issues weren't for the telling. I fussed with some strands of my hair that had fallen over my shoulder. "It's more a *lack of family* issue for me, honestly."

After a beat, he said, "I'm going to guess the *real* issue is with your extended *Sententia* family." Nailed it. "Is that why you only went to Northbrook for two years?"

"Um, no, not exactly. It's a long story."

"I've got nowhere to be." He checked the time on his phone to confirm. Neither did I. My classes were over for the day.

What the hell, I thought. *Why not?* I took one deep breath and plunged. "See, I didn't even know I was Sententia until I got to Northbrook. It was…well, it was a lot of things, but I'll just go with overwhelming. I thought I was getting away from it when I left there. So, yeah, when you said you went to Webber, I freaked."

"That's actually true? You really didn't know what you, what *we* were until, what, two years ago?" I shook my head. "That's crazy."

"Pretty much."

With the toe of his shoe, Jack absently moved his chair back and forth. "So, how did you even…?"

How to explain without spending the entire night in his cramped, dark office? "It really is a long story. How about I give you the high-lights?"

"I'm listening."

"Okay. Listen really closely, because I don't repeat myself." He stilled his chair and leaned forward, arms resting on his knees and hands folded. I grinned at him. "Perfect. Ready? Once there was a lit-tle girl whose parents died and was raised by her world-traveling Godmother, and when the girl turned thirteen and started to grow up and go crazy in the brain, her doctors decided she couldn't be a world traveler anymore and an opportunity from her *dad's* past came up and landed her at a special school where she found out she *wasn't* crazy, fell in love, met her best friend, saved a girl's life, broke a heart, and doesn't ever plan to go back. The end." I leaned my head back and took a deep breath, winded by the time I finished. It felt good, though, to unburden.

Jack sat up and was quiet for a few seconds, his toe moving his chair again as if he didn't realize he was doing it. Finally, "Saved a life?"

"Another long story, but yes." And really, I should have said *ruined*. I was hardly the hero of that story.

After another pause, Jack said, "I'm sorry about your parents."

"Thanks. And me too, but it's been a long time."

He stopped rolling his chair and cocked his head to the side. "Fell in love?"

I sighed. "It's the 'broke a heart' that's really more important."

"So you *are* dangerous." His tiny half-smile taunted me and made my stomach twist. It felt strange to talk about Carter while thinking about that smile.

"Amy doesn't call me 'heartbreaker' for nothing."

"Is your friend…?"

I shook my head. "No, but…she knows. She's cool though. Promise." When he didn't say anything for another second, I took the opportunity. "Okay, your turn." I assumed the same waiting pose he'd taken before my story.

Jack laughed and crossed his arm over his chest. "You'll have to listen carefully, just so you don't fall asleep. My story is pretty boring, actually."

I doubted that. "I'd still like to hear it."

"Once," he said, "there was a boy whose father, no, whose *grandfather* was a wealthy patriarch in a long line of them and when *his* son turned out to be a disappointment, all the family expectations landed on the boy and so far he's living up to them."

Interesting. "Does he want to, the boy?"

Jack rubbed his hands across his thighs. "Do you know, in twenty-three years, no one's ever asked me that so directly?"

"Do you know the answer?"

"Yes."

I laughed. "Yes you know, or yes you…?"

"Yes. I want to. So far. No one's forcing me, not really. My father went his own way and I could too."

"So you chose Webber?"

"Well, we have a Legacy longer than the state of California, so really, it chose me. My dad went too. I *did* choose to live with my grandparents while I was there. Get some quality time drinking the family Kool-Aid, I guess."

"Was it…bitter?" The way he said that made it sound like it was.

He smiled and looked at me, *really* looked at me, as if this whole conversation was an unexpected surprise. "You're too perceptive for your own good, you know?" With a few pushes of his foot, he rolled his chair over until he was next to me, in the small space between my chair and the door. When he put his arm down, it touched mine and neither of us moved them for a few seconds. "Honestly," Jack continued, "it wasn't except maybe in retrospect, or maybe aftertaste? Yeah. That. Don't feel bad for me. I don't."

"Really?" I didn't believe him.

"Really." He leaned closer to me, his arm pressing against mine once more and our heads nearly touching. "I'm just telling a sob story to a pretty girl."

I breathed out. "It's working."

Jack stayed like that, next to me, for another second before sitting straight and rolling himself away. From the safety of his desk, he said, "Then I think my job is probably done for today." A glance at my watch told me this was true. We'd been talking for a long time and I stood and stretched. "To make this official," he added, "good job on your assignment. Keep that up. Come see me again if you need more help."

"No, thank *you* Mr. Kensington. I feel much better…about class now." Which reminded me of something I'd wanted to ask since the first day. "Is the J. really for John?"

He laughed. "Not at all. It's Jarvis. Jarvis Ablemoor Kensington the Third, actually," he pronounced and I couldn't keep my eyebrows from shooting up. That was a heavy name for a guy who seemed so carefree. "I know. It's terribly pretentious, right? Dad's homage to Grandfather. Mom gave in on the full name but refused the nick-names—Father is Javvy." It sounded almost Spanish when he pronounced it, Haa-vy, the J like an H. "If I was from around here and went by that, people would think my name was 'Harvey'. Anyway, J.A.K. makes Jack. That's what stuck."

"It fits you. Much better than Jarvis. Or Ablemoor." I snickered and was rewarded by the sexy upturn at the corner of his mouth that had fascinated me since the first time I'd seen it.

Yeah, I was in so much trouble. Except he was Sententia and that was trouble I'd promised myself I *wouldn't* get into.

I resolved all over again to keep my distance.

Chapter Ten

Carter

Fridays I had only one morning class, so I spent the afternoon with money. Hypothetical money. *Other people's* hypothetical money. I may have owned a bookstore, but numbers were a second language I spoke fluently. No one remembered how, before the Sententia genes had sparked, I'd been best at *math*.

My uncle did though. Of course he did. With Alexis's help, I modeled donation projections. Together we were not only accurate, we were killer at maximizing. I wondered what the world would think if they knew the reason Senator Astor's fund raising efforts were so successful was two kids who couldn't legally drink.

I was in my cube when I heard Uncle Dan coming down the hall. This happened often because my cube was so close to his office. Which was another reason the interns all secretly hated me. It was strange, going from an environment where everyone liked me to one where inherently they *didn't* while being essentially the same person. I supposed that was politics.

I began to suspect I'd made a mistake, majoring in Political Science. I *wanted* to be good at it. I *was* good at the *science* part. But actual politics, I wasn't cut out for. I added that to my list of self-disappointments. Then, because I was alone and already wallowing, I pulled out the note and stared at it while listening to my uncle approach.

"Where's your protégé, Dan?" His companion was from somewhere south of the Mason-Dixon Line, I could tell that much.

"My nephew Carter, you mean?" he replied. "He's just across the hall."

"No. I thought—"

"Let me introduce you."

I was standing in front of my desk by the time they appeared in my doorway. Uncle's companion looked close to his age, in a suit even more expensive than his, with the build and tanned face of someone who didn't sit behind a desk all day.

"Ah good, you are here." Uncle Dan stepped forward to embrace me. "How was your trip, son?"

"Fine, sir, but I'm glad to be back. Headmaster Stewart sends her regards."

"Yes, I'm sure she does," he said, nodding, before he gestured to expensive suit. "Cartwright, this is Harlan Waites."

Ah ha. It's funny how, after my years of genealogy work for the Perceptum, I could close my eyes and picture a man's entire family tree yet not know what he looked like until that moment. He shook my hand. It was firm, well-practiced. He was born shaking hands.

"It's nice to finally meet you, sir," I said. "My condolences on the loss of your father." Winston Waites had passed away just a few

months ago, after I'd moved. Harlan had taken his seat on the Perceptum Council. That explained why he was here.

"Likewise, and I appreciate that," Harlan replied with a solemn nod
of his head. He eyed me with keener interest than I liked before turning to my uncle with his grin as wide as the Texas sky. "Daniel, I was
hoping to get that tour you're always promising."

Uncle nodded. "Of course, Harlan. Let me ask Marita who's available."

"How about your nephew here? He looks available. Care to show
me the sights, young man?"

I looked toward my uncle, unsure if I should agree immediately or
not. Harlan Waites wasn't exactly a friend. Uncle Dan inclined his
head, briefly considering, before nodding to me, "If you can step
away?"

"Of course, sir," was the only answer I ever gave. "It would be my
pleasure."

TOURS WERE NOT my usual duty, but I was good at them. I was
charming enough for the constituents and flattering enough to the
donors and, unlike most everyone else, I knew all the facts. Harlan
listened to my spiel all the way through the tunnels, through the Capitol, and up until we stepped outside. It was a beautiful day. Warm, to
me. I couldn't get used to fall in the near-South.

"So," Harlan said. "You're the boy he's been hiding away in New
Hampshire."

"Massachusetts, sir."

"Yes, right. New England. You're not who I was expecting."

I didn't know what that meant. "I'll try to make up for that."

He laughed. "No, no. I thought—well, Daniel always has his surprises, doesn't he?"

"I suppose he does." His voice was silky smooth with a Southern lilt that made it easy to underestimate him. Except for the accent, he and my uncle had much in common. No wonder they didn't really like each other.

"How are you finding life in the South?"

"Hot, sir."

He laughed, genuinely. "And you've never even been to Texas."

"Not yet. Where do you recommend I start?"

"You look like a boy who'd love ranching. Ever ridden a horse?" I was embarrassed to say no. "We'll have to change that. You walk like you'd be a natural at it. Tell your uncle you need to come visit me. You'll be a guest of me and my wife."

I nodded, knowing this would never happen. I was surprised my uncle had sent me on this errand, alone with Harlan Waites. Either he wanted my opinion on something, or he hadn't wanted Harlan to question why he'd keep us apart.

"Speaking of horses," I said, "in the original plan, the Mall was intended to be half the length and end not with that"—I gestured toward the tall, white spire in the distance—"but a statue of Washington on horseback."

Harlan nodded along while I spoke, appearing interested until I finished. "That's fascinating. But you know I've been on this tour before. Maybe we could just talk about some other things, get to know each other and all. I feel we're a little bit like family, but Daniel's been keeping you quiet up in the cold weather for so long. Jillian used to talk novels about you."

In actuality, Harlan *was* almost family. We had as much relation as my Uncle Dan and I—by blood, none at all—but it wasn't always about that. In this case, it was about Jillian. She called him Uncle Harlan, but he was technically her cousin. Her mother Angela's first cousin, the only male in his generation of the Waites and also the oldest. His and Uncle Dan's complex rivalry ran deep.

"I didn't think Jill talked novels about anything." It still hurt to think about Jill, and still felt bitter when I said her name. I missed her and hated her in the same breath.

Harlan's smile melted butter. "About you, she came close. I suppose you know what I can do?"

"Of course." And everyone in your bloodline. Harlan Waites was a Sensor with a talent for reading a person's skills. It's the point from which I always assumed Jill's gift branched.

"You have quite a few skills, son."

"I know."

"Politicking isn't one of them."

I cleared my throat. "I think I know that too."

"You're charming enough—had a good teacher—but if it isn't in you, well, it isn't. I know."

"Thank you for the confirmation. Sir."

"That's not why Daniel's been hiding you though."

"Oh?" I was sure he didn't know why. Unlike Jill, he couldn't sense Sententia gifts specifically, but skills in a broad sense, like *memory* or *dexterity*. If he could read my most secret ability, Uncle Dan would never have introduced us.

"Nah. You're dangerous in plenty of other ways, and your uncle doesn't like to show his cards until he's ready to play them."

For how many times in one conversation, now? I didn't know how to take what he'd said. I glanced at Harlan from the corner of my eye, but he wasn't even looking at me. His expression was placid and comfortable. "My uncle thinks more of his family than a deck of cards."

"'Course he does," Harlan agreed, nodding like it was the most obvious statement. "But see, Carter, you don't realize you're in the game. Our granddaddies, and on up, they started it. Daniel and I, we've been playing since we were in our cradles. You don't realize that *family* are the *best* cards. You treat them right and protect them, because you can't just toss them away."

I felt myself frowning and worked my face back into a neutral expression. Were we all part of a game? Maybe everything *was* a game to men like Harlan, born into the laps of luxury and the pressure of keeping it. But that described my uncle too, and he'd never once pressured me to do *anything* for him.

"I'll keep that in mind, sir."

"Don't suppose you play poker, do you?"

"Not really." Nobody wanted to play cards with the guy with a photographic memory.

"When you come to Texas, we'll play. I can teach you all about cards."

"I look forward to it." Not that it would ever happen.

After a few steps in silence, Harlan said, "It was you who found the Marwood girl, isn't that right?" as casually as he'd ask about the weather.

My mouth went dry. I swallowed before saying, "Yes, sir." It wasn't accurate, but close enough. And now I knew why he'd asked for this tour, from *me*.

"I'm curious about her. What's she doing now?"

"She's in Boston, sir."

"You keep in touch?"

"No."

"Shame. I'm a little disappointed the senator has been unable to convince her to join. Seems like a job he could have used your help with."

"Apparently," I told him, "I wasn't convincing enough either."

"I'm taking it she broke your heart?"

Broke? No. She stole it, trampled it, then tossed it back at me in a fiery heap of ruin. "Something like that."

"Well. That *is* a shame. She must be something special." He already knew these things, I realized, every detail. Of course he did. In fact, I was certain Harlan Waites knew more about everything than he'd ever admit. "Who do you suppose is her father?"

"You mean Allen Young? He's dead."

"Yes, sure. I mean who *is* he. Who was *his* father?"

"There are no records, no testimony from anyone who knew Virginia about a boyfriend or anything. I've searched. I even met his adoptive mother. She said she didn't know and I believed her."

"Do you have a theory?"

"He was a Diviner. Wealthy. Likely married, or about to be. *He* knew she was pregnant even if no one else did. And he's dead too." Otherwise he'd have come forward when she claimed the Legacy.

"Sounds about right. You ever see him, Allen Young?"

I almost said no, Lainey wasn't a picture person, not like that but: "I did, once. In a picture at his mother's house, Chastine Young's house, I mean. He was a kid. Dark haired, like Virginia."

"Mmmhmm." Harlan nodded, stroking his chin in a way too practiced to be entirely natural. The same way Uncle Dan made his lopsided scholar's grin that charmed the world.

We continued in silence for a while. We'd rounded the reflecting pool and were headed down the Mall. The grass was dry, brown in patches. It was strange being here almost daily, among the icons and monuments that seemed so grand and untouchable from far away. Up close, they weren't perfect, much like the people who lived and worked here. It made me feel better, somehow, not worse. This place was as real as anywhere else.

I was pretending not to be sweating and Harlan, a true Southerner, didn't appear to be at all. I was no longer sure I was leading. Probably I hadn't been the whole time. His next question confirmed it.

"How well did you know Senator Astor the senior?"

"Not that well," I answered, before I registered the tone in his voice and knew that was not a random change of subject. I froze. Was he suggesting *Jacob Astor*...was that *possible*? And that would mean *Lainey* was...Too late, I realized what my standing there, mouth open, had given away.

"I guess you *didn't* know him that well."

"I—" I shook my head. No, I didn't. I'd met him once, but I was too young to remember more than how he'd ruffled my hair and asked me about my soccer game. I knew the stories my uncle told and what little Grandma Evelyn told me. I knew what had happened to him. But.

He was a Diviner. He was wealthy. He was dead. He loved secrets. He was...a possibility. How had I never seen it before? He *was* a philanderer, I knew that. Everyone knew that. Virginia Marwood would have been young, but she was beautiful and she was the last Marwood. She'd have been a trophy, a power play. God, it fit *too* well. It was so obvious I'd ignored it. Maybe everyone had.

Everyone but Harlan Waites.

He clapped me on the back and started walking again, a comfortable, leisurely pace that said he was enjoying everything about this walk, even the way it was making me sweat. "Know who did know Jacob Astor? My daddy. Pretty good guess, don't you think? Now my real question is: how well did your *uncle* know his daddy?"

"Mr. Astor liked his secrets."

"Don't we all, son. Secrets are like wine. You save them until they're just the right vintage, however long it takes. Too early and you waste them, passing up the best drinking time. Too late and they're spoiled."

"Is this the right vintage?"

"Hard to say. But this one tastes pretty good to me. Aged almost fifty years now."

"Why are you telling me this?"

"I'm not *telling* you anything. This isn't *my* secret, just a guess. And I had a feeling you'd be interested."

"Why me?"

"Besides the obvious?" He gave me one of those grins that was meant to convey sympathy in the face of being punched in the gut. The strangest part was, I believed it. Harlan Waites felt *bad* for me, which felt worse than anything.

"Besides that. I've moved on," I lied, Lainey's note burning in my pocket. "But I'm sure you know that too."

Harlan chuckled. "I might have heard. The Morrow girl is a rare gem too. But to answer your question," he said, turning to look me in the eye, "I like your skill set. You're smart as they come, but there's not an ounce of natural manipulator in you. We could really use a Hangman, and I'm betting on the last Penrose to find another one or convince the one we've got."

Find one. God knew I'd been searching the world for years. "I'll do my best."

We'd strolled nearly the entire distance of the park, the Washington Monument now looming. Harlan stopped and put his hand on my shoulder like we were old friends.

"I don't doubt you will. Well, Cartwright, it sure has been nice talking to you, but this is where I'm going leave."

"Are you sure, sir? It's a long walk back to the Capitol or where are you staying?" The Council usually met at the private offices of one of the Perceptum's official charities.

"Don't you worry. I know exactly where I am and where I'm going."

I was sure that was true. I put out my hand. "Mr. Waites, it was nice to meet you."

"I doubt that. But I bet it was interesting."

"It was definitely that."

"Son, before I go, can I give you some advice?"

"I'd be glad for it, sir."

"You know, you're just smooth enough you might make a politician yet. But don't try. It wouldn't be a failure. *That's* what I'm telling you."

THE WALK BACK to the office *was* long, but I needed it to collect my thoughts. Harlan Waites was not what I expected. He was every bit the Southern Gentleman, and everything my uncle had warned me about, but it was hard to dislike him. He wasn't lying to me. He didn't see all the way through me, either. No one ever did.

Manipulation might not have come naturally to me, but I did it. Every hour of every day. Secrets were my best friends. They kept me alive and I treated them like lovers, not wine. They weren't for sharing.

I didn't know yet what to do with Harlan's secret, but for now, I planned to keep it.

By the time I returned, I thought my uncle would be gone. But I could see he was still there, sitting with his feet up on his desk and leafing through a file. He'd replaced the original heavy wooden door with a glass one as a nod toward transparency. He worked for the people and everyone could see it. Then again, he could see us too.

When he saw me outside, he waved me in.

Truth be told, I loved and hated my uncle's office. It reflected him. He eschewed the common heavy, formal style except for the requisite flags, country and state, flanking his window. He favored instead a room that felt like a cross between a Montana lodge and my own bookstore. If not for the barely controlled mess, I'd have wanted to spend more time in it. Files and books were everywhere, great, precarious stacks of them.

Uncle closed his folder and tossed it onto the closest pile. "You were gone a rather long time. I wasn't sure if I should be worried."

"Isn't worrying part of your job description?" I poured water from the pitcher on the sideboard and sank into my usual chair.

"When it comes to the Waites family, absolutely." Uncle Dan grinned and propped his feet back on the desk. "So, what did you think?"

"Honestly, I liked him. I'm not sure I can entirely trust him, but I did like him."

"That sounds exactly right. More importantly—what did he want?"

"Mostly I think he was curious. He wanted to meet me. Because of Jillian."

He raised his eyebrows. "And? I'm sure he was curious about you, but I doubt that was the whole of his motivation."

I swallowed. "And he asked about Lainey."

"Ah." At the mention of her, Uncle Dan's smile wasn't fond. "I should have guessed as much. Everyone's curious about the last Hangman, most assuredly him. What did you tell him?"

I did not like keeping anything from my uncle. But Harlan's "guess" wasn't something to toss around casually. I needed to look into it. So I looked him in the eye and said: "There was nothing I could tell him that he didn't already know."

"Well then,"—Uncle Dan put his feet down and closed his computer with a snap—"let's not worry about it."

Out the window, over my uncle's shoulder, a bird swooped into view and disappeared just as fast. From my perspective, I couldn't see much of anything but the clear, blue sky. Harlan had been wearing a tie of the same color.

"Carter? Did you hear me?" My uncle's voice interrupted whatever I'd just been thinking about, something about Lainey, and fathers, and the color blue. I snapped to attention.

"Yes, sir," I said automatically. I'd heard him, hadn't I? He wanted me to get my projections for the upcoming event. Harlan and some of the other Council members would be attending it. "I've done preliminaries, but Alexis hasn't gone over them yet."

"That's fine. I'd like to review them on the drive home." He came around the desk to walk with me out of the office. "You seem distracted, son. Everything all right?"

I shook my head, not sure it was true. I *felt* distracted, like the entire afternoon was rattling around in my head. "Sorry, sir. I was just thinking about…card games." Uncle Dan raised his eyebrows. "Just something Harlan said. He invited me to visit him. Learn to ride horses and play poker."

Uncle Dan chuckled. "One little walk and he's 'Harlan' now?" He rested his hand on my shoulder. "Don't be putting too much stock in anything from the mouth of Harlan Waites. Invitations from the Devil always sound the prettiest and end the worst."

Chapter Eleven

Lainey

G ot it!" I shouted and threw myself toward the spinning ball. My knees slammed into the ground, but I *did* get it. I passed it cleanly back into court and popped up just in time to see the super tall guy on the other team block our shot back at us. I dove to my left and got my wrist on the ball before it hit the ground. This time, we put it away, and my team hauled me off the ground and cheered.

Intramural volleyball was actually hard core.

"Yeah, Lanes!" Our captain, Wendell, grabbed my shoulders and shook them harder than necessary. He was Navy ROTC and excitable. I was taller than he was.

"Secret weapon!" one of the guys shouted. He held out his fist, and I bumped it with mine.

Everyone else hugged me or knocked fists. I was breathing hard and trying not to rub my hip. I knew it would hurt later, but I was feeling good, high on adrenaline and victory. We'd just beaten the best team in our group and I was proud to have saved the point.

"Victory drinks at twenty-two hundred!" Wendell called while everyone was grabbing their things after we'd shaken hands with the opposing team.

Annnd that was that. "Okay, so, I'll see you guys next week," I said, the same lame thing I said every week. Being the only underage undergrad on the team was kind of a downer at the end of the night.

"Awww, Lanes, c'mon." Wendell put his arm around my shoulder, which was kind of funny with the way he had to reach up. "Join us. If Sadler's at the door tonight, I can get him to let you in." He must have seen me preparing a variation of *no*, because he broke in, "C'mon! You saved the game! You can bring your boyfriend too."

"I'm sorry, who?"

"Your boyfriend," he repeated, not sounding excited about it. He pointed over his shoulder toward the court entrance.

Standing there was Jack Kensington. Of course. When our eyes met, he smiled and waved.

"He's not my boyfriend! He's my TA," I said, but I could feel my already warm cheeks growing warmer.

"Good!" Wendell said, though he was still looking skeptically at where Jack lounged against the wall.

"Um, I'd better see what he wants." An awkward hug and goodbye later, I followed Wendell and the rest of the team toward the door where Jack waited.

Jack. Damn him. Despite my vow to keep my distance, *avoiding* him, I discovered, was completely impossible. Jack was *everywhere*. I saw him in the student union while I was getting coffee and in the hallway after my classes. I bumped into him at the bookstore, and once, even, in line at the Post Office. And now he was here, crooked smiling at me.

I stopped in front of him. "If I didn't know better, I'd say you were following me."

"I'd say you might be right," he said, his dimple deepening as the smile spread. "Or, maybe, *you're* following *me*."

He leaned forward, just enough for him to feel close to me, and his voice dropped in a flirty way. I became acutely aware of how little my volleyball shorts and tank top covered.

"The team thought you were my boyfriend."

"Is that so?"

"I think Wendell might have been jealous."

"Hm. Was that his name? I think you're right. Do you *want* him to be jealous?"

"Not really," I admitted.

"Because that could be arranged," he said. "Your pretend boyfriend could show up *every* week."

"Talk about going above and beyond for one of your students."

Despite that it was ten o'clock, Jack leaned on the wall like this was exactly what he needed to be doing and where. He looked less put together than I'd ever seen him, in mesh shorts and a non-designer t-shirt, with hair hanging in his eyes. For the first time, I could see his legs. It's a strange thing, to see a usually hidden part of someone.

"There's nothing," he said, "I wouldn't do for you."

I snorted. "What *are* you doing here anyway?" We were alone in court four, though they were still going in the court next to us.

"Besides following you? Playing basketball." Ah, yes. He'd mentioned that the night of the concert. And it explained the muscular legs, different from Carter's long, lean runner's legs. Jack was shaped for agility and bursts of speed. His clinging t-shirt made it obvious he spent regular time here.

"How'd you do?"

He chuckled. "I won the swearing portion of the game," he joked, but I didn't actually believe him. "*You*, on the other hand, are clearly some kind of volleyball ninja." He reached out, almost like he was going to touch me, but his hand kept going, just brushing my shoulder as he tapped one of the knee pads sticking out of my bag.

Right about then the lights went out.

I gasped. Because we were looking at each other, I watched Jack's eyes as they adjusted to the dark. His pupils grew large, swallowing up the warm brown of his irises. When I was younger, I'd stand at the bathroom mirror watching my own eyes change as I turned the light on and off. It was a game, something childish, but this did not feel childish. It felt…intimate. The kind of thing you saw in bedrooms right before you were kissed.

And I had the terrifying, thrilling feeling that he *would* kiss me. I leaned toward him, breaching the space between us. Close, closer now, and I was sure I could feel the gentle puff of his breath on my lips.

Click. The lights snapped on and I jumped back as if I'd been caught doing something I shouldn't. Which I *had*. Behind me, an escaped ball from court three bounced across the floor and a girl called "Sorry!" as she chased it down.

"No problem," Jack said. Our eyes met again, but the moment had disintegrated. I became unsure it had existed at all.

The neighboring player retrieved the lost ball and breezed back by us with a "Thanks!" though we hadn't done anything to help her. "No problem," Jack repeated and I laughed. He cleared his throat and a light fog of awkwardness drifted into the space between us. "So." he said. "Are you supposed to meet your friends?"

"No," I admitted. "The rest of the team is mostly seniors and they always go for beers."

"Leaving you out after you save the game? That's shitty."

I shrugged. "Wendell offered to get me in."

"I bet he did." A sly grin crested like a wave across his features and a flush appeared on my cheeks in response. I would have hated him if I didn't like that smile so much. It occurred to me that I might have had a thing for boys and their smiles. "How did you even end up on a team of upperclassmen?"

"They needed one more girl. At the meeting, Wendell came over to me and the other few looking for teams and said, 'So, which one of you can jump serve?' When I said I could, he laughed, and I realized he'd been joking."

"But you weren't." I grinned and he matched it. "Full of surprises, you are." Glancing away, he said, "Pizza, volleyball ninja?" When he looked back at me, he cocked his head to the side, adorably.

I opened my mouth, realized the word *Yes* was about to tumble out of it, and caught myself just in time. I bit my lip to keep my mouth from betraying me. Jack's eyes darted to the movement, and lower, to where my fingers furiously slid my necklace back and forth. I dropped the necklace and he met my eyes again with his pretty brown ones. My resolve felt about as strong as wet paper.

No, damn it. *No.* No TAs, and definitely no Sententia. Right?

"I can't," I said finally.

"Can't?" he said. "Or won't?"

Damn him for knowing. But this was my choice and I was keeping it. I stood up a little straighter. "Won't. I have homework, and also, boundaries. You're my TA."

He nodded. "For now. But—just so you know—I looked in my handy TA handbook and there's nothing in it that says we can't be friends."

"Well, I looked in *my* Lainey Young handbook and it says no, we shouldn't." I threw on my sweatshirt and started walking toward the exit. Jack fell into step beside me. I should have told him not to follow me, but my willpower only went so far. It dawned on me then that I was flirting and I didn't want to stop. That didn't hurt, right, flirting? Just flirting. I hadn't made any rule against that.

"Okay, not friends then. Got it. Purely professional. So," he drawled, "out of professional interest only, if someone, like a dedicated TA for example, wanted to obtain a copy of the Lainey Young Handbook, how would he go about that?"

I looked at my feet to cover my stupid smile and muttered, "Don't you have somewhere to be?"

"Yes."

"Good." He held the door open for me, and I stepped onto the sidewalk, only half prepared for the slap of cold air against my too-bare legs. It was late, and the autumn night had lost all the day's warmth and then some. "Thanks," I told him, fighting a chatter in my teeth. "So, see you in discussion."

"You're welcome," he said, and fell into step next to me again as I hurried down the street.

"I thought you had somewhere to be?!"

I could feel the cut of his eyes over to me and hear the amusement in his voice. "And it can't be in this direction?"

"Where are you going?"

"Where are *you* going?"

"The *library*," I blurted, and I could see the flash of his grin in the streetlights.

"Well, what do you know." Jack hitched his bag higher and strode ahead of me like he'd been leading the whole time. Over his shoulder, he called, "Coming?"

I shook my head, flustered and amused and wishing I was neither. "You are *maddening*," I told him as soon as I caught up.

He nodded, saying mildly, "So are you."

"*Are* you following me?"

"I'm not," he said and nudged me with his elbow. "I'm next to you." I elbowed him back, harder, and he laughed while rubbing his arm. "Easy, killer."

"You know what I mean."

He rubbed his chin with his hand, and I watched his fingers scrape across the light stubble there. For a single second, I allowed myself to imagine what it would feel like to have his rough cheek brush against *my* skin. I shivered at the same time as he said, "I know *I* have grading to do."

"Okay," I said. I wasn't sure I believed him, but I wasn't sure I *didn't* either. I mean, I didn't really think he was *following me*. Surely he had better things to do.

We'd made it to the library, ugly as it was on the outside and tucked between campus and the river, much like my dorm. Inside though, it was bright and warm and had a few spots with surprisingly good views. As I pulled my bag off my shoulders to show the attendant, Jack spoke behind me, voice lower than before. "I know I'm not sorry I got to walk here with you either."

Maybe I was imagining it just like earlier, but I swore I'd felt his breath move my hair and the heat of his body close to mine. I resisted the terrible urge to lean back until whatever small space was left between us disappeared. Twice tonight, I'd wanted him to touch me, though I knew he shouldn't, and I'd sworn not to let him. I was losing this battle so hard.

Did it really matter whether or not Jack was Sententia, whether *anyone* was? I'd told myself I'd given up Carter to escape the Sententia, but Amy was right. I never could, not unless I could be free of *myself*. What I'd thought was my meager reward was starting to feel like penance. One I was choosing to make myself pay. Had I just been forcing myself into an equally limited box?

The library attendant cleared her throat. "Thanks," she said pointedly and I realized I was standing there, bag open, waiting for something that wasn't coming.

"Sorry," I muttered, and moved through the gate, glancing at Jack as I went.

"See you in discussion, Lainey," he said, stepping past me into the library. "Chapter eight," he called over his shoulder, giving me one more smile before he slipped around a corner and was gone.

He didn't look back.

At the information desk, another girl in the ridiculous coats they made the staff wear was watching me watch him. She raised her eyebrows when I walked by and I looked away. And then I kept walking, past the elevators, past the stairs I usually took to the third floor, heading in the same direction as Jack.

When I realized what I was doing, I stopped. I closed my eyes and took three yoga breaths but when I opened them, I still didn't want to turn around. "Shit," I muttered and kept going.

I rounded the corner but didn't see anywhere he would have gone. It was nothing but a few reference stacks and mostly display cases, housing the letters and artifacts of someone dead but interesting.

"Boo," came from right behind me and I screamed. I whirled around to find Jack leaning there between the last row of shelves and laughing softly. "Shhh," he said, holding a finger to his lips.

"You asshole," I whispered, and he laughed more.

"See, told you—you *were* following me."

"I was *not*," I huffed. Lied. "I need to look at the Faulkner papers for my lit class." I spun on my heel and headed in the direction of the display cases. I didn't have to look to know he was next to me again. "What now? Do you need to look at them too?" I hissed. I pulled out a notebook and dropped my bag at the end of the row.

"No," he whispered. He leaned over the last case, propping his elbows on it. "And neither," he added, "do you."

I glared. "What would you know about my assignment?"

"Nothing," he agreed. "Except I *do* know"—he tapped lightly on the case with one knuckle—"that this is a Marie Curie exhibit."

"*Shit*," I muttered again and closed my eyes in a long blink. I could feel the case shake with Jack's laughter. Why the hell did he know what this display was? Who even *looked* at these? Wait. I opened my eyes and peered at the case. "This stuff isn't from Marie Curie!"

He laughed out loud, loud enough that if there'd been anyone around it would have gotten us shushed. "No," he admitted. "But it's not Faulkner either."

I couldn't help it. I laughed too. Leaning next to him on the case, I said, "So, what is it?"

He squinted. "It's..." He shrugged, smiling. "Who knows? I'm no historian. I didn't even know these were over here."

Historian. I swallowed. It didn't mean anything. Or did it? Either way, it was a reminder: I had to get away from him. As soon as he'd said the word, visions of another boy's smile danced behind my eyes, kind of like sugarplums, except they tasted bitter, like baker's chocolate or heartbreak.

I took a deep breath, fortifying my crumbling wall of resolve. *No Sententia.* I'd had a moment of weakness tonight, okay, *several* moments, but it was over. Picking up my bag, I said, "I have to go."

His smile faltered. "Wait. Don't you really have homework?"

"*Yes.*"

He straightened and gestured grandly back toward the main library, like a tux-clad maitre'd, not a TA in basketball shorts with sexy legs and messy hair. "So. You need to be here and, believe it or not, I need to be here. Want to share a table with me?"

I want to share a lot more than that with you, I thought. *And that is your whole problem, Young.* "I have to go," I repeated.

"Okay." He nodded, resigned, and I turned. "But Lainey?" I looked back at him. "What are you running away from?"

"Trouble," I told him, though that was only half the truth. The real answer was something more like the past. Like myself.

His lips curved again into that crooked smile, the one that chipped so mercilessly at the bricks around my heart. "Oh, Lainey. You know trouble follows you."

Chapter Twelve

Carter

I t was no surprise the restaurant where my uncle asked me to meet him was posh and expensive.

The surprise was finding Tessa Espinosa waiting alone at the bar.

I saw her first. She was a woman who stood out, and not only because she was beautiful. She exuded a presence, a sense of being much larger than she was. Because she was tiny, except for her hair. The unmistakable tumble of deep brown waves spilled over the shoulders of a purple velvet jacket that was probably meant to be described as something like *aubergine*. I paused about halfway to where she sat, regarding her back while I took a few breaths. The smile I was trying to maintain felt brittle.

She must have felt my eyes on her because she turned around. A warm and genuine smile brightened her face. Her eyes teared, growing shiny and wavering in the light from the small candles lined up on the bar. I didn't know how to feel about that.

"Carter!" she called and I raised my hand in greeting, pretending like I hadn't just been staring at her. When I got close enough, she pulled me into a hug. It, too, felt genuine. Maybe even fierce. The high bar chair where she sat meant I didn't even have to lean over.

"It's so good to see you," she said as she held me. There was a thickness to her voice that made me have to swallow before I could reply.

"It's good to see you, Tessa." She released her grip on my shoulders, finishing with a kiss to my cheek before she pulled away. I smiled. "It's actually a surprise. I thought I was meeting my uncle. Are you joining us?" She really did look beautiful, in the carefree way that was always so distinct from Lainey. I wondered if Lainey had grown so reserved in contrast. She and her adoptive mother were like complementary angles.

"Yes, I'll be joining you. If you don't mind," she added.

"Of course not."

"Oh, good!" She cleared her throat, a feminine sound that only added to her sense of perpetual youth. I wondered if she wasn't slightly nervous. I wondered, too, if my uncle had chosen this place just for her, with its walls covered in paintings. The dark tones of the art deco room were made to flatter her.

I began to wonder if their relationship was more than friendly. Was Tessa the woman he'd met at the coffee shop? She was certainly beautiful. And she did have ties to Arizona. Her parents and brother still lived there.

"Can I get you something? A beer?" Tessa asked, sipping her own glass of something clear with lime. It seemed out of place for her. She drank red wine, or dark things with more passion than coolness.

I grinned. "Thank you, but the bar would probably rather I didn't. Water will be fine." She tilted her head and I said, "It's still a couple months until I'm old enough. Legally."

She laughed. "I'm sorry. I forget how young you still are!"

"It's fine. I don't really drink anyway."

"No," she said. "I suppose you wouldn't." She looked at me like she saw deeper into my thoughts than I wanted her to. "You look, well, you look great, Carter." She glanced at her drink, stirring it idly, before she looked back up at me. "I hope it's okay for me to say that. I...I've missed you, but I thought it best if I kept my distance for a while. I hope you understand."

I nodded, grateful for the distraction of the bartender. I sipped my water to delay having to say anything else. I did understand. I did not want to talk about it. Tessa made a sound in the back of her throat, something frighteningly close to pity, and patted my hand before changing the subject.

"Martin is on his way too." I'd barely had the chance to get to know Martin Schearer before graduation and Lainey had... But I'd liked him—everyone did—and he was deeply involved in the Astor Arts charity now. It wasn't unusual for him to dine with Uncle Dan, or probably both him and Tessa. Now I was wondering why I was here. My sense that this night was *something*, something serious, began to grow.

"Tess!" Uncle Dan's voice came from behind me and Tessa's face lit up. I glanced over my shoulder to see my uncle weaving his way to the bar, Manny following a discreet distance behind. It was a particular skill of Manny's that he could blend so seamlessly into a crowd, despite his watchful eyes and size forty-six jacket that covered more than one weapon. "And good, I see you've collected my nephew."

He kissed Tessa on the cheek in greeting. I glanced around to see if anyone else noticed. If someone was watching, would they see how she looked at him? Observe how his hand lingered on her back?

Maybe my idea had merit.

Uncle Dan clapped one hand on my shoulder. "Son, I hope you don't mind, but Tessa and Martin will be joining us as well."

"No, sir. Not at all. Tessa even offered to get me a drink. So I'm starting to wonder what you have to tell me."

When Daniel Astor laughed, people noticed. People noticed now. He laughed like someone whose life was perfectly in control, because it was. I hadn't laughed like that since I was thirteen years old and I envied it. Next to him, Tessa was grinning. "Then we shouldn't keep you in suspense. Let's sit down." He caught the eye of the hostess, who lingered just outside Manny's shadow, before meeting my own. "I hope you're going to like it."

WE WERE SEATED in another room of the restaurant, one I imagined was called The Federal Room. The walls were still covered in art, but it was brighter and more Americana. Except for the huge fireplace warming my back and reminding me of home, I liked the dark bar better. In this room it would be harder to keep lying to myself that this was fine.

Martin arrived a few minutes later, as our waiter poured the bottle of wine Uncle Dan had ordered ahead. It was expensive. Extravagant, actually. I'd gotten a glance at the wine list when I returned it to the hostess. This was a celebration wine.

The server filled my glass without asking, but Tessa gave a slight shake of her head when he moved to hers. He skipped on to Martin's glass without a pause, but Martin was not looking at him or the wine. He was staring at Tessa in a way that made me stare too.

"Tess?" he said. "You're not having any?" There was something in his voice, something barely contained.

"No, Martin, I'm not," she answered. That was all she said, but she was smiling, darting glances at my uncle, and her eyes filled with tears again. Martin made this noise, a shocked-gasp-hiccup, and clapped his hands together like her not-drinking a glass of wine was the greatest thing in the world. He, too, seemed ready to cry.

And just like that, it hit me: she's *pregnant.*

Holy fucking shit.

I was standing, I realized, looking back and forth between Tessa and my uncle. But everyone else was standing too, Martin hugging Tess, saying words like *congratulations* and *dreamed of this* and *perfect, just perfect.*

Was this perfect? I wasn't sure.

Uncle Dan was smiling, but he was watching me with a guarded expression. He put a hand on my shoulder and I became very aware of the fact that I hadn't said anything yet.

I cleared my throat and held out my hand. "Congratulations, sir." I sounded so formal, like we were still in the office, in senator and intern mode.

He grasped my hand and pulled me toward him, throwing his arm around my shoulder like he did so often when I was younger. He was barely taller than me now, and my shoulders were broader than his, but next to him, I still felt small.

"Surprise," he said. "That wasn't exactly how we wanted this to go. I should have anticipated the wine better."

"It's been a while since you had to think about those kind of logistics."

He chuckled. "Sixteen years. How do you feel about the news?"

"Surprised," I admitted.

"Pleased?"

"Of course," I said automatically, and then repeated it, deciding it was true. "Yeah, of course." He nodded when our eyes met.

"I'm glad," Uncle said. "And relieved. I know this might be a bit awkward for you."

Rather than lie, I said, "The media's going to go crazy, you know. *I* didn't even know you were…" I gestured to Tessa. "Though I probably should have suspected."

He smiled and steered me back toward my chair. "We weren't, not exactly. Let's sit down and explain."

THE MEDIA *WAS* going to go crazy. They would fucking love this. I'd almost have suspected Anton Williams, Uncle Dan's campaign manager, of orchestrating the whole thing, but Tessa would never have agreed to that. I tried to keep my face neutral while she talked about asking my uncle to father her baby—through in vitro fertilization.

"Needless to say, I was surprised—and immensely flattered," Uncle Dan said.

"I was already in the process," Tessa explained. "Actually, I'd prepared for it some years ago, but decided to wait. And I kept waiting, thinking, I don't know, maybe I wouldn't need it."

"You're forever romantic, Tess," Martin said and she chuckled.

"I do like surprises, and I guess Dan was one." They beamed at each other and I had to look at my hands. "But my doctor told me I'd waited long enough—much more and I'd be practically fifty years old with a *toddler* and my first baby would be graduated from *college.*"

There it was. She didn't say her name, but we'd been edging around her all night. I was prepared for it, though. *Not* reacting outwardly to mention of Lainey Young was a skill I practiced actively. Tessa darted a glance in my direction but seemed encouraged by my non-reaction. I may have even smiled. Below the table, my hands gripped each other to keep from rubbing the achy spot in my chest.

"So, I just knew if anyone, it would be Dan. He reminded me so much of—" She paused. "Well, let's just say he was the first man I'd met in a long time who made me think of the possibility."

Uncle Dan reminded Tessa so much of *whom*? I wondered. I knew many things about Tessa, like how she used to date a banker from California who'd fly all over the world to see her, but it certainly wasn't him.

"Of course he did, Tess. We all knew it was fate." Martin toasted to each of them—Tessa, Uncle Dan, and fate, along with the as-yet-undetermined baby. Tessa's club soda and lime made an off-note when it clunked our wine glasses and she laughed.

Fate. Fuck fate. Lainey had been right when she said it felt more like chaos. I understood now.

"When?" I asked. It was the first time I'd spoken since we sat back down. The waiter had just cleared our salad plates.

"We're due the end of May," Tessa said, rubbing her still-flat stomach. Belly? "Almost twelve weeks now. I'm feeling great, just a little tired, and, well, morning sickness does *not* occur only in the *morning*." She shook her club soda and laughed again, while my uncle rubbed her back. "That has to be the biggest lie about pregnancy ever told."

I nodded. "I meant: when did you ask him?"

"Oh." Her cheeks flushed and she couldn't meet my eyes, so I knew. After a breath, she said, "It was right before Lainey's"—she dragged the L out when she said her name, as if her tongue hesitated to say it to me—"graduation. And the announcement. So much was happening then…" She stopped and took a gulp of her drink.

"It was a very busy time," Uncle Dan concurred.

No kidding. "And when did things…change?" I said, looking between the two them, and the way Uncle's hand covered Tessa's. They hadn't told the whole story yet, how they went from partners in an arrangement to having a child *together*.

Tessa blushed, and it was the only time I thought she and Lainey looked like mother and daughter. She cleared her throat. "After the procedure, when my doctors told me it was official, I called Dan to let him know. He asked me to dinner, and then…" She smiled, shrugging her tiny shoulders. "We thought it best if we didn't make a big deal out of it."

I swallowed hard not to laugh, but Martin actually chuckled. This was most definitely a big deal. In fact, it was nothing short of insane.

"We haven't told *anyone*," she was saying. "Except my parents, last weekend."

"Anyone?" I said.

Tessa glanced at my uncle. "We're going to Boston this weekend." So Lainey didn't even know yet.

"So you understand we'd appreciate if we kept this news between us," Uncle Dan said in his gentle command voice, the one that meant *of course* we would.

"I'm always discreet," I reminded him, at the same time Martin nodded vigorous assent. He wasn't Sententia, but he wasn't stupid either. This was about more than telling the families. Uncle Dan was running for *president*, for God's sake.

"Carter—" Tessa started. Stopped. Those big brown eyes of hers were imploring me, and I was afraid she might cry again. I was gripping my wine glass too hard, so I set it down. "You're not upset, are you?"

"Of course not."

"It's just—" She did cry. Big tears that plopped from her eyes even as she grinned and wiped them away.

"Tess," my uncle said. It was his most private tone of voice, the one I sometimes thought was reserved for me.

"I'm sorry!" She swiped more tears and gulped her fizzy water, setting it down with a heavy thud that made her grimace. "Damn these hormones. Carter, I am sorry."

"It's okay," I said, because what else could I say?

"No. Ack." She fanned her eyes with her hand and took a familiar deep yoga breath. "This isn't going at all how I wanted it to."

Did anything, ever? I considered inviting her to join my club. I'd been president for nearly twenty-one years. Instead, I said, "It really is okay. It's a surprise, but"—I looked at my uncle—"you know I can't be anything but happy for you."

"Thank you," he said.

Tessa echoed him, adding, "I just hope you understand. We didn't go into this planning to keep secrets from you, and, well, I wonder if I shouldn't have asked for your blessing."

"I'm not sure it works that way."

"Maybe it should."

"I think what Tessa is saying, son," Uncle Dan interjected, "is we'd like you to be a big part of the baby's life. We'd like your blessing, too, albeit we're asking a tad late."

I grabbed my wine and lifted it. The firelight behind me winked off the glass, throwing warm red shadows across the table.

Even I thought I sounded perfectly genuine when I said: "To fate and late blessings—and healthy babies," and we all clinked glasses one more time.

Chapter Thirteen

Lainey

Y ou know you're going to regret sitting like that some-day, right? You're so tall, it will probably be worse for you."

I sat up straight and found Natalie watching me from our doorway. "Thanks for the reminder," I said. *Again*, I thought and had to clamp my mouth shut to keep from snap-ping at her.

I'd been sitting cross-legged on my bed and leaning over my lap-top, a position I adopted too often if Nat's constant reminders were any indication. She was right, of course—I *shouldn't* sit like that. She was also, however, annoying. I slipped on my headphones and pre-tended like I was alone again.

College so far had been so many things: enlightening, liberating, fun, frightening, and, also, disappointing. I hated thinking that about my roommates, but it was the truth. Without Amy, I was afraid I might actually be lonely, and that made me a little sad.

Was I doing this wrong? I *liked* college, a lot. I loved classes and campus and pretty much everything except for Natalie. I liked Jack, more than I wanted to. I hung out with Serena and her friends sometimes, but I still felt a little separate from her group. The truth was, I *still* didn't know how to make friends. Maybe no one knew how. It was just something you did, naturally. Or not.

The biggest problem was that I missed Carter. He would have—*should* have—filled in the small spaces that now were empty. Like tonight, when I had no plans except to read a book and feel sorry for myself.

Nat tapped me on the shoulder and I jumped high enough to rock the bed. Though I wasn't actually listening to anything, I pressed mute on my computer just for show and took my headphones off. "Hey. What's up?"

"I was going to get coffee. Want to come?" Maybe Natalie was lonely too. Actually, I was sure she was. She rarely sought out my company, or any really. What I should have said was yes, but I'd opened a sad door in my head and I needed Amy to help close it.

"Not right now, I'm sorry." She dropped her eyes, making her look sadder than usual, so I added, "Maybe tomorrow? Or later?"

"I'm going to the play with Kendra later." She hesitated a second. "It's just at Fine Arts, if you want to come."

"Yeah," I said. "I'd like that. And actually…" I tugged my bag over and scrounged a five out of my wallet. "Would you maybe bring a coffee back for me?"

As soon as she was gone, I closed our door and called Amy. I laid back on my bed while the phone rang and stared at the photo collage on Nat's dresser that I could see reflected in my mirror. The faces were fuzzy from my angle, but I knew she was smiling in most of them.

Finally Amy picked up. I was afraid I'd missed her before she left to spend the long weekend in Iowa. "Lainey-baby. Just when I was sure you were avoiding me, you call me back. Finally."

"Sorry." I ran my finger along the edge of the *Out of Africa* poster over my bed. I had a theme, one for each of my roommates. Turned out we were all a little international, not just Ginny. Kendra had been born in Ethiopia. I had Pearl S. Buck's *The New Year* for Ginny and *Like Water for Chocolate* for me. For Natalie, whose mom was Italian, I had *Roman Holiday*. "It's been a busy week."

"Busy avoiding me."

I didn't want to tell her she was right, but she knew she was. "I'm sorry."

Amy sighed. "I know. So. Let's get it out of the way. Go ahead, ask."

"Did you have fun?"

She sighed again. "Yes. It was freaking great. But to answer the *real* question, yes, Carter was there. Yes, I talked to him."

I dropped an arm over my eyes. For some reason, it was easier to have these conversations with my eyes closed. "What's he doing?"

"Besides Alex-bitch Morrow?"

"God, Amy."

In softer tones she said, "Besides studying, he's doing data analysis and statistics, he says. He reads a lot." My stomach churned and I pressed down on it. That was it? Daniel Astor was ready to kill me to have Carter do math and *read* for him? Like I would have kept him from any of that! "Lane?" I was quiet for too long.

Finally I said, "Did he…did he seem happy?"

"Truth?"

"Always."

It was her turn to be quiet. After a few seconds, she said, "I think so. He said he doesn't know, but I think he just doesn't realize it. He loves classes and feeling like he's helping Senator Astor. He *looks* amazing. And I think…" She hesitated. "I think he likes Alexis more than he should."

"I'm…glad," I said, because what else could I say?

She laughed. "Well at least that makes one of us." She regaled me with the rest of Homecoming, which really did sound like a good time, and I dutifully filled her in on my boring life, leaving out the ruminating and feeling sorry for myself. By the time I got to my volleyball match, my stomach was feeling better.

"And then I saw Jack," I admitted.

"*Again?* I think he's following you." On the other end of the phone, I could hear the sounds of her last-minute packing.

"That's what I said!"

"There are worse things to follow you around." She huffed as she zipped up a bag. "Like rumors and syphilis." I laughed. "Mr. H.O.T. is more like a puppy. A sexy puppy."

"He's pretty fit," I added casually.

"No shit. So what's he do again?"

"He plays basketball and lifts—"

"*Sentimentally* I mean, Lane." That was her code for Sententia. "You know I don't care *how* he works out. He's not a sex demon, right?" Amy was still rightfully bitter about her experience last year with Alexis's cousin Mandi, a Siren who'd tried really hard—and nearly succeeded—to ruin her year. "Though in *this* case maybe that wouldn't be so bad."

"Amy."

"I'm just saying—you could use a sex demon."

"Jesus, Ame."

"What? You could."

I pulled a tack from the corner of the poster and pushed it back in. Finally, I said, "I'm not ready for that yet."

Amy made this throaty noise of dismissal. "Sure you are. *You* broke up with *him*, or did you forget? Sometimes you act like you didn't want to and I don't get it at all." She cursed under her breath as it sounded like she stacked her bags. I could hear her door open and close.

"I didn't forget," I said. I never forgot. This is when it hurt most that I couldn't tell her what happened. "I'm just…trying to adjust to college and everything. I'm not ready to throw relationshipping into it. Plus, he's still my TA." I took a sip of water to help me swallow the lump in my throat.

"I know. That just means it's going to be *awesome* when you finally do it." I choked on that water. "All the waiting will be *totally* worth it," she went on, oblivious. "And besides, I really wasn't talking about a *relationship*."

"God, you're impossible."

"I think the same thing about you, you know." I knew. It was part of why we loved each other. After a pause, she said, "I gotta go, babe. My ride's here."

I could hear the wind and traffic as she stepped out of her dorm, swallowing up our goodbyes. I tossed my phone on the end of the bed. It bounced and slipped over the side, through the little space next to the wall. *Shit.*

I flopped backwards onto my pillows. From beneath the bed, I heard my phone buzzing but I didn't have the energy to retrieve it. With one hand, I smoothed the corner of the poster I'd been worrying.

Even though she was impossible, I was sorry it took so long for me to call Amy back. I hated that she was involuntarily caught in the middle of Carter and me. It wasn't *her* fault. Hell, it wasn't even *my* fault. It was Daniel Astor's fault, that manipulating, lying, asshole uncle of mine, among other choice terms. I refrained from using *son-of-a-bitch*, though it flowed so nicely, because his mother Evelyn was actually a gem of a woman. I refrained from using *life-ruining* too, because he wasn't in control of my life anymore. He wasn't even part of it.

My phone was buzzing again. *Crap.* I squeezed my arm down between the bed and the wall, but when I tried to grab it, I pushed it out of reach. It stopped buzzing. With a sigh, I heaved off my bed to retrieve it. The two missed calls were from Aunt Tessa. Huh. I was just getting off my hands and knees when our door buzzer rang. I just could not win.

I skipped down the stairs to see who it was, but even before I'd opened the vestibule door, I could see behind the glass wasn't a friend, or pizza delivery guy, or even Natalie, forgotten her keys. It was a man, clearly not a student, and he looked…almost like a police officer, standing straight and with a serious kind of intensity. The missed calls from my aunt! I rushed to the door and threw it open without a second thought.

"Miss Young?" the man said as soon as I opened it.

But I didn't even see him.

Beyond his broad shoulders, waiting at the bottom of the steps in an eggplant colored velvet coat, was a petite brunette alive, unblemished, and beaming at me. And she wasn't alone.

I gripped the door frame until my fingers were white. "Auntie?"

"Surprise!" she called, though I barely heard her.

Because behind her was Daniel Astor. His razor smile was the last thing I saw before I passed out.

I WOKE UP in a nightmare. Halloween wasn't until next weekend, but I felt like I was being tricked right *now*. This couldn't be real.

My aunt was having Daniel Astor's baby.

This. Could not. Be real.

"I know it's a shock, honey." My aunt was sitting next to me on my bed and petting my hair. Quietly in a corner and safely out of my reach stood the baby's father, making the room look shabbier and more beige just with his presence. I kept darting glances in his direction and blinking in hopes that when I opened my eyes he'd disappear and I was, in fact, dreaming. Nightmaring. Was that a verb? If not, it should have been.

I couldn't make my mouth work, so my aunt just kept talking. "This is something I'd been thinking about for a long time—you knew that. I wanted to talk to you about it sooner, I did, but there was so much...*happening*, and then, well"—she flapped her hand toward the corner—"with Dan, and the *sensitivity* of his situation, and so we just *waited* until we were sure, and you understand, don't you, sweetheart?"

Finally, what I managed to say was "Who's he?"

Aunt Tessa blinked. "I'm sorry, honey, what?"

"Him." I nodded my chin at the big man, though he wasn't taller than me, who'd rung my doorbell and seemed to eschew sitting. He stood just outside the bedroom door, not at attention, but not lounging either.

"Oh," my aunt said.

Obviously, he was at least half listening and not required to pretend he wasn't, because he turned his head and smiled. He had a nice smile, actually. "I'm the one who caught you, Miss." And that, I supposed was true, because if not for him, my head probably would have hit the stairs pretty hard.

The man in the corner I was trying to pretend didn't exist cleared his throat. "Manuel is with the Service. There've been some security...concerns, so he's been with me for a while."

My brain wasn't processing the importance of *security* and *concerns*, but I understood Service, capital S, as in *Secret*. That made a lot of sense, actually, the way such a large man could so easily blend into the wall. "Where are your sunglasses?" I asked him.

He cracked another smile and you could tell he was trying, really hard, not to laugh. He coughed a little before he said, "I prefer not to wear them at night, Miss."

"You can call me Lainey."

"Thank you," he said, though I could tell he'd probably keep up with the Miss thing.

Next to me, my aunt's forehead looked a bit like an accordion. "Sweetie, I think—that is, are you having migraines again? Do you need one of your pills?"

I looked at her. "I'm fine. I just need some coffee."

"Er. Okay! We'll get some!" she said, too brightly. She, too, kept flicking glances at the senator in the corner. "I mean," she amended, "I'll have decaf." Her hand fluttered to her stomach and I had this horrible, horrible feeling I might throw up.

I stood too quickly, making my head swim, and when my fingers failed to grab hold of my dresser, I sat right back down again. The bed gave a muted squeak underneath me and my little, pregnant aunt rocked back and forth. Right about then, the front door banged open and Natalie said, "Whoa," before calling, "Lainey?"

"In here, Nat. Don't mind him."

"Um," she said and appeared in the doorway, fairly clutching a tray of white and green cups. Nat glanced at Manuel before her gaze traveled to me and Aunt T. "Oh, um, hi. I think you're—" she was saying when she realized there was still one more person in the room. "Holy shit!" Her eyes grew so wide I thought a blood vessel might burst. The coffee tray tipped precariously toward the floor, and Manuel, very graciously, reached out a hand and tilted it back up. Nat didn't even notice. "You're running for *president*!"

Mr. President smiled. "Daniel Astor," he said, with an affable wave of his hand. "Pleased to meet you."

"Holy shit," she repeated.

"That," he said, "would be my opposition. You can just call me Dan."

"I—um, hi. Dan," she said. It barely came out as a breath. I hated him all over again right then for being so damned charming. "I'm just going to sit out here." She backed out of the room, squeaking as she bumped into Manuel, who once again saved the coffees.

"Which one is Miss Young's?" he murmured, in a voice much more soothing than you'd expect from him.

"Lainey," I reminded.

Eyes wide, Nat swallowed as she held out my cup. "This one, um, I'm not sure who you are."

"Security," he said, smiling that nice smile again and plucking my coffee out of her hand. I *really* didn't think Secret Service were supposed to have senses of humor. Mr. Funny Man breached the doorway and brought me my coffee.

"Thanks, Manuel."

"My friends call me Manny."

"My friends call me Lainey."

"Touché." His eyes crinkled when he smiled, and I thought that so far, he was the best part of this whole rotten deal.

"Lainey." My aunt was still next to me. I hadn't exactly forgotten her, but I was doing a good job of trying. I'd *never* felt that way before, ever. But then she'd never sprung a surprise brother or sister fathered by an evil Sententia sociopath on me either.

My aunt was having my uncle's baby.

It sounded really weird when I thought of it that way.

"Lainey," she repeated.

"Yeah?" Out in the front room, I heard the door open again and Kendra's confused *um* before Natalie interceded in whispers. "Holy *shit*," Kendra said, and I kind of wanted to laugh/cry.

"Sweetie," Aunt Tessa continued. If she wasn't touching me, she was wringing her hands in her lap. "Maybe we could go somewhere? To have dinner and talk about this? We made a reserv—"

"I have to go to a play."

"What?" She glanced at Dan again, who made a throat clearing sound, and that's officially when I lost my shit.

"I'm going to a play." I stood, and even though I wasn't remotely ready to go out in public, I gathered my things to leave.

Eventually my aunt was going to cry. She cried at everything. "I *know* this is a surprise, Elaine," she said. "I—I should have done this differently. I thought you'd be happy, and we could talk—"

"What's there to talk about?" As soon as I opened my mouth, the threatening tears spilled down her face, but I couldn't stop myself. "This is kind of a done deal—you're having a baby! It's a little late for *talking* about it, unless you want me to help pick out names! We have like seven *months* to do that. I'm going to a play. I'll see you tomorrow."

I tossed my bag over my shoulder and walked out, past Manny, past my whispering roommates, and straight out of the building.

I hadn't said a word to Daniel Astor the entire time.

NOT HALF A block later, I ran into Jack Kensington. Of course. He was walking down my street wearing a plaid shirt, an expensive coat, and a serious expression. As usual, he seemed primed for a photo shoot, as if a woman with a camera should be walking backwards in front of him, capturing the perfect shot every time the leaves gusted around him in the October wind. I, on the other hand, was wearing sweat pants and possibly mis-matched shoes, and I for sure hadn't brushed my hair. I stopped and waited for him because why not?

"Seriously? You're walking down my street right now?" At the sound of my voice, surprise slid across his features. He looked around like he was in the wrong place.

"Lainey?" His eyes traced me up and down as he came to a stop, like he had to verify it was actually me. "What are you doing out here?"

"Running away," I said. "But I live here. What are *you* doing out here?"

He stuffed his hands in his pockets. "I—Are you crying?"

"What?" I swiped my hand across my face. "No." Though maybe I had been.

"What happened?"

I told him the basics because, again, why not? "I probably could have handled it better," I admitted.

"Probably," he agreed. Looking over my shoulder, he added, "But I think you have a chance to rectify that." He put a hand on my shoulder and spun me around. Sure enough, Aunt T, the devil, and his bodyguard were pouring out of my building and heading our way. "You ruined your grand exit by stopping to talk to me."

"I just—*fuck*." Behind me, Jack made this coughing sound, like he was trying not to laugh, though there was nothing funny about this situation. "This sucks."

"Don't want to be a big sister?"

"What? No! That's not i—" I went to glare over my shoulder at him, but he was gone. I whipped my head the other way to see he'd moved up next to me, and was trying not to laugh again. "This isn't *funny*."

"C'mon. That was funny." He imitated my confusion and I stamped my foot hard enough to crack the concrete.

"Argh! What is it with me and guys who can't be serious when things are going wrong?!"

"I don't know," Jack said, "but it's probably a good thing."

"Argh!" I wiped my face with the back of my hand and took a deep breath, then another.

"Lainey!" My aunt was still crying. I held open my arms and she tumbled into them. "I'm sorry! This went so wron—"

"Shhhh," I soothed as she cried, and I felt strangely comforted. I'd always been the strong one, the one who hugged *her* when she cried. This was familiar. Not *everything* had gone to hell. "*I'm* sorry," I said, and I repeated it over and over until her tears began to slow.

Over my aunt's shoulder, I locked eyes with the senator. I'd told him to stay away from my family. I'd *told* him. I'd done what he wanted, earned my freedom, and *this* is what I ended up with anyway. I held his gaze, hoping my eyes conveyed all the hatred they possibly could. But if they did, it didn't scare him, because he didn't flinch. He might even have smiled.

We stood like that, an awkward family reunion on the windy city street, until Aunt Tessa croaked a muffled, "Lainey?"

"Yeah?"

She picked up her head and wiped her eyes. "Who's this?" She gestured to Jack, quiet, handsome, and still standing next to me.

"Oh." I'd forgotten he was there.

"Jack Kensington," he said smoothly, topping it off with a perfect smile that showed his dimple. "It's a pleasure to meet you." He held out his hand to Auntie, and she took it, a little smile growing on her face.

"You as well," she replied. She patted her own mussed hair and swiped under her eyes once more. "Sorry about this." She held up a hand, as if to indicate, I didn't know what. The circumstances, I supposed, including her tears, and my own ragged appearance.

"He's my TA," I said stupidly.

"Is he now," said Aunt Tessa. She still had one arm around my waist and she tapped her fingers against my side. I tried not to squirm. After a short lull, because obviously I was not going to do it, Auntie introduced our illustrious companion. "Jack, this is Daniel Astor."

Dan stepped forward and held out his hand. "Mr. Kensington."

"Sir. It's an honor to—to see you," Jack stuttered, like he was embarrassed or, possibly, star-struck.

"You *know* each other?" I blurted out. I could *not* handle that too.

Jack glanced at me, a little sheepish grin playing on his face. "Doesn't everyone recognize Senator Astor?"

"Oh." *Duh.* Of *course.* Naturally, Jack would recognize him. Probably *every* kid who went to a Sententia school would.

"You're too kind," Dan demurred, and my fingers tightened into a fist at my side. I wished I could punch him. "Well. Perhaps we could move on to a less breezy location?"

"Is Jack joining us?" Aunt Tessa said, a little more hopefully than I liked.

"He's my *TA*," I repeated. Why did that only seem to matter to me? "And I don't know what he's doing here—I just ran into him on the street."

Jack shifted the bag slung over his shoulder. "I was meeting…someone at the Castle. For a drink." The way Jack hesitated over *someone* made me sure it was a girl he was meeting and I wished the idea didn't make my stomach clench.

"Oh," I said, and my aunt squeezed my side.

"A drink, eh?" Dan interjected. "A drink sounds perfect right now, doesn't it Manny?"

"It definitely does, sir," Manny agreed.

"Well then." Dan smoothed his coat. "If I may be so bold as to invite myself, may we join you, Mr. Kensington? If it won't upset your companion, of course," he added.

Jack coughed. "That sounds fine."

Dan nodded, our plans determined. "Tess," he said, and I hated the way he said her name. There was affection in it, the kind I wasn't sure even he could feign. "Perhaps you and Lainey would like some time together?"

"Yes, I think we would. Does that sound okay, honey?"

"Yeah," I agreed, because alone time with my aunt sounded good. And besides, what else could I say? I'd lost control of this situation a long time ago.

Chapter Fourteen

Carter

Halloween was sexier than I remembered it, if Alexis's costume was any indication. Which wasn't a bad thing. At least there was some reward for what I'd let her do to me.

I watched myself in the mirror as she applied the finishing touches to my face. She stepped back, satisfied. "All right, done. Let's go before it gets any later."

"I look ridiculous," I informed her.

God help me, but I'd agreed to let Lex pick my costume. I had not expected to turn out as a Lothario pirate in pants too tight—*way* too tight—and shirt too loose. And with not enough buttons. And boots that laced up to my knees. I should have been more concerned when she asked for my shoe size.

"You look *perfect*. Come on." She dragged me out the door of her dorm room and slammed it behind her. I didn't visit her dorm often, because I had a luxury apartment and Lex liked luxury. She hated her roommate and barely called, "Bye," to her as we escaped into the hall-way. "God, she could have left an hour ago. You have to stop being nice to her."

"Maybe you need to *start*," I suggested and she huffed.

"Are you kidding? She's boring. And stalker-y. She just likes to stare at you. Seriously, she asks me if you're coming over every single day."

"Maybe because I'm nice to her."

"No. Because she hopes to get a peek of you in your tight little boxer briefs. Know who she reminds me of? Your creepy kissing-cousin, Jill."

I didn't reply. Alexis knew it upset me when she talked about Jill, but she thought it was because she never said anything nice. *Niceness* was something we argued about regularly. We were both on a mission to get the other to be more/less of it.

Outside her building, we headed in the direction of the party, walking fast while scanning for taxis. Speaking of little and tight, I tugged as discreetly as possible on the leather pants she'd squeezed me into.

"I think you ordered the pieces in the wrong size."

She raked her eyes up and down my get up, lingering on one of the too-tight places. "Trust me, you're the only one who'll think that. You look hot." I looked like an asshole, but I didn't tell her that.

I slapped her nearly bare ass with the plastic sword strapped to my belt. "You don't look like a Raven."

"Shut *up*. *I* look hot." She did.

We were on our way to the *Rogues and Ravens* party, whatever the hell that meant. Probably whoever thought it up wanted to say *Maid-ens*, but then someone got to rhyming and *Ravens* had the nicer alliteration. Who cared if it made sense?

"What, exactly, are you supposed to be again?"

She glared the truly perfect glare of a debutante. "A *chef*." She gestured at her ensemble, from the tiny white dress with offset-buttons, to the scarf that rested artfully against her cleavage, ending with the little white barrette in the shape of a chef hat. It glittered against her dark hair, which was the closest thing to "raven" about her.

"I think the length of your uniform is a health code violation."

"Fuck off. You like it." I did. She tugged on the fool scarf tied around my head. "Your old hair would have been perfect with this. I *should* have gotten you a wig. Damn."

"No, you shouldn't have. That's where I would have drawn the line." Which was likely not true, because I'd let her go so far as to line my eyes with dark pencil. What was a wig on top of guyliner?

Alexis knew this. "Add some nice dark, flowing hair and those baby blues would pop even more. Maybe you were born for this pirate thing."

Probably not, because I got sea-sick. I didn't mention that. It was more embarrassing than the costume. Growing up in New England with a father who was afraid to fly and a life without much room for vacations, I'd been on my first whale watch in first grade. I'd seen no whales but become intimately friendly with the toilet. When I was fourteen, I'd humored Aunt Mel and tried again, thinking maybe I'd grown out of it. Same results, but worse somehow. I was almost six feet tall and supposed to be a man.

"By the way, Michael Jackson called—he wants his jacket back." It was a deep red velvet and, like everything I was wearing, felt expensive. Intentionally shabby brocade bits lined the cuffs. Lex was visibly shivering by now, so I slipped it off and draped it over her shoulders. She gave me a look but didn't protest.

"I was going more for Captain Morgan," she said, pulling the jacket tight around her.

"Who?" I tried to keep a straight face but it didn't work.

"Seriously? Captain *Mor*—Oh, shut up. I'll introduce you to him tonight. But no fighting," she reminded me for the fifth time.

I slapped her with the sword again. "Probably couldn't anyway. My range of motion is impaired and I'd lose. And I'm getting concerned about my future ability to father children. It would be pretty tragic for the Penrose line to end with *me*."

Lex hesitated. "I'm pretty sure your future children are still intact," she said finally, but it lacked the spark of everything before it.

"Hey? What'd I do?" Uncle Jeff had taught me to claim responsibility.

"Nothing." Lex tugged the coat tighter and I added my arm over her shoulder. "It's just weird to joke about your future children, that's all."

"I'm sorry, babe. I didn't mean anything by it."

"I know," she said, with this measure of defeat in her voice.

"Hey." She shivered and I hugged her close to me. We *had* to get a taxi soon. At this rate, by the time we got there, Lex would have frostbite and I'd really have fucked something up. "I don't know what I did here, I'm sorry. Could you maybe tell me? So if I do it again at least it will be on purpose?"

A bubble of laughter floated up from the folds of my ridiculous silk shirt, so I knew I hadn't dug my hole any deeper. Yet. "It's just—arrrgh!" She thumped her head against my chest. "Okay, listen, because this is the kind of girly breakdown shit I just don't *do* so I'm going to say it one time and then we'll forget about it. Right?"

"Right." I held very still. Alexis *admitting* to doubt was rare, like unicorn blood, but chinks in her armor were *good* for her. They let out some of the things she'd been burying since she was fifteen. The imperfections made her more *her*, the girl I'd always liked underneath, even during the years when I hadn't much liked the rest of her.

"Here's the thing—you're joking about kids and the future, and it's just, well, am *I* the future? I know that's, like, far away, but I...I don't want to be a joke. Okay? God, I need a drink now. Let's go." She tried to twist out of my grip, but I tugged her back.

"No. Wait." I couldn't go on without saying *something*. "You're not a joke or a, a fling. I swear you're not. I *was* joking, but *not* about you. I'm sorry. I—" *haven't thought about this before* I started to say. But I had.

I had imagined a whole future, could see it so clearly I'd thought it was guaranteed. I saw my apartment filled with antiques and dark haired children with green-blue eyes running around the store like I had as a kid. But it turned out to be just *my* imagination. I hadn't thought beyond *now* in any real way since.

Finally, I said, "I'm just figuring things out as we go. And I thought we were going good?"

She smiled. Tentatively at first, but it spread into a champion of a grin. "Yeah," she said. "We are."

"You say that like it surprises you," I joked, and gave a little tug on her cleavage scarf.

She bumped me with her hip. "It does."

"I know," I said. Because it surprised me too, in a good way.

"I'm not even sure why I bother. You're too serious and work too much and are too prone to brooding—"

"But I look good."

"Don't interrupt! *But*, I was going to say, you look, like, *scandalously* good in those pants."

"Arrrr. And what lassie can resist a brooding, tight-panted rogue?" I poked her with my sword again, which was proving to be the most fun part of the costume.

"Get your cutlass away from my ass before I reconsider!"

"Seriously though, I'm working on those first things."

"I know."

"I mean, I'm wearing this."

"Admit you love it."

I kind of did. Pretending to be someone else had its advantages. I hadn't done a proper Halloween since I *was* a kid. Last year I'd ducked out of candy duty at the store long enough to see Lainey in her evil witch costume, and that was as close as I'd come in years. Funny though, I hadn't thought of that until just now, and the memory *didn't* make my chest constrict.

I took a deep breath and felt…okay. Good, even.

"Carter?"

"Yeah?"

"*Now* what are you brooding about?"

"You," I said, and for the first time, it was mostly true.

"WHERE ARE WE going again?" I became concerned when the taxi we finally caught stopped on a street in Arlington where Important People lived. An enormous Tudor mansion loomed in front of us, decked in artfully lit cobwebs and flickering pumpkins that were probably professionally carved. Raven figurines with glowing eyes watched our approach from perches all over the trees. "The *Rogues and Ravens* are *here?*"

Lex glanced sideways at me. "Do you seriously listen to *none* of the talk at the office? This is Janelle Roberts's party. Everyone wanted an invite. Remember?"

Fuck. Janelle's father was the senior senator from Virginia. Every congressional relative and big money donor's kid between the ages of sixteen and twenty-five would be here, along with their retinues and hangers-on. I *hated* these parties. I resigned myself as the door man guarding Halloween Wonderland carefully checked his guest list before waving us inside. Almost as soon as we walked through the door, Lex was dragged off by a squealing gaggle of girls dressed in costumes as small or smaller than hers. She disappeared into the artificial fog with a final glimpse of her dark, swinging hair.

The image danced behind my eyelids, and I couldn't help thinking of *another* girl's raven black hair. For one fleeting second I allowed myself to wonder what Lainey was doing. She'd never choose a costume as overtly sexy as Lex's. Would she? And if she did, was someone else there to appreciate it?

I shook my head, unsure how I wanted that question answered. I slipped my jacket back on and ran my fingers over the interior pocket, ensuring my wallet—and the note—were still there. With a promise that I wouldn't touch it again tonight, I plunged into the party. Finding Lex was a half macabre, half sexy game of hide-and-seek. Ghouls, fools, and sexy-somethings popped up in surprise singles and packs all over the fog-filled mansion.

"Misch!" I heard her voice, high and excited. A white flash shot into my line of vision, not toward me, but to hug a pretty boy "mechanic" whose hands had obviously never wielded a wrench but did land far too low on Alexis's back when he kissed her cheek. I didn't like that at all.

Who knew I was the jealous type? I'd felt the same way…months ago, right after I'd gotten here. At the time I'd thought it was because I wasn't used to Lex flirting with someone else. But now here was the feeling again. I *really* didn't like how his hand was still resting on her hip.

"Hey," I said, inclining my chin as he met my eyes over her shoulder. I looked at his hand and looked back at him.

"Babe!" Lex squealed. She turned around to hug me, and I left my arm around her shoulders. She was wobbly like she'd had too much punch already and talking louder than usual. "*There* you are. This is the best party of the year! Have you met Mischa? Wait, of *course* you have. He played soccer at Andover."

On closer inspection, I realized I had. It had been years, and he was older and taller now. His simpering smile was still the same though. "Yeah. Hey," I repeated.

"Boo," came a small voice behind me. It was comic how such a soft noise had all three of us turning around together. Standing there was a ghost. A little blonde wisp of a thing in an ethereal white dress with white-painted face, black-lined eyes, and red lips.

It was Jillian.

I closed my eyes and opened them again, but she was still there, smiling a bloody smile.

Jillian. Here. In front of me.

As if Lex mentioning her earlier had conjured her, in real life.

Lex stared at her for a few seconds with her best bitchy eyes, until finally they widened in recognition. "Holy shit!" She looked her up and down. "Where the hell have you been hiding? I thought maybe you *were* dead."

"France," Jill said, though I knew where she'd been. Hidden away, first at a psyche ward, then boarding school.

"*Mais oui?*" Lex replied, eyebrows raised.

"Father thought it was best I go somewhere nicer. For my recovery, you know." Casually, she added, "*Aussi, les étudiants sont beaucoup plus sophistiquée que dans les États-Unis.*"

Lex's bitch eyes reappeared even narrower than before, so I could tell whatever Jill had said, she didn't like it. "*Alors, je suppose que vous n'avez rien appris,*" she said, and made a cursory glance around. "Oh, Mischa, look! There's—" She gestured vaguely toward the crowd. "Let's go get a drink." And she marched away, dragging her confused but happy acquaintance along behind her.

I still had not moved.

"Carter?" Jill said. "How are you?"

Paralyzed. That's how I was. Except for the skyrocketing rate of my heartbeats. Blood thundered in my ears and pushed at my temples. Somehow over the noise of it, I heard myself say, "What are you doing here?"

"What do you mean? Janelle invited me." She stared up at me with those big blue eyes, wide and innocent-looking as ever. Like she wasn't an attempted murderer and I didn't know it. I gripped my stupid sword tightly with both hands, to keep from doing I didn't know what. Something I'd regret. I let go only long enough to run my hand over my hair because I just couldn't stop myself. I did it a couple times and felt better.

"No." I shook my head, more times than necessary. "I mean, what are you doing here." I spread my arms and hoped they encompassed what I meant—here, in this house, in this city, in this *country*.

She shifted on her feet, tucking a strand of blond hair behind her whitened ear. It was the first time she looked like the Jillian I remembered. "Father wanted me to come home. To tell me the good news. And for the announcement." She looked back up at me, meeting my eyes in a way that wasn't like the old Jillian at all.

I nodded. Of course. I should have known. Since Jill almost died and her father began running for president, Jill's mother had made a complete about-face in her dealings with Uncle Dan. Some combination of guilt and Sententia solidarity. Everyone needed to support his candidacy, her most of all. Of course Jill would be here.

But someone should have warned me.

"I asked Father not to tell you," Jill said, reading my mind. "I…I've missed you. I wanted to surprise you."

A harsh laugh I barely recognized escaped my throat. "Congratulations," I said. "I'm surprised."

I meant to go then, but her small hand on my arm stopped me. "Please," she said. "Please don't walk away. L-let me say some things."

"Why?" My anger boiled over then. I used to love Jill, legitimately love her. *Seeing* her still triggered those feelings, conflicting with a near-ly all-consuming rage I could barely suppress. I'd loved her, and protected her, and she'd tried to take *everything* from me. "Tell me *why* I should do that?"

Simply she said, "Because you can't make a scene."

Fuck. And this was why she'd wanted to surprise me. Here. Harlan Waites's words came back to me: *You have many skills, but politicking isn't one of them.* Maybe it really was in the blood. Even Jill was a million times better at it than I was.

I took a deep breath and another, running my hand over my head. "You have five minutes."

I FOLLOWED HER down hallways, past the bustling kitchen, to a quiet room, a study not decked out for the party. When she tried to shut the door, I stopped her. "No. Leave it open."

"But—"

"I don't care if it's not discreet. Leave it open."

She nodded. I followed her again to a set of chairs by the window. It was dark outside, so instead I saw the two of us reflected in the glass. I didn't like my expression. I knew I had a temper, but I'd never considered myself *violent*. But I'd never been so betrayed by someone either. Looking at Jill, I was afraid. That *I* would do something terrible and, worse, not regret it.

We looked at each other for a while, ticking away another minute. We'd passed the five I'd given her already, and sitting there was tor-ture, which was why I wouldn't move. I wanted to hear whatever Jill was going to say, knowing it would hurt. It had been a year and a half since I'd seen her. She'd changed. I could tell, even with the makeup. She was small as ever, but older. She was prettier, actually. She sat up straighter.

"You look good," she said finally. When I didn't respond, she took a breath and kept going. "I think you're even taller. I-I've missed you."

I laughed, a coughed out sound that was bitter and touched with menace. I felt blood in my cheeks, angry splotches I couldn't control. Missed me? As if she had the right. "The feeling is not mutual."

She sighed. "Isn't it? You don't miss me at all?"

"No."

"But I *know* you. How many people can say that? Can your new girlfriend?"

"*No!*" I blurted out, meaning *stop*, but giving away the truth anyway. Though I'd come close to exposing them, Lex still didn't know my secrets. "We're not talking about her. *Don't* talk about her. Say what you wanted to say, or I'm leaving."

Softly, she told me, "I'm sorry. I know—what I did, I know it was wrong. I'm sorry."

"You tried to kill someone. It takes more than sorry to make up for it."

"I know," she squeaked out. She looked up at me from where her hands gripped each other. Her knuckles were so white, they looked painted, like her face. "I'm trying. My doctors—they're helping. I swear. I needed help. I'm sorry."

I nodded, unsure what to say. She did need help. In most ways she hadn't been punished enough, but in others…Jill may have been re-suscitated after Lainey was forced to use her Hangman gift to save herself, but not all of her came back. Though sometimes I fantasized about it, I couldn't imagine losing my Sententia gifts, like she had. It would be like ripping away vital pieces of myself, an arm or half my soul. Who was I without them? They were part of what defined me, and all Sententia. Curiosity got the better of me.

"How are you handling your—loss?"

Jill shifted in her seat. "It's—" Tears welled in her eyes and she squeezed them shut, grimacing. "It's hard. I'm not going to lie about it. I forget. I meet someone, and when nothing happens, I think 'oh, they're not one of us' but it's *me*." Her voice cracked. "It's me who's not one of us anymore."

I opened my mouth. Closed it. *I'm sorry*, I started to say, but I wasn't. Not entirely. *Maybe you deserve it*, I thought next, but did anyone deserve that? Finally, I said, "It sounds hard."

A breathy huff-laugh escaped her. "It's like there's a little empty piece of me right here"—she touched the center of her chest—"and I can't find anything to fill in the hole all the way."

Bam. She was leaning forward in her seat, looking at me when she said that. Despite everything, she knew *I* was the one who could understand. And I did; I had the same hole. My hand was halfway toward the note tucked in my jacket pocket when I realized what it was doing. I ran it over my hair instead.

Jill nodded and sat back, exhausted or maybe satisfied. "So. You know what it's like."

"I suppose I do." My voice came out like I had sand paper in my throat. I cleared it.

After a few beats she said casually, "Father is much happier with your current match anyway."

"Because I'm happy."

Jill grinned, and for the first time ever, I saw the cool madness lurking under her facade. "No," she said. "Because she's easy to control."

I shot up, the chair behind me making an ugly squeak as it scraped backwards too fast. "Stay away from her."

The crazy look slipped away, replaced with Jill's usual innocence. I shivered. "Gladly," she said. "Maybe I should say that to you. She's just a tool. *And* she's a bitch. Always has been."

"You don't know her."

Jill shook her head. "No. *You* don't know *anyone*."

I rocked on my heels as her words punched into me. Without another word, I backed toward the door. I wouldn't take my eyes off Jill until I was gone. She was standing now too. "I'm sorry, Carter. I'm sorry!" She held out her hands. "This is what I needed to say! I'm trying to make up for what I did, to *help* you. It's never been me you need to be protected from. I *love*—"

I slammed the door and was gone.

Chapter Fifteen

Lainey

It was weird how life worked. A day, a weekend, a single minute, even a single second could change everything, take something from you or give it, maybe even both. When I looked back on it, I'd see that weekend shoved me over a precipice. I'd gained a brother or sister, but lost the feeling of freedom I'd only just started to grasp.

So much had happened that was out of my control. But it had never *been* in my control anyway. I couldn't keep Daniel Astor or the Sententia out of my life. All I could control was *me*. Grasping that was a different kind of freedom. The question I still hadn't answered was: who was I? Maybe we spent our entire lives trying to figure it out.

Halloween was exactly what I needed, the chance to pretend to be someone else, to be *anyone*.

"You have brothers and sisters, right?" I asked Serena as we browsed a vintage shop in Cambridge, looking for the final touches for her flapper costume.

"Yeah, three. Two sisters and a brother." She picked up a midnight blue cloche from the bin in front of her and held it up.

"What's it like?" The thing about my aunt's impending baby was that I wanted to talk about it but I *couldn't*. I shook my head at the hat. "You need a headband," I said. "Sparkles."

"And feathers!" She moved on to a rack of vintage outerwear, stoles and coats and things. "I don't know. It just is. I've always had them, so I don't know what it would be like without them. Why?"

"Just curious. I'm the opposite, so I was just…wondering." I slid my necklace back and forth on its chain.

Serena glanced up at me, pausing at a fox fur wrap. She held it up. "This is nice."

It was rather nice, actually. Average condition, so wearable but not collectible. It was perfect. That is, until I swiped a finger down the fur and a tell-tale hum rose beneath it. *Shit.* I wavered, not wanting to loose my Grim Diviner senses I'd been suppressing for months, but I was just so tired. Tired of resisting. Tired of everything. If I couldn't use my gifts for my friend, what good was I?

I watched the vision for only a second. She passed peacefully, this fur draped around her shoulders and another one across her lap. I thought she might have been the second generation owner. A young girl sat by her side, waiting.

I shook my head at Serena. "Not that one."

"But—"

"Trust me. We'll find a nicer one." I flipped quickly through a few pieces on the rack. "Tell me more about your siblings?"

"My little sister is my favorite. She's only nine. She was a surprise, but she's the best."

"I'm sure she is." I could only hope to be half as cool a big sister as Serena must be.

"She dances better than me. But I'm boring. Let's talk about how *you* are on a first name basis with the guy who might be president." Right then, her eyes lit on a sparkling beaded bolero, so I didn't think she saw me flinch. "I knew you were fancy, but that was a surprise. So how did your aunt meet him? At some big DC charity event?"

"It's a long story, but the short version is I introduced them." Much to my chagrin.

"*You* did? You get more interesting by the minute."

I inspected Serena's find. The wrap was black and teal with an art deco rose motif, and in below average condition—which is to say, perfect, because the price was reasonable I tapped some of the pulled edges, but no more beads fell off and, good news, no one had died while wearing it. "That's the one."

"Yes! I love this." She held it in front of her and did a little pirouette. When she came to a stop she said, "So then how do you know a senator?"

Different answers ran through my head: *he's my long-lost uncle. He tried to kill me. He's the leader of the secret organization that wants me to be their assassin.* Ultimately what I said was, "He's my—ex-boyfriend's uncle." I stumbled over the ex- part, even though I should have been used to it by now.

A thoughtful look crossed Serena's face, like she wanted to say something more, but she shook her head and chuckled. "You really are fancy."

"Fancy enough to wear *this*?" Desperate for a change of subject, I pulled the last coat off the rack, a fluffy white monstrosity that looked like it was made of Abominable Snowman hide and had probably belonged to a seventies porn star.

"If *anyone* is fancy enough to wear that, it's you." She slipped it over my shoulders. The lining was expensive—the *coat* was expensive—and it fit me perfectly. Serena laughed again. "That's so ridiculous, it's actually great. It looks good with your hair."

With a grin, I said, "I'm buying it."

Next to the register was a rack of kitschy, retro cards that I spun idly while we waited to cash out. Serena pointed to one with Dorothy from the *Wizard of Oz*. "You should totally go as Dorothy for Halloween. You've already got her whole innocent-sexy thing down perfectly."

Laughing, I said, "I already have a costume, but maybe next year." I was about to spin the carousel again, when I noticed the card just below Dorothy. If not for Serena, I'd have missed it. On the front was a ridiculous snowman, wearing sunglasses and flowered shorts, carrying a surf board. I hesitated before I pulled it from the rack. Inside it read *Feliz Navidad!* That was it. I closed my eyes and held the card to my chest before I plucked out an envelope.

Serena watched me curiously. "Early Christmas shopping?"

"Something like that."

I bought the coat, and the card too.

ON THE T ride back, Serena eyed me where I was wedged in a corner, trying not to touch anyone. I didn't like the T very much, packed with people in various stages of living and dying. Crowded public places were a challenge for any Diviner, and often morbid for a Grim one like me. Serena thought I was a germophobe.

"Did you hurt your wrist?" she asked as our train rumbled its way underground.

"Huh?"

"Your wrist. Does it hurt? You keep rubbing it."

I looked down to see I was, in fact, rubbing my wrist and stopped. No, it didn't hurt. But rubbing it made the phantom pains in my heart feel a little better. The card had me thinking about…things. Carter, last

Christmas, the accident. "It's the cold today," I lied. "I broke it last year, and sometimes when it's cold, or rainy, it aches."

Serena nodded, like that made sense, and I hitched my new fluffy coat from one arm to the other. After a hesitation, she said, "Can I ask you something else?"

"Sure."

"Is ex-boyfriend the one who gave you that necklace?" She looked down toward my chest, where instead of my wrist, my fingers were clutching the diamond again. I dropped it.

I cleared my throat. "Um, yeah."

"It's pretty. I get why you wear it, but then, maybe I don't?"

"It's…complicated," I hedged.

Serena paused again. Finally, she said, "Did he abuse you?"

"God, no! He was the best. Why do people keep thinking that?"

Holding up her hand and ticking off a list on her fingers, she swept her eyes first down toward my feet and said, "Uh, the tattoo,"—up to my hands—"the broken wrist,"—and finished at my neck—"and the expensive present you don't want to let go. It's okay. I understand. It's hard to leave behind—"

I held up my hand. "I swear, he was great. He the opposite of abused me."

And then, the question: "So…well then, why did you break up with him?" Why indeed. If only I could tell her.

"He was…*too* good," is what I said, and I liked that it wasn't a complete lie. "Too soon. I needed to do this on my own." I refrained from adding *but I miss him*. I wanted to admit it, out loud. It felt like it would be good to stop denying it, just like it had felt perversely good to use my Diviner gift at the store.

"Hmmm," she said, and I broke in before she could ask any more questions I didn't really want to answer.

"So are you *sure* it's okay if I come with you?" Serena had scored VIP invitations to the biggest Halloween party in the city, something she excelled at. She danced better than anyone I'd ever seen, so promoters shoved passes at her every time she went out. I barely managed to keep up with her and her other friends. "I don't want to intrude—"

"Lane," she interrupted, laughing. "You're coming. And I get it. You don't want to talk about ex-boyfriend. So. What are you going as again?"

I smiled. "I have this great Malificent costume."

"Who?"

"Malificent?" I said, smile faltering. "You know, the witch from *Sleeping Beauty*?"

"Oh. Right." After a pause for the train announcement for the next station, she said, "Is it sexy?"

"Not exactly," I admitted. We couldn't really do sexy at Northbrook's Halloween Bazaar, where I'd worn it last year.

"Then no," Serena said.

"What?"

"I said no. No way." She leaned toward me, hanging onto the train bar with both hands. "Have you seen yourself? You're not going as some creepy not-sexy Disney witch. You need to shake things up. Do something to forget about Mr. Too-Good and be Miss All-Bad."

I swallowed. Hadn't I wanted just that? To be someone else? "Well, I don't have another costume…"

Serena eyed me up and down, like she was sizing me for something. Something I should be worried about. "*I* do. Let's get off here." The doors opened at Park Street and she headed toward the tunnel to Downtown Crossing. "You're going to need boots and…accessories."

"I CAN'T DO this," I said later as I stood in Serena's room, wearing a string bikini and feeling ridiculous. And cold. I watched myself shiver in the mirror as Serena finished braiding my hair.

"Oh yeah you can. You look amazing."

"I look *naked*." The bikini was nearly the color of my skin, which on Serena surely looked amazing. On me, it looked basically like I was wearing nothing.

"That's the point. That's what she looked like." She snapped a rubber band into place and draped the long braid over my shoulder. "You look *perfect*."

I certainly looked…something. Serena had brought up images on the way off the train, and we'd come home with suede boots, two silk scarves, and some chain necklaces. Add in the bikini she already owned and *voila*! I was Princess Leia in the dessert.

"I can't do this," I repeated.

Serena tied her own scarf around her head and twisted a few curls into place on her forehead. Her flapper ensemble complete, she said, "Too late. Time to go!"

"Fine," I relented. "But I'm wearing the coat." Serena rolled her eyes and pulled me out the door by my chains.

The party was at a rock club on Lansdowne Street, where I'd been to concerts but never something like this. In fact, I'd never been to anything like this party *ever*. The "VIP" room was a riot of color and texture, and that was just the walls. Chairs, tables, rugs, pillows—*everything* was a vibrant, exotic rainbow, like a Moroccan palace and a gay pride parade met and fell in love. And then there were the *people*.

Everyone was in elaborate states of dress—or mostly closer to *un*-dress. The entire place was *packed* with partygoers, far more than I expected. We escaped into the main party as soon as we'd eaten, because Serena and her other friends wanted to dance.

"I'll meet you in a minute," I told them. "I have to do something with this." I shook my coat at them and Serena nodded.

"Sure. Find us on the flooooor!" she called over her shoulder, already moving to the beat as the others dragged her away.

On the way to the coat check, I spotted an out-of-the-way bathroom and slipped inside. It was semi-quiet compared to outside and, blessedly, empty of people waiting. The two stalls were occupied, so I draped my coat over my shoulders and leaned against the wall, waiting for a turn but mostly just taking a minute to gather my courage. I wasn't sure why I had no problem spending all day and night at the beach in a bikini but was afraid to relinquish my fuzzy white shield here at the party. Being Miss All-Bad was easier for Serena to say than for me to do.

Two girls tumbled out of the stalls, their laughter replaced by glares for me and my coat. I squeezed closer to the wall to let them pass. "*Whore*," I heard one of them whisper just as I was closing the stall door.

And that was it. The push that sent me tumbling. Something inside me snapped, all my frustration, anger, bitterness. *Fuck them*, I thought. Fuck *everyone*. Miss All-Bad? She was awake now, and she was *pissed*.

I slammed the door open and stalked up behind them. They both had these fake innocent expressions on their faces, but they were watching me in the mirror, nervous. I was tall, and I was angry, and I *hoped* I intimidated them. "If I'm a whore," I mused, eying their barely-larger-than-mine devil and kitty cat costumes, "what are you two? Nuns? Good luck with that." And I left them there, with their mouths hanging open. *Good.*

By the time I fought my way back from the coat check, Serena was already surrounded on the dance floor. Still flushed from my mean-girl encounter, I stopped at one of the bars for a Coke. Nearby was a tiny open space against the wall with an unexpectedly good view. I leaned there, assessing my options. Of course, that was when I saw him. By now, I wasn't even surprised.

Halloween suited Jack Kensington. In fact, I was willing to bet it was his favorite holiday. His pants were *tight* and stuffed into motorcycle boots that weren't exactly period. A red, possibly velvet jacket topped an appropriately—if you were a pirate captain, anyway—frilly shirt that was open nearly to his stomach. A plastic sword slapped at his waist, and tied around his head was a shimmery silver scarf, not unlike Serena's.

In truth, he looked as comfortable and natural as a flamboyant pirate as he did in his button downs and ties, striding through the throngs to order a drink at the bar. When he turned, after gracing the bartender with a rakish smile, he saw me, and the smile grew by degrees.

"Ahoy, me beauty!" he called in his best talk-like-a-pirate voice, stopping in front of me and striking a pose. I fought the urge to smile.

"You look ridiculous."

"I was thinking swarthy? No?"

"Do you even know what that means?"

He thought for a second. "Swashbuckling?"

"Swash-something."

With a raise of his glass, he said, "Just trolling these fine waters for grog and booty." I couldn't help myself; I laughed. Quite suddenly, I was having a good time. In fact, I was pretty sure if I did nothing more than flirt with him for the rest of the night, I'd have my best Halloween in memory.

I glanced in the general vicinity of his waistband. "That's quite a cutlass you've got there."

He nodded, grinning like the devil. "The wenches do love me sword."

"I bet."

"Ah, a wager then!" He tilted his glass at me, something dark that I suspected was a rum and Coke, because what else would a pirate drink? "I bet thee I'll leave here with the prettiest maiden in the tavern."

I patted my completely non-existent pockets. "I'm afraid I left all my doubloons at home." In truth, they were stuffed in my boot, along with my key, ID, and phone.

"Aye, but we can wager with other things."

"Like?"

Jack made himself comfortable, wedging into the space next to me, so it was impossible not to touch him. My arm pressed against his, informing me that the jacket was indeed velvet, and soft. He leaned in closer when he answered, "Kisses be as fine tender as jewels…" and waggled his eyebrows at me.

I sucked in a breath, thrilled and frightened by the mere thought of it. Most of me wanted to make that bet, just to see how far he'd go. But the night was early, so instead I said, "I'm sorry sir; I don't think you're allowed to trade those with me at this time."

He laughed, dropping the pirate voice but not moving any further away from me. "I'm not allowed to say how you look tonight, either."

"You don't seem to worry much about what you're allowed or not allowed to do."

Jack's smile nearly filled the room. "You're right." His eyes washed over me again, gleaming like a kind of sleek cat that prowls in the dark, a jaguar maybe. "And telling you how not-ridiculous you look in that suit might even be worth getting fired over."

Damn damn damn my blushing red cheeks. I hid them by looking down into my soda, but it was pointless. Possibly the worst thing about wearing a bikini in October is when your whole body flushes, anyone can see it. But I was smiling, too.

Jack bumped me lightly with his shoulder. "You know what? It's *Halloween.* I think you need to loosen up, relax a little."

I laughed. "You're saying this to the girl dressed like *this*?"

"I'm saying this to the girl dressed like *this* and hiding in a corner." He reached over and gave a gentle tug on my long braid. I hadn't been hiding, but let him think that.

"And I suppose you're the one who's going to show me how?"

"That's why I'm here." He held his arms out, but the gesture seemed bigger than the party. More like that's why he was here, in my city.

"Oh yeah?"

"Yes."

He smiled then, that crooked tilt to his lips that I dreamed about. Something about *this* smile was so terribly true, and wickedly tempting. He was right; I did need to loosen up. Hadn't Amy been saying that for, basically, ever? Wasn't that why Serena put me in this outfit in the first place? I was Miss All-Bad tonight.

"So. What do you think, Leia? Want to get out of here?" He looked down at his watch, as if he had somewhere else to be, or was bored, but it was neither. The sexy upturn to his lips and the way he glanced up at me told me the truth.

No, I can't. I'm here with friends, I should have said. "Yes," is what I told him. Once I said it, I knew just how true it was. "Yeah, I do."

His dimple grew as deep as his smile was wide. "Let's go, then."

WE EXITED THE club into the chilly night and a cloud of smoke. People huddled with their cigarettes in one of the funny little corrals erected next to anywhere with a cover charge. When we stepped past it, the bouncer called, "No re-entry."

Jack and I looked at each other. "That's okay, thank you," I said and he said, "I don't think we're coming back." I was pretty sure a few people waiting in line cheered.

"Thank God we got there early. I wouldn't have wanted to wait in that line."

"You're kidding, right?" Jack threw a glance back over his shoulder. "*You* wouldn't have had to wait in that."

"Only because we had invites."

"That's just why you got in *early*. You don't go to many clubs, do you?"

I shook my head. "Is it obvious?"

"Yes. Because you didn't even notice that eighty percent of the line was guys hoping to get let in just for the chance to see girls like you and Serena who don't have to wait in line."

"That's gross."

"Sure," Jack agreed.

"So how did *you* get in so easily?"

"I have my secrets." An exaggerated wink punctuated this pronouncement and I laughed.

"Like twenty dollar bills and a Herald's smile?"

He flashed the smile at me. "See? You're catching on."

A gorilla passed by going the other way and Jack gave him a high five. His sexy angel companion eyed my coat with un-angelic envy. I shivered just looking at her bare arms and...most everything else. I never thought I'd be glad for the Abominable fur joke, but I pulled it close around my shoulders. Next to us, Fenway Park loomed. I looked up at the wall that looked black in the dark, not green, and said, "It's an antique."

"What?" Jack followed my gaze. "The Green Monster?"

"Yeah. It's an antique. The wall, the original parts, not the chairs on top. Did you know that? Over a hundred years old. 1912."

He watched me for a second and smiled. "I think I did know that, but I'd never thought of it that way before."

"It's cool, right? You can sit on top of an antique wall and watch baseball. That's part of what I love about this city. You can walk down the sidewalk basically anywhere and trip over historic buildings. But then"—I pointed my thumb to the right—"right over there is a highway that goes *under* a fifty-two stories tall building. It's *all* right here in just fifty square miles of land. The whole modern world collected in an antique teacup."

After a silence that stretched until its edges were frayed, I started walking again, too fast and with my head down. "That probably sounded silly, huh? My ode to Boston. You're a New York guy, so maybe it just feels small here."

Jack cleared his throat. "No." He touched my hand and I stopped, turning to see he'd stopped too. He stood very still. In fact, it was this strange moment where *time* seemed to still. There was Jack, and me, and the city lights glowing like stars. "It feels beautiful," he said softly, looking right at me. "Everyone should be so lucky to see the city with you."

"It's dark. We can't see anything."

"That doesn't matter. I can see it in the way you love it. You see the cracks and tiny details and that makes you love it more."

The corners of my mouth, and my spirits, lifted. "My Aunt Tessa says this city was made for me."

"She was right." He was smiling too, his teeth shining in the light but face mostly in darkness from the shadows of the buildings. I was afraid for a second that he'd disappear, like the Cheshire Cat, or that I was crazy, and everything would disintegrate. Because I'd said something real, something private even, and instead of a stupid *wanna get Leia-d?* joke like the ones I'd endured at the party we'd just left, Jack said: "I never *wanted* to be here until just now."

My heart gave this mighty thump, as if those words had hugged it tight and then set it free to pound again. I was glad once more for my coat covering me, or I was sure he'd see it beating fast. I wished I could see him better, so I took a step, heading out of the shadows and toward the city proper. "So why did you?" I asked. "Come here, if you didn't want to."

With a harsh laugh, he said, "The wrong reasons." He'd said something like this before, in his office that day. Something about how it had been his Grandfather's idea and he didn't want to disappoint him.

"Maybe," I said, "the wrong reasons can lead us to the right thing."

"If only," he replied. After a second, he blew out a breath with a shake of his head and the moment was over. The tension broke and the lightness that seemed natural to him, so opposite of Carter's inherent seriousness, flowed back in around us. The *feeling*, however, the one bouncing between my internal organs like a pinball, stayed. Jack tugged on a piece of my coat's white fur. "You look like something from Hoth in this, you know."

"What's a Hoth?" I said, and his face puckered like I'd just insulted his mother.

"Have you even *seen Star Wars?*"

No. I honestly hadn't and I was suddenly embarrassed about that. But I said, "Maybe?"

Jack groaned. "We're watching it. *All* of them."

"Right now?"

"No," he laughed. "It's a little late tonight."

"So what *are* we doing?" I felt so good, champagne bubbly but, also, bold. I had the *feeling*, but on top of that was the giddiness of having done something I shouldn't have. I left a club with a guy with nothing more than a text to my friend. *Saw H.O.T. and left with him. Don't tell. xo* After that, I'd turned off my phone. I was doing something bad. I *liked* it. I felt like I could do *anything*.

"Are you hungry?"

"Aye, matey," I replied, and he whooped. So help me, I loved making him laugh.

I wasn't sure where a grad TA pirate and an underage undergrad in a fluffy fur coat and bikini could go, but as we headed into the brightly lit beacon of Kenmore Square, Jack led us up the stairs of the big chain restaurant on the corner.

"Really?" I couldn't help laughing. "Here?"

"Don't you like pizza?" he countered, arching an eyebrow in the most ridiculous way and making me laugh harder. I admitted I did and followed him inside.

We were lucky to be squished into a table in the single unoccupied corner in the entire place. Before we sat, Jack tugged the chairs side-by-side, so we could both appreciate the menagerie that filled the restaurant tonight. Servers bustled around, dark figures darting between lobsters, vampires, witches, sexy just-about-anything, a giant condom, a box of crayons, a TV remote, and a smattering of just regular people, though they were probably tourists.

"Is that a sexy *nun*?" Jack said, pointing to a girl at the edge of the bar, and I was laughing before I even saw her, because of *course* there was a sexy nun.

"Wow. I think it is." The sexiest thing at the Northbrook Halloween was my friend Brooke's fake accent. *This* was a sexy free-for-all. The girl's rosary belt was longer than her "habit."

"Kind of makes you look modest, doesn't it?"

"Thank God," I said and we both laughed.

"Whose idea was your costume, anyway?" His eyes flicked over me again, and I couldn't help but flush. "I'm guessing not yours."

I looked down at all the bare skin barely covered by my coat and tugged it tighter around my shoulders. In the light of the restaurant, my outfit felt more ridiculous than ever. "Serena's."

Jack nodded and leaned closer. "Remind me to thank her."

Blushing even more furiously, I plucked at the soft velvet of his jacket. It felt expensive. "And where did *you* get *this?*"

"Hugo Boss," Jack admitted.

"So you're a *fancy* pirate, eh?" I teased, though I'd always suspected it. His clothes fit way too well for anything else.

He looked back at me with a lopsided grin as he twirled a piece of my coat's abominable fur around his finger. "Takes one to know one, I think."

The harried server returned with two sodas and we ordered a chicken thumb platter to share, which clearly didn't impress her. I frowned as I watched her retreating back, hurrying to the station to input our crappy order.

"Somebody," Jack commented, "is not having nearly as much fun as we are."

"I should have ordered something else. I feel bad."

"Why? We didn't do anything wrong."

I supposed that was true. At Dad's Diner, people could come and sit at my counter all morning ordering nothing but coffee and toast. "But we could have done better, I guess. It's got to be a hard night to do her job."

He sipped his Coke from a straw and it made him seem younger. But then I watched his lips as he did it, which didn't make me feel younger at *all*. He seemed to realize what I was doing, maybe even what I was thinking, and grinned. I flushed and looked away.

"You," he said, "have to learn that you're not responsible for everyone else's happiness. Just your own. I can tell that about you. You worry too much." He tapped a finger in the middle of my forehead.

"And you don't seem to worry at all."

"As little as possible."

Maybe I could learn some things from him. It was a hard habit to turn off. "Like you don't seem worried that someone might see us together," I said.

He shrugged. "I told you, it's not illegal for us to be friends. Plus, whose fault is it we keep running into each other? Fate? I'm not going to fight it."

"But—"

"Lainey." Jack touched my hand, just for a second. "*If* there was a problem, it would be *my* problem. No worrying about my problem. In fact, no worrying at *all* tonight. Deal?" He held out his hand. I stared at it for a moment, wanting to take it but knowing that everything about this night *was* something to worry about.

I shook anyway. "Deal." His hand was warm and slightly calloused from basketball and weights. He held on longer than necessary, or even appropriate, and I started to wonder what that hand would feel like spread across my skin. Heat crept from my belly all the way to my cheeks.

Finally, with a satisfied grin, he said, "Good. Let's talk about other things." He still hadn't let go.

"Like?" I said, and I gently, regretfully, extricated my hand. But it was like it didn't want to be far from him, so instead of in my lap or somewhere out of reaching distance, it came to rest on the table between us.

He sipped his soda, considering. "What's the baddest thing you've done?"

I laughed. "'Baddest?'"

"As opposed to worst." And I understood. I'd been thinking about 'bad' things all night. I wondered if he knew that. Or maybe he had too. The fluttering feeling in my stomach came back.

"Ever?"

"Recently. Say, since the semester started." He looked down at the table, where my hand rested, and traced the outline of it with his finger. Not touching, but nearly. I wanted to reach my pinky over and let it catch his on the way by.

What *was* the baddest thing I'd done? Put on this costume? Had impure thoughts about my TA? I didn't *do* many bad things. That was when a whisper in my head said to *kiss him*. Really kiss him, right there, in the restaurant crowded with people pretending to be something other than what they were. That would be deliciously bad, forbidden. He was still my teacher. The voice was strong, and I leaned forward. He did too, almost as if he was waiting for it. My pulse quickened and we hung there, a breath apart.

But no. I didn't want to, not like this. If I was going to kiss him, I didn't want it to be a stolen moment or broken rule. I wanted to be able to do it again. At the last second, I covered his hand with mine. My lips just grazed the edge of his as they brushed over the stubble on his cheek and stopped at his ear.

"This," I whispered, and then I Thought, making him forget it happened at all.

If I was going to do bad, I was doing it all the way.

Chapter Sixteen

Carter

Without Grandma Evelyn, Thanksgiving was strange and quiet. I couldn't remember a holiday that didn't include Uncle Jeff's mother. She was dining this year with her first born—Uncle Dan—along with her real grandchildren, both born and unborn. I'd been invited to join them, but declined. I was a lot of things now: senator's analyst, college student, Washington DC resident, but I'd forever be a bookseller. There were two weekends a year I'd never miss at the store, and this was one of them. Black Friday was still black, even at Penrose Books.

Also, I assumed Lainey would be there, and therefore, I would not.

"Do you want more pie?" Aunt Mel asked hopefully. "I have apple-cranberry and pecan."

I shook my head. "No thanks," I said while Uncle Jeff said, "Cranberry, please." Aunt Mel patted his hand and jumped up to get it with a fond smile. It wasn't that her pies weren't good—they were—but they weren't Grandma's. Aunt Mel knew that as much as anyone and she was trying extra hard.

When pie had been meted out, I poured each of them more wine. The dining room table felt too-large and lonely for just the three of us. After I set down the bottle, I finally said, "Can I ask you both something?"

Aunt Mel looked up, ready to make a joke, but something on my face must have stopped her. "What is it?"

"Harlan Waites said something to me."

"You met him?" Aunt Mel looked intrigued. Uncle Jeff paused with his fork halfway from his plate to his mouth.

"A few weeks ago." Though it felt like half of forever. "He asked me to give him a tour, but he really wanted to see if I knew something."

"And did you?" Uncle Jeff's quiet, deep voice rumbled in the too-empty room.

"No, but it makes sense. Theoretically." I told them Harlan's "guess" and Aunt Mel gripped her wine glass hard enough for me to worry for it. They looked at each other then back at me. Their silence hung heavy for a long moment.

Finally, Aunt Mel admitted, "It does make sense. I don't know if it's true, but…it sounds like it could be. Jeff?"

He shook his head. He didn't know, but he didn't deny the plausibility. "How far have you looked into it?" he asked.

"As far as I can discreetly." As far as I knew how, in fact, which was pretty far. I'd been researching Allen Young since the day Lainey showed up at Northbrook. He was truly a mystery, an intentional one. I folded my napkin into a perfect triangle.

Aunt Mel said, "So what do you think?"

"Allen Young was intensely private," I told them. "No public pictures; no articles, despite his success; courthouse wedding with two witnesses, Tessa and Martin. He established an elaborate trust for Lainey before she was even born, ensuring his fortune would go to her and her guardianship to Tessa if anything were to happen. Aside from Lainey, Tessa, and charities for foster children and victims of domestic violence, Chastine Young was the only other person mentioned in his will. I don't think she was lying when she said she didn't know who his father was. But *Allen* did. He knew and he wanted nothing to do with him."

"Say it was Jacob," Uncle Jeff pronounced. "He didn't give a damn what anyone else wanted. He'd have wanted his son. Why would he stay away?"

I thought about this. I'd *been* thinking about it, but mentioning her name made her words drift back into my consciousness. *That was all it took*, Allen's adoptive mother, Chastine Young, had said the day Lainey and I visited her. The day Allen left her for good, he'd shoved her abusive husband away from her. *Willie stumbled, fell, and never got back up.* One touch—one *Thought*—was all it took. I looked at my uncle. "Because Allen knew how to use his Hangman gift."

The soft music Aunt Mel had put on to make the apartment feel less empty drifted around us, incongruous to our topic. Softly, she said, "Knowing how doesn't mean he would have," because she liked to believe that everyone was good despite knowing that they weren't.

"He would have." I knew that as well as I knew anything. He'd have protected his family without hesitation. He'd done it once. The first time, I didn't think he'd meant to *kill* Willie Young. But he'd known about his gift. Maybe Allen hadn't believed it, or maybe desperation turned a thought into a Thought. But once he'd used it, he knew how to do it again.

Assuming Jacob Astor was Allen's biological father, I was willing to bet Allen had seen him again. Jacob couldn't have done much while Allen was still a minor, without risking a kind of exposure he wouldn't have wanted. But when Allen turned eighteen and left home? He set-tled in Baltimore. He was in Jacob Astor's back yard. They had to have met. And Allen had to have said something to scare even Jacob Astor away.

"Did you ever see a picture of him?" I asked Aunt Mel and she shook her head.

"No. And you didn't either? Not even, um—" She glanced in the general direction of campus, and the dorm I used to sneak into. "Not even in Lainey's room?"

"No." I'd never thought to wonder about it until it was too late. I didn't walk around showing everyone pictures of my dead parents ei-ther. Lainey was more likely to hang art or travel posters on her walls. "Not one when he was older than about eight, anyway."

"Can you call her?"

"No."

"Not even for this?"

"*No.*"

Aunt Mel looked like she wanted to say something else, but Uncle Jeff interjected. "So, what's next?"

"Grandma?"

He shook his head. "If she knew, we would too." It was true. Grandma Evelyn knew her ex-husband's infidelities were extensive, but she didn't have a roster. The only one who might know the names was my uncle, but there was no way he knew this one. Was there? If this were true, it would make Lainey... I couldn't even think about that.

"Dan—" Aunt Mel said and stopped.

"There's no way," I said. He'd have told *me.*

"Honey, I know you think...Listen, Dan isn't always honest."

"He is with me."

"Not with anyone." She spun her glass between her fingers, not looking at me. The movement caught the candlelight, throwing a warm red kaleidescope across the table cloth, not unlike the color of blood. I watched it until the patterns came to a halt and she met my eyes.

"He's not like that anymore."

"No. He's *less* like that than he was. He's not perfect. He never was. He—he'd *not* tell you a lot of things if he thought it was better."

"Not *this*."

Aunt Mel shrugged, conceding the point or giving up. Uncle Jeff cleared his throat. "I don't think he knows," he said, though he didn't contradict anything else Aunt Mel had just said.

"Are you certain?" Aunt Mel asked. "You realize what it would mean if it were true?"

"Of course," he said. In his deep, quiet voice, it sounded so final and true. "You've been looking for signs of a Hangman your whole life. If my brother had any knowledge there was one out there, and she was *related* to him, he'd have had me *find her*, no matter what it took. He doesn't know. That doesn't mean it's not true though."

Uncle Jeff glanced at me and I looked away. When we were together, Uncle Dan had treated Lainey like one of the family. But what if she already was? And now with Tessa…Lainey could be more my uncle's family than *I* was. My stomach rolled, full of snakes fighting their way out, and needles pricked behind my eyes.

Elaine Young had already stolen my heart; would she steal my uncle too?

Under the table, I gripped my napkin in a tight fist to keep from running my fingers through my hair. More specifically, to keep Aunt Mel from seeing me do it. She was at least as shrewd as she was sweet, possibly more.

Proving that point, she said, "Assuming it's true, and accepting Jacob was frightened enough not to approach his son, why wouldn't he *tell* his other one?"

"He didn't have the chance," I suggested. "The secret died with him. Or Allen's threat was great enough for him to want to take it to the grave."

"Or," Uncle Jeff said, "Jacob divined the outcome of telling Dan— or anyone—and it wasn't favorable at the time."

"Should *we* tell him?" I asked, because even though I hadn't yet and didn't want to, it was the next logical thing to say.

Uncle Jeff shook his head at the same time Aunt Mel said "No!"

"You made the right choice, keeping it to yourself," Uncle Jeff finished. "Considering the source. Harlan Waites wants something too. It might be a good guess, but it's still a guess. No need to raise an alarm. Dan has plenty on his plate right now."

I nodded, feeling immeasurably relieved but trying not to show it. "That was my read. So, what *is* next?"

"I'll see what I can find."

"Me too," Aunt Mel said as she moved from her chair to stand behind me, hugging me tighter than necessary. I didn't mind, even when her elbows poked into me. Somehow her arms stayed chicken-thin despite all the books she'd hoisted in her lifetime. "So *now* do you want some pie?"

How could I refuse? "Some of both," I said. It felt good to see her real smile.

Chapter Seventeen

Lainey

How did one give thanks when forced to break bread with her mortal enemy? I was about to find out. Thanksgiving at my aunt's apartment was shaping up to be lavish, possibly our most extravagant ever. No, *definitely*. Three caterers rushed around mincing and stuffing and plating, since Aunt Tessa's greatest skills in the kitchen were ordering take out and making coffee, while she and I put the finishing touches on the decor. It looked like an expensive holiday catalog had exploded, showering all the flat surfaces in artfully arranged gourds, candles, and shiny fine silver.

But it did look beautiful, and smelled *heavenly*, the combined scents of savory roasting turkey, tart cranberry, exotic nutmeg and cardamom floated through the air, cutting a relaxing path through Aunt Tessa's manic energy and my unease. We had a table set for ten squeezed into the dining room, and enough hors d'oeuvres for approximately the entire Senate in the living room, though I could count only seven coming for dinner. In the center gleamed a metal cornucopia sculpture Aunt Tessa had created just for today.

"I think we're ready," Aunt Tessa said, rushing past me to deposit a variety of breads—muffins, rolls, sticks—in the belly of her horn-o-plenty. Sometimes it was strange to picture my aunt, decadent as she was today in a burnt-orange velvet dress and magenta heels, with her long waves tumbling and her burgeoning belly on full display, in a welding helmet, holding a blow torch and swinging a hammer while she worked.

I grabbed her in a hug as she tried to flit past again. "We're ready," I assured her, squeezing her tiny shoulders. Her little baby bump pressed into my hip and I shifted, half horrified and half guilty for feeling that way. Plus, I didn't want to dent the baby's head or something. "Relax. Sit down, take some yoga breaths. I feel like I'm talking to myself." I laughed, and she did too.

"You're right." Though she did settle onto one of the too many chairs, her back was still straight like she might jump up and adjust something at any moment. "It's all going to be fine. Why am I so nervous? God, I wish I had a glass of wine right now."

"I'll get you one—Oh." I blushed. "I guess you can't have that."

She sighed, absently petting her belly. "I'd probably just throw it up anyway."

Ew. But I nodded like I understood. "Maybe the turkey will make you feel better. That's supposed to be calming, right?"

"Let's hope so." She eyed me then with a familiar look, the one that meant whatever she was going to say was certain to embarrass me. "You're still using birth control, right?"

"Auntie!" I hissed, ducking my eyes as one of the eager-to-please caterers deposited a glass of club soda and lime at my aunt's elbow.

"What? You are, aren't you?! Thank you," she added, taking a tiny sip and setting the glass back down.

I stood, knocking the chair back a little further than I meant to, and went to the bar set up on the side of the room. I poured *myself* a glass of wine because I could. "There's *nothing* to worry about," I muttered. "Trust me." Before she could embarrass me anymore, I said, "There are too many chairs, you realize, right? Shouldn't we put some away?"

"What?!" She appraised the table, lips moving as she counted. "No, that's right."

"Then who are the extra for? Did you invite friends?"

"No, it's not that. Actually, it's a surprise for you."

"Oh," I said, dubious. I hadn't done a very good job with the *last* surprise she'd sprung on me. I took a big gulp of the wine, something white the caterers had opened that was fruity and sweet. I liked it. "Wait!" An idea came to me. "Is Uncle Tommy bringing a *date*?"

She shook her head. "Though don't you and I and my mother wish it. But I think you'll love it. I—" Right on cue, the doorbell rang, and she smiled. "And maybe they're here."

They were not. My grandparents and dateless Uncle Tommy spilled in, Abuela ready to fuss and still a little peeved Aunt Tessa hadn't let her cook. Uncle Tommy immediately started teasing his sister, and Abuelo put his arm around me and kissed my head. They filled all the lonely spaces in the house with love and an occasional smattering of Spanish, and everything seemed warmer and brighter just by their being there. For a few minutes anyway, Thanksgiving was perfect.

When the doorbell rang again, Aunt Tessa's already glowing face brightened more. She didn't even notice how the conversation fell to a hush. "Why don't you get it, Lainey?" she said, excitement wrapped around every word.

Behind the door, once again, was a set of shoulders barely contained by a dark suit. Manny was holding three white boxes tied with string in one hand and when he saw me, he smiled. He still was not wearing sunglasses.

"Miss Young, Happy Thanksgiving. These are for you." He handed me the boxes and I took them automatically. They were heavier than they looked when he'd been holding them.

"Thank you. Happy Thanksgiving to you, too, Manuel." Strangely, I wanted to hug him, but I didn't think that was appropriate. He flowed into the apartment not like the bull you'd expect, but with grace counterintuitive to his size. Also, like someone who'd been here before, and with a start I realized of course he had.

Behind him towered Daniel Astor, looking casual and relaxed and just like my father, as always. "Lainey," he said, nodding. He, too, carried tied up boxes in both hands, and when he bent to kiss my cheek, I was too stunned to stop him. Also I had eyes only for the woman behind him, still tall and elegant despite her age, and also, undoubtedly the source of the boxes.

"Evelyn!" I rushed forward to hug her. Now I understood why the caterers had brought no dessert. Evelyn Revell was the kind of woman one was lucky to know, even luckier to call family, and not just because she made the best pies in the entire world. I'd been sure I'd never get to see her again. "I didn't know you were coming!"

"Surprise," she said in her Long Island lilt, and it was a great surprise, my aunt had actually been right. "It's so good to see you, dear. And I brought a pecan just for you," she added in a hushed tone, like it was a secret. I laughed and hugged her fiercely, before leading her toward the crowd.

My aunt said, "Lainey," at the same time an unfamiliar voice delicately cleared her throat. I turned back to the door, confused. I hadn't even realized there were more people here, and I definitely didn't recognize the woman.

"Hello, I'm Angela," she said, and held out her hand. I took it automatically, trying to figure out if she was the senator's secretary or something, and trying to remember where I'd heard that name before.

She was pretty and petite like my aunt, but with fair skin that made me think of peaches and strawberry blond hair. She had a smile like a beauty queen, or, possibly, a Southern Belle, but with enough character lines around her wide, blue eyes that—

I dropped Angela's hand and mine involuntarily flew to my throat.

There was a tiny blond girl with matching blue eyes standing solemnly behind her.

It was *Jill*.

"Oh my God," I said, the words choked and barely audible. I couldn't breathe.

I stumbled backwards and caught my hip on a table, hard enough to leave a bruise. My knees were wobbly beneath me and if not for one hand desperately gripping the table, I would have slid to the ground right then. The other hand still scraped at my throat while black and white spots floated in front of my eyes. I. Could not. Breathe.

"Hello, Lainey," Jillian Christensen said, stepping through the door into the full light of the apartment. "It's good to see you." She smiled then, the one so like her father's, like the unsheathing of a knife. And that was it for me. The blackness filled my vision and I fell.

I AWOKE IN my room, my head throbbing in a way it hadn't almost since the day Jill had tried to kill me. My hand went to my throat again, but though it felt raw inside, it wasn't bruised. I could breathe. I closed my eyes and repeated that to myself like a mantra, taking Auntie's yoga breaths while I did it. I. Could. Breathe. I could breatheIcould-*breatheIcouldbreatheIcouldbreathe.*

My aunt's voice snapped me out of nearly hyperventilating. Outside the slightly opened door, I could hear her babbling softly about shock and migraines and saying things like *overcome* and *saved her life*, and oh, *God*, I didn't want to open my eyes. It dawned on me that I'd had a panic attack. I'd never done *that* before. Amy would be proud of me for trying something new.

If I never thought I'd see Evelyn again, I *really* never thought I'd see Jill. She haunted my nightmares, but I never believed I'd have to confront them in real life. A delicate cough, one I recognized, came from the corner of my room and my eyes flew open. There was Jill, watching me. My hands flew up again, one to my mouth, one to my throat, and I barely stifled a scream.

"I'm sorry," she said softly. "I didn't mean to frighten you." I wanted to scramble farther away, to fly from not just the room but the whole apartment, but how in the world would I explain that? Instead I stayed frozen, observing her.

It had been nearly two years since I'd seen Jill. She still looked like the girl I knew, if a few years older and maybe prettier, but she was different. Not just older, but more sophisticated. I didn't think she was any taller, but she seemed to sit up straighter now. Maybe she was more herself than ever. Was she more sane? I couldn't tell.

When I didn't say anything, she continued talking as if we were the friends I once thought she wanted to be. "Manny carried you in here. It was really heroic. That's always your luck, isn't it? Handsome guys sweeping in to save you. Your aunt asked me to stay with you. Just so you know, it wasn't my idea. None of this was. Not Father's either. He *told* her it wasn't a good idea." When I still said nothing, Jill glanced toward the door and then back at me. "You *don't* have to be afraid. I'm just here to talk."

I snorted. Jill might have wanted to talk to me, and but I didn't have to endure it. She didn't hold all the power in this situation. Yet even as I tried, my legs and voice refused to march me out of the room and tell her to buzz off. Maybe a small, strange part of me want-ed to talk to her too. After a long few seconds, I told her honestly, "I don't know what to say."

"*I* do," she said. "'How have you been, Jillian?' is a start."

"How have you been?" I repeated automatically.

"*Better*," she spat, and I flinched. Stupid. Stupid stupid to play along. "I'm sorry," she said immediately. "I didn't mean it to come out that way. I didn't." She closed her eyes and took a breath, opening them again slowly. "It's harder to pretend when, for a few minutes, you don't have to." She took a breath again. "I *have* been better. But I've also been worse. So. I am okay." She didn't ask how I'd been, and I suspected she knew quite a bit more about me than I did about her. She always had.

"I thought you were in Europe," I said, finding my voice again. It occurred to me she might be on drugs—the psychiatric kind. I hoped so.

"I was." She shrugged, her stiff shoulders relaxing a fraction when they came back down. "Father needed me to come home. I live in Alexandria, with Mother, for now. She hates it and just wants to go back to Wyoming."

"But you don't," I said slowly, remembering there was always more in what Jill *didn't* say than what she did.

"No. I like it here. I liked France, but I'm *someone* here. I'm going to live in the White House." After a pause she said, "You could, too, you know. We could be sisters. Isn't that funny?"

"Funny?" I coughed out. Ironic, maybe, but I saw no humor in the prospect of living with Daniel Astor, or any of the rest of it. "Why is it *funny*?" Jill's smile slashed again.

"Because we're already related. Aren't we, cousin?"

I sucked in a breath hard enough to make myself cough. "*What* did you say?"

She smiled, blindingly, achingly pretty, almost like the way she'd smiled when she was choking the life out of me. "You know," she breathed. "*You* figured it out first, didn't you?"

She was right. I didn't even know why I was surprised, but I was. I thought the secret of me, of our connection, was the *one thing* Dan would honor. But that was stupid—he had no honor at all.

"I can't believe—" *he told you*, I started to say, but I heard light steps and whispers on the other side of the door. My aunt appeared with a glass of water and a prescription bottle, as if summoned by my coughing. Daniel Astor hovered behind her.

"Oh, honey. I'm so sorry. How's your head?" She sat on the bed, handing me the water and shaking out one of the migraine pills I rarely took anymore. "I'm *terrible* at surprises. It must have been so emotional to see Jillian again. Are you catching up?"

I opened my mouth to say something, but couldn't before Jill piped up, "We are, Ms. Espinosa. It's nice to be able to talk about things with someone who knows me. Feels like we're sisters already." Jill beamed and I sipped the water to keep from grimacing.

My aunt beamed right back. "I'm so glad. And Jillian, please, you know it's just Tessa."

"Why don't we give them a little longer together, Tess?" Dan suggested. "Lainey could probably use a few more minutes of rest." Over my aunt's shoulder he smiled at me, falsely benevolent. I didn't know if Jill was playing his game or her own. Maybe they were one in the same.

I opened my mouth then, finally ready to scream in frustration that they were all liars, that this whole *thing* was a lie. Not for the first time I wondered *why* I was still keeping the secrets. But the simple answer came to me immediately: Carter. Always Carter. My fingers ached from how hard I was clutching his necklace. I hadn't been brave enough to fight for him, but I loved him too much to hurt him further. Hadn't I sacrificed him to the wolves, to ignorant bliss, to save my own skin? And would I do it again?

I slapped on a smile, or the approximation of one. "I'd like that," I said and my aunt nodded.

"Of course, girls. Join us whenever you're ready." Aunt Tessa patted my hair and backed out of the room, shutting the door behind her.

Ever-shrewd Jill locked eyes with me. If one's expression could be smug sadness, that was hers. "It's pretty," she said, tilting her head at my chest, where Carter's necklace rested. "Looks expensive. Did he give it to you?"

I nodded, fingering the diamond again. After a second, I said, "Does he know?" For some foolish reason, I couldn't say his name.

She shrugged. "I doubt it. Father didn't tell me, you know. I guessed. If your aunt keeps blabbing about how much Father looks like *your* father, everyone else will too. You should tell her to quit it. But I don't think he wants Carter to know. He doesn't want him to think about *you* at all."

Ouch. I closed my eyes for a long blink. "If that's true," I said, opening them again, "then why start an affair with my aunt?"

Jill shrugged again, a delicate lift of her tiny shoulders. "I think he might kind of love her? It's hard to say. Or *maybe*"—she leaned forward—"he just wanted to give *you* one more reason to join us."

"You mean the Perceptum?"

"Obviously."

"I'll never do it," I told her. "He knows that. It was our deal."

Jill laughed. "Well then maybe *I'm* not the crazy one."

Automatically, I wanted to say *you're not crazy*, but she *was*. At least she recognized that now. "That's not funny," I said.

She watched me for a few seconds. "You know, I don't hate you anymore." I must have looked skeptical because she repeated, "I don't. And I'm sorry. I need to say that. I am sorry for what I did. It was wrong and I am sorry." She said the words like a recitation she'd been forced to memorize. I had a feeling she *wasn't* entirely sorry, but she did know it was wrong.

"Okay," I told her, because there didn't seem to be any other answer.

Jill nodded, as if she'd checked an assignment off her list. "I'm almost glad we're going to be sisters," she went on. "I meant what I said earlier, about it being nice not having to pretend. I'm *good* at pretending, but it's nice to have a break, you know?" She looked at me with these big, open eyes, like she was really asking that question and hoping I'd say yes.

Because she was right, I realized. I *did* know. And this was why I couldn't make myself leave the room.

"I do," I murmured. I really, really did.

"Isn't that funny too?" She stood, pacing the small end of the room. It reminded me of Carter, and I wanted to look away. "You took *everything* from me," she said, stopping for a brief second to fix her gaze on me. "But I don't hate you anymore, because you *understand*. You've lost everything now too, haven't you? You *gave it up*."

I closed my eyes, Jill's words piercing me again. If we'd been in a fight, I'd have said she was winning, but we'd both already *lost*. So much. This wasn't something either of us could win. And as weird as it was, it felt *good* to hear her say painful things and *acknowledge* them. How could you move on if you kept everything locked inside?

Finally, I said, "I had no choice."

"Ha!" she laughed, once, hard, and it made me jump. I met her eyes again. "You had a choice. You made one. If there's one thing crazy class has taught me, it's that."

"Do you *really* know what my options were?" I couldn't tell if she was guessing again. Or maybe Dan liked having someone he didn't have to pretend with either.

Jill sat again, hesitating. "I know enough," she said, "and I know my father. And I also know, for you, it would be *so easy* to get it all back." Then she added, "So maybe I do still hate you a little."

"How would I get *anything* back?"

"Duh! What have we been talking about this whole time? All you have to do is what you were *born for.*"

"You mean killing people."

"*Bad* people." She leered at me. "First time's the hardest, and you've already gotten it out of the way."

I cringed. "That was different! You tried to *kill* me. It was self-defense!"

Jill came to sit on the end of the bed, leaning toward me. "Self-defense? What about all the poor, *defenseless* people being hurt by malicious Thought users? *You're* their defense."

I pulled my knees up in front of me and shook my head. "But I'd still have to kill them, and I—I can't do that. It's not right."

"But they all know what they're doing is *wrong.* They *all* get warned; they all get a *choice.* Besides, do you really think most of them would fear death if they saw it was *you?*" She shook her head. "Yeah, I do still kind of hate you. I'm sorry, cousin. I'll work on that."

"It doesn't matter what I *look* like," I told her. "I'd still be a monster."

"No," she said. "You'd be an avenging angel. It's quick, and it doesn't hurt." She wiggled her fingers in my direction. "*I* know. Life in prison has to be worse. I kind of know that, too."

"Then maybe," I added carefully, "*that's* what they deserve."

Jill smiled. "So. What's more monstrous then?" I opened my mouth and closed it while I could feel whatever color was there drain from my face. Was she right, or more right than I was? Why was this so *complex?* Shouldn't murder automatically equal the wrong choice?

"And anyway," she went on, "these people don't *go* to prison, or don't *stay* there. Don't you listen to *anything*?"

"I—I just can't." Jill started to say something and I amended, "I *won't*. Your father knows this. And I'm keeping my end of our bargain."

Jill sighed. "This is what you were *born* for," she repeated. "You're the *last* one. Did you *really* think Father was just going to let you *walk away*? For *good*?"

A puff of air escaped me. I had thought that. That had been our bargain, hadn't it? That I'd give him Carter and keep his secrets and he'd let me go. But no, I realized now, too late. He'd let me *live*, not let me *go*. That wasn't the same thing at all. Brain seething, I slid off the bed and moved to the door. "It's time for dinner," I said. "Let's go."

"You know, Lainey," Jill said softly before I stepped into the hall. I paused with my hand on the doorknob. "Killing isn't the *only* way. If you really wanted to torture someone, you could just do to them what you did to me."

BY THE TIME I returned to my dorm on the Monday after Thanksgiving, the news had broken.

"Lainey!" all of my roommates practically screamed before I'd even closed the door. The strangest part was they were all home. Nat ran over and dragged me toward the futon where they were huddled around Ginny's laptop, because hers was the biggest. Three sets of wide eyes alternately stared at me or the screen.

"Your mom was on TV," Kendra said. There was awe in her voice, more than usual. She'd had a little crush on my aunt since the beginning because she was a successful artist. It's amazing, and sad, how many kids who want to *be* artists have never met one who makes a living at it.

"Your mom is having the future president's *baby*," Ginny clarified.

"Why didn't you *tell* us?!" Kendra added. "Actually, why weren't you, like, *there?*"

"I was already on my way back here when they planned the press conference." It wasn't exactly the truth, but close enough for them. Speculation had broken over the weekend, when pictures of Dan leaving dinner, hastily snapped by one of Auntie's curious neighbors, had surfaced and spread. The only control *I* had was asking to be left *out* of the media circus. But I couldn't avoid the people I lived with, or the news, forever. It was finally time to watch.

Auntie looked good, of course. Happy and beautiful and not nervous at all, even while the cameras in the room flashed every few seconds. She wore a flowing kind of top that might have been labeled *"For telling the world you're pregnant!"* at the store. She was talking about me, saying, "Yes, my daughter's excited too. She had classes today; her education comes first, as well as her privacy."

"She's a remarkable young woman," Dan added. "I'd be lucky to call her family," he said, and I wanted to be sick. He was a natural at speaking to the camera, and it felt like he was looking right at me. Mocking me. I half expected him to wink.

A reporter asked a question the microphones didn't pick up, and Kendra giggled. "Here comes my favorite part."

"I'm sorry, what was that?" I heard him first, before the camera had zoomed all the way out to show the rest of the 'family' at the press conference, standing behind my aunt and Senator Astor. My heart flew into my throat, and I had to swallow to keep it from escaping.

There he was. Carter. Standing next to Jill, wearing a neat blue button down—God he looked good in blue—and a smile. My neck burned as my fingers pulled on my necklace, too hard.

"Do you know if it's a boy or girl? Have they told you?"

Kendra giggled again. "The senator's son is super hot."

"Nephew," I whispered, but my eyes were glued to the TV.

"*No*," he said, shaking his head, the smile never wavering. "*I don't know. Not yet.*"

"*Do you have a preference?*"

Carter laughed. "*I hope it's a boy, just because I know* nothing *about girls.*"

Everyone laughed, my aunt, the reporters, my roommates, even though they'd already seen this who knew how many times. Dan looked over a shoulder with a fond and charming smile that made me want to throw up all over again. I'd seen that smile so many times on the boy he was looking at. Carter had learned it from him.

"I bet that is *not* true," Kendra pronounced and Ginny laughed.

Nat was still glancing between me and the TV, suspecting. "Do you know him, too?"

The reporters had moved on to Jill, asking her how she was feeling, if she was excited, and I couldn't watch anymore. "Excuse me."

I picked up my bag and walked away, shutting the door to our room behind me. I could hear them whispering outside but Nat didn't follow. I flopped on my bed and put my arm over my eyes.

Carter hated it, being on TV. Despite his winning smile, I could tell in the stiffness of his shoulders and the way he kept lifting his hand like he was ready to run it through his hair. Probably Dan even knew he hated it, but he wanted him to be there. Of course he did. Carter was brilliant and beautiful. The camera loved his face. So did I.

And Jill. Jill Jill Jill. I hadn't been able to stop thinking about her since I left Baltimore. Worse somehow was seeing her there on TV, standing next to Carter, looking healthy and normal and *happy*. How was it fair that *she* got to be happy, got to stand next to Carter, and I didn't?

Frustration brimming, I got up and rooted around the perpetual mess of my desk until I found the card I'd bought with the smiling snowman in his ridiculous beach-wear. Before I knew it, I had a pen in my hand and was filling it out, sealing the envelope, and carefully writing out the address Carter had given me before he gave up contacting me at all.

Dan didn't want him to even *think* of me? Well, he couldn't be with him twenty-four hours a day, controlling his thoughts. He couldn't stop me from sending this card.

I'd spent almost an entire year contemplating my mortality. Not just contemplating it, but *facing* it. I'd almost been *murdered. Twice.* Both times, I'd averted it by doing something horrible. And I knew I'd do it all again, because what would be stupider than dying just for defiance? I might not have exactly the life I wanted, but I had most of it. At least I had it at all. I had my thoughts, and they were the one thing Daniel Astor couldn't take from me.

Chapter Eighteen

Carter

What are you working on, son?"

Startled, I looked up to see my uncle's tall frame leaning in the doorway to my cube. He'd snuck up on me. That was rare. I put on a smile. "I didn't hear you coming."

He smiled back. "I know. Come work with me in my office. I don't get to spend enough of that kind of time with you lately."

True. He didn't. In some ways, I felt like I talked to him less now, when I worked for him, than before I'd moved here. He hadn't been running for president then. Or in love.

Everything had been nuts since the news broke. The headlines were ridiculous, like romance novels. THE SENATOR IN LOVE. THE SENATOR'S BABY. Some of the less friendly publications added SECRET to that one. In the worst, it was THE SENATOR'S MISTRESS.

Tessa was handling it remarkably well, a true media darling. Her face was everywhere within seeming hours. Magazines, tabloids, TV. Despite some analysts calling it a stunt to attract women and minority voters, and some religious groups painting her as little more than a whore, the response was positive. I imagined the value of Tessa's work was climbing along with Uncle Dan's numbers in the polls. He'd moved solidly into second place, just out of first.

Williams had orchestrated us all at the emergency press conference, down to our outfits, an unconventional but delighted "family." He'd practically begged for Lainey to be there but she'd refused, for which I was glad. I'd never smiled so much, and I wasn't sure I could have kept it up if she'd been standing next to me. It was exhausting. I'd hated it, but most of all I'd hated myself for hating it. For not being good at it.

In Uncle Dan's office, I dropped my spreadsheets at the small table by the window, the one with the best view in the entire building. He didn't settle behind his desk right away but instead stood beside me. We stayed quiet for a second, looking out at a dreary city day. The biggest spot of color was a tour bus—belonging to Uncle Dan's leading competitor—resting at the curb.

Uncle Dan nodded at it. "Ostentatious, no?"

"I wouldn't think they're allowed to park there."

Uncle chuckled. "Allegedly, he's treating the touring staff to their own tour of the Capitol and lunch in the cafeteria. The guards are 'keeping an eye on it.'"

"He just wants us all to see it," I said, and Uncle full-on laughed.

After another few beats of silence, he said, "How are you doing?"

I glanced at him. The fact that he was asking told me he knew the answer. "I'm looking forward to going back home for a while, sir."

"Son, it's just us. You don't need the 'sir.' And you can just go ahead and tell me you hate the attention."

"I hate the attention," I admitted, and felt some tension leave my shoulders. It felt good to say it out loud after so much forced smiling. "Harlan told me that I wasn't cut out for this. He's probably right."

"You're doing beautifully," Uncle Dan said. "And I appreciate that you're doing it for me. You and Jill. I couldn't be doing this *without* you."

"Sir—" He made a light *tsk*-ing sound. "Sorry. I—About Jill. I wish you'd told me she was coming home."

He touched my shoulder. "I know. I'm sorry. I should have told you right away. I didn't expect you'd see each other before I could speak to you or that Angela would allow her to go to that blasted party. She shouldn't have."

"It was a surprise, is all. It's hard for me. Being around her." It felt good to say that out loud too.

Jillian handled the media with surprising ease, which made me feel even more a failure. She was Uncle's first heartwarming story, with her near-death and their subsequent reconciliation. If only they knew. No one suspected her of anything, with her big blue eyes, tiny little self, and new French-influenced sense of style. Finally, she had what she'd wanted all along: her father *needed* her.

"I know, son. And I thank you for understanding about why we've handled her…situation the way we have. There was no other way to be discreet, and I promise you, she's getting help and being monitored. The party was a lapse. It won't happen again."

I nodded, not knowing what else to say. *Thank you* wasn't the right sentiment. I couldn't remember having felt more awkward in my uncle's company. I wasn't used to being a disappointment, and that's what I felt like. I thought more than I should have about what Jill had said to me on Halloween. I couldn't trust anything from her, I knew that much, but I still wondered who she'd been talking about. Who didn't I know? Who did I need protection from? Lainey? I thought I'd known her, but she'd left me anyway.

"You still think about her, don't you?" Uncle Dan's voice interrupted my internal confusion.

"Yes." There was no question whom he meant, and it wasn't Jill. I touched the pocket with her note in it.

Uncle Dan sighed. I was surprised when his hand fell again on my shoulder and stayed there. "I'm sorry. For bringing her up and for not thinking more about how Jillian's presence would affect you. I don't want to be as careless with your trust as Elaine was." I let out an involuntary puff of air when he said their names and he squeezed my shoulder. "Is she why you wouldn't join us for Thanksgiving? Or Jillian?"

I shook my head. "No. I needed to be home." I said it so convincingly, I almost believed it was the whole truth.

"Your sense of duty is admirable. One of your best qualities. I'm proud of you, son." He paused. As if it hadn't occurred to him before, he added, "Miss Morrow really does suit you better. I'm proud you've realized that, too."

Had I realized that? I wasn't sure. But I was trying. Not wanting to disappoint him, I sat down and arranged the spreadsheets on the table. "Sorry—I want to finish this before we leave."

He hesitated as if he might say something else, but finally said, "You're right—let's get to work." With one last glance out the window, he added, "It really is ostentatious, isn't it?"

Nodding, I put my head down and got to work. I barely remembered the rest of the afternoon passing until we said goodbye.

The next day, a wheel fell off the tour bus. Improperly tightened lug nuts, according to reports. There were no serious injuries except to Uncle's competitor's schedule and pride. He was late to a charity appearance and Uncle Dan got all the good coverage on the news that day. He was really on a roll.

Chapter Nineteen

Lainey

A ny more questions?" Jack asked, looking at each one of us in turn. The last day of classes had finally arrived, cold and bitter and gray, much like how I'd been feeling. We huddled in our basement classroom, cramming in our last review before the exam.

It was a big one. This class would be a heavy part of my first semester GPA and that mattered to me. I wanted to do well. I *always* wanted to do well, but especially now that I was in college, studying the things *I* wanted for the future I'd chosen for myself. Maybe it was silly, but I wanted to do well for Jack, too, to impress him or reflect on him as one of his students, or probably both.

When none of us said anything, he smiled. "Good. You're ready. And in case you're *not*, here's a neat study sheet along with your last assignments. Good luck everyone—it's been a pleasure." His eyes stopped on me when he said that, and I smiled down at the table as I passed the stack of papers over to Serena.

The yellow sticky note over my grade bore a smiley face, so I knew it was good. Underneath was a surprise second note. I pushed it up carefully, so I could just see it.

Meet me Friday night?

Friday was the day of our exam, and the last official day of the semester. Jack stood at the front, listening to another student. I couldn't help looking up at him, and he caught my gaze from the corner of his eye. He was smiling, and I was pretty sure it was at me. In the last few weeks, I'd done *plenty* of thinking about Jack Kensington.

With no more thought at all, I nodded and his smile widened. He nodded back, just a tiny bob of his head, and I couldn't stifle my silly grin as I looked back at my paper. A third note read:

If no, please?

If still no, okay. At least I tried.

If YES, followed by a club name and time.

Underneath all that was finally my grade, an A-. I was still smiling when Serena cleared her throat. She was already standing, tying her scarf and waiting for me. My cheeks were hot before I even managed to meet her eyes, and she raised her eyebrows.

"That must be a pretty good grade…"

I laugh-coughed to hide my embarrassment. "Something like that."

Since she pretty much knew anyway, I let her peek at my stickies while I shrugged into my coat. She made that approving noise of hers, softly sucking air through her teeth, and cut a glance between me and Jack. He winked at us, and I felt a little bad for the kid who only had half his attention. Serena handed back my paper, which I folded in half twice before sliding it in my bag between my notebook and the card I'd been carrying around for more than a week.

"I never thought I'd want an exam to hurry up and get here, but maybe I do now," she said.

"Me too," I breathed. *Me. Too.* I practically vibrated with…something. Excitement? Nervousness? Possibility? We both peeked at Jack once more before we were out the door.

"Bye, ladies," he called. "Until Friday." We waved to him as we passed into the hall. "And Lainey?" I paused, wavering at the threshold.

"Yes?" I sounded breathy to myself and felt a little embarrassed by that.

He smiled, showing me the dimple and all his perfect teeth. "Don't be late."

I waved again, and I could feel my cheeks flush once more. I knew he wasn't talking about the exam. Serena slipped her arm through mine. "Well," she said. "Looks like we've got some work to do."

"Studying?"

"No!" She laughed. "*Shopping.* Studying can *so* wait. That place is as H.O.T. as your date. Let's go pick out what you're going to wear."

Out on the street, we stopped for traffic before crossing to catch the T. Next to us was a post box, navy blue and slightly dinged up from years of students mistreating it. It was nothing out of the ordinary, but the longer we waited, the more *it* seemed to be waiting for *me.* In my bag, I could practically feel the card shaking to get out, to get into the box and away from the paper with the stickies in Jack's handwriting.

Traffic broke and Serena started across. "Lainey! C'mon," she called.

"I'll be right there!" I promised. And then, before I could think about it a single second longer, I yanked the card out of my bag and slipped it into the mail box's waiting mouth. I rushed across the street, narrowly dodging a car and getting honked at, but who cared? I was doing *all* the dangerous things now.

Chapter Twenty

Carter

There was a bomb in my mailbox. I stood frozen in my vestibule, staring at the envelope. It looked like a Christmas card, but no, it was a bomb, ticking inside me. My memory easily called up the handwriting and did moronic cartwheels at the sight of it. My memory *loved* this handwriting, the awful, messy scratch of it.

I blinked. The envelope was still there. I didn't want to believe my eyes, but they were the thing that never lied to me.

Of course I knew who it was from.

What I couldn't fathom was *why?*

"You okay, man?" I turned to see another resident closing his mailbox door and watching me with an expression that fell somewhere between mild concern and wariness.

"No," I told him. "Excuse me." I stepped past him without looking back and skipped the elevator, taking the stairs two at a time to the fifth floor. I had to get to my apartment before something exploded.

Alone behind a closed door, I tore the envelope open fast enough to slice my finger on the thick card inside. I wanted to laugh as I shook my hand from the sting. Of course it cut me. It was a weapon designed for the task.

The front read FELIZ NAVIDAD below a picture of a stupid fucking snow man in surf shorts and sunglasses, just like the one stuffed in my closet back home. Inside was blank but for her scrawl of

Happy Birthday
Love,
Lainey

That was all. Four words and a thousand pounds of heartache.

The stove burner came to life with a satisfying *whoosh*. I tried to burn the card, but I couldn't do it. Which made me want to burn something all the more, so I settled for the envelope. I held the corner of the starched white paper in the flame until it caught. Watching my name in her handwriting disintegrate felt perfectly awful. I held on to it for a few seconds, until the first bit of flame licked at my fingers, then dropped it in the sink and watched it burn.

Why? Why the fuck why? Why *now*?

I did not understand. In May, she'd driven away without looking back and had refused all contact with me. Then she'd shown up at the office in August without warning and I hadn't heard from her since. Until today, the last day of finals and a few days before Christmas. I was supposed to drive eight hours home tomorrow.

I get to where I don't think of her *every* second of the day and now this.

I emptied my backpack, sorted the rest of the mail, changed into running gear, all with one hand while I carried the card around with the other. I took it all the way down to the gym. I'd already run that morning, but that was before *this*. I ran again, until sweat dripped into my eyes and my lungs hurt from the exertion, not from anything else. But funny thing about running on a treadmill—you never get anywhere, or away from anything. Especially the thing you carried with you.

Back upstairs and showered, I laid on the couch with the TV on, trying not to obsess. And failing. I turned the volume off on the TV and gave in.

I wished for a switch to turn off my brain.

I wished for some magic to erase Elaine Rachel Young from it.

I wished I could hold her again.

I wished I hadn't thought that, or that it wasn't true.

Would I feel better if I'd never met her? Where would I be if it wasn't for her?

And the big one: would I be happy?

There were signs I could be, and without her. It was a different feeling from what I'd had with her, but still a good one. Still one I wanted back. And that made me feel, what? Guilty? Maybe that was it. I had guilt for being happy without my own permission, without Lainey. Part of me—*most* of me—didn't want to move on. That was the part staring at the four scrawled words and aching.

But the other part...now it was pissed off.

I hated that I didn't know what to do or, worse, that there wasn't even anything I could do. I needed to get up, move. *Anything* was healthier than this.

Chapter Twenty-One

Lainey

I was late. Heart pounding, I stepped out of the taxi. I'd never been here before, this club on the south side of the city. I had no ID to come here. The line for the door told me it was popular, and I had to trust Jack's magic would somehow get me in. That, and my getup.

I *never* dressed like this, pants like skin, boots like stilts, and a tissue-thin shirt over a contrasting bra. It felt like a costume, like I was auditioning for a role I had *no* idea how to play. But at the same time, it felt good. Carefree and dangerous, the two things Jack seemed to inspire.

"Latecomer!" he called, pushing away from the shadow of the wall. "I was getting worried."

He looked his usual in a button down and expensive jeans under a snug wool coat, dark hair unstyled to perfection. He looked *good*. Before I could say anything at all, he walked right up and kissed me on the cheek, as if it were the most natural thing in the world. With a whistle, soft and low, he said, "Good God, you are tall, aren't you?"

I blushed. He was right. In my heels, I was taller than him and I wanted to kick myself with their pointy tips. First late, and now this. "Sor—"

"Nope. No apologizing. That's a terrible way to start a date. And besides, I *like* it." He slid his arm around my shoulder and turned me toward the front of the line. "Dante!" he called. "She's here!" To me he said, "The bouncer. Dante and I go way back."

"All the way to September?"

He laughed. "Yeah. We're kindred, though. I told him you were coming." He called again to Dante, "I'll take that twenty now! Thanks." The big bouncer, whose job was to let as little as possible amuse him and he was undoubtedly good at it, looked amused. "We made a little wager," Jack told me, smiling a politician's grin.

"On whether I'd show?"

"On the fact that you'd be the hottest girl here."

I didn't know whether to laugh or be insulted. "So no pressure or anything."

"Nope," Jack said. His lips were very close to my ear. "You win without even trying."

"I actually *did* try."

"I know." And this time those lips grazed my neck. I shivered. I couldn't stop thinking about how officially he wasn't my TA anymore.

When we reached him, Dante wordlessly removed twenty dollars from his wallet, though he handed the money not to Jack but the guy collecting the cover. "You're all set, my friend, but…"

Dante was giving me another appraisal, the one that would finish with his asking, politely, for my ID, when Jack reached out a hand. "Thanks, man." They knocked fists. "We're good, right?" As he said it, the warm brown of his eyes flashed a soft gold color. I suppressed a gasp.

And then after a tiny hesitation, barely time for a blink, Dante said, "Yeah. Of course, yeah." He inclined his head toward the door. "Have fun."

"Always," Jack said, smiling once more before following me inside.

THE KIND OF place I pictured Jack, somewhere expensive, filled with leather and wood and specializing in something like bourbon—this was not that place. This was a club, the kind of place with a one-word name that implied what you'd be feeling tomorrow. The kind of place filled with beautiful youth, exposed skin, laughter too loud so it could compete with the music, and fifteen dollar mixed drinks being tossed down as casually as water. The kind of place where sex floated on the air and filled in all the empty spaces.

I fidgeted my way through the crowd, yet Jack seemed as comfortable here as anywhere. He led me to an area of seating guarded by a relentlessly pretty girl. Probably "hostess" was her job title, but the job description was more like *hotness*.

And she was happy to see Jack.

"Oh, there you are, *Mr.* Kensington!" The wattage of her smile was blinding, as was the shimmer of the lights off her acres of smooth skin.

"Hello, Char."

With daring familiarity, she reached for his arm and purred, "I see you'd like a banquette tonight." I had no idea why that was so suggestive, but Char did. The second she noticed me behind him, that smile dimmed. "Oh. And I see you've brought a *friend.*"

"Indeed." Jack slipped his arm around my waist and pulled me next to him. "This is Lainey. You'll be seeing us often," he said and her smile dimmed even more.

"Of course. Follow me. And what would you like this evening?"

"Lainey?" he said and I nearly stumbled. Was that his answer? When I didn't respond, he said, "What's your poison tonight? Vodka maybe?"

"Vodka," I echoed, and Jack obligingly ordered a bottle.

I fell onto the soft and improbably white banquette, feeling breathless. It did not escape my attention that the first and only word I'd uttered in my entire club experience so far was vodka. Around me, music pounded and lights pulsed, briefly illuminating people writhing on a sunken dance floor. Servers expertly wove between it all, delivering drinks and wearing little. I felt over dressed, which when I left my dorm, I wouldn't have thought possible.

I slipped off my leather jacket and Jack slipped his arm around my shoulders. It was comfortable there, his arm, like it had always wanted to be there. I liked the weight of it, the potential.

"What do you think?" In the privacy of our booth, he didn't even have to shout.

"It's a lot to take in."

Jack laughed and the vibration of it flowed between us, joining the reverberations from the music. "That," he said, "is the point. Places like this specialize in excess and abandon."

"And you like that?"

"Like is a strong word." Our heads leaned toward each other while we watched the drama of the club play out. My neck rested on his arm, his fingers still light and warm on my shoulder. "Appreciate, maybe? Enjoy? Everyone can benefit from a little of both sometimes."

I nodded. Amy and Serena would both agree I needed to. I was starting to believe they might be right. "What the hell was that, by the way, earlier?"

Our eyes met for a glance and Jack dipped his chin. "Sorry. It's possible I might have flirted with Charlotte on previous visits and she—"

I rolled my eyes. "Not *that*. I mean *outside*. With Dante. I *saw* you, your eyes, I mean. And he decided not to ask for my ID or whatever. So—"

Before I could finish that question, our *entire bottle of vodka* arrived. Jesus. Our own *bottle*, guarded and delivered by a private brigade of servers, along with an assortment of things to mix with it. *This* is what clubs were like?

"Cheers," Jack said, clinking his newly minted vodka-tonic-with-a-twist with mine. I took a tiny sip and put it down.

"I'd say you were trying to impress me with all"—I looked around at the spectacle, pausing on Charlotte, who stood nearby pretending not to be disappointed—"*this*, but you've obviously been here enough times for her to hope *she'd* be joining you in this banquette."

Jack coughed, abashed and amused. "I just thought we'd have fun. Plus, I'm fairly certain *this*"—he gestured toward the club with his drink and then tilted it at me in salute—"isn't the kind of thing that impresses you. And I'm sorry, again, about Char—"

"If you feel like you have to apologize, you should probably do it to *her*."

For a moment, Jack regarded me, and I tried very hard not to get sucked into the depth of his eyes. "You," he said, "are even more amazing than I realized. And you're right. Excuse me for a second." And then he walked over to the lovelorn hostess.

I watched as he did it, apologized and sincerely. He ran his hand down his hair to the back of his neck while he spoke and she toyed with the reservations book in her hand, shifting on her high heels. But ultimately she nodded, smiled, and Jack lightly touched her elbow before returning to our table.

"*Now*, I'm impressed," I told him as he slid in next to me. "She didn't even slap you."

"It's a gift."

"About that. As I was saying before our bottle of abandon and excess arrived, I saw you in action outside. I know you're a no-good Herald, but what exactly is it you *do*?"

Jack took a deliberate pull from his drink and set it down. With a smile that brought out the dimple, he said, "People say I'm trustworthy."

"Now I don't trust you at *all*."

"Good. You shouldn't." After a second he said, "Do you want to go somewhere else?"

"What? No. Why?"

"You seem…" He looked at my fingers, which were absently sliding my necklace, and I stopped. "Nervous," he finished. "I'm not your TA anymore, remember?"

I remembered. Oh, did I remember. "I guess I'm out of practice with all this."

"I can't imagine why," he said, eyebrows raised. "I can't be the only guy who fell all over himself this semester wanting to ask you out."

I swallowed, trying to ignore how hard my heart was beating. I *should* have left it at that, but for some reason, I couldn't. Amy would kill me for talking about this on a first—whatever this was. Finally, I said, "I was…with someone. Before."

Jack sighed. "I know," he said, and before my pounding heart could go into free fall, he tickled my side. I shrieked like a stupid girl before I laughed. He leaned close, like he was going to tell me a secret. "I've been 'with' other someones too, you know."

I raised my eyebrows, unable to resist asking, "How many?"

He held his hand to his chest in mock horror. "A gentleman never kisses and tells. The past is past."

"So a lot then?"

He chuckled. "Definitely fewer than you're imagining right now. Probably by a lot."

I considered him for a moment, and the openness in his face, not his gift, made me believe him. And it made me want to be honest too. "I only brought it up because I wondered if you know him is all. Know who he is, I mean. My ex."

"I don't want to."

"He's—wait, what?" Jack's response finally registered.

He tapped my nose with a finger. "I said, 'I don't want to.' I don't want to talk about it. I'm sure he's a great guy, but he was someone else. The past. And that's over. I like *now*."

"But you might already know anyway. He's Sen—"

"Lane." Jack silenced me with a look, his eyes so deep and intense my thoughts of anything—or any*one*—else evaporated. "The past is past," he repeated. "Let's just be *now*. Let's not talk about exes. In fact, let's *not talk*. You know, people *also* say I'm a good dancer. Want to try?" He held out his hand in invitation. After a moment, I took it.

We danced.

He really was good at it, and I had rhythm. Better than that, I had an excuse to touch him, and that was the best part. At touching, we were awfully good. Naturals.

The club music was loud and insistent, each song morphing into the next, so there was no beginning or end and no reason to stop. We danced until my shirt clung to me, even more see-through than when I arrived. The pulsing lights, blue—green—blue—red, bounced around, reflecting off my skin below. I felt lit up from within, glowing, and this, I thought, was happiness.

I was having fun and I was happy. When Jack was touching me, I was even happier. He pulled me back against him with one arm, and pushed my hair to the side.

"You're pretty good at this, too," he said into my ear.

"It's mostly you."

"Ah, flattery." I could just feel his lips moving as I leaned back into him. He was solid behind me, strong. I could feel that as we moved to the music together. He was shorter than Carter, but bulkier, not in a bad way. Carter was a V, all broad shoulders down to slim hips. Jack was a pillar, a column of muscle and agility. "I know it doesn't do much for you, but it'll get you *everywhere* with me."

I peeked at him, over my shoulder. "Are you looking down my shirt as you say that?"

"Just admiring the view."

I laughed and spun away, hoping he'd chase me. And he did.

After a long time that felt not long at all, we settled back in the banquette, where we were descended upon by our servers with drinks and waters. I rolled one glass over my neck, absorbing the cold into my overheated skin.

"How did you choose this place anyway?" I yelled, half deaf from the music.

"You could say it chose me. I have the good fortune of living around the corner."

Not long after that, I trailed Jack up the stairs of his building.

Chapter Twenty-Two

Carter

The bar a few blocks from my apartment wasn't the kind of place that carded at the door. I ordered a Coke and sat waiting, watching two girls watching me. If I ever planned to frequent a bar, I thought this one would do. It was close enough to walk to, with thick wood paneling that made it comfortable and relaxed. Everyone was casual, young but not too young, alternately drowning their sorrows or finding some trouble.

When the girls called the bartender over and peeked at me while they talked to him, I knew what was coming. He nodded and crossed back to me.

"The ladies there"—he gestured unnecessarily—"would like to get you a drink. Another Coke, or…?"

I sat a moment, deciding. I *should* have declined, but I wasn't sure if that would be ruder than accepting. Finally, I said, "Scotch." I hesitated, almost adding *for my uncle*, but ultimately just said, "Please." The bartender nodded and set a heavy tumbler knuckle full of amber liquid in front of me.

I picked it up and tipped it in the girls' direction with a smile. I caught their return smiles with a feeling somewhere between pleasure and guilt. When it dawned on me that they might *recognize* me, the feeling tilted toward the latter. I'd meant to set the drink down, but my fingers didn't want to. I swallowed a gulp.

Gah. It was awful, like black coffee, and burned like fire. I liked it.

Most of the drink later, the center of my chest started to thaw. All of me started to thaw. My fingers relaxed, no longer white where they gripped the glass, shoulders loosened. Just about the time I caught myself smiling at the girls again, when I should have gone to talk to them, I saw him come in.

I thought about how this might be the only time we ever did something like this. Pretty soon, Uncle Dan wouldn't be able to. Eventually, he might be president, and they weren't afforded the luxury of meeting wayward nephews in bars late at night.

"Son." Uncle Dan embraced me before taking the seat next to mine. Manny nodded at me, but kept far enough away to give us some privacy.

"Thanks for coming."

The bartender's eyes widened when he arrived to take my uncle's order. "Sir? I, uh, what can I get you?" I wondered if this was a second job, if he was on staff somewhere. Probably. He looked barely out of college, older than me but not much, and vaguely familiar.

"We'll have another round," Uncle Dan said, nodding toward my near-empty tumbler. He glanced at me. "What is it?"

"Scotch," I told him and he smiled.

"What else is there, eh?" To the bartender, he said, "Make it a good one, if you would."

"Of course, sir. On the house."

Uncle smiled. "That really won't be necessary, but thank you. If you'd like to do something for me, vote."

"Of course, sir. I'm with Congressman Statern. You have my support."

He poured our drinks then, considerably more than my first one and from a different bottle, pulled from the back of the top row. Uncle Dan raised his glass first toward the bartender and then me.

We drank. Uncle Dan took a healthy slug and made a face, like a grimace but satisfied. It seemed to be the face one made when drinking Scotch. "That's not bad." He was right. It was better than my first one, still awful, but smoother. More like lava than fire. I loved it. "So," he said as if nothing was unusual about our meeting at all, "how were finals?"

I smiled. "Great. I'm sure I did well. But..." I hesitated. "I'm thinking of changing my major. To History, or Statistics. Maybe." I'd been considering it for weeks, but was afraid to admit that I'd made the wrong choice, and also to disappoint my uncle.

But he nodded like this was unsurprising, even welcome news. He'd been a history major, after all. "Why not both?" he said. "If anyone's capable, it's you. And I'm sure the university will accommodate whatever schedule you want."

Yes, they probably would. They already had, really. "Maybe," I conceded. "I'll think about it over break." It felt good, just talking like this. I wanted to keep doing it, so I said, "I'm going to New York, finally. For New Year's. Did I tell you that?"

He took another swallow of his drink, smiled. "Miss Morrow might have mentioned it the other night. I should have taken you to the city myself, when you were younger. I regret that. Alexis is growing up well," he mused. "An unparalleled beauty. Her mother cried when she was born with brown hair, did you know?"

I shook my head. "I didn't, but it doesn't surprise me." Her name was Barbie, after all.

"Much better this way, though. No one takes blondes seriously." He smoothed a hand over his own fair hair and laughed. This was why people loved him.

We both took another drink. I appreciated how he was waiting for me. He hadn't asked what was wrong, hadn't pushed me to get to the point. He hadn't even commented on the card sitting in front of me on the bar, though surely he'd seen it. I took a step closer to the real issue and asked, "How's Tessa?"

"Healthy. Vibrant. Determined." Uncle Dan made no effort to hide his proud grin. "She's quite amazing, really. Anton thinks I should marry her, propose."

"I know." Uncle's campaign manager thought the public would love a White House Wedding, even more than a White House Baby. He was probably right. I wasn't sure Tessa was on that page yet, but what did I know about women?

"It's a boy, Cartwright," he said softly, meeting my eyes, and for some reason I had to look away. "I would like you to be his Godfather."

My head snapped up. "Sir, I—"

"Don't protest. Just say yes."

"I'm honored. I just..." What? What did I tell him? That I could barely manage myself without his guidance, so how could I take care of his son? That I couldn't be Godfather because it would inevitably mean interacting with the girl who broke my heart? What kind of pussy was I? Instead of answering that, I took a huge slug of Scotch. Better. "Don't you think Uncle Jeff would be a better choice?"

He watched me while sipping from his drink, an excuse to give me the look I'd tried to emulate since I was a kid. To me, it always said more than he was saying. It was, I realized, a presidential look, one he turned on me now.

"Nothing," he said, "has pleased me more than having you join me here, Cartwright. I know it was your second choice, and a painful one, but I hope you've found it the right one. I know you're the right choice to mentor my son. None better, even my brother."

I looked down, unable to hold his gaze. I really was transparent. Finally, I cleared my throat and met his eyes again. "Thank you. That's high praise."

"And also true. So." He set down his glass, the heavy bottom thudding on the glossy wood of the bar. When he nodded to the bartender for another round, I should have recognized I was in trouble. But I was already drowning tonight. Uncle Dan knew that, or why else would I have called him? "How are you?"

I thought about my answer while I watched the amber fire rise in my glass. I nodded at the bartender as he left. "Confused," I finally answered. Another slug of the Scotch made my voice raspy.

"What's happened?"

I pushed Lainey's card at him. Its edges were starting to wear from my fingers. He opened it and made a noise somewhere between a tongue cluck and an *ah*, though his face remained carefully neutral.

"I see," he said. He tapped a finger on one of the worn edges while I stumbled through figuring out what I wanted to say.

"And I, I just want to know why? It's been months and now this and I guess...I don't understand what it means."

"I think that's fairly clear. It means she's cruel."

I stared at the card, frowning. Cruel. The word sounded harsh and whole, applied to Lainey in my uncle's voice. I still wanted to defend her.

"Don't you think she maybe, because of the baby—"

"I think, son, that she likes twisting the knife."

I coughed. Hearing him say it hurt as much as anything. I took another drink. Then another, rolling the tumbler in my hands. When it started to feel weightless, imaginary in my fingers, I set it down. "I miss her," I admitted. "Love her, still." After a pause, and the last of the liquid in my glass disappeared, I asked the eternal question: "What did I do wrong?"

He set down his own glass and put a hand on my shoulder. "You loved a girl before you knew her. Loved a girl more than she could love you. We don't choose those things. I was heartbroken when Angela left me, but I was at fault. I've been atoning for it for sixteen years. You, on the other hand, are blameless. The only thing you've done wrong is let her keep doing this to you."

"I don't know how to stop."

"You stop by doing. Your life is full. Embrace what you have. Change your major if you'd like. Enjoy your holiday in New York." He slipped the card from under my fingers and into his coat pocket. "And you let go of things like this."

For a long time I stared at the empty space on the bar where it had been. *Let go.* Was it that simple? Was the problem that I was *holding on?* Finally, I met his eyes. "You're right."

He nodded. "I've made all your mistakes and more, son."

"Thank you. For this. For coming here and...understanding."

"I should have done this sooner. Another regret." He stood, and when I tried to join him, I swayed and had to catch myself on the bar. Uncle embraced me. "Manny will see you home."

"But—"

"I'll be fine. Good night, son." Before he left me to Manny's care, he rested his hand on my shoulder one last time. "Remember, she's not the end. Only the beginning."

Chapter Twenty-Three

Lainey

Unlike I imagined most apartments of graduate assistants, Jack's was beautiful, with exposed brick walls, gleaming hardwood floors, and enough windows to offer peeks of the nearby waterfront. The place was small, but open, with high ceilings and a decently appointed kitchen that looked too shiny to be used often. Though not as nice as mine, Jack's apartment was pretty nice. I said as much.

"Compliments of the *III* at the end of my name. Turns out grandchildren are a decent tax shelter. Not that I'm complaining. But don't worry," he said, settling next to me on his expensive couch and handing me a drink. "I do work for it."

"I'm the last person to judge you if you didn't."

He clinked his glass against mine. I didn't really want it, but I took a sip anyway. "Another thing I like about you."

I laughed. "That I'm rich?"

Over the rim of his glass, I watched his lips as they smiled. He shook his head. "No." He shifted in his seat, so that our legs were touching. "That you don't care that I am, through the sheer dumb luck of my last name."

"To last names and luck," I said, touching my glass to his again. "I doubt anyone's ever called you dumb."

He chuckled. "More times than I care to remember. I'd tell you stories, but they're all family failures or involve girls, neither of which I want to bore you with." He set his glass, half finished, on the coffee table.

"Girls, eh?"

"What can I say?" There. The crooked smile I dreamed about appeared. "You're the only one I've brought here, though."

I laughed again. "Sure I am." After another sip from my drink, I traced shapes in the condensation on the outside of the glass.

"Scout's honor," he said, letting his fingers graze my thigh as he brought them up in the salute. Softer, leaning closer, he said, "You're the only one I've even wanted to. And that's the truth."

At that moment, a drop of water from my glass fell from my finger tip. I gasped. It landed near my collar bone and slid down. Jack's eyes followed it, and then, slowly and light as breath, his finger. His eyes came back to meet mine, but his finger kept going, and I gasped again. He followed the drop's path, dipping into the V of my shirt and tracing between my breasts before reaching up to pluck the glass from my hand.

And then he kissed me.

His lips were soft, *so freaking soft*, as they pressed against mine. He lingered there, tasting like sweet tonic and lime, until I leaned into him. When my lips finally parted and his tongue slipped between them, I was sure I'd already known how *perfect* it would feel. I closed my eyes and let him kiss me.

Good *God*, he knew how to kiss. I'd been waiting for this. Since I stepped out of the cab a few hours ago or, honestly, a lot longer than that. When his lips trailed across my cheek, I whispered, "That was worth the wait."

He paused, tickling me with his nose as he met my eyes and I drowned in the warm brown depths of his. "If I was a gentleman, I'd have asked first."

"It would have ruined the surprise."

Jack leaned forward, closer, until I thought he was going to kiss me again without permission. But he turned to the side, lips grazing my ear as he said, "I know." He held there, fingers tickling my side until I giggled. Then, on an impulse that seemed to surprise us both, I slipped my shirt over my head and dropped it over the side of the couch.

I wasn't sure why I did that. I wasn't drunk. I hadn't planned on removing clothing, not tonight, but in the heat of the moment, I realized *I didn't care*. I *wanted* to, and wasn't that reason enough?

Jack surveyed the new development with delight, grinning like he'd gotten away with something. "May I?" he asked.

"Please."

His kiss was deeper this time, confident and eager. He pulled me onto his lap, crushing me to him, and I didn't resist. My arms twined around his neck as his hand slid up my stomach, fingers brushing my breast first over, then under, my bra until my breathing was ragged. He unhooked it neatly and I tossed it away.

I was desperate for this, for heat and closeness and touch. It had been so long, months, since I'd been with anyone—with Carter—and the only person I'd really wanted to kiss since then was kissing me now.

I kept kissing him until kissing wasn't enough. I shifted my hips, pressing against him, and he groaned. His lips broke from mine, traveling down my neck, and lower, while his hands made the rest of me feel like I was on fire.

I did not want to put it out.

So I didn't.

Instead, I tugged on his shirt, unbuttoning it as quickly as I could between his kisses, and then his jeans, too. He stilled, just for a second, when my fingers found the button and undid it. He pulled back, looking in my eyes before slowly, *so* slowly, leaning forward until I was pressed into the couch and his solid body hovered over mine.

Jack cleared his throat lightly, one finger tracing under the edge of my waistband, as he asked, "Would you like to see my bedroom?"

"Yes," I told him. "Please."

Chapter Twenty-Four

Carter

Hangovers were worse than the fucking flu.

I woke early the next morning at my usual time, barely knowing where I was. I didn't remember getting there. I didn't get up and run. I didn't answer the phone. I didn't text Alexis. I didn't move from my bed until eventually I threw up.

After that, I found coffee and a few bottles of water and moved to the couch, watching the sky lighten outside. It was still early to most people. I felt not better, but less like I'd rather be dead. It was a different feeling, laying on the couch hating myself for something I understood. This was concrete. I drank too much, too fast. Lesson learned.

I did, however, remember seeing my uncle.

Thinking hurt, but it hurt less than moving. I could obsess in relative stillness. For once, though, it wasn't Lainey's words on replay in my head. That alone was a miracle. Not the end, only the beginning. Not the end.

Not. The. End.

I laid there longer than I should have, past the point where it was time to go. But I'd been past that point for a long time, hadn't I? I'd wasted seven months on something I couldn't change, spent too many hours trying to understand when it would never make sense to me. I thought I'd lost The One, when she was only The Beginning.

I'd let myself become my father.

It was time to let go.

I used to send her signs all the time when we were together, to let her know I was thinking of her. Push her pen onto the floor in class. Move the pages of her notebook. Knock a favorite book off her shelf in her room. Maybe it was stupid, but I thought she liked it, this secret communication only we understood. Having this damned Thought Mover gift was probably going to get me killed one day, so I might as well get a *little* enjoyment out of it.

I wasn't sure if it would matter now, if she'd ever know. But she'd been wearing the necklace the last time I saw her and maybe she was still. I closed my eyes and pictured it, the perfect diamond resting against her smooth skin. In my mind, I followed the delicate chain up over her clavicle, under her heavy dark hair. Then to the sturdy clasp at the back of her neck, I Thought: *open*.

Finished, I let the necklace slip from my thoughts and disappear into the past.

Happy birthday to me.

Chapter Twenty-Five

Lainey

Later, I stared at the high ceiling of Jack's bedroom and imagined constellations in the pattern of its cracks. The noises of a waking city filtered in, mingling with the gentle sound of Jack's breathing. He looked younger when he slept. Maybe everyone did. I wished I could sleep, too.

I had, for a while, when I'd been warm and snuggled against Jack's even warmer skin after…just *after*, before my brain woke up. Now it would not shut up.

What had I done?

I mean, I knew what I—what *we* had done. I'd been *thinking* about it for weeks. Looking at Jack there, tousled and content in sleep, I wanted to wake him and do it again. I also wanted to rewind this night and make sure it didn't happen.

What happened to my mind-heart-body alliance? The one I'd been so faithfully devoted to in the past? My mind was punishing me now, and my heart was thumping strange, erratic beats that sounded suspiciously like *Cart-er, Jack, Cart-er, Jack.*

I wanted so many things, and suddenly they all felt wrong. *Everything* felt wrong, except the weight of Jack's arm across my stomach, and I felt guilty that that *didn't* feel wrong. I still wanted Carter, and that felt the most wrong, wanting two men at the same time. But it *wasn't.* It wasn't wrong. It was human. I hadn't done anything wrong.

But I had, hadn't I? I'd done one thing wrong. I thought about the card I'd sent Carter and how I shouldn't have done it. I really, really shouldn't have done it. But much like visiting him at the end of the summer, I couldn't seem to stop myself, no matter how suspect my motivations. I wondered if he'd gotten it and hoped it had been lost.

Jack's room grew lighter by pale gray degrees. A slow turn of my head and I could see the clock, which told me it was still early, barely nine o'clock. I knew I wasn't going to sleep probably at all anymore, but definitely not in Jack's bed. Carefully, I slipped from under his arm and padded to the bathroom.

I was leaning over the sink, looking in the mirror and trying to figure myself out, when my necklace fell off.

I caught it easily, a reflex. It landed in my fingers and I stared at it. I shouldn't have been wearing it tonight, when I was with another man. Which was a joke. I shouldn't have been wearing it at *all.* Maybe the necklace knew that.

Inspecting it, I found it wasn't actually broken. The chain was intact and the clasp worked perfectly fine. I pinched it a few times between my fingers. Odd. It must have just opened, accidentally let go.

And that's when it hit me: Carter.

I knew it was him. I felt it, a zinging in my veins and cracking in my heart. It was a sign, the first one he'd tried to send me in months, the way he used to make books fall off my shelves. Carter *had* gotten the card I shouldn't have sent and this was his answer. And I heard it, loud and clear.

Let go.

Numbly and quiet as a ninja, I dressed in the living room and fled. Just as I was closing the door behind me, I heard a groggy call of, "Lainey?" I tugged on my boots and ran down the stairs.

I barely made it to a bus stop bench before the sobs burst out of me, choking my throat and squeezing the breath from my lungs. My heart pounded, hard, beating my ribs as the tears clogged my eyes and flooded over. I dropped my face into my hands and cried the ocean onto the sidewalk below.

I WAS HOME at my apartment, trying and failing not to think about two men at once, when Amy finally called me. It dawned on me then that I was leaving for Mexico in less than twenty-four hours and Jack didn't even have my phone number.

"That text was pretttty early this morning," she said by way of hello.

What could I say? "Yeah. Yeah, it was."

"So. Is it still a *Walk of Shame* if no one sees you, or if you didn't do it? Discuss." I chuckled, but it sounded forced even to me. "Oh," she said. "Um, so did you? Do it?"

"Yeah," I admitted. "We did."

She paused. "Did he… pressure you?"

"What? No. Not at all."

"Heh. So, I guess you *are* that kind of girl." I could picture her, in her big, white bedroom on the third floor of her parents' house, leaning forward and smiling like I was the canary she'd just caught in her polished cat claws. "So then the question is, why don't you sound more excited about it?! Wasn't it good? Tell me it was good."

Was it good? It was fantastic. It made me sorry I'd had to wait an entire semester for it to be possible. It wasn't *better* than being with Carter, or worse, or the same. It was new, and—*Jesus*. I should *not* be comparing them.

I couldn't stop thinking about them.

Finally, I said, "It was great."

"Are you just placating me or what here?"

"No, I mean it. It was great."

"So, then, where are the exclamation points?!" Amy huffed. "Why aren't you sighing and going on about tasting and stroking and what not."

"What? Are you drunk?"

"No." She sighed, and I heard the soft, squishy sound of her million pillows as she flopped onto them. "I've been reading romances in my loneliness. They're *always* going on about tasting him, tasting her, and what the hell? This isn't dinner. But anyway, are you going to taste that again, or are you one and done?"

"I'm not anything." That was a lie. "I'm...confused." I told her how I left and she whistled.

"You really are my heartbreaker, aren't you."

"It was one night."

"One you *both* waited for months to have—don't try to deny it." I wasn't denying. "He's been following you around awfully faithfully if all he wanted was to ba—"

"Amy. It's not about him."

She was quiet for a few, considering. Finally, "Is it Carter? Are you...regretting?"

"It's just...me." And it was. I did regret everything in relation to Carter, but Jill had been right—ultimately, I'd chosen. I'd chosen everything, including last night. I'd been *thinking* about Jack for weeks and weeks, but that was abstract, fantasy. A crush. Reality was scary. There was so much that could go wrong.

"Lane," she said, paused, then started again. "Remember our conversation over the summer? I'm starting to worry again."

On our summer "Yes Day", the crazy day I got my tattoo and kissed a random stranger, Amy had been brave enough to ask me if I was fighting depression. And I'd told her the truth—I didn't know. Was it depression when the thing causing your inner-darkness had a name and a face and was running for president? And, now, worse, dating your mother-figure and fathering your brother or sister? But that wasn't what was wrong.

My problem was fear. Fear and sadness. I lamented what I'd given up and was afraid what I'd found would just be taken from me again. "I'm afraid," I told her. "What if he's too good to be true?"

"Oh, Lane. What if he isn't?" she countered. "What if he's just…true?"

What if he was? Maybe I was afraid of that, too.

Chapter Twenty-Six

Carter

For the first time in—ever, the New Year felt entirely new. New city, new sites, new pressure of meeting your girlfriend's parents. I'd met them many times before, but never as Alexis's boyfriend, someone who should be worthy of her. I wasn't, but I was trying. More every day.

Uncle Dan had taken the birthday card from me, but I couldn't bring myself to destroy the note. The idea alone made me feel bereft, incomplete. Instead, I relegated it to a tiny slot in my wallet and left it there, untouched. Someday maybe I'd have the courage to let it go, too.

I thought about this as I sat alone drinking coffee and reading a newspaper at the approximate acre of Carrera marble that made up the Morrows' kitchen island. The room was all so much gleaming white and blinding chrome. It looked like no one ever used it because the staff cleaned it faithfully every day. I had never been in a home with a full-time staff before. Uncle Dan's ranch in Montana had a staff, but I'd never been there.

"Up early again, I see." My head snapped up to find Alexis's mother in the doorway and I nearly spilled my coffee. She was wearing what I believed was called a peignoir. Whatever it was, for certain it left too little to the imagination. Jesus Christ. "Alexis told me that about you."

"Guilty," I said, making sure not to look anywhere but her eyes or the counter. "It's a habit. I can't sleep late even if I want to."

"Enterprising. Brendan sleeps like the dead. He never even knows when I come and go." She moved past me into the kitchen, making her own cup of coffee, before settling next to me at the island. She stirred in a heap of some sugar substitute, took a sip, and closed her eyes, making a contented sigh, like it was the best thing she'd taste all day. When she opened her eyes again, she said, "My daughter hasn't brought a boy home in years you know."

"I'm honored. And hope I'm not a disappointment."

She smiled, flicking her eyes over me in a way that made me want to shift in my seat. "Not yet." I held tight to my coffee and kept my eyes level. Barbie Morrow's job was to be beautiful and she succeeded. Her daughter had inherited much from her, despite her father's brown hair, but it all worked *better* on Alexis. I couldn't tell which Barbie was more, jealous or proud. "Dan coming to the city soon?"

There was a hopefulness in her voice that gave me pause. "I'm not sure. He offered me his apartment this week, though. Gave me the elevator code."

"Yes, well." She waved her fingers. "I'm familiar with the code." Before I could really think about that, she said, alarmed, "He hasn't given it to my daughter, has he?"

"I'm not—"

"Who hasn't given me what?" Lex said from the doorway. She was dressed already, a clinging dark sweater, pants, and boots, and it always amazed me how head-to-toe winter gear could be so sexy. She breezed past us to the coffee machine, like a sleek, black bird aiming for her prey. "And mother, really?" She pushed a discreet button on the counter and said, "Carmen, could you find mother's robe? She seems to have misplaced it."

Not a minute later, Carmen bustled in with a blessedly opaque cashmere robe. "Here you are, Mrs. Morrow. It's freezing out! Would you like me to find your slippers?"

"Thank you, Carmen, this will be fine." She slipped it over her shoulders and I was finally able to relax. "I don't know what I'd do without you. You or my thoughtful daughter."

Lex rolled her eyes. "Yes, mother, wouldn't want you to be cold."

Carmen turned her attention on me. "Mr. Penrose, tomorrow I'll have your breakfast ready for you, after your morning run."

I almost coughed my mouthful of coffee across the marble counter. "Thank you, Carmen." Not for the first time, I felt entirely out of my depth. I wanted to tell Carmen not to worry about it, I was used to doing it myself, but I suspected that would be rude. Learning to negotiate social mores about accepting what was offered was a challenge. "Thank you," I repeated.

She nodded and disappeared back to whatever she'd been doing to keep the Good Ship Morrow running at peak performance. Alexis called her "the housekeeper" but Carmen was more like a household executive assistant. She had a staff of three and I suspected she made more in yearly salary than I did. Deservedly.

"So you run *every* morning," Barbie said, "even on vacation? Maybe I'll—"

"Mom!" Alexis's mug rattled as she set it on the counter.

"What?" She looked at her daughter with these innocent saucer eyes. Lex and her mother's relationship, the entire Morrow family dynamic, was complex.

"Just—isn't it time for yoga?"

Barbie sighed and carried her mug to the sink. "Probably. What are you kids doing today? I'll be at the club for lunch if you—"

"Mom. No. We're doing the city. We'll see you at dinner." She turned to me before her mother could say anything else. "Ready, babe?"

"WHAT'S THAT ONE?"

Lex sighed. "It's *Rockefeller Center*. See—giant Christmas tree, ice skaters? Jesus, babe, don't you watch TV either?"

Alexis found my lack of New York knowledge both hysterical and infuriating. I was having fun irritating her and, though she wouldn't admit it, she was having fun showing off her city. It was cold, but bright, starkly beautiful and sexy, in its way. Kind of like Lex. Everything seemed to be black and white and yellow, with windows and taxis and puffs of breath glittering in the sun.

"Let's skate," I said. Her look could have murdered. "C'mon. It will be fun. Let me do something quintessentially New York."

"It is quintessentially *tourist*."

"Well, I'm a tourist. Let's skate. I'll buy you hot chocolate or something expensive afterward."

"No."

"Can't you skate?" I poked her side and she crossed her arms.

"Of *course* I can skate."

"Good. You can teach me."

"No."

"C'mon. You can watch me fall down."

I dragged her toward the rink but eventually she was leading. For a decidedly non-tourist, she knew right where to go.

"So you have done this before," I teased.

After a sigh, she admitted, "Every little girl in New York does this."

I found that unlikely, considering I handed over nearly a hundred dollars before we took our first glide on the ice, but it was reality for Alexis. Her sphere of wealth and privilege extended so far, she had trouble remembering there was more beyond the edges of it. It was different from Lainey, who was alternately forgetting about her fortune or buying an armoire worth more than her car like it was nothing. I knew from living next door to it for my entire life that money wasn't magic, but it was a better problem to have than some others.

We stepped onto the ice together and I inched forward, away from the entrance, holding Lex's hand. She tugged on my arm. "Watch my feet and push off. See?" She pulled me along for a few feet while I did as instructed, watching her skates make smooth strokes despite my extra weight. I was guessing she took lessons as a kid, possibly right here, and despite her protests, she liked this. "Ready?"

"Yes." I dropped her hand and my pretense, easily skating past her and into the flow of traffic.

"Hey!" A glance over my shoulder showed the round O of surprise on her lips before they flattened into a pissed off line. She hurried to catch me. "You liar! You *can* skate!"

When she got up next to me, I grinned and took her hand again. "I'm from New England—*rural* New England—remember? We play hockey."

"Well, I'm from New York. We don't play fair." She shoved me and dashed away while I caught my balance.

I almost didn't want to catch her, she looked so just...*perfect* weaving between the other skaters, her brown hair flowing behind her from under her little hat, having fun. Happy. She was happy and, I realized, so was I.

Out here on a cold afternoon, chasing Lex through the crowds of tourists, I was happy. I couldn't remember the last time I'd been happy without trying, without thinking about it first. Alex was right in front of me now, letting herself be caught, and I wrapped my arms around her waist. She leaned back and let me push us along.

"You're such a cheater."

"Says the girl who doesn't play fair."

"But you already knew that about me."

"So what's something I don't know?"

She straightened and I let her go. "Watch!" she called as she gained some speed and distance, angling toward the inner ring of skaters. After making a tight circle around the more open center of the ice, she lifted one foot, sliding for a few feet before planting it and performing a perfect little spin jump. She twirled in a circle once more after landing and skated back to me, flushed and smiling.

"I used to be able to do two revolutions, but still pretty good, huh?"

I kissed her hand before we moved back into the flow. "Amazing, actually, Miss didn't-want-to-do-this."

With a smile like daggers, she tugged her hand from mine. "Okay, your turn."

I laughed. "I can't do *that*."

"So show me what you *can* do, Mr. I-can't-skate." She slapped my ass and pushed me forward.

I *could* skate, really skate, a skill kind of like bike riding. Even if it had been a while, once I got back on the ice, the motion came back to me. I was as good skating backwards as forwards.

I spun around, or at least I tried. It should have been easy. But I usually wore hockey skates when I did it and these were…not. My feet tangled and stuck, sending me tripping forward until I crashed to the ice in a pathetic imitation of Prometheus on the bronze statue behind me. From my supine position, it looked like he might be trying to help me up, or light me on fire. Lex skated over, not even pretending not to laugh, and did a circle around me.

"Impressive, right?" I coughed out, trying not to wince.

"Amazing," she said, giggling, and reached down a hand. The other skaters parted and flowed around us, some of them laughing too. I couldn't help but join in.

Upright again, I pulled Alexis close, not even caring about the road block we'd become. "See? Told you you'd get to watch me fall down." Then I kissed her, and the happy was complete.

From up above, someone whistled. A familiar voice called, "Hey lovebirds, get out of the way!" We looked up to see Brooke Barros waving from behind the observation railing. Lex squealed and dragged us off the ice.

BROOKE LOOKED MUCH more Manhattan when we were *in* Manhattan. She'd always been one of the prettier girls at Northbrook, but it was sloppier, somehow, when she was there. More relaxed. I liked that about her. Today, she looked more like Lex, with salon-straight hair and high black boots.

I sipped coffee while the girls gossiped over cappuccinos and made fun of me.

"You need, like, a signature cocktail or something," Alexis said, eying my coffee like it was offensive.

"An old-fashioned?" Brooke suggested and Lex laughed.

"Totally!"

"What's wrong with black coffee?" I asked. "It's manly. We should talk about the four spoons of sweetener you stirred into that tiny cup." I clinked Lex's with my own cup and took a sip.

"Carter, seriously, you're twenty-one now. You *can* order a drink and you don't even *want* to."

"It's barely past lunch."

She rolled her eyes. "Which is a perfectly acceptable time for a drink. I'd kill for a champagne right now."

I flagged our server. "A glass of champagne, please? My girlfriend has informed me that I'm no fun." He nodded and didn't even ask for my ID.

The champagne came and I took an obligatory sip. Except for the bubbles, it was nothing like the sweet stuff Amy'd gotten everyone drunk with at every Winter Ball. Not bad, but, "I think," I said slowly, "I'm more of a Scotch guy."

"Yes!" Brooke nodded. "Dad drinks it all the time, Scotch. It would look good in front of you, yeah? And it would match your hair."

"And your eyes," I said and tilted my champagne at her. Lex shoved me.

"Don't flirt with my friends."

"I've been flirting with your friends for *years*. It used to be my job, remember?"

"Yeah, well, you work with *me* now, remember?"

"Yes, m'lady." Lex narrowed her eyes but it lasted only half a second, as she only half hated it when I called her that. If anyone was aware of her princess station in life, it was Alexis Elizabeth Morrow.

"Good," she pronounced. "Now do me a favor and order another one of those while I go to the ladies'."

One thing you had to respect about Lex was she could go to the bathroom, or do anything really, by herself. At Northbrook, she'd always been surrounded by an entourage, but she didn't need them. She *liked* them, because if she liked anything, it was an audience. But independence was not something she lacked. I watched her pause to talk to the Maitre'd, like *they* were old friends, not that he was friends with her father, and it struck me how very good she must be at events with my uncle.

Brooke watched me watching Lex and said, "Sooo…Holidays with the families, yeah?" She turned big eyes and a big grin on me and I couldn't help but smile.

"Just New Year's, really. I'd never been to New York before, so how could I refuse?"

"What do you think?"

"It's big. Loud. Sexy, in its way. Different from DC and Boston. I don't have a lot to compare it to otherwise. I can see how it would be addictive though."

"Some of us just call it home."

I swirled the champagne in front of me, watching the bubbles. "I think it's different if you grow up in a place versus adopt a place. Like a primary language. You speak it, other people learn it. They might eventually sound like they've always been here, but it takes a long time."

"Carter Penrose, philosopher."

I smiled. "I do like how *everyone* lives in apartments. Back home, I'm the *only* one. And I like Central Park. Hard not to, right?"

"I think you'd learn the language here pretty easily. How's Mr. Morrow?"

"I believe his exact words were, 'Glad you've finally come to your senses. Don't fuck this up.'"

Brooke had this girly laugh that was petty, like she was, and it made you want to make her do it often. "That sounds about right."

"But he's refrained from asking me my net worth or offering me a more lucrative job, so I think he doesn't hate me."

"Of course he doesn't. He's always liked you. Everyone likes you. Has Barbie made a pass at you yet?" I looked away. I didn't want to talk about how friendly her kiss had been at the turn of New Year's. I thought it was because she was drunk, but then this morning happened and I wasn't so sure anymore. Brooke chuckled. "Obviously that's a yes. You'd be hard to resist. God, she's such a cliché." She leaned in and lowered her voice. "You know she slept with Rex?"

I did not know that.

She shook her head and crumbled the little cookie thing on her plate. "I don't think anyone but me does. It was here. He was visiting at Winter Break, and Lex went to sneak down to his room one night...except her mom was already there. She didn't tell me until last year."

"Jesus Christ." I rubbed my eyes. That would explain a lot. Theodore Madsen was Alexis's first, maybe only, love. He was also the dipshit male Siren who slept his way through Alexis's freshman class, starting with her. Also, apparently, with her *mother*. And I thought *I* was an asshole? He was King Asshole, and I a lowly prince.

"Yeah," Brooke said. "I, well, I know it wasn't my secret to tell, but I kind of thought you should know. You...care. Lex needs that. She wants this to work."

I did care. Even if Alexis deserved so much better than me. To Brooke I said, "It wouldn't have before."

"I know. I'm sorry, by the way. About Lainey. I never got to say that before."

"It doesn't matter anymore," I said, though it still did. Just not as much as it used to.

"No, maybe not. I mean, I'm pissed at her too. But I wanted to say it anyway. She texted me the other day, you know? Out of the blue, after not talking to me all that time."

Seemed Lainey was contacting a lot of people. I didn't mention the card, though. "*I'm* sorry about that. That she stopped talking to you. Because of me."

Brooke shook her head. "No, it wasn't you. I don't think anyway. I think it was just...*her*."

"Maybe you're right." I glanced over Brooke's shoulder, but saw no sign of Lex. I did, however, see an opportunity to investigate a resource I hadn't considered before. Besides me, Brooke had been Lainey's *only* real Sententia friend. Would that make her a confidant? "Since you brought her up...can I ask you something possibly strange?"

Brooke's eyebrows rose an inch. "Man, you have *no* idea how much I want to check what you want right now! But I won't. Sure, ask anything."

"Did she—" I forced myself to say her name. "Did *Lainey* ever say anything to you, anything at all, about my Uncle Dan?"

"Senator Astor? Um." She considered. "*Say* anything? Nothing specific I can remember, but I swore she was really freaked out when she first saw him. At the art thing, with her aunt? And then...on SAT day, I saw her, with a note from him. She was weird then too, but I know she wanted him to like her." When a Sensor like Brooke said things like that, she meant it. That was her talent, knowing what people wanted, at one particular time anyway. What people wanted often changed. "Why? Did something happen?"

"I don't know," I said, but thought, *What note?* Uncle loved to send them, said they were more personal and powerful than anything else. Except Lainey had never mentioned one to me. To Brooke I said, "It's probably nothing. But thank you for playing along."

"Now I'm curious. So. Should I text her back?"

I chuckled. "Depends. Are you a glutton for punishment?"

Brooke's eyes gleamed as she picked up her mug and looked me up and down while she sipped from it. "You look good, Carter, you know?"

I smiled. "It's the champagne. Brings out my eyes."

"Seriously though. If someone asked me a year ago if I'd be sitting in New York with you and Lex, like this, I'd have *laughed*. And when I saw you at Homecoming, I never would have *said* any of this to you. But today when you smile, you mean it. This was fun. I think, right now, you just want to have fun."

"I thought that's what girls wanted?"

"What do girls want?" Lex said, appearing behind me and slipping her arms around my neck.

I grabbed one of her hands and kissed it. "More champagne?"

"Duh," she said, and we all laughed again.

Happy, I thought. *This is what it feels like.*

Chapter Twenty-Seven

Lainey

My aunt glowed. I thought that was like a metaphor or cliché, or just something people said to make pregnant women feel better, but seriously, she glowed. I couldn't get over how beautiful she looked, her skin dewy and bright with color, her belly turning rounder every day. I swore her hair was even thicker, which I wouldn't have thought possible.

I watched as she ran and splashed in the ocean, playing with her little cousins with more enthusiasm than ever. I wondered if pregnant women were supposed to do that, run and play like they were little kids themselves, but Abuela didn't stop her, so it must have been okay. She was so happy.

What, I wondered, was I?

Happy had been an elusive state since...May. Sometimes it snuck up on me; sometimes I was so busy I forgot I was looking for it;

sometimes I faked it. But that night with Jack—for a while, happiness was right there.

It was here, now, lurking, tangled with pain. Could I be happy *for* my aunt, despite everything? And if my *aunt* could be happy, with the constant baby sickness and half the world's media calling her a *whore*— why couldn't I be happy too?

Still laughing, she ran back to her chaise next to mine, kicking sand on my feet as she lay down. She put her hand on her belly. "Whew! One second you're having a good time, and the next you can't decide if you need to eat lunch or throw up."

"But your hair looks awesome," I said. "So at least there's that."

She lifted all the awesome hair off her neck then dropped it again. "It's just more to hold out of the way when I puke," she said and I wrinkled my nose. I idly rubbed my ankle with my foot, brushing sand off the broken noose that circled it.

"Oh, sweetie," she sighed. She dipped her toes off her chaise and kicked sand at me again. "I'm sorry, but you know I just hate that tattoo."

I sighed too. This argument was already old. "Then you'll have to draw me a better one."

"It's just, what's it even mean? Is it—"

"It's about my migraines," I lied, a pretty freaking great lie, too, I thought. I'd had to come up with some explanation, because like the tattoo artist, people kept thinking I'd been in an abusive relationship. "I had this debilitating thing and I broke free." The bitterest part was that I hadn't, not really. I'd just been roped in a different way.

"But why *that* symbol? It's so macabre. Why not, I don't know, a butterfly emerging from a cocoon?"

"We can't all be butterflies, Auntie." She was. She had more than one in an elaborate garden on her back. To end the conversation, I said, "So, what do you think? Do you want some—Hey!"

The sleek, black sanate trying to steal from our lunch plate had only one foot, the other leg ending in a rough white stump on which he hopped, seemingly unaffected. He wasn't even afraid of me.

"He's a determined bird," Auntie said.

"Determined to eat your lunch!"

She waved her hand and the bird hopped closer. "Give it to him."

I frowned. "You don't want anything?"

"Oh, I *want* lunch." She rested her hand on her belly again. "My stomach says no."

I stood and swept up the plate, the bird cawing at me angrily. "I'm going to take it inside, or he'll never go away."

"Bring me a seltzer?" Auntie called and I felt guilty about the bite I'd just stolen from her sandwich.

Once inside, I deposited the plate in the kitchen and, sure that no one else was around, slunk to my bedroom like a thief, or a fool. Quietly, I closed the door and slipped my contraband out of the drawer where I'd buried it. I pretended I wouldn't be tempted to look at them, my phone and my necklace, if they were out of sight. I lied to everyone all the time, so might as well lie to myself too.

I lay on my narrow bed and held up the necklace, watching the diamond glimmer in the sunlight. It felt cold, not having been resting against my skin. I wanted to put it back on; I wanted to be able to put it away for good. For now, I dropped it back into the drawer and turned over my phone.

Blinking—a message! I nearly dropped it, my fingers were so clumsy and desperate. I wasn't even sure what I was hoping for most, but there was no reason to rush. It wasn't a text from Carter or an email from Jack. I'd done terrible things to both of them; neither was going to contact me, no matter how many times I checked. It wasn't even from Amy. It was from Natalie.

Hope you had a good Christmas. I just wanted to let you know that my par-
ents and I talked and I'm not coming back. I'm transferring to Richmond. I'll miss
you.

I kept up my lies when I texted back how I'd miss her too, though I was afraid I actually would. Nat had been challenging, but she wasn't all bad. I felt guilty for not trying harder, and guilty for not feeling worse. Could this break, I wondered, get any worse?

By the time I went back outside, Daniel Astor had arrived.

Later, his shadow fell across my beach chair. "May I sit with you?"

Manny was around somewhere, but for the first time since he'd almost killed me, Daniel Astor and I were as alone as we'd probably ever be again. I even welcomed it, because we needed to talk.

"When are you going to tell her?"

"I'm sorry?" He settled comfortably on Aunt Tessa's chaise, crossing his ankles and shading his eyes with his hand. I hated looking at him, so I watched the ocean instead.

"What we are. What her baby's going to be. When are you going to tell her?"

He smiled. "Ah. I'm glad you asked. When were *you* going to tell her?"

I opened my mouth to snap at him then registered what he said. "What?"

He folded his hands across his stomach like he was the most content man in the world. I hated him. "As you just said, this is *your* secret too. Isn't it a courtesy I should afford you, discussing when it will be revealed?"

Two waves crashed before I said, "The answer is never. I planned to tell her never. I didn't want her to be part of this. She deserves to live a normal life."

He chuckled. "I daresay 'normal' is not the life she's pursued. In fact, I think she'd consider that an insult. But to answer your question,

I planned to tell her when it became necessary, or whenever you were ready. The baby may not inherit, you know. No guarantees."

"Did you make her do this?" I asked quietly. *This* is what I wanted to know.

"Excuse me?"

"You know exactly what I'm asking."

He did. After a pause, he said, "My dear Lainey, even I don't have the ability to maintain such an elaborate ruse. That's not how Thought works."

"You know if you're hurting her or using her or just with her to torture me, I will kill you." He had the nerve to chuckle again and I hated him more. In fact, whenever I saw him, I seemed to find new depths to my hatred. "I *will*."

"That's not why I'm laughing. True, I'm not sure I believe you, since you've had any number of chances. Even now." He reached out and put a hand on my bare shoulder in a fatherly, condescending way. "You could do it, if you wanted to."

I stared at him, wishing I really had it in me. But I didn't. Not yet. I was afraid my aunt loved him and, regardless, he was the father of my unborn brother. I. Hated. Him. But I couldn't kill him. I also hated myself for taking the bait. "Why are you laughing?"

"Because, my dear, you know a bit about torture, don't you?" From his pocket he produced Carter's birthday card and I wanted to vomit. I inhaled one, two, three times, to keep the tears from spilling.

"Where did you get that?"

"I relieved the burden from my nephew after I found him at a bar, knee deep in a bottle of Scotch."

Carter? Drinking? Alone at a bar? I struggled again to keep the tears at bay. "That's not—that's not why I sent it!"

"No? What effect did you think it would have?" I kicked little puffs of sand onto one foot with the other. The problem was I hadn't really been thinking about *Carter* when I sent it. I couldn't look at Dan, but I could feel that he was grinning. "Precisely."

Finally, I raised my eyes to meet his. "I didn't mean to hurt him. I never wanted to at all."

"Yet you're doing a remarkable job. Has it occurred to you that he might be happier if you'd leave him be?" Probably he could have stabbed me and it would have hurt less than those words. But then he added, "Or that I am here to be with Tessa because she's the most amazing woman I've been lucky enough to meet in this lifetime?" Which is when, finally, I did cry. I turned my back to him and mashed away tears while he said, "I'm sorry, Elaine. Eventually you'll learn there are times when it's *not* about you."

LATER THAT WEEK, when Dan had gone to smoke cigars with Abuelo and Uncle Tommy, leaving my aunt and me at the dining table alone, I asked her, "Are you happy, Auntie?" Not that it wasn't obvious, but I needed to hear it, from her, in her own words.

She regarded me for a while before she answered. "Do you know, when your father first showed up at the café where we worked, I was the one who had a crush on him? Julie had a boyfriend, of course. She barely even glanced at Allen, but she'd always talk to him, mostly about me, until one day she realized she'd stopped talking me up and started, simply, talking. The next thing she knew, the boyfriend was gone and it was like your father had always been there, the missing part of her. It was hard even to be jealous, I loved your mother so much, and they were obviously meant to be together."

"I didn't know that," I whispered. I had no idea. She'd never included this detail in the story before.

"So," she continued, "when I met Dan, it was like that moment again, so many years ago, when your father walked in, tall, and handsome, and radiating success. Something in my heart thumped. In a way it hadn't since probably that day."

"Were you... were you in love with my father?"

She laughed. "No, honey. I was attracted to him once, before it was impossible to think of him separately from Julie and, eventually, from you. But I did love him. And I miss them both, every day still. When I saw Dan, it just flooded me, the same attraction. I wanted to know him. He's nothing like your father, and yet, so similar. Sometimes in the way he'll tilt his head or wave his hand..." She absently rubbed her belly, while I sipped my wine. "So this is all to say, yes, I'm happy. So perfectly happy."

"Do you love... are you in love with *him*?" I had to know. I could barely handle the idea that my aunt was carrying Satan's baby, but the fact that she might actually be in *love* with him...It was all too late for me to change, but I had to know.

Auntie chuckled again. "I suppose I might be. But, you know, it wasn't until I was already pregnant, after he'd agreed to father my baby, that we actually started doing the thing that leads to babies."

I dropped my glass. The heavy blue base hit the table edge with a thud and started to tip over the side, the last of the wine sloshing onto the tablecloth and my leg, before I caught it. Auntie made this clucking sound with her tongue as she handed me her napkin.

I dabbed at the spill and said, "Sorry."

"Really, Lainey, it shouldn't be a surprise."

"It's not," I admitted. "But still weird."

"Psh. It's perfectly natural."

"Should pregnant ladies even be doing that?"

"Elaine, seriously."

"Sorry," I repeated. I rubbed aggressively at the wine spot on the tablecloth until she stilled my hand with her own.

"I know it's strange for you. Because of Carter."

There. She'd said it. She couldn't know it was so much more than Carter that made her affair strange and terrible to me, but I wouldn't deny that he was part of it. "Yeah, a little."

"Do you ever talk to him?"

"Not really."

"Do you think you could, for me? And your brother?" A *brother*. It was a boy. When she asked me to be his Godmother, and said that Carter and I together would be the Godparents, I wasn't really surprised.

I swallowed my unease, pushed it so far down I could barely feel it, so that my smile was genuine when I said, "I would do anything for you."

"So that's a yes?"

"There's no other answer, Auntie."

She beamed, that glow of well-being and happiness so intense it made my eyes, and my heart, hurt. She pulled me into a hug, the bump that was my baby brother poking into me as she squeezed, saying, "Thank you, sweetie. Thank you so so much. This means...I can't..."

"Please don't cry, Auntie."

She cried anyway, little sniffles that shook her shoulders while I stroked her soft, dark waves. I loved her hair, everything about her, even the little brother she carried, though it scared me to admit it. It didn't matter who his father was; he was *my* brother. I prayed then, harder than I'd prayed for anything except maybe my life, that the only thing he'd inherit from his father was a healthy trust fund.

"I'll be there for him, for everything," I promised.

"Thank you," she sniffled again and finally pulled away. With her napkin, she wiped her eyes and her nose, crumpling it on the table. After a deep breath, her smile returned, true and beautiful. Her eyes twinkled when she grabbed my hand and said, "Do you want to come with me tomorrow? To see him?" Because of a number of things, including her age, her wealth, and also the baby's father, Aunt Tessa had an absurd number of checkups, arranged even while on holiday.

I eyed the men through the doorway to the other room. "Just the two of us?"

"The three of us—me, you, and your brother."

"Then there's nothing I'd like more."

After more hugging and tear wiping, Auntie released me to arm's length. As she spoke, she leaned over the table to retrieve a not yet empty wine bottle to refill my glass. "And what about you, sweetie? Are you happy?"

"I'm so happy for you. I mean it!"

"That's not what I'm asking." She glanced at my bare neck, where my fingers had reached automatically for the necklace that was no longer there.

I'd known what she was asking. I just didn't know the answer.

I sipped the new wine, a different one than I'd had before. It was peppery and strong, something Dan had chosen and seemed to fit him. I didn't want to admit I liked it. I thought about the necklace, about seeing my baby brother tomorrow, about everything I'd left in Boston.

Let go, Carter had told me.

Could I do it?

I was holding onto something I wanted, wanted so hard, but couldn't have. Even when I'd been with Jack, I was still grasping at the threads of Carter, clinging to them with a grip that made my heart ache. It was unfair to both of us, strangling me and, maybe, him too.

It was time to break this other noose. I understood now that finding freedom wasn't a one-time deal. Freedom was a journey, a series of choices, and sometimes what holds you back turns out to be yourself.

I thought once more about Carter, about how I loved him. *That* was something I didn't have to let go—loving him. It would always be a part of me, locked into a private place in my heart just like his necklace was locked away in my room. But loving Carter wasn't all I was ever going to do or be.

And, I realized, though I would always love him, maybe I wouldn't *only* love him.

Finally, I said, "I think I could be."

Chapter Twenty-Eight

Carter

College had so much vacation time it was a wonder anyone learned anything. After my New York sojourn, I went back home again, still days before my return to DC. It was busy in the store as the Academy students filtered back to campus after being away for all of break. Chelsea Agro was one of the first to arrive.

She sat behind our counter, watching me with a little frown on her face. Seeing her there, with that look on her face, reminded me intensely of Jillian. I forced myself not to look away before I ducked under the counter and sat next to her.

"Hey, Chels. Welcome back. Aunt Mel says you're doing a great job here." In a rare show of generosity, Dr. Stewart had helped solve our staffing issues with an allotment of student work hours. Applications had been legion. For the first time ever, Aunt Mel had an overrun of help.

"Thanks," Chelsea said. Her voice was small, like she was, and sweet. Her dark hair was longer than last year, but except for her big brown eyes, she didn't seem any bigger. Or maybe it was just that I'd grown some, too. Going under the counter was harder than it used to be. "I like working here. A lot. Sometimes I help even when it's not my turn. Mom says it's okay, as long as my grades are good. Melinda lets me take some of the galleys."

I smiled. "I'm glad they're going to a good place. And that Aunt Mel has such good company."

"She misses you."

"I miss her too."

Chelsea paused, like she was going to say something else and changed her mind. "I saw you on TV."

"Yeah? How'd I do?"

"Good. Super good. You were, like, so funny."

"Honest?"

She nodded emphatically. "Yeah, honest. We all cheered when they started talking to you."

"Thanks."

Watching the press conference, or any of the times the camera had caught me since, was like torture. So of course I'd done it repeatedly. What surprised me most was how decent even I thought I performed. I was a better actor than I gave myself credit for. It made me wonder how many others were.

Chelsea darted a glance at me and away, the little frown returning to her face. I had a feeling she wouldn't tell me whatever she really wanted to say unless I encouraged her. "Is something the matter?" I asked.

Chelsea's eyes widened and she looked down at her hands, shaking her head. "No. It's just"—she glanced out at the lounge and raised her chin a fraction—"not the same."

The *not the same* she indicated was Lex, who was laughing on one of the good couches, just like old times. Alexis had needed zero convincing to ditch her parents and come with me to see her Northbrook friends before we went back to school. Plus, I felt better about the flying when she was with me, though I didn't tell her that.

I didn't say anything for a moment. I hadn't forgotten that little Chelsea was a Cupid. Lainey called them love detectors. Finally, I said, "Not the same how?"

Chelsea shook her head again. "Just, you know—I'm sorry. I should keep my mouth shut. Mom tells me that, too."

"No, it's okay." Damn curiosity to hell.

She took a deep breath and went on. "It's just, I liked her, you know? Lainey. She was always so nice to me."

"I liked her too."

"I know." Chelsea nodded. "And I—I'm sorry. It's not the same. With Alexis. You're mostly an orangey shade, and she's, well, she's really hard to read. She doesn't know what she feels about anyone. She feels more about *you* than anyone else though," she added quickly. "So there's that. She always has."

"And orange is bad?"

"No! It's not," she said slowly, a blush creeping up her cheeks. "It's just—God I can't believe I'm saying this to you, but it's more…physical," she practically whispered, darting her eyes at me and away again. "But it's more than that. Pure lust," she whispered the last word again, "is yellow. Plenty of married people are shades of orange."

I twirled a pencil from the counter across my fingers and thought about that while Chelsea rang out a customer. What she said seemed accurate, maybe better than I'd hoped. I tried not to think too hard about my feelings for Lex out of fear they were less than they should be.

"And Lex?" I asked when we were alone again, part out of curiosity and partly to delay talking about Lainey.

Chelsea thought for a moment. "It's not bad either, not really. Before she used to feel what we call covetous of you. And now that

you're together… she feels so many different things nothing has settled. She's, um, plenty orange too though." Chelsea rushed through the
last words and I looked down at the counter to try to hide my grin. "I
think," she went on, "that Alexis is really strong willed and everything
is a competition, even her feelings. Like Brooke? She loves her—in the
friend way—but it's a fight between the kind of love that makes you
happy for someone or jealous of someone."

I regarded Chelsea, with all her self-possession and maturity yet only in the eighth grade, and couldn't help thinking of Jillian again. "That
sounds about right," I finally said and Chelsea's face went pale.

"God, I must sound—I don't mean it in a bad way—I was just—"

"Chelsea." She stopped fidgeting and looked back at me. "You
sound incredibly perceptive. And mature, I might add. I'll never look
at oranges the same again."

"Oh, God." Blood rushed back into her face. I tried not to laugh
but couldn't keep from smiling.

"Sorry," I said and bumped her lightly with my shoulder. "And I'm
glad you're here to keep Aunt Mel company. She loves to talk about
love."

Chelsea grinned back. "I know."

After another customer and a few moments to prepare myself, I finally asked, "So how is it different?"

"What?"

I cleared my throat. When I realized I was playing with the pencil
again, I put it down. "It's not the same, you said. And I wondered…how."

"Oh! Oh." She toyed with one of the levers on the ancient register.
"Are…are you sure you want to hear it?"

The longer I talked to her, the more I liked Chelsea. "You *are* perceptive. But yeah, I'm sure."

She took a breath. "It used to be perfect," she said and I think I flinched. If Chelsea noticed, she didn't show it. Her game face was better than mine. "It really was. Just pure, perfect red. Those are the highest forms: red, gold, and white. And you guys glowed. I liked to watch you—sorry, that sounds creepy—but it's just because it's so rare. Your aunt and uncle are like that too and I thought, how lucky to have *two* couples who *really* loved each other."

"I guess Lainey didn't really feel the same way." I slipped off the stool and leaned my elbows on the counter.

"That's the thing," Chelsea said, "she did." My eyes snapped back to her and then away again.

"Something must have changed."

Chelsea nodded. "Something, I guess, but it wasn't how she felt about you. I was at graduation. So I saw you, that day. The two of you, on the field. Nothing had changed. If anything, it was *stronger*. And, well, I heard later that she—what happened—and it made no sense to me. So—I don't know. I probably shouldn't have said all this. Sorry. Sometimes I wish I was a real Empath. I'd know so much more." She shrugged her little shoulders and returned to toying with the register.

"Hey." I bumped her again. "Don't apologize. Never apologize for your gift, or for being brave enough to talk about it. Most people are afraid to talk about emotions. I…appreciate it."

"Did it help?"

"No." I laughed, a real one, and she smiled big enough to show me all her braces. "But I'm glad you told me. Your gift must be very strong if you're so good with it this early."

Chelsea blushed again. "I practice a lot."

"Good. Remind me to introduce you to my uncle. He'd love you."

"You mean Senator Astor?" Chelsea looked at her hands. "I think I'd be too scared to meet him."

"What? Why? He really would love you." After a second, she met my eye, and in her brown ones I saw all the thoughtfulness of a girl who pays attention all the time.

"That's what I'm afraid of," she said. "He's silver. Always silver. About everything, even you."

"What's silver?"

"Covetous," she said. It came out breathy and soft, but I felt like I'd been slapped. I must have looked like it too, because Chelsea's eyes went enormous. "I—I'm sorry. I shouldn't have said that. Mom will be so mad! I'm sorry," she repeated, before she slipped past me to busy herself in the store.

When she glanced back over her shoulder, I hadn't moved.

I still hadn't moved when my always-quiet Uncle Jeff came up behind me. "Ready to go?" he said, and I startled. "Sorry."

"Yeah, I'm ready."

FOR ALL IT seemed contrary, I found a peacefulness to holding a gun. At the range, I guaranteed myself total concentration and a respite from whatever noise was crowding my head. Coupled with the private thrill of being able to use *all* my gifts in a public place made shooting one of my top three favorite things to do.

It was also the thing Uncle Jeff and I did together, and the time I felt closest to him. After my talk with Chelsea, I was more glad than ever I'd asked him to go. We were lucky to snag the private range for an hour this afternoon.

I hesitated at the door. She was already in my head from earlier, and I couldn't help but think about Lainey. Last time we'd been here, something strange had happened. She told me this story: she dropped a bullet, I slipped on it. I hit my head hard enough to momentarily knock me out.

When I came to, she was crying harder than seemed necessary for a pretty minor accident. I had a wicked headache, but not even a lump or bruise or any memory of the fall. She'd claimed she was so upset over her clumsiness and how it could easily have been worse. But for maybe the first time, I didn't believe her.

I remembered—*something*. I remembered turning, not falling. I remembered her eyes going wide like she was afraid—*of* me, not for me. I remembered the clock over the door. The placement of the hands and how it seemed like too much time had passed for what little happened. I remembered—

"Plenty of spaces in the main room," Uncle Jeff suggested benignly.

I shook my head. "No, I'm good." I pulled the door handle and it flew open with a whoosh, so hard I almost stumbled. "I've missed this place."

Three quick rounds of fifteen later and I had shaking arms and a light sweat going. In other words, I finally felt pretty good.

Three rounds after that, Uncle Jeff said, "So. Do you want to talk about it?"

The thing about being quiet all the time is it makes you observant.

"About what?" I stalled.

"Whatever it is that's bothering you."

Did I? If anyone would listen, it would be Uncle Jeff. More than what Chelsea had said, more than being here, I had this growing feeling of—something. Something I couldn't fully explain. Finally, I said, "Have you had any luck? With what we talked about in November, the...Marwood question." I said *Marwood question*, like it wasn't about Lainey, or by extension, his half brother.

Uncle Jeff didn't raise an eyebrow at my verbal tiptoeing, like Aunt Mel would have. He shook his head. "There's nothing left for me to find, or if there is, we don't have access to the places I'd need to look."

All the relevant people were dead, and their things lost or inaccessible. If Uncle Jeff, with his *Venator's* gift for finding things, couldn't track down the answer, there was no way I could.

"So what's next?"

"There *is* an 'easy' way to find out." He paused for only a moment in his reloading to look at me. "DNA."

DNA. I wondered why I hadn't thought of it sooner. "You can do that?" I asked.

He shrugged. "Zeus will do it."

"Discreetly?" Ezekiel Usunat, affectionately known as Zeus, was the Perceptum's geneticist. Members often chose to contribute their DNA to the project. As lead investigator of unreported Sententia, Uncle Dan worked with him often.

"For me, yes."

"What about *getting* the DNA?"

"It's only the Marwood side that's…problematic." He paused. "I don't suppose you have anything that might…?" I shook my head. Definitely not anymore. "*If* we can get it, I can have it tested against my brother. The family markers will show, or not."

"I'll get it," I said with more confidence than I felt.

Uncle Jeff nodded. "I know you will."

He finished his reload and snapped the clip in place but hesitated before donning his sound gear, waiting for me. I was only halfway done. I could reload in my sleep, or with my eyes closed. My fingers knew what to do. But they weren't doing it. Embarrassed, I quickly packed the rest of the clip.

"It's okay, you know," Uncle Jeff said.

I glanced over at him. "What is?"

"How you're feeling."

"I'm fine."

"You've stopped reloading again."

Shit. "Sorry."

"Don't be." When I didn't respond, he said, "I heard a little bit of what Chelsea was saying."

My fingers stilled again. I took a breath. It was weird, but something about this distracted reloading felt…familiar. I couldn't understand the sense of deja vu that settled on me, like my fingers had disobeyed me once before. I stared at the wall of the shooting lane because I couldn't look at Uncle Jeff when I asked, "Do you think she was right?" My voice was smaller, younger than I remembered. I cleared my throat.

"She's a perceptive girl." He paused. Slowly, he said, "My brother is a lot of things. Perfect isn't one of them. None of us are. It's okay to recognize that."

I nodded. I wanted to respond, to say *something* that would make at least one of us feel better, but I couldn't stop staring at the wall. My brain automatically did calculations and comparisons even when I didn't ask it to. I could tell you there were seven new holes since the last time I was here.

No. There were eight.

Seven, my brain insisted. *One was already there.*

I stared at the wall until I could see it, could understand what my brain was telling me and what it had recorded. In the commotion, I hadn't consciously noticed. I mentally layered images until the truth appeared:

One new bullet hole had appeared in the wall between when Lainey and I entered the room and when we left.

Except I didn't remember the shot.

Chapter Twenty-Nine

Lainey

Returning to campus was strange and disconcerting. Everything felt different. Everything *was* different. Even me. It was freezing out, icy and gray, having finally snowed while I was gone. City snow was ugly, clumped and dirty within hours of falling, not at all like winter at Northbrook. The wind bit with teeth that were sharp, gusting up between buildings and slamming you when you turned corners.

Under my coat and hat, I was tan, still warm inside from vacation and the rapid pounding of my heart. Anticipation made my pulse race and palms sweat as soon as I returned to the city. I didn't know if I dared to hope for anything with Jack, after how I'd left him.

But at the same time, I felt new. Freer. It was like by taking off the necklace, I could breathe again. I'd trapped myself on top of a mountain and grown used to it there. When I finally came down, I realized how thin my air had been. Possibility felt like something I could reach out and not just find, but take.

I closed the door to my room and sighed. Nat really was gone, her side of our room barren and depressing. I tossed my coat on her naked bed. *Could* I have done more to help her? I mean, I'd known she was unhappy. I wondered if this would be my curse forever, wishing I'd helped someone more when I had the chance. But at the same time, I couldn't have forced her to classes or to be happy either. Nat, I reminded myself, wasn't ultimately my responsibility. I flopped back on my own bed and called Amy.

"Do you want to move in with me?"

"What?"

"My roommate is gone. If they're replacing her, the new girl hasn't shown up yet. Classes start in the morning, so..."

"Let me get this straight—you basically have a single now, you're in college, and you want someone to move *in*?"

"Well, yeah." Though mostly I just wanted her.

"You're crazy. Oh, that's right." She snapped her fingers. "I forget you already *have* a single. In a building down the street. With a doorman."

"The whole reason I'm here is to have roommates."

"You have two."

"But now my bedroom is ugly and lonely."

"Invite Jack over. Then it will be neither."

If only it were that easy. "He probably doesn't want to see me."

She made this clucking sound. "You don't know that, heartbreaker. You just need to apologize."

I flipped over onto my back. "I don't have his number."

"You realize this is the 21st century, right? There are other means of communication. And also, seriously?"

We never exchanged them. We used email for class and then, when we met at the club, I thought it seemed...special, maybe even daring, just to show up at the time he said and assume he'd be there. It would have ruined the feeling to have called to confirm, texted I was on my way, etc., etc. But then, I went and ruined it anyway. I didn't want to say any of that to Amy, so what I said was, "Do you think I'm self-absorbed?"

She laughed. "Way to change the subject, Lane. Also, you realize the irony in our talking about you being self-absorbed, right?"

"Could you just tell me?"

"Yes. Sometimes you are. But I love you. And your life is weird, so maybe you get a little leeway."

"I miss you," I told her.

"I'm right here."

"It's not the same as is if you were on the bed across from me."

"I know." She paused. "But things can't always stay the same, can they?"

WHAT HAPPENED WAS I ran into him in the hall.

He was standing outside a lecture room, alternately glancing at a sheet of paper and watching me approach, looking his usual perfect. For just a second, I pictured him the last time I'd seen him: asleep, lips slightly parted, body tangled and bare under a midnight blue comforter. A flush began to creep up my face, starting from my neck or possibly lower.

How did one do this? How did one talk to a guy for the first time since slipping out of his bed without even saying goodbye? I could hardly recognize myself as the girl in this situation. Yet I was, and now he was right in front of me.

So I said, "Hey." I tried a smile, but it felt tentative and uncertain.

Jack was not smiling as he glanced at the paper again. I tugged on my ponytail while he said, "Please don't tell me you're in this class."

"What? No, I'm not. I just left Intro to Finance."

He blew out a breath. "Thank God."

Ouch. My smile lost its tentative hold and my stomach felt like it was somewhere around my feet. I'd known this might be his reaction. "Listen, I'm sor—"

But I didn't finish what I was going to say because Jack was already kissing me. Right there, in the hallway, where every and anyone could see. I was so surprised I forgot to blink, but my lips knew what to do. They parted happily, pressing against Jack's, which were warm and soft and smiling. His arm slipped behind my back, pulling me closer.

Behind me, I became aware of cheering and clapping. I heard someone call, "Yeah, Lainey!" as Jack and I broke apart. Over my shoulder, I saw Serena and a few other kids from discussion making the noise. Serena winked at me.

Grinning and blushing, I turned back to Jack. "You forgot to ask permission again."

His lips curved into the perfect, crooked smile. "Sorry. But I didn't forget. I just really wanted to do that one more time before you gave me the awkward let down. It's okay if you want to slap me; I'd deserve it."

I smoothed his tie. "That's not what I want to do."

"Oh?" he said, one eyebrow perfectly arched and I flushed what had to be an electric shade of red. Behind us, the last kids filtered slowly into his class, and I prayed they weren't listening too closely.

"I want to apolog—"

"Not now," he said, pressing one finger to my lips.

"But—"

"Later. Like on Friday. Friday night." He leaned closer, saying, "I kind of feel like you owe me a do over," and my already red face burst into flames. "For the *date*," he amended, suppressing a snicker. "Dinner? The club didn't work out so well for me last time. Unless you don't want to."

"No, I-I'd love to," I stuttered. I bobbed my head and realized I was behaving kind of like one of those weird desk toys, where you tap the bird and it dunks its beak in some water, all jerky and without rhythm. I took a deep breath, tried to still myself. "And I *am* sorry, for...disappearing."

He tucked the class sheet under his arm and pulled his phone from his pocket. "Do you think," Jack said, "maybe I could get your number? So I could find you, if it happens again."

As I walked away, my phone rang. I glanced behind me and, sure enough, Jack's was to his ear. "Who is this?" I answered, though I'd turned around to watch him.

He smiled. "Your destiny."

Chapter Thirty

Carter

I obsessed. There were many secrets about me, but that was not one of them. I loved mysteries, too. An extra bullet hole? What *happened* that day at the range? That was a true mystery, one whose only answer rested with a girl I'd been trying to forget.

I thought about driving to the city and waiting outside her apartment until I saw her. I thought about breaking *in* to her apartment. Uncle Jeff could tell me how. I started writing her a letter, but I couldn't figure out what to write. So instead, I obsessed. Maybe my brain just needed something to do. It was like a kid brother that looked continually for the next way to annoy me.

Or possibly my brain was trying to distract me from something else:

Doubt.

I began to doubt my uncle.

Voices fought for attention in my head. Uncle Jeff first: *my brother is a lot of things. Perfect isn't one of them.*

My aunt had said it before, but I wasn't ready to listen then. None of us were perfect. I wasn't, not even close. I knew, intellectually, Uncle Dan wasn't either. But in some part of my hyper-active brain—the part that had been looking up to him since I was a kid—I expected him to be. Other whispers I'd been ignoring grew in volume until they were all I could hear:

Jill: *you don't know anyone.* Uncle Dan: *Miss Morrow really does suit you better.* Harlan: *your uncle doesn't like to show his cards until he's ready to play them.*

Chelsea: *he's silver. Always silver. About everything, even you.*

Aunt Mel: *he'd not tell you a lot of things if he thought it was better.*

Were they right and I was wrong? Or was my uncle just protecting me?

I knew Dan loved me. More than that. He'd been there for me whenever I needed him, since my own father couldn't and even before then. He'd arranged for me to come to DC when I couldn't do it myself. He valued my opinion. He trusted me with tasks that rightfully belonged to people far more superior.

Why was I doubting him? Why was I doubting *myself?*

Now was the wrong fucking time for an identity crisis.

I figured the week-long headache I had upon returning to DC was what it felt like when everything you'd been convinced you knew—about yourself and the people who were important to you—started to crack. I *thought* I'd known myself. I thought I'd had everything figured out, too. But maybe I'd been too isolated to really know anything.

The crumbling of so many convincing illusions fucking *hurt.*

I tried to conjure a single image of my uncle that corroborated what Chelsea had said about him, what Harlan and *everyone* had said, but I couldn't. He didn't want to use me; he wanted the best for me. Always had.

But then, there *was* an image. Not of me, but of Lainey. Standing with Uncle Dan on the graduation stage. I closed my eyes and it floated to the surface. I hadn't understood her expression at the time, but my brain called it up now with shocking clarity: revulsion. She looked as if his arm around her shoulder burned her skin.

She looked like she hated him.

"Surely you're enjoying yourself."

My eyes popped open at the sound of his voice, and I remembered where I was. *When* I was. Uncle Dan was coming through the office. He was on the phone, on one end of a conversation that amused him. I'd heard him this way many times, and I pitied whoever was disappointing him now.

"No? Then what is it?…Of course you do. I knew you would."

I pictured him, his patiently expectant expression as he waited for the person to come around.

"All the better…Than you? Perhaps. But in the meantime, you can reap the benefits." Uncle Dan's face split into a grin when he saw me waiting at my cube. He nodded at me as he passed, and I dutifully followed.

"Then you need to keep trying…As long as it takes…The truth is," he drawled, "I have an eager line for this job out my door right now." He looked at me while he said this, and I wondered if he'd summoned me just to make that statement true.

"What would you do if you quit now? What do you think would happen?" There was a long pause, presumably while the caller pondered what would happen—and that it wasn't good.

"It's not *me* you should feel bad for disappointing. The old man…No, of course not." He was smiling now, reeling in whoever had gone off track.

"No, no. I understand perfectly. But you're doing fine. Just relax. Enjoy the opportunity."

After one last pause, Uncle Dan said, more kindly than before, "They never are." He hung up then, shaking his head but smiling. The outcome was satisfactory. It always was.

From the doorway, I said, "Uncle, *is* that something I could help with?"

Just my asking pleased him. His grin transformed to the wide and charming one that generally made women flutter and men irritated. "No, no. You're beyond such trifling as that."

"Well, if there's any way I can help—"

"Believe me, you have helped enough in that regard." He pecked out his computer password as he spoke, index fingers hunting for the keys. People didn't believe me when I told them he wrote all his memos, even his books, in long hand. He glanced back up at me, still smiling. "But there is something you can do for me."

THE *ZZZZHP* OF a tape measure through expert hands was an intimidating sound. I thought this as I stood on a wooden box, in my underwear, surrounded by mirrors and mahogany paneling. For a guy who did little more than glance—if that—at what he wore on a daily basis, being fitted for a custom tuxedo felt ridiculous.

Uncle's tailor was old enough to be my grandfather and looked like he'd been born wearing a suit vest. He stepped around me in a complicated waltz, taking stock of my body and my measurements with an efficiency I admired.

"You don't take any notes?"

Mr. Melawi—Sam, he liked to be called—tapped the side of his head. "Perfect recall," he said, though I knew Sam's gift was from years of practice, not Sententia genes.

"I never thought I'd be doing this," I admitted. Something about the quiet fitting room brought to mind a confessional. It was the kind of place one could speak freely and did.

He clucked. "I've been waiting for the senator to send you since you arrived here. And then I asked him to, after the press conference. That shirt you wore…" He shook his head. I shifted on the box, feeling sorry for disappointing someone I'd only just met.

"What was wrong with it?"

"Everything," he pronounced, and I resisted the temptation to laugh. Williams would probably be insulted; he'd chosen it, after all. "You're obviously an athlete—all that hard work, your body deserves clothes that fit."

"I guess I thought they did."

He clucked again. "*Now* they will." He bent to measure my legs, pausing at the point of my inseam. "And to which side do you dress? The left?"

"I'm sorry?"

He met my eyes and glanced back to where he held his tape measure. "Do you rest on the left or right? Preferably."

Jesus Christ. He meant my—My face grew hot. Maybe I *didn't* know anything about how clothes fit, if something as personal as that was a factor. Uncle Dan could have warned me about it. But then, he'd grown up in custom suits, probably made right here. Like Lex, he'd never known anything but having money.

"Um, left, yes," I squeaked out, sounding like a fucking thirteen year old. I cleared my throat. "May I ask how much this will cost?"

"It's taken care of," Sam assured me, and indeed it was. Uncle had insisted I attend the upcoming gala his charity was sponsoring, and that he buy me a *real* tuxedo to wear to it. "No need for concern."

"I understand. I'd just like to know, for future reference. In case I'd like to become a regular customer." After Sam's comments, my entire wardrobe seemed shabby.

Sam smiled to himself. "I can see why you're Daniel's favorite."

I flushed further, a reflex. My battle with doubt had not reduced my pleasure at hearing those things. "Am I?"

"Always have been. You're the most *and* least like him, I think."

"It's just that there's no competition. I'm his only nephew." I didn't go into how technically I wasn't even that.

Sam dismissed this with a wave of his hand. "He's always grooming someone to follow in his footsteps, just like his father." Which was true. Uncle's slate of interns was always full partly because he enjoyed being a mentor. Was I no different? Over an armful of wool samples that looked almost identical to me, Sam said, "To answer your question, bespoke suits are an investment. This tuxedo will last your entire life if you treat it right. With the three shirts…"

He quoted a number approximately the value of my car. I nodded, hoping my skin hadn't turned green. I'd known Uncle spent thousands even on his day suits, but hearing it out loud was still a shock. At least it wasn't over five figures.

"Amazing to see their dream finally about to happen." Sam's comment interrupted my mental calculations.

"What dream?"

"President, of course. I've been waiting to add that title to my resume of clients for a long time. Maybe I can finally retire." He chuckled, then sighed. "Sorry Jacob isn't here to see it. You can step down now, redress."

I folded my arms over my chest, curious. "This was never Uncle Dan's dream, you know."

"Oh?" Sam's tone was mild, but I could see his expression reflected in the mirrors. He looked like he was as curious about what I was going to say as I was about why he thought that.

"No," I said. "It was Mr. Astor's. Uncle used to think he was crazy. It was only after he…passed, Uncle Dan reconsidered. As a way to honor him." That's what he'd always told me.

"I see," Sam said, but it was nothing more than platitude. "I must have misunderstood. I'm sure Jacob would be proud."

"Yeah," I said, pondering what was more likely: that this man, with perfect recall and years of suiting Mr. Astor and his son, had misunderstood…or that I'd been misled.

Maybe I really didn't know anyone at all. And what had happened to my life if, of all people, *Jillian* turned out to be the one telling me the truth.

Chapter Thirty-One

Lainey

I'd missed touching. Not *that* kind—though I'd missed that too. No, the everyday kind. The kind that starts out as flirting, as *thrilling*, and then becomes comfortable. Unconscious, even. An arm around the shoulders, twined fingers, a touch on the back. The kind you do without thinking, just because you *can*.

I'd missed fun, too, and Jack was nothing if not a good sport. "Hee-ya!" I shouted as I threw him to the ground. Again.

"You don't seriously say that?" he coughed, pushing himself up to his knees on the practice mat rolled over the floor.

"Only when I'm thrashing you."

"This isn't thrashing. I'm a novice!" He coughed again and peered up at me through his messy hair. We were in my favorite private studio room that students could reserve for things like dance or, if you were me, martial arts practice. I liked how this one was covered in mirrors and I could watch Jack flounder from all angles. "And how tall are you again? I swear your legs are infinite."

"The doctor did once tell me they were longer than average." I stretched in front of him just to show them off, which was my mistake. Quicker than I expected, he threw a hand out and caught my wrist, tugging me off balance and onto the mat next to him.

"Oof! Not fair!"

Jack laughed, crawling over until he was looking down at me. "Says the girl who's thrashing me." He leaned down as if he'd pin me, or kiss me, but just as quick as he'd grabbed me, I snaked my long legs around him and rolled until he was beneath me. His eyes were wide, impressed even, and his lips spread into the dimpled smile that now I got to see whenever I wanted.

"Got you." I leaned over until my hair tickled his face and he laughed again.

"You fight *dirty*." He tugged my wrists again until I was flush against him. His arms slid around my waist and held me in place. "I like it," he said into my ear before he kissed me to show me just how much. Lips free again, he said, "Where'd you learn that move anyway? It didn't seem like karate. And can we practice it again?"

I shoved his shoulder and rolled to the side until I was lying next to him, head on his arm, and about as content as I knew how to be. I'd been teaching Jack martial arts for weeks now, and this was how we seemed to finish every session. And despite the obvious temptations, he was actually improving.

"It's not karate," I admitted. "I learned it in the self-defense class my aunt made me take. Sort of. I left out the part where I knee you in the crotch and run away."

He tickled my ribs, making me squirm. "And I thank you for that."

The beginning of the semester, that I'd expected to be so dreary, had flown by in a blur. All the loneliness I'd felt first semester, all the longing, floated away in a haze of laughter and touch and Jack Kensington. Every spare minute, I spent with him, and even some that weren't.

In my bag where I'd dropped it by the door, my phone buzzed, interrupting my ruminating. "You want to get that?" Jack asked and I shook my head. Whoever it was could wait. "Despite, you know, the bruises and the ass kicking," Jack went on, "this was fun." Then he kissed my cheek, the gentle kind, and absently brushed away a piece of my hair. I closed my eyes and wished every moment were this simple.

This. This is what I'd missed. And I had no idea just how much I missed it until I had it again. And that was why I was so afraid to lose it. Again.

Because I had secrets, mountains of damnable secrets, some that I'd never share, but some that I needed to. He needed to know who I was. I couldn't stand the feeling anymore, the secrets like acid, eating up my insides and willing themselves to be poured out.

"What's up, latecomer? You're awfully quiet over there." Despite his general playfulness, Jack was no idiot.

I took a deep breath. Could I do it? Could I tell him everything, despite what it might cost me? Regardless, I *had* to. I'd waited long enough—it was almost spring break already—and here was as good a place as any.

Finally, I said, "Can we talk for a while?"

"Uh oh." He chuckled, but he sat up, pulling me up with him. He scrubbed a hand across his eyes. "If you want me to pack my bags, please just say it quick."

"No! Of course not. We were just…" I gestured to the mats, where we'd just been tangled up together.

"Yeah, I know. It seemed like you were into it, but…" He shrugged, grinning, but then his face turned the color of fire-place ashes and he grabbed my hand, squeezing a bit too hard. "Are you pregnant?"

I shook my head. "No," I said softly. "It's nothing like that."

Jack flopped back on the mat. "Oh, thank God. I mean, if you were, we'd figure it out, together. I'm not the kind of guy who—and you—and I'd probably be a hero—and—" He shook his head and dragged a hand through his hair. My heart thumped, once, hard. It was a gesture so reminiscent of Carter I had to look away. "I'm just glad that's not—wait." He sat up again. "Are you okay? You're not, are you sick?"

I looked back at him. His hand drifted toward his hair again and I trapped his fingers with my own. "No, I'm fine. Really. But there are some things I need to tell you."

Jack squeezed my fingers. "Tell them. I'm here. I'm not going anywhere."

"It's just that you don't know who I really am."

"I doubt that." He gazed at me with those deep brown eyes and I was so afraid that when I told him, they wouldn't look at me the same anymore.

"No, really. I…I haven't been totally honest with you." I pulled my hands out of his and crossed them over my stomach. "Well, I haven't been *dis*honest. But here's the thing: I'm not just a Thought Mover."

His dimple flashed along with my favorite half-smile. "*Just* a Thought Mover? I've never heard anyone treat it so lightly."

"I mean that I'm more. Oh, let me just tell the story from the beginning." So I did, explaining how I got to Northbrook and the terrible vision of Ashley Thayer that started it all.

Jack's eyebrows drew together. "So you're a Grim Diviner, not a Thought Mover?"

"No. I'm both. I'm dual-gifted. But it's more than that. I say I'm a Thought Mover, but really, I'm the *last* of my kind. Or so they tell me."

Jack's eyes stayed with me, thoughtful. "What kind would that be?"

"I'm the last Marwood, Jack. That's who I am." I took a breath, ready to tell the rest of the story. "If you don't know the name—"

"I know the name." He reached for my hands, stilling their wringing. "We've all heard the great Sententia mystery." He looked away, toward our reflections in the mirrors. "It's not common knowledge it's been *solved* though."

I shook my head. "I don't know who knows now, but I don't tell people."

"I'll take that as a compliment."

It was. Oh, how it was. And I'd told him and he didn't run. Words fell from my lips without my planning. "You're still touching me."

"What?" He leaned closer, turning his head to hear me.

"You're still touching me," I repeated, louder. Part of me couldn't believe it. He knew what I could do, and he'd reached *for* me. Willingly.

His head snapped back around, eyes meeting mine. "You thought I wouldn't?" I opened my mouth, closed it, and shrugged instead. Gently, he turned my hands over, setting them in his lap. "You thought I'd be afraid of you? Of these?" He placed his palms flat to mine. His fingers grazed the skin at the inside of my wrist and warmth flashed through me.

"I'd understand if you were. If you wanted to…" I looked toward the door and shrugged again.

Jack tapped that spot on my wrist lightly and my eyes came back to his. "All I want to do right now is kiss the last Hangman. If she'll let me."

I wanted to pinch myself, to make sure I wasn't dreaming. That had been almost too easy. *Carter hadn't pulled away either*, my traitor brain snuck into my head. But that was different. He'd known I was a mystery even before I did. He'd held my hand through death visions and caught me when I'd blacked out from them. He'd shielded me from Dr. Stewart and hugged me when I cried. When we finally discovered my heritage, Carter had already loved me.

But this wasn't his moment. It was Jack's. This, between us, it was too new for the L-word. I didn't know what all he felt for me, or might someday, but he'd proved it *wasn't* fear. He didn't deserve to share this moment with a memory. And speaking of memories...I shook my head.

"There's more."

Jack chuckled. "More than *that?*"

"Yeah."

"Okay." He paused. "Are you supposed to kill me?"

"*What?* No!" I could feel the color drain from my face. I shoved him and he toppled back onto his elbows. "Be serious for five minutes."

"I was. And I'm still listening."

I took a deep breath, and then another, calming myself. "You know what I can do?"

"Sure." He shrugged. "Every Sententia kid knows. Hang—excuse me, *Carnifex* have the death touch."

I nodded, watching him as I explained. "I do. But it's not just, well, living things. I can kill memories too, kind of like Thought Moving in reverse."

"Really?"

"Yeah. It's pretty scary."

"That's what makes this such a rush."

"What?"

He cleared his throat and sat up. "You, I mean. You *are* dangerous. So do it. Show me." He held out his wrist, almost the same way Amy had nearly a year ago, and I laughed.

"You won't remember anyway."

"But I'll *know* I don't remember, right? How much can you erase?"

"Just immediate. It's a…delicate balance."

"I should think so. So do it. Make me forget. Then I can wonder what I'm missing."

At this point, what the hell? Maybe nothing I said or did was as shocking as I thought it was. "Okay." I pushed up onto my knees, so I was looking down at him, and grabbed his hand. His palm was warm and smooth where my fingers rested against it. I leaned over, eyes locked with his, and whispered in his ear. He was smiling when I kissed him.

And then I made him forget.

I was still looking at him as his eyebrows drew together and his free hand came up to touch his forehead. Then his grin returned and he pulled me down on top of him.

"That was *amazing*! I saw your eyes. I remember *that*, I know you did it, but…so what did I miss?"

"You'll never know."

"Was it this?" And then he was kissing me, nothing like the one I'd given him and erased, but deep and long and something I did *not* want to forget.

Something about that kiss, the realness of it, the honesty, made me feel boneless and free. As free as I'd felt when I thought I'd left Sententia behind. Jack *knew me*, the *whole me*, even the part I thought I'd have to keep secret forever. He knew everything I could do, and I didn't have to hide it from him. I was free to be myself. I was free. *This* was freedom.

Chapter Thirty-Two

Carter

T he phone was ringing when I stepped out of the shower. Only four people called me with regularity, and it was way too early to be Alexis. That meant family. Towel in hand, I snatched the phone off the counter before it could stop.

"Hello?" I swiped at my face, blinking in surprise at the caller. Uncle Dan. I hadn't expected to hear from him until later. The gala was tonight.

"Ah, Son. Good, you're there. You've already run?" He sounded in good spirits.

"I just got back."

"Perfect. Manny and I will be outside in twenty minutes."

I blinked at the phone again. "Why? Is everything all right?"

"Quite. I know it's your day off but I...need your help with something."

The magic words. Uncle Dan knew I'd never say no to him, but even his dullest tasks seemed more interesting when he said he needed help. "What is it?"

He chuckled. "Let's just say it's a field in which you have far more expertise than I. And I'm afraid I'm dreadfully out of practice."

FROM THE OUTSIDE, the Secret Service's Rowley Training Center looked like a National Park. In a way, it was—acres of trees and trails disguised an enormous, deadly amusement park of law enforcement. Manny took us on a tour before our appointment at the most exclusive shooting range of them all.

As I watched agents and trainees run, climb, shoot and other things I was sworn not to talk about, I thought this was a job I would probably be very good at. I'd never really considered any other job but the one I was born with.

In the mirror, Manny caught my eye. He was so quiet, and such a common fixture, I often forgot he was there, even when he was piloting the car. "Want to sign up?"

I felt my cheeks warm and felt even more embarrassed because of it. Next to me, Uncle chuckled. "And you haven't even seen him shoot yet."

Manny's eyebrows went up. "Oh?" I grinned at him and his interest piqued. "All right. Loser buys the drinks, Mr. Penrose."

"I like the Lagavulin," I said, and he laughed.

"Yes, you do. All right," he repeated. "You're on."

I flipped my sunglasses down and looked back out the window, trying to hide my smile. Uncle didn't try at all. "Well, gentlemen. I'm looking forward to this."

They'd arranged some dozen firearms for this unexpected field trip, most I'd never handled before. It was strange, seeing a row of weapons laid out like presents on a table. Stranger still, it was broad daylight. Despite being still technically winter, it was a nice day, almost sixty degrees. We were able to shoot outside.

I walked up and down the row, awed at the selection. Our choices included semi- and automatic handguns and rifles in a range of sizes, and—

"Is that an Uzi?!" I never expected to see them anywhere other than TV, let alone *shoot* one. I was reluctant to touch it.

Manny laughed as he inspected the submachine gun. "Technically, no. It's an MP5." He set it back down. "But let's start a little smaller, work our way up."

Shooting wasn't a skill I ever expected to apply to the real world; it was just something I enjoyed. Like running, it helped that I was good at it. After a few rounds, I found my rhythm. I felt good, relaxed even. That nagging asshole, Doubt, actually shut the fuck up for a while. Until I set the safety and took off my ear guards, I didn't even realize I had an audience.

"Fucking A, kid!" Someone clapped me on the back, and I turned to find Manny's partner, John, had joined us. He wasn't the only other agent on Uncle Dan's detail, but the only one I saw with regularity.

Over his shoulder, Uncle Dan was smiling like a proud father, and Manny looked impressed and kind of pissed. "Beginner's luck," he muttered, and Uncle Dan laughed out loud.

"Can you do that again?" John asked.

"Sure." There was a satisfying *click* as I popped in another clip.

"And move the target back," Uncle Dan suggested.

You know what? It felt good to show off. John was already laughing by the time I finished the next round. "More like tough luck, Manny. Kid's sure as hell not a beginner."

Manny was too good natured to hold a grudge. Smiling, he said, "You're a better shot than I am. Maybe the whole team."

And it was true. I scanned his targets. He was excellent, but I was better. Even without my particular talents. Though I *could* use Thought Moving to my advantage, it was basically useless today because I hadn't loaded the clips myself. I could pull any of the triggers from, well, anywhere, now that I'd seen the guns. To really enhance my aim, I had to have seen the bullets.

"I'll thank you, Manuel," Uncle Dan said idly, "not to be recruiting my nephew." He shouldered a rifle, testing the sights. I could tell he was enjoying this. "Ignoring that *I* need him, my mother and sister-in-law would likely attempt to kill me if you succeeded, and wouldn't that make your job difficult?"

"Yes, Senator." Manny tipped his chin in deference and we all laughed. "If anyone's going to try to kill you, we prefer strangers."

We secured our ear guards once more and everyone took turns, including John. He wielded the machine gun better than anyone. When my turn came, he showed me how to use it.

"This," he explained, flipping a switch, "is your selector. Single shot, burst, or auto. Not all SMPs can do single shot. Try it on burst."

He turned it over to me. The metal was warm. It felt like danger in solid form. "Will you carry one of these tonight?"

He winked. "I'll carry this one. Make it lucky."

RAT TAT TAT. The gun leaped in my grip, and I barely hit the target. Adrenaline rushed through my system and my heart pounded. Fright blended with a sort of perverse thrill. How simple it was to spray round after round of death. Just a few pounds of pull.

Behind me, Manny hooted. "Looks like we've found one you're not so good at!"

I took a deep breath and fired again. Better. Again again again. Perfect. I felt like I'd tamed some kind of animal, a fierce and desperate one. My arms shook by the time we were done and I thought they might actually be sore tomorrow. I hoped they would. I was having fun, happy again without effort for the first time since New Year's. I suspected Uncle Dan had done this for me, and I couldn't say I minded.

"Thank you," I told him in the car on the way back. Manny and John were in front, conferring with the divider up, leaving Uncle and me in relative privacy.

He glanced at me from the papers he was reviewing. "That was enjoyable, wasn't it? Just what we needed."

"I just hope we never have to see them put their skills to use."

"If we ever do, you know they're more than capable," he assured me. "I had Manuel and John begin planning that since…well, your birthday, we'll call it." The night at the bar, he meant. It felt like years ago, even thought it was only a few weeks.

"About that. I'm sor—"

He held up a hand. "No need, son. I know this has been hard for you. And she hasn't made it easier. I think she'll not bother you any more, though."

His words were like a rubber band snapping in my chest. I gaped at him, though I wished I hadn't. "Why?"

"I spoke with her, of course." Of course. He'd seen Lainey over the holiday. In fact, he'd seen her with greater frequency than I had since graduation. "She recognizes her selfishness now," he continued before I could respond. "And besides." He waved his hand. "I understand she's found other amusements."

I swallowed. Amy had mentioned there was another guy. "Did you—" I halted. Doubting my uncle was foreign ground. I had no idea how to question him. "Did the two of you have a disagreement?"

Uncle looked at me for a moment before putting his papers back into his bag. "We've had a disagreement since she so wantonly cast you aside."

"Before that," I pressed. "Before graduation."

"Before graduation and she showed her true colors," he said slowly, "I was welcoming her into our family with open arms. Why do you ask?"

The image of them together on the graduation stage blazed behind my eyes. I tried to shake it away, but couldn't. Something had happened, beyond the phantom bullet hole, something I didn't understand.

But I understood this: my uncle was lying. Now I had to find out why.

Chapter Thirty-Three

Lainey

L ater on, I finally checked my phone. Two calls from Amy, crap. I vaguely recalled saying maybe to doing something tonight. I glanced at Jack next to me, still rumpled and cute from our sparring session, and knew I wasn't going anywhere else. I'd call her later.

The third call was from my aunt, and I returned it. "Hi, sweetie!" she answered, sounding buoyant and vaguely echo-y. In the background, I thought I heard someone say, "Still a while longer, sir."

"Auntie? Where are you? You sound like you're underwater."

"Just in a limo on the way to pick up, um, I mean to an event, honey. Stuck in traffic! Where are you?"

"Same," I laughed, "though I'm just in a taxi and on my way to Jack's."

"Spending a lot of time there, hmmm?" I could practically hear her smiling over the phone.

"A limo, huh?" I said, ignoring her question. I wondered just how often she traveled by limo these days.

"A nice one, too. You'd love it. Actually, you'd love tonight's event." Another phone rang on her end, muted conversation competing with my aunt's voice. "The annual ball for the Metropolitan Ballet. Astor Arts is a principle sponsor. And you should see my dress! It's designer. Pregnancy haute couture."

The same man's voice as before said, "Additional security is in place, sir."

"It sounds awesome, Auntie—wait. Did someone just say something about additional security?"

She hesitated a second, as if she didn't want to tell me, or maybe she didn't know. "I'm sure it's standard for big events," she finally said. "Nothing to worry about. Anyway, I just wanted to say hi before things got busy. I wish you were here with us."

"Maybe next year," I lied.

She sighed, and I knew she didn't believe me. "I love you, sweetie. I'll call you tomorrow and tell you all about it. I can't wait to see you over break." The murmur of Senator Astor's voice snaked over the line, and my aunt said, "Oh, wait. Dan says hi and also that he'd like to speak with Jack, if that's okay?"

The taxi suddenly felt too small and very, very hot. The deep feeling of ease I'd been carrying since the studio flew straight out the window and drowned in the nearby harbor. Wordlessly, I held the phone out to Jack.

He looked at it, confused, but took it without question or complaint. "Hello? Oh," he said, softly, clearing his throat. "Sir, yes, good to speak to you too…Yes, I know; I'm still not sure about the timing…Of course. I'll talk to you soon."

He said good night and ended the call just as the taxi pulled up to his building. I held my tongue all the way up to his apartment. For some reason I couldn't ask questions whose answers I feared in a stairwell. As soon as we were through the door, I blurted, "What was that about?" My voice sounded thin and high to me.

Jack dropped his bag, flicked through his mail, and rooted around for take-out menus, seemingly oblivious to my angst. "When we met in October, you know, when we had drinks so you could talk with your aunt? The senator talked to me about the Perceptum Council internship. The position is…available. Okay," he said, holding up three papers like a fan, "sushi, sushi, or—why do you look so freaked out?"

I opened my mouth to answer and then snapped it shut. I'd told so many secrets today it was easy to forget about all the ones I couldn't. What could I actually say that would make sense? "It's just, you know, the Council." I waved my hand like this should be obvious. "And he's—Senator Astor—he's my…ex's uncle. It's weird, is all. For me. It's just…weird. I tried to tell you before."

Jack plopped down onto the couch next to me and pulled the piece of hair I'd been playing with out of my hand. "Okay. Well, now it's weird for me too."

"It is?"

He nodded solemnly. "I've seen this nephew of his and if what I once overheard the girls in my discussion groups saying about him is true, I leave a lot to desire in comparison."

Oh, the wonderful restorative properties of laughter. It bubbled up and over without my permission. "You know they talk the same way about you when you're not around, right?"

"Do they now?" His crooked smile slid into place and he leaned closer. "Did you?"

"Absolutely."

"*Good.*" His lips were so close I could feel the puff of the word against mine, but he didn't kiss me. He leaned back, and I let out a sigh of air. "Now," he said, grinning like the devil, "sushi?"

After dinner, we relaxed on the couch, listening to music, while I read a book and Jack graded papers. My head rested in his lap and he played, absently, with my hair. "Can I ask you something?" he said.

"Sure."

"Why are you so afraid of the Perceptum?" My fingers froze on the pages, and I lowered the book to my chest before I dropped it. "See," he said. "You tense up every time I mention it."

"They want me to kill people," I said, giving my answer as much truth as I possibly could. "That's enough to make anyone tense. And now they want you to work for them, too."

"Don't you believe in their mission?"

Did I? I didn't know. But for sure I didn't believe in their leader. "I don't believe in my part in it."

"Do you think there's another way?"

"I don't know," I admitted.

"We could do it," he said softly. "Together. I could help you." I didn't know what to say, so I said nothing. I didn't know what to feel either. It was either the sweetest or most terrifying thing anyone had ever said to me. "Okay," he said. "I guess…just think about it."

I threw a hand up over my eyes. I didn't want to tell him how, since talking with Jill, I'd *been* thinking about it. "Will you leave?" I whispered. Would Daniel Astor take Jack from me too?

Jack pulled the hand away and looked down at me. "I'm not going anywhere."

"Oh," I said, and he kissed my nose.

"You're not getting rid of me yet."

I smiled up at him and he kissed my hand before setting it back over my eyes. With a chuckle, I picked up my book, but the words wouldn't come into focus. My brain was in a million places: with Senator Astor in the shooting range, staring down a gun; at my aunt's apartment with Jill, and her sweet voice saying *who'll protect them?*; with

Jack, in the studio, and the way he'd accepted me. Thinking about our afternoon reminded me of something.

"Can I ask *you* something?" I said, and his eyes flicked down to meet mine.

"Do you want to show me what you erased from my memory again?"

I bumped his stomach with my head. "What did you mean you'd probably be a hero?"

"What?"

"If I was pregnant, you said—"

"Oh." This flash of—*something* flew across his face. Guilt? No, of course not. He shook his head and smiled. "Nothing. I just—my mom would probably throw a party. My grandfather too, if it was a boy."

"You're only twenty-three!" Not to mention how not-old *I* was. My *aunt* was about to have a baby.

"When it comes to bearing grandchildren, the earlier and more often the better. When they know *you*, they'd be even more excited about it."

"Even when they know you're dating the grim reaper?" I said, flushing red.

Jack touched my neck, his fingers a cool flash against the heat that had bloomed there. "Even then." He scooped me upright so he could kiss the spot he'd just touched. I shivered. "You said I didn't really know you, but I *do*. I know the person you are here." Feather light fingers touched approximately the spot where my heart was, then moved to my temple. "And here, and she's *incredible*. I don't deserve her. You're special, Lainey," he finished, his lips just brushing my ear. "And it has *nothing* to do with your gifts. Don't forget that."

He kissed me then, slow and deliberate, the kind of kiss that made me forget about anything besides the feel of his lips, his tongue, his hands slipping beneath the hem of my shirt, cool then warm against the sensitive skin at my waist. His skin on mine was almost as effective as my memory erasing. Before long, I forgot how my clothes, and his clothes, ended up on the floor and all I did was feel.

LATER, I HEARD my phone buzzing from the depths of my bag. Again. I'd heard it a few times before but ignored it all. Guilt got the better of me, and I got up to fish it out. Holy shit! *Twenty* missed calls? It started buzzing again while I stared at it stupidly. Amy.

"Something up?" Jack asked, an unusual touch of concern in his voice, and I answered the call.

"Hello?"

"Jesus Christ, Lainey!" Amy shouted. "Where the hell have you *been*? Are you on your way there?!"

"Where?" I asked. I didn't understand the hysteria in Amy's voice. "I'm at Jack's. Sorry I didn't—"

"Jesus Christ!" she repeated. "Do you even *know*?" She plowed right through anything I might have said. "You don't want to take my calls anymore, fine. But turn on the fucking TV!" And then she hung up.

Jack was standing now as I stared at my phone again, a feeling like frigid fingers tickling down my spine. "What's going on? Was she shouting?"

"I—I don't know." My voice sounded far away to my ears. Most of the missed calls were from Amy, and some from numbers I didn't know. "She said to turn on the TV."

"Okay," Jack said, perplexed but accommodating. He clicked on a news channel and had just enough time to catch me when I started to scream.

Chapter Thirty-Four

Carter

Lights, camera, action. Finally. So far attending the ballet gala had felt exactly like Northbrook's Winter Ball, right down to my waiting around in a tuxedo, reading a book and trying not to get wrinkly. Alexis had insisted we get picked up at her dorm, because she had classes and it was closer to her salon, she'd claimed, but I knew it was so everyone could see us.

The sleek, black limo pulled to the curb, looking imposing and very, very expensive. Just like Uncle Dan, who stepped out to hold the door himself.

"Alexis, my dear, you're an absolute vision," he said, kissing her cheek before handing her into the car. He inspected me, too, brushing non-existent lint off my shoulders.

"Well?" Maybe I was an asshole, but I knew I looked good.

"Sam does fine work," he replied, grinning. He clapped a hand on my back. "Remember to stay close to us tonight, all right? Save Manny some stress." He'd said the same thing to me this afternoon, when they'd dropped me off. While I endured a final fitting, Uncle Dan had gone with Manny and John to meet with the private security covering the event.

"We'll be right behind you," I promised and ducked into the limo.

"Oh," Tessa gasped. "Oh, my." She put a knuckle to her lips and I prayed she wouldn't cry. "You look—both of you. Just beautiful. Alexis, that *dress.*"

Lex leaned forward to kiss her cheek. The amazing thing about Tessa was how she never even flinched. "Thank you!" She wore this dress of tulle and satin that hugged her like a cocoon. It was a strange and magnificent combination of green and gold that sounded fancier when she called it *oro verde*. "Do you like it? It's vintage," she added.

At that, finally, Tess's mask cracked. A look like accidentally swallowing a too-large piece of ice flashed across her face. She should rightfully have hated Alexis, and I wondered if Lainey had never told her the things that happened. But then, if not for Lainey, *Alexis* wouldn't be the one wearing a vintage dress and getting into this limo with me. So maybe Tess understood.

"It was made for you." Tessa's smooth smile slid back into place. All her time with Uncle was paying off. "And *you.*" She turned to me, eyes alight with the genuine affection that forever made my heart ache.

"This *was* made for me," I said, running a finger over the smooth lapel, and she laughed.

"I was going to say *you* were made for formal wear. I'm so glad you're with us tonight." She tried to reach forward to squeeze my hand, but fell back with an *oof.* She patted her rapidly growing bump. "Between baby and this dress, I can't be doing that!"

"Relax while you still have the chance," Uncle Dan said. I wasn't sure if he meant before we got there, or before the baby came.

"I feel like I've been in this car forever!" Tessa fanned her face as we herked and jerked toward the event. If only Uncle Dan were president already, we'd have had a police escort to speed up the trip.

"Funny how quickly you forget the awful things about home—like the traffic—when you move away for a few years."

"How long is it now?" Alexis asked. She sipped the champagne she'd found chilling next to her seat, another thing just like the Winter Ball. Except her glass was real crystal and the vintage was fine. "Until the baby, I mean."

Tessa smoothed her hand over her bump again. "Oh, about 56 days, but who's counting, right?" We all laughed. "So around eight weeks," she said, "give or take. The home stretch. My doctor thinks I might go a little early."

"Is that bad?" Alexis asked.

"Not as far as I'm concerned!" Tessa said. "I look forward to being able to eat again. Anything I manage to keep down goes straight to the little guy." She was joking, but she *did* look thin. Her arms were skinnier than I remembered them. Pregnant women were supposed to *gain* weight, I thought.

Before I could ask a probably stupid question, the divider slid down and John's voice drifted through. "All right, folks. Rolling up to the show at last. One more turn and it's go time."

Spotlights drifted back and forth across the darkening sky, a sure indication we were finally close. Idling limos crammed the side streets, their drivers clustered in groups, enjoying the warm night. And then we turned the corner and the limo slid to a halt. Manny opened our door with a flourish.

"About time," I heard him quip as my uncle led Tessa into the melee.

Stepping out of the limo was the closest I'd ever felt to a celebrity. I'd been on TV, was occasionally recognized in public, but that was nothing. Dozens of spotlights glanced off the imposing white stone building hosting this year's jazz-themed event, creating peek-a-boo shadows with the thick columns that lined the front. Cameras popped and flashed. Voices shouted, sometimes even my name.

The red carpet, plusher than I expected, was dotted with men in black and women in the entire spectrum of colors, looking disconcertingly like pretty flowers floating up a river of blood. Jazz musicians drifted through the crowd, chased by dancers in costume, doing ballet versions of Foxtrots or Charlestons, or some other dances I had no idea the names of. I turned and extended my hand to help Lex out of the limo. It felt gentlemanly, and looked good for those watching.

The atmosphere was unbelievable, the kind of thing Lex was born to attend but usually made me feel like a fraud. But not tonight. I looked the part, and I *felt* it. Maybe Sam was right, and the clothes made the man. Maybe I was still riding the adrenaline of the shooting range. Hell, maybe I was just hungry and had become delusional. Whatever it was, it felt good. Like good things could happen. I breathed it in and let it carry me forward.

Up ahead, Uncle had one hand free for shaking and one on Tessa's waist, guiding her along as she smiled and waved. She stood out, in a dress red as a raspberry that hugged her pregnant belly, like a cupcake or a Christmas present. I made sure to stay only a few feet away, as promised. Martin was here too, just in front of them, his smile as bright as the spotlights.

Uncle Dan caught my eye and inclined his chin as if to say *I told you you'd enjoy this.* I nodded back, because he was right. I was. I put my arm around Alexis's shoulder and stopped, taking it all in. I truly couldn't believe I was here.

And then I blinked and it all changed.

RAT TAT TAT.

For one moment, silence fell on the crowd like a blanket smothering flames. It could almost have been applause, or part of the music. But I knew the sound of a gun.

I'd fired one just like it that afternoon.

RAT TAT TAT RAT TAT TAT

Shots echoed over the ground.

I blinked again and the entire world erupted into screaming. Instinctively, I dove on top of Alexis. Beneath me, she screamed, adding her voice to the other screams filling the night. Feet pounded in every direction, shaking the ground.

"*STAY DOWN!*" John shouted as he sprinted past us. The lucky MP5 was already in his hands.

"It's okay," I could hear myself repeating to Lex, which was ridiculous, because we could be dead at any moment. My body screamed at me to *do something*, but I couldn't leave her.

I raised my head until I could see Uncle Dan and Tessa buried under someone's broad shoulders. The edge of Tessa's red dress peeked from the bottom of the pile and flapped in the breeze of rushing feet. Just past them was Martin, his face contorted in pain. *Oh, God.*

Manny stood over them, waving his hands toward the side of the building. It was yards away, but I could just make out someone holding up a machine gun, ready to shoot again or—

BANG BANG BangBang BangBangBang

Guns fired, closer now, and I hugged Alexis as tight as I could, praying her screams wouldn't be the last thing I ever heard.

And then it was done. The noise changed, the running feet shifted directions. Tangles of limbs and chiffon unfurled into people. A few seconds from the first shots until now. That was it.

"*GO, GO!*" Manny was shouting. "*LIMO, NOW!*"

I hauled Alexis to her feet but I couldn't move, not until I saw that my uncle was okay. John and the other agent were pulling him up, practically carrying him off Tessa and back the way we'd come. Someone was helping Martin stand, thank God. One arm was clutched to his to his chest.

People with cameras and professionally concerned voices pressed around us. Alexis tugged me toward the cars screaming back up to the curb.

"Carter, c'mon! *Please!*" she pleaded.

But I still couldn't move.

Because Tessa was still on the ground. She was screaming. Screaming and screaming, a sinister stain darkening the bright red of her dress and pooling around her.

I was wrong. The carpet wasn't the color of blood at all.

"*TESSA! NO!*" my uncle screamed even as John lifted all six foot five inches of him off the ground and dragged him toward the limo. "*NO!*" My uncle was still screaming. "This can't have happened, this wasn't meant to hap—"

The car door slammed and tires peeled away, louder even than the gunfire. Tessa's cry rose over the noise and I sprinted to her, shoving through the growing crowd of people.

"*TESSA!*" I landed hard on my knees next to her.

She looked at me, face the color of a chalk outline and arms clutched to her abdomen. Her breaths were quick rasps.

"The baby," she gasped out. "Carter, *the baby!*"

And then she screamed again, gripped by another contraction.

Chapter Thirty-Five

Lainey

llen Jacob Fernando Astor Espinosa had a name longer than he was and would never have the chance to grow into it. He was buried on a day so clear and beautiful it was painful even to open your eyes.

I stood apart from the others in the cemetery, alone, or almost. My parents' grave stood before me, looking more cheerful than it had any right to in the bright sun. Fresh flowers surrounded the heavy stone, complementing the soft rose color of the marble. My mother had been so bright and beautiful, Aunt Tessa had once told me, she couldn't stand the idea of her spending the rest of forever under a drab gray piece of rock. So pink it was. My brother's stone would be white.

Even with my dark sunglasses, I had to shade my eyes with my hand so I could read their names. Allen, my brother's namesake, was on the left. My mother was on the right. I wanted to kneel down, to trace the letters, to be closer to them, but I knew if I did that, I wouldn't have the energy to get back up. And it wouldn't matter anyway. They weren't really here, except for their bones and their memory.

"Take care of him, mom," I whispered, knowing wherever they were, she would. She already was. I'd never spent much time thinking about the afterlife. Before today, I wasn't sure I even believed in one. But now? How could I not. There had to be *something* more for my brother than a few measly hours.

I kissed my fingertips and pressed them to the cold top of my parents' stone before I turned back toward the others, arranged in a loose line before the too-small hole in the ground. Family only had been invited. My grandparents, Uncle Tommy, and Uncle Martin on our side. Abuela wept openly, as she had nearly every moment since she'd arrived. I wondered if she'd ever stop.

My aunt was in the middle, looking absurdly small in her black wool coat without her pregnant belly rounding the front or joy rounding her cheeks. Her skin was the color of wheat flower and her usually proud shoulders sagged under the burden of burying her baby. Why the hell didn't we have chairs? Aunt Tessa had just had an emergency cesarean, had just lost her *child*. She shouldn't be forced to stand through this. Despite that Dan was by her side, his hand on her back, she seemed alone in the world. We looked like piano keys that had gotten all mixed up, the tall and pale ones standing straight on one side, and the smaller, dark, passionate notes leaning against each other on the left.

Next to her son, Evelyn Revell stood stoically, but I could see how tightly her fingers gripped her handkerchief. Jillian's arm was looped through her grandmother's. Jeff Revell stood to her right, as straight and tall as ever, and then, on the end, was Carter. My eyes skimmed over his broad shoulders, stiff with tension, and glanced off his hair, glinting in the sun. I avoided looking at him directly, even from the back, because it just hurt too much.

Grief and rage performed a brutal dance in my chest, trampling the spaces around my heart that had just been starting to mend. The unfairness washed over me in waves, and I wondered if I ever had the chance to confront the person who did this, could I kill him? Would I? Except I'd never really know the answer, because he was already dead. The part of me that wanted to *do* something, anything, seethed at this.

The rest of me wondered if *I* was to blame. *I'd* been meant to die; I'd seen it myself. Was *this* my payment for thwarting fate? I didn't really know how it worked, fate. Maybe it didn't appreciate my meddling. Or maybe death simply required an even exchange. Had I traded *my* life for my brother's? If that was true, would Aunt Tessa ever forgive me? Could I ever forgive myself?

My aunt turned her head in my direction, almost as if my thoughts had drawn her attention. Over her shoulder, the priest looked at me too, and I knew it was past time to begin. I started the walk back to join them, slower than I should have. An acre of flower arrangements surrounded our gathering, all white and pastel, like we were at a baby shower gone far awry. I wavered, wanting to go to my aunt, to offer her comfort, but not knowing how. I took the spot on the end, next to Uncle Tommy, instead. As soon as I stepped into line, the priest began the ceremony. He said things, about death and life and resurrection, but I didn't really hear them. I couldn't stop looking at my brother.

It didn't seem possible for a coffin to be so small. It looked like a macabre toy, a salesman's portable demo. How could this fancy little box be the place where my brother would spend eternity? He hadn't even lived.

And then it was over and the little toy box was lowered into the ground, showered with dirt and flowers from our own hands. My brother was buried and we were all still here. We were supposed to go to lunch because even though the worst thing in the world had just happened, we still had to do things like eat.

Everyone was hugging and crying again before we left. My grandparents hugged me, and Uncle Martin, Evelyn, Uncle Tommy, everyone. Did they all say things to me? I wasn't sure. I wasn't sure if I hugged any of them back. All I knew was I couldn't move.

If I moved this would be real.

"Lainey." His voice was so soft. I blinked.

What was wrong with me that I thought about how good he looked? Even with red eyes and somberness sitting on him heavier than his long wool coat. The coat was unbuttoned, despite the cold, and his gray shirt competed with the bright blue of the sky to make his eyes look like a stormy Caribbean Sea. Cut short like it was, Carter's hair looked darker, like burnt caramel, but the bright sunshine lit up the golden bits.

He'd been there the whole time, only a few people away, but it might as well have been miles. We were so far apart now. But then here he was, right in front of me, and it was like something snapped with a twang in my chest.

"Carter—" I started, but even I didn't know what else I meant to say. The tears I'd held in so tightly burst from my eyes and I crumpled into his arms.

Chapter Thirty-Six

Carter

There was no funeral. Tessa, bless her, had refused anything but the committal ceremony where we all now stood. I fucking hated funerals. When you've been attending them literally since your birth that tended to happen. I felt like I'd spent half my lifetime saying goodbye, putting people I loved in the ground.

Today, it was my Godson.

People sometimes said *you can't miss what you never had*, but that was a lie. I was about to watch them bury the boy who was the closest I'd ever come to having a brother and I already missed him. I missed the chance to hold him, watch him grow, teach him to play soccer and ice skate. I missed that he was something Lainey and I would have shared, when otherwise it felt like the entire world was between us.

I could feel her behind us now, watching from the nearby grave that was surrounded in almost as many flowers as this one. I assumed it was her parents'. After we'd unloaded from the limos, she'd marched straight past the open grave to that one, like she had an appointment.

She hadn't met my eyes once yet, and I wondered if she would. And if she did, what it would feel like.

That's how I felt about Uncle Dan too. I darted glances at him, trying to decipher what he was thinking, feeling, wanting. What he needed, and if I could provide it. I couldn't shake the desire to please him, just like I couldn't shake the doubt still plaguing me, not that he deserved it today.

The priest cleared his throat and looked at Tessa. She glanced behind us, saying nothing, and the priest followed her gaze. I resisted the urge to do the same. As Lainey's footsteps drew near, Uncle Jeff's attention snapped to a space between us and the police perimeter.

"What is it?" I whispered.

"A person," he said. "The angel mausoleum. Don't look."

Bastard. "Should we do something?"

"I will." His voice was colder than I'd ever heard it, and it reminded me that he was a soldier. Dangerous if he wanted to be. Whoever was intruding on our tragedy was a fool.

Lainey finally rejoined the end of the line, and the priest started his bullshit. They all said the same things, and none of it made any difference. The dead were still dead and we were still here, living. If we saw them again, met them in the afterlife or joined them in spirit or whatever the hell, we'd be dead, too. That was supposed to be a comfort? If death was so great, why was suicide a sin?

Ashes to ashes, dust to dust. I was the last in the line to pay respects. I took only a handful of earth, tossing it onto the tiny coffin and feeling guilty. I scrubbed my eyes with the heel of my hand. *I'm sorry*, I thought. What else was there? A hand fell on my shoulder, and I turned to find Uncle Jeff.

"It's over, Carter," was all he said. I wondered how long I'd been standing there. All around us were tears and hugging, the sound of sobs and murmured assurances. I joined the melee, touching everyone, even Jillian. Somewhere in the distance bagpipes played.

Uncle Dan looked less in control than I'd ever seen him. "I'm sorry, Uncle," I said for a countless time. It was so inadequate.

"Carter." He looked at me with eyes that were haunted and distant. If he hadn't said my name, I'd have wondered if he saw me at all. He gripped my shoulders tightly before pulling me to him. "I need you more than ever now," he said, before he released me and was gone.

Tessa was the hardest. She felt weightless in my arms but hugged more fiercely than anyone. I didn't understand how she was still standing, let alone hugging me in a way that seemed more like giving comfort than receiving it. She said nothing—I wasn't sure she'd spoken the entire time—but she patted my cheek and stepped away, turning to take Uncle Dan's side and start the trudge back to the limos.

And then all that was left was Lainey. She was there, off to the side, in body at least. She hugged and was hugged, but it was all reflex. A light wind gusted, blowing her hair across her face, but she didn't move to brush it away. One hand wiped absently against her thigh and her eyes never strayed from the small hole in the ground.

I stepped next to her, wanting to touch her but knowing I shouldn't. "Lainey."

Slowly, her eyes came back into focus, and she looked at me, really *looked* at me. I'd wanted to know what it would feel like, and it felt like this: heartbreak. But I knew right then that everything was forgiven, too. All of it. I might never understand, but I no longer needed to.

"Carter—" she said. Her mouth opened and closed like there was something more, but instead of words, all that came out was tears. She fell into my arms and I didn't let go.

She shook, quaked like an earthquake, sobbing so hard I was the only thing that kept her upright. It had hurt seeing her in pain and not being able to comfort her. It hurt more holding her now and still knowing there was nothing I could do. Nothing would change this. It wasn't even me who should be holding her, but I wanted to. And there was no one else here.

"I'm sorry," I said into Lainey's ear. I said it over and over while she cried onto my chest.

Automatically, I ran my hand down her hair, just like old times. It was soft like I remembered, but cut differently. There were shorter pieces—layers—and little streaks of a color like honey at the ends. When she didn't protest, I did it again. I kept it up the whole time. I'd have held her until the next day, or forever, however long it took. Eventually her breathing slowed and the shaking subsided into tremors. They vibrated from her body to mine.

Abruptly, she pulled back. "I'm sorry—Ow," she said as her hair caught in the exposed cuff of my shirt. A clump of strands dangled from it, wrapped around the button. I stuffed my hand in my pocket. I opened my mouth to say something but there were so many things I wanted to say, to ask her about, in the jumble of my head, I couldn't find the words.

"I'm sorry," Lainey repeated, wiping swiftly under her eyes. She looked a wreck, face red and blotchy, eyes puffed nearly closed and ringed by makeup, nose running. A line ran down her cheek from where it had pressed into the edge of my lapel. When she noticed the patch of my shirt wet with tears and mucus, she groaned. "Oh, God, I'm sorry." She lifted her hand as if to brush it away but instead pulled a tissue from her pocket and wiped her nose. "We should go."

"Wait—" I said. But she was already striding away. I followed her toward the idling limousine, the hand still in my pocket curled into a fist.

"...NO FURTHER EVIDENCE or witnesses have surfaced..."

The TV was on as it always was now, though I barely heard it anymore.

"…at this time, investigators still believe the failed assassination to have been the work of a lone individual. No groups have yet come forward to claim responsibility. Some are hinting the incident was an accident—a tragic accident…"

They were saying that because most of the shots fired inexplicably went into the ground. The shooter had been a relatively new member of the private security team. It was his first, and last, time working a high profile event. He couldn't explain whether it was an inept assassination attempt or a weapon malfunction because now he was dead.

I watched the screen intently, staring hard at the images replaying again and again. Nothing ever changed, but still I watched, hoping for a new angle or a new video to surface.

Because if there was one thing I knew it was this: what happened was no accident.

"…Senator Astor and his fiancée, Teresa Espinosa, ask for your understanding and respect of their privacy in their time of grief…"

Fiancée. That was new. I'd not heard anything official, but I'd never been first to learn anything about them. Maybe Tessa had relented, or Williams had begged them hard enough. It could hardly improve Uncle Dan's standing in the polls at this point. His popularity had surged since the tragedy, vaulting him to the top of the polls.

The video on this channel slowed down and zoomed in, though for what purpose, I couldn't say. So people could see Tessa screaming? So everyone could watch Manny pointing right before they shot a possibly innocent man?

Or was everyone watching what I was: me, looking straight at the shooter before a single shot was fired.

I paused, rewound, and watched again. *There.* I'd noticed it a few days after the incident, standing in line for coffee. I'd been trying *not* to watch the coverage, considering I'd been there. But that TV wasn't mine, and I couldn't click it off. The news channel I was watching now must have been covering the gala live. Their video was excellent. And then there I was, in the middle of the screen.

I couldn't remember anything about those seconds before the hysteria, but I couldn't deny what I could see with my own eyes. There was my uncle, smiling at me, lifting his chin and then I—*Why* had I looked across the lawn, toward the shooter?

Halfway through replaying it again, the phone rang. Uncle Jeff.

I picked it up and paced the living room, wondering if now was the time to tell him. "Hello?"

"Carter." He cleared his throat, an absolutely un-Uncle Jeff thing to do. Like he was nervous or didn't know what to say. Uncle Jeff planned every word before he spoke it. "The results are in."

"What? Already?" I'd carefully transferred the strands of Lainey's hair that caught on my sleeve at the cemetery to Uncle Jeff before he left. Zeus couldn't have had it for very long.

He cleared his throat again and I decided I should probably sit down. "It turns out," he said, "the sample was already in the database."

"*What?* How?" There was *no way* Lainey had donated it. If I knew *anything*, I knew that. Which meant someone had submitted it without her permission. "Or, no, *who?*"

"It was my brother, Carter." I sucked in a breath. "It was Dan." I couldn't believe it. How could he do that to her? "There's more," he said.

I knew what he was going to say before he said it.

"It's a match."

A match. So it really was true. Lainey was part Astor.

And Uncle Dan had known all along.

Chapter Thirty-Seven

Lainey

Jack was waiting for me. That thought kept me going for the rest of the week I spent with Aunt Tessa through the plane ride home. Otherwise, I closed my eyes and saw the tiny coffin slipping below the dirt and the destroyed look on my aunt's face. I heard Abuela sobbing and Uncle Tommy whispering "okay, okay" over and over. I felt the familiar weight of Carter's arms holding me and Daniel Astor's eyes following me. All of those sensations pressed on me from inside my head, crushing and expanding at the same time, getting louder and sharper and heavier until I was afraid I might explode.

It was all I could do not to scream.

So instead, I thought about Jack. There was something *good* waiting for me at home. At least I had that.

When he flung his apartment door open and crushed me to him, I couldn't contain the tears anymore. I'd kept them in the whole flight, the whole mercifully short taxi ride from the airport, but the pressure had built and built until the sobs erupted from me like a geyser.

"At least I have you," I hiccupped out, the words broken and garbled between breaths. "At least I have you."

"You do," he said into my ear. "I swear it. You do. Only you matter."

Jack held on, and I clung to him. It was different from when Carter held me, because I didn't have to let go. Carter was just one more thing I'd lost, the first thing. Like being held up by a ghost. Jack was mine. He was real, and here, and I could stay.

I stayed. Safe in Jack's arms, and knowing they'd still be there when I woke up, I slept the first decent hours since my brother had died.

FROM MY BEDSIDE table, my phone blared, the ring so loud it made the phone bounce and me jump to answer it. I always answered now. I'd never miss a call again.

"Hello?" I said groggily.

"Lane?" Amy's voice faded in and out, the way it did sometimes when she was in her dorm, making her seem farther away than just the few miles across the river. She seemed farther away than ever lately, and a little voice I didn't much like said that was my fault. "Were you sleeping?"

I rubbed my eyes, hoping that would ease the dull ache behind them. "Yeah."

"It's five o'clock. PM."

"It was...a late night," I admitted. Fun though. One of Serena's regular clubs had Salsa Night and a rather lenient ID policy. It was the kind of place you'd be afraid to see in the light of day, but after dark and a couple of shots it was great.

After a pause Amy said, "On a Wednesday. Did you go to class?"

"Yeah. Of course."

I wasn't proud of the way I responded to what happened. Though that was something I only thought of distantly, in the down moments when I wasn't actively pursuing distractions. I still went to classes, always, even if I was tired or hungover or not prepared, which was most of the time. My grades were dropping, though not as much as they *should* have, if not for my "extenuating circumstances."

Amy sighed. "So I guess we're not going to that show tonight?"

"What?" I sat up, regretting the throb it caused in my head. "Yeah, we are! Why do you think I was taking a nap?"

"Lane—" I knew that tone of voice.

"You *can't* bail on me."

"I don't want to, just—are you sure?" She said it in a way that made it obvious *she* wasn't sure. Irritation tickled at me like a stray hair. I wanted to brush it away but couldn't. "Two nights in a row? And, I mean, you're *napping.* You never nap."

I never used to do a lot of things, but things change. *Maybe that's just what happens*, I thought. How could we ever stay as close as we were in high school? Our lives were different now. Separate. I still missed her, but it was an entirely different feeling than before. I think what I really missed was how things used to be easy.

"Ame," I said, trying to keep the irritation from my voice. "I want to go! You love this band! I'll be fine."

"Will you?" she said softly, more like a thought than a question. "I don't think you're fine, Lane. I'm worried."

I stood, stretched, searching for my sweatshirt so I could go for a quick run. "Aspirin, exercise, and dinner. That's all I need. I'll be fine," I repeated.

"That's not what I meant," she muttered, and then sighed. "Okay. Meet before dinner or after?"

"Um. Jack will be here…" I quickly scanned my messages. "Any minute, actually. So whichever you want. We can meet you. Thai maybe? And yes," I added as she started to respond, "you can stay at my apartment. Of course." At this point it was as much Amy's apartment as mine.

"That's not—" Amy sighed again. "So, Jack's coming too? I thought it was just us."

"Oh." I hadn't thought that. Truthfully, I hadn't thought about it at all. "I'm sorry. He's already on his way." She didn't say anything, but tension hung on the line. "What?"

"It's just—is he ever not 'on his way' or already there anymore? Ever?"

What the hell? I yanked hard on the laces as I tied my sneakers. "He has class, just like I do. More than I do."

"That's not—*argh*!" I could hear her moving on the other end, pacing, or maybe getting ready to leave. "Maybe we could take *one* night off without him. I'd like to see you. *Just* you. I meant that I'm worried about you."

It was true that I spent a lot of time with Jack, but he was my boyfriend. And I needed him a lot more right now than I needed her guilt trip. "Are you jealous?"

"Jesus, Lainey." The noise on her end stopped, and she took a breath, and another. "What happened to being by yourself, doing this alone?"

I burst out laughing, incredulous. "You were all *about* Jack before!"

"I was all about...*fun*."

"I'm *having* fun!" Funny how Amy had always been the one trying to get me to loosen up, and the one who didn't like it when I did.

"I know, I know." I could almost see her holding up her hands or tugging her curls. "And I mean I *like* Jack, but it's—dangerous. Not healthy. You needed, like, a rebound, not, not *this*. You're so serious about this guy and maybe—"

"What?!"

"Maybe it's not good for you."

"Are *you* serious?" Not good for me? Jack was just about the only thing keeping me sane.

But Amy said, "Yeah, I am. You never say no anymore! You're just...not you."

If I wasn't me, who the hell was I? "Maybe I *am*. Maybe this *is* me and you just don't like it." Above me, my upstairs neighbor took heavy steps across the floor and I realized I was shouting.

Amy was quiet for long enough I thought she may have hung up and I might not have minded. Finally, she said, "You're right. I'll give you that. Maybe this is you...but not the *best* you." Ouch. "It's, it's *part* of you," she went on, faster, her words catching up with her thoughts, "like we all have those parts. And all I know is when I wasn't being the best me, when the not-as-good-parts were showing, you called me on it. You were *there* for me! I'm trying—"

Blessedly, the door buzzer rang. "You know what?" I interrupted. I'd had enough. "Jack's here. For me. Right now. I gotta go."

"Lane—"

"Bye."

And I hung up.

By the time I made it down the stairs to the entryway, I fumbled twice trying to turn the knob to open the door for him. I couldn't manage to raise my eyes from the floor.

"Hey," he said, and tipped my chin up to look at me before tugging me straight to his chest. I leaned there, soaking in his warmth and the scent of his fancy cologne, like expensive whiskey and nature. "What's up? You're vibrating. It's okay now, whatever it is. I'm here."

And he was. Amy was crazy. Jack wasn't dangerous; he was my savior. How could spending so much time with someone who made me *happy* be less healthy than being depressed? Somehow, I'd lucked into a guy who made it easier *not* to think. Just to do. Be. Give my overactive psyche a break. I wasn't sure what it was about him, his carefree nature or maybe even just his age. He was older and had done more. He did things like go to clubs and attend graduate school.

Or maybe it was all of those things, or *none* of those things. Maybe, no, *definitely* I was over-thinking it. Maybe it was just me. I'd been through tragedies. I was growing up. I gave myself permission to stop thinking sometimes.

"Do you want to talk about it?" Jack murmured and I pulled backwards.

"No." I met his eyes so he'd know I meant it. "I want to go have fun."

He smiled and held out his hand. "Then let's go."

Chapter Thirty-Eight

Carter

I t's amazing how fast your entire life can unravel. The edges had been fraying for a while, but I'd ignored it, tucked the little dangling strings inside to hide them. But once one was pulled, it all came apart. That's what happened when the foundation was built on lies.

There were a dozen reasons Uncle Dan would not have told me about his relation to Lainey; a few were even decent. I couldn't think of one for why he'd have checked in the first place. Unless—I pictured Lainey's face again, something I'd been doing more and more, looking revolted on the graduation podium. Had *she* known and told him? And how? *When?* I needed proof, some kind of evidence, before I confronted him.

It took me longer than I wanted to break into Uncle Dan's office. Getting in was simple; or it would have been if I could bring myself to do it. Every time I made the decision to go in and poke around, I started to hyperventilate. I was standing with my back to my cube wall, practicing Lainey's ridiculous yoga breathing to calm myself down, when two staffers passed by. They were whispering to each other and oblivious to my presence.

"Did you see the latest poll today?"

"Yeah. Nomination looks like a lock now. At least *something* good came out of…Oh. Hey, Marita."

"What do you need, Daly?" Marita, Uncle Dan's assistant, said. "The senator is out for the rest of the afternoon and I'm on my way to lunch."

"Oh, never mind then. I'll come back later."

This was it. As soon as they were gone, I slipped out of my cube and crossed the short distance to Uncle Dan's door. It opened quietly with a Thought, like it had never been locked at all.

The office was familiar to me as my apartment, but once inside I stood still like a fool, looking around like I'd never been there before. The problem was I didn't know what I was looking *for*. On impulse, I crossed the room to his desk and tapped the computer to wake it.

The password was no challenge. I'd watched Uncle Dan hunt and peck for the keys enough times, all I had to do was call up the memories and recreate the keystrokes. A few seconds later, I was in. His email was open on the screen, so I started there.

I scrolled through the recent messages, but nothing jumped out at me. Near the top was one that looked like spam, from a generic email address with no name and the subject line UPDATE. The rest were obviously Senate-related or condolences. Pages and pages of condolences. I kept going, still not sure what I expected to find, until a familiar name caught my eye. John Abernathy, Manny's partner, two days before the gala: ITINERARY FOR REVIEW.

I opened the message. It was as described, a detailed itinerary for the day, planned almost to the second. There I was, listed bright and early. *08:00-08:30 Pick up C. Penrose.* At the bottom was the text of the previous messages in the exchange. I scrolled down to read them in chronological order. John wrote:

Sir-

I'm completing arrangements for your visit, as requested. I'm not sure the date is the best choice. We need extra time that day to review security protocols for the event. The next weekend would be more flexible if you'll consider it.

Uncle Dan replied:

That date is essential; it is the only time in my schedule. We will start early and I plan to oversee the security review. Also, ensure a nice range of weapons, including a submachine gun, if you would? I'd like to try my hand at one and I'm sure my nephew would as well.

—DA

Why, I wondered, was that date so important?

"Uh, hey, Carter. What are you doing in here?"

Shit. I started at the voice and cursed myself for it. Might as well have printed *GUILTY* on my forehead. I was such a terrible sneak, I'd left the damned door open. In it was the staff assistant who'd been whispering in the hall, a young hopeful distinguishable from the interns only because he drew a paycheck. An intern wouldn't have questioned me. I glared at him like he was the one who shouldn't be there right now. "My uncle forgot to leave a file for me." I emphasized *uncle* slightly.

He cleared his throat. "I was told no one should be in the senator's office without—"

"Well, Davey, I'm not no one."

"Daly," he corrected. I knew his name.

"Right. *Daly.* Do *you* know where the latest Budget Committee file is?"

He stepped further into the office and I risked a distraction. When he passed a stack of files on the floor, they toppled with a thud and whoosh of paper scattering. We watched a few escaped pieces float to the floor. Daly made a strangled sound while I exhaled an aggrieved sigh.

"Great. Just *great*." I leaned on the desk and sighed again.

"I didn't—I…*shit*!" Daly fumbled, and he was right. He didn't. *I* did. But how else could he explain what happened? I was on the other side of the room. When he bent to sort the paper disaster, I bumped Uncle's mouse forward until it lined up to close the message. I blinked a few times, using Thought to push the buttons so it wouldn't be obvious what I was doing.

From the floor, Daly was muttering, "I can't believe this. I *swear* I didn't touch them—"

"Just pick them up," I said sharply, feeling like a dick but knowing I had to keep acting that way. "And I won't mention to my uncle what a mess you made."

"Do you think you could hel—?"

"Here it is," I said. No, I couldn't help him, because I was about to do something the old Carter, the one who trusted his uncle to a fault, would never have considered. Something likely illegal. When I bent over the desk, I noticed the top file folder in the stack on the floor next to Uncle Dan's chair. In neat, block handwriting I recognized as Manny's were the words OFFICIAL REPORT followed by the date of the gala.

I took it.

"Sorry, but this is important," I sneered at poor Daly as I breezed past him out the door. I walked calmly back to my cube, sat down, and opened the folder like I hadn't just broken the law.

Evan Smith—such an unremarkable name for someone who'd changed my world so completely—was twenty-three years old. No evidence explained why he'd fired the gun. Tests showed the weapon was in perfect working order. Manny, or whoever prepared the report, postulated·Smith, a junior member of the security team, had not been properly trained in semiautomatic weapons, resulting in the erratic discharge. Though none had surfaced at this time, they would continue to seek a motive for an attack, including evidence of radicalization or personal vendetta. Until then, the incident was considered an accident.

Of course, they hadn't shown the evidence to me. I'd already known it wasn't an accident, and as soon as I flipped to the photos, I knew exactly what happened. All the pieces fell into place.

I did it.

I fired the gun.

Because the gun pictured in a big, full color, eight by ten glossy and labeled as the weapon in question was the same "lucky" MP5 I'd used that morning. John Abernathy hadn't been holding it after all—Evan Smith had.

Maybe guns of the same model were indistinguishable to most eyes, but I had *Lumen*-perfect recall. Every tiny scratch and line and imperfection was a marker for me, and I'd inspected that gun *thoroughly*. It was the first of its kind I'd ever held. And it was responsible for what happened—for my Godson's death, for everything.

I was responsible.

The entire scenario clicked into my mind with the easy conviction of something you'd already known in your heart. It all added up:

The importance of our visiting the range *that* day, using *that* weapon, why Uncle Dan personally attended the security review. Why he'd insisted, more than once, that I stick close to him at the gala. Why all the shots went into the dirt, like the weapon had fired itself. And why *I'd* looked at the shooter before he'd even fired.

Because he didn't.

I did.

Only one person could ensure a weapon belonging in a Secret Service agent's hands ended up in poor fucking Evan Smith's without anyone noticing. The same person who'd guaranteed I could fire it from anywhere in the world. But the reach of *his* gift was limited to direct sight.

Uncle Dan was likely the most powerful Thought Mover in the last fifty years, not counting me I supposed. But his gift was different. With the right Thought at the right time, he could do practically anything he wanted to someone's *mind*—change it, make it forget, make it remember something else. But even *he* couldn't make someone do and forget something if he was more than a few feet away.

The kid with the gun had been yards across the grass, at a lonely corner of the building, too far away for Uncle Dan's gift to reach. But I'd been *right there* next to my uncle, just like he'd wanted, his trump card waiting to be played.

He's used me to fire that gun and he'd nearly gotten away with it.

What better way to propel yourself to the lead in the polls than to fake an assassination attempt? It was almost perfect. He couldn't have predicted what happened to the baby, but hell if it didn't help his campaign even *more*.

Somehow I made it home before I threw up. I retched again and again until my stomach was barren, kneeling in the shower while the water went tepid, then cold, then frigid. Shivering, I dragged the soggy husk of myself out to my couch and cried.

Had anything—*any damn thing*—in my life been true? Did my uncle love me, or just want to use me? Had he been helping me, or *shaping* me? And the worst: who was I, if not just like him? I'd spent years observing and emulating him, building the foundation of myself on his example.

God, I was such a fool.

And now, was I a murderer, or was he? Did it matter? I was what he made me.

It was my worst nightmare come true. I'd been made a weapon. I'd always believed my Thought Moving would eventually kill *me*, not others, not my *Godson*. For a while as I laid there on my couch, I wished it had. I wished I'd just turned myself in years ago and let the Council vote. None of this would have happened. I retrieved the bottle of Scotch I'd won off Manny and wondered how long it would take me to kill that too.

About half the bottle later, my door opened, startling me awake. "'Lo?" Alexis stood in the doorway, twinkling in a silver sequin dress. It barely reached mid-thigh and looked like starlight. I rubbed my eyes. I could still be sleeping.

"Carter?" she said, as if she wasn't standing in my apartment.

"Hey, babe." I didn't even slur that badly. "What are you doing here?"

She took a few steps inside and dropped her bags on the floor. "Your uncle just dropped me off. After the Pendergest dinner? Remember?" *Idiot*, her tone implied, and I knew I was awake. She sparkled into the spot on the couch next to me, a distraction even more beautiful than the Scotch. I put an arm around her, drawing her close. "What are *you* doing?"

I nodded at the bottle. "Having a drink."

"*Alone?*"

"Not anymore," I said and pulled her closer.

IN THE MORNING, while Alexis and most of the city still slept, I ran. It was drizzling, gray and cold, making it a perfectly miserable day. My head pounded in time with my steps, thud, thud, thud, on the wet sidewalk. It was awful, running after drinking, but in the way black coffee and Scotch were awful. Which is to say, I didn't mind. I deserved it. It was less awful than thinking about—I forced myself to run faster.

But if anyone knew you couldn't outrun or drink away your thoughts, *I* did. They always caught up. *These* thoughts didn't so much catch as plow into me with the force of my entire world crumbling. All the things I'd lost pounded down on me, demanding to be acknowledged, starting with my Godson. My independence. My dignity. My thoughts. My trust. And Lainey. Selfish as it was, I couldn't stop thinking about her. He was responsible for that too; I knew it as well as I knew the words of her goodbye note.

Sometimes a puzzle piece fits *almost* perfectly, so you let it stay. You *want* it to stay. Until you realize, too long later, you were forcing it the entire time. I pulled out memories that were vague, or incomplete, or didn't quite line up. *Years* of them, since I was *thirteen*, up through the last few months. The inexplicable bullet hole in the shooting range wall. A tour bus wheel falling off the day after I'd lost minutes while looking at it. And finally: the fuzzy seconds at the gala, right before the person I'd trusted more than anyone in the world betrayed me.

I'd fallen to my knees on the stiff grass median, retching and shaking for God knew how long. Long enough for the back of my shirt to soak through. Long enough for a guy from the convenience store in front of which I crouched to become concerned.

I heard the door open and his few steps onto the sidewalk before his voice saying, "Kid, you okay?"

No, I was not okay. Did I fucking *look* okay? Anger boiled up from my empty stomach, but I realized it wasn't at this guy. What was I doing, cowering on the ground and crying? Drinking myself stupid and running away wouldn't change *anything*. I'd done enough fucking wallowing in the last year, in my whole *life*, and look where it had gotten me. I couldn't change anything, but I could do something better than *this*.

I looked up at the guy, shaking my head. "Not yet," I said with a smile that felt grim, and dangerous. "But I will be."

WHEN I GOT back to my apartment, Alexis was awake, balanced on the edge of the couch with her knees bent and feet propped on the coffee table. She grinned when I came through the door, but she looked bleary, her long legs bare as they descended from my t-shirt and her eyes smudged with yesterday's makeup. Usually I found this sexy, but today I found it painful.

"Ugh, why did we do that?" she said, nudging the mostly empty bottle in front of her with her toe. "I can't believe you *ran*. I think I missed a quiz this morning." She ran her hand across her forehead and through her rumpled hair before holding it out for the coffee I carried.

"I fixed it, but be careful. It's hot."

She sipped the sweet concoction with her eyes closed. "Mmmm, good job, babe." Finally, she looked up. "Hey, you're soaked!"

I peeled off my top layer before sinking down next to her. "Your coffee waits for no weather."

"You've been gone for, like, an *hour*." More like two. She set her coffee on the table. "Carter, what's going on?"

"I need to go away for a few days."

"What? Why?! Did something happen."

"It's what's already happened," I said, trying desperately not to lie to her. When you grew up keeping secrets for your own good, it became second nature. I didn't know how to stop. And I couldn't tell her *this* secret without telling her mine. She was safer if she didn't know. "I just…yesterday I realized I need a break. To work through it."

"Oh, babe," she said. She put her head on my shoulder and hand on my knee. "You should have done this before."

"I wasn't ready before."

"Are you going home? How long will you be gone?"

"A few days. I'll miss you." I cleared my throat, unsure how to say what I wanted to say. "Listen, do me a favor while I'm gone? Don't spend too much time around my uncle."

Her head snapped up and her forehead wrinkled. "What?"

"I just...I'm worried about you. After what happened. That it could happen again, and you'd be there."

Lex smiled, broad and true and so big her eyes crinkled at the corners. "Why Carter Penrose," she said in her best Scarlet O'Hara. "If I'm not mistaken, you're trying to say you love me."

I looked back at her for a long time, memorizing that smile and the beautiful tangle of things that added up to her and only *her*. "Maybe," I said, "I am."

But it was too late.

I knew what I needed to do. And where I would start.

Chapter Thirty-Nine

Lainey

Ridiculous as it was, pretty much the only rule I still abided by was the one I'd set for myself at the beginning of the year: no staying at my apartment during the week. I hardly stayed there at all. The weird thing was, Jack didn't seem to mind. Amy had been right about the advantages of having a single.

"This brings back memories," Jack said. He had a book in his lap as he sat behind me on my extra-long twin bed.

"Spent a lot of time studying in girls' rooms, did you?" Sometimes I forgot Jack was a student, too. All TAs were. He never seemed overly concerned about it. But then, he rarely seemed concerned about anything.

"That was *definitely* the best place to study. You couldn't do *this* in the library." He tossed his book aside and grabbed me around the waist, dragging me backward to nuzzle his face into my neck. He made a long inhale as I settled against him. "There. This is perfect."

I giggled. "What about your studying?"

"I'd much rather study this," he said, kissing my neck. "And *these*." Quick as a thief, his hand dashed up my shirt.

I squeaked and swatted at him. "Before you can study *that*, I have to study *this*." I shook my Finance book. "I don't have much time left."

He turned his face into my skin and sighed. "You worry too much."

"Lately, I don't worry enough," I said without planning to. The truth always found its own way out.

"Everyone understands."

I frowned. Not exactly. I'd blown Amy off last week, but her words still echoed in my head. Finally, I said, "I—I want, no *need* to pass my exams. It's important to me." As long as I passed my exams, I'd pass for the semester.

He nodded, holding me tighter, and we stayed like that. After a moment of quiet, he said, "Have you thought about it anymore? The Perceptum, I mean."

I stiffened, but didn't pull away. Yes, I'd thought about it. I'd been thinking about it more and more after the funeral, and pretty much non-stop since Jack had told me he was taking the Council intern offer. Up until a month ago, I truly believed I'd *never*, never ever ever, be able to do what they wanted. But something in me changed as I watched them lower my brother into the ground. The need not just to *do something*, but something that *mattered*, swelled in my heart until it burst into my arteries and spread, filling me with the crackling restlessness I'd since been mollifying with partying and drinking and Jack and sex.

In fact, it would be so easy to just turn around, drop my book and lift my shirt, and let Jack "study" me so I wouldn't have to talk or think about any of this anymore. But my mouth had spoken the truth once tonight and it wanted to keep going.

"Yeah," I said. "I've thought about it. I'm…considering."

I felt Jack's eyelashes brush my skin as his eyes popped open. "You are?"

"Yeah. Yeah," I repeated, softer. Part of me couldn't believe I was about to say this, but the rest, the hot, angry center blistering in my chest, knew it was true. "I am. I'm ready to talk to them."

Jack inhaled hard, the breath rushing against my neck in a cold breeze, and his arms tightened around me until they were almost too tight. "Thank you," he whispered, so soft I almost didn't hear it.

And then he kissed me, and I heard that loud and clear. My Finance book slipped from my fingers and landed with a thud.

LATER, I FELT myself slipping toward sleep and didn't bother to fight it. Jack shut off the light and I snuggled into his arms, tired, warm, and content. My eyes drifted closed.

"Lainey." Jack's voice. I felt it, like a breath in my ear, or a whisper in my brain.

"Hmmm?"

It was quiet for a long time before: "I love you."

Was I dreaming? Was I awake? I wasn't sure. I wasn't sure I'd heard those words or just thought them. But I knew they'd been there, below the surface, waiting to be said. *Love.* Jack loved me.

"I lo—"

"*Lainey.*" It wasn't Jack this time. It was Kendra's voice, outside the door. She was tapping, quiet but insistent. I sat up, rubbing my eyes, and felt Jack sit up too. "*Lainey,*" she whispered again. She sounded so urgent.

"Coming," I called softly and got out of bed.

Behind me, Jack murmured, "What's going on?"

"I don't know. Kendra needs me." I threw on my robe without turning on the light and slipped out the door. Kendra's eyes were wide and startled. From the fresh charcoal on her hands, I could tell she hadn't been sleeping. "What's wrong?"

Her eyes slid from me to the front of the apartment and back. "There's someone at the door for you," she said, still whispering despite that everyone in the apartment was awake, like she was telling me a secret.

"What?" How odd. "Right now? I didn't hear the bell."

"He didn't ring it."

He? Amy was the only person I knew who'd show up unannounced and she wasn't exactly speaking to me at the moment. "Who is it?" I asked.

Kendra opened her mouth and then shook her head. "Maybe you could just go talk to him? He seems kind of…upset."

Confused yet curious, I tightened my robe and tiptoed to the door. I didn't know why we were being so quiet but I couldn't stop. I cracked the door open and a tall, tall boy with blonde-brown hair folded himself off the wall at the sound.

Oh. My. God.

"Lainey," he said. He was whispering too.

Oh. My. God. I must have been dreaming.

"Lainey," Carter repeated. "Please. I have to talk to you."

My shock broke, and I gasped in a stuttering breath. "Carter? What are you *doing* here?"

He ran a hand over his short hair once, twice, three times, like he couldn't stop himself. "I really need to talk to you," he said again. "Please. Just listen."

I pushed the door open a little further, drenching him in light, and had to stifle another gasp. He looked like *hell*, with plum-colored circles under his eyes and deep lines that should *not* have been on his young face. Like he hadn't slept in a week.

"Please." Carter touched my arm, where I was still holding the door handle, and I jerked away from him, backing into the suite. He followed, though I wasn't sure I meant it as an invitation. "I'm sorry, it's late. I know I should have called or something but—"

"You shouldn't *be* here!" I said, backing up another step. I shook my head, trying to work some sense into it, and tightened my robe again. A desperate sense of fear was clawing down my throat and under my skin. Goosebumps jumped out on my arms and I hugged myself.

"I know," Carter said. "I know, it's just, please. Lainey, I *know*. I know about my uncle, that something happened at the range, that—"

"Lainey?" In the hall, my bedroom door was opening. We both turned toward the voice. Carter went absolutely rigid, eyes wide as moons and filled with something like…recognition. "What's going on?"

Jack stepped into the common room and froze.

"Jack?" Carter said. Blood rushed to his face at same time Jack's went white.

"You—what? You know each other?" My eyes flicked between the two of them, finally landing on Jack. He took a step toward me, hands held out in front of him.

"Lainey, it's not what, I swear, I was going to tell you—"

Carter stepped between us, his hands closing into fists. "So *this* is what the Perceptum Council intern has been doing all year? Kensington, you son of a bitch!"

And then Carter launched himself at Jack and they hit the ground with a crash.

About the Author

Cara Bertrand is a former middle school literacy teacher who now lives in the woods outside Boston with: one awesome husband, two large dogs, one small daughter, and lots of words. She is the author of TANGLED THOUGHTS, SECOND THOUGHTS and LOST IN THOUGHT, the first novel in the Sententia and one of three finalists for the Amazon/Penguin Breakthrough Novel Award in the Young Adult category.

Visit her online at www.carabertrand.com or on Twitter @carabertrand